RADIANCE

Books by Catherynne M. Valente

The Orphan's Tales:
In the Night Garden

The Orphan's Tales:
In the Cities of Coin and Spice

Palimpsest

Deathless

The Dirge for Prester John: The Habitation of the Blessed

The Dirge for Prester John: The Folded World

Six-Gun Snow White

Silently and Very Fast

The Fairyland Books

The Girl Who Circumnavigated Fairyland
in a Ship of Her Own Making

The Girl Who Fell Beneath Fairyland
and Led the Revels There

The Girl Who Soared Over Fairyland
and Cut the Moon in Two

The Boy Who Lost Fairyland

RADIANCE

CATHERYNNE M. VALENTE

corsair

CORSAIR

First published in the US in 2015 by Tor
First published in Great Britain in 2016 by Corsair

1 3 5 7 9 10 8 6 4 2

Copyright © 2015 by Catherynne M. Valente

The moral right of the author has been asserted.
Sappho translation on page 413 by Francis Fawkes

A CIP catalogue record for this book
is available from the British Library.

ISBN: 978-1-47211-514-0 (hardback)
ISBN: 978-1-47215-182-7 (trade paperback)
ISBN: 978-1-4721-1516-4 (ebook)

Printed and bound in Great Britain by CPI Group (UK) Ltd., Croydon, CR0 4YY

Papers used by Corsair are from well-managed forests
and other responsible sources

MIX
Paper from
responsible sources
FSC® C104740

Corsair
An imprint of
Little, Brown Book Group
Carmelite House
50 Victoria Embankment
London EC4Y 0DZ

An Hachette UK Company
www.hachette.co.uk
www.littlebrown.co.uk

For Heath, who taught me about light
and my father, who taught me how to get the shot

Chronology

(Some dates are approximate due to known issues with reconciling standard and sub-light transit calendars.)

1858: Conrad Wernyhora and Carlotta Xanthea launch the *Tree of Knowledge* from the Hawaiian islands, Earth

1872: Violet El-Hashem born in Marrakech, Earth

1876: Hathor Callowmilk Corporation founded

1883: Percival Unck born

1891: Mary Pellam born

1902: Proserpine, an American colony on Pluto, is destroyed. Cause unknown.

August 1908: Mary Pellam's first significant role (*Meet Me on Ganymede,* dir. Hester Jimenez-Stern)

24 March 1914: First episode of *How Many Miles to Babylon?* broadcast throughout the inner Solar System

29 October 1914: Severin born in the Lunar city of Tithonus

6 January 1915: Premiere of *The Red Beast of Saturn* (dir. Percival Unck)

25 January 1916: Erasmo St. John born on location in Guan Yu, Mars

1917: Enyo, a Russian mining settlement on Mars, is destroyed. Cause unknown.

3 July 1919: Premiere of *Hope Has No Master* (dir. Percival Unck)

1921: Severin sees Mary Pellam for the first time in *The Seduction of Madame Mortimer* (dir. Thaddeus Irigaray)

1922: Percival Unck and Mary Pellam wed

1924: *The Abduction of Proserpine* (dir. Percival Unck) released

3 July 1924: Anchises St. John born in Adonis, Venus

14 January 1930: The *Achelois* sets sail from Tithonus Harbour for *The Miranda Affair* (dir. Thaddeus Irigaray) wrap party

1936: *Self-Portrait with Saturn* (dir. Severin Unck) released

Christmas 1937: Erasmo and Severin become romantically involved

1938: *The Famine Queen of Phobos* (dir. Severin Unck) released

1939: The *Stone in Swaddling Clothes* departs for the Outer System

1940: The *Clamshell* built

1940: Fifth Venusian census, the last to record the village of Adonis

1941: *And the Sea Remembered, Suddenly* (dir. Severin Unck) released

1943: *The Sleeping Peacock* (dir. Severin Unck) released

June 1944: Moscow Worlds' Fair / The *Clamshell* departs for filming of *The Radiant Car Thy Sparrows Drew* (dir. Severin Unck)

16 November 1944: The *Clamshell* lands at White Peony Station for *Radiant Car* principal photography

21 November 1944: *Radiant Car* film crew sets out from White Peony Station

1 December 1944: Crew arrives in Adonis, Venus, first contact made

2 December 1944: Auditory phenomena commences

3 December 1944: Severin disappears

1946: Erasmo St. John debriefed by Oxblood Films

10 October 1947: Severin's funeral *in absentia*

1951: Severin's funeral

1959: Production begins on *The Deep Blue Devil* (dir. Percival Unck)

Spring 1959: Posthumous publication of Erasmo St. John's book *The Sound of a Voice That Is Still*

1960: Major rewrite on *The Deep Blue Devil*, retitled *The Man in the Malachite Mask* (dir. Percival Unck)

Winter 1961: Major rewrite on *The Man in the Malachite Mask*, retitled *Doctor Callow's Dream* (dir. Percival Unck)

Summer 1961: Major rewrite on *Doctor Callow's Dream*, retitled *And if She's Not Gone, She Lives There Still* (dir. Percival Unck)

December 1961–October 1962: The action of ~~*The Deep Blue Devil* *The Man in the Malachite Mask* *Doctor Callow's Dream*~~ *And If She's Not Gone, She Lives There Still* takes place

Locations

The Moon	☽
Mercury	☿
Venus	♀
Earth	⊕
Mars	♂
Jupiter	♃
Saturn	♄
Uranus	♅
Neptune	♆
Pluto	♇

Being unable to retrace our steps in Time, we decided to move forward in Space. Shall we never be able to glide back *up* the stream of Time, and peep into the old home, and gaze on the old faces? Perhaps when the phonograph and the kinesigraph are perfected, and some future worker has solved the problem of colour photography, our descendants will be able to deceive themselves with something very like it: but it will be but a barren husk, a soulless phantasm and nothing more. "Oh for the touch of a vanished hand, and the sound of a voice that is still!"

—Wordsworth Donisthorpe,
inventor of the kinesigraph camera

Light makes photography. Embrace light. Admire it. Love it. But above all, know light. Know it for all you are worth, and you will know the key to photography.

—George Eastman

Talking pictures are like lip rouge on the Venus de Milo.

—Mary Pickford

RADIANCE

Come Forward!

Come forward. Come in from the summer heat and the flies. Come in from that assault on all senses, that pummelling of rod and cone and drum and cilia. Come in from the great spotlight of the sun, sweeping across the white sands, making everyone, and therefore no one, a star.

Come inside and meet the prologue.

It is dark inside the prologue. Dark and cool and welcoming. Whatever is to come, the prologue welcomes you absolutely, accepts you unconditionally, receives you graciously, providing all that is necessary to endure the rest. The prologue is patient. She has been told often that she is wholly unnecessary, a growth upon the story that the wise doctor must cut off. She has time and again found the doors to more fashionable establishments closed to her, while tables are set with candles and crystal for a top-hatted in medias res, a pedigreed murder at midnight, a well-heeled musical number. This does not trouble the prologue. She was fashionable when plays still began with sacrifices—and if you catch her in her cups, she will tell you that any show that jumps into the action without a brace of heifers burning centre front still strikes her as a rather tawdry affair. The prologue is the mother of the tale and the governess of the audience. She knows you have to bring them in slow, teach them how to behave. All it takes is a little music; a soft play of *lights; a flash of skin; a good, beefy monologue to bring everyone up to speed before you expect them to give a witch's third tit who's king of Scotland.*

The prologue is where you take your coats off. Relax. Leave your shoes at the door. Invoke the muse, call down whatever royal flush of gods you want pulling the action between them. O Muse, O Goddess. Sing, Speak, Weep. Give unto me the song of rage. Hand over the arms and the man on the double-quick. Hit that horn and play me the voice of the many-minded traveller who could not get home. Keep a front-row seat for that masked demiurge, a plum spot for that jazzy old Word in the Void, or let it be on your head.

So come in. Let your eyes adjust. We need your eyes. Let the chartreuse pop of the sun's afterimage fade into the blackness we have thoughtfully provided. The floor creaks underfoot: slick, yielding wood, green as an olive in a martini, fresh from the forests of Ganymede. You can smell it lightly, under the lime polish. Ashes and copper. Let the dark scoop your ears clean, scrub out the bubbling champagne-cacophony of the world you have only just left behind. We need your ears. And we want your hands as well. We are all primates, after all. We love to touch; we love to interfere with objects. Nothing is real until you can touch it. Your sight will sharpen in time; the shadows will lift and separate like curtains. You will find pages under your eager fingers: pages, phonographs, objects great and small but mostly small, resting on pillars of Uranian saltrock carved into cresting, foam-gnarled waves, trusting their flotsam to your keeping.

Come in, come in, there is so much to see.

No sitting down, though. We need you standing. There's a projector here, just there—have a care, sir—to your right. Another—mind your hems, madam—to your left. But you will find no screen. You're it. If you'll gather in . . . yes, just so, all in a row like good little daisies. Tall folk to the rear, small folk up front. Now, if you are comfortable, we can begin.

This is a story about seeing. This is a story about being seen. All else is subservient. The ears assist; the hands comfort. The only verbs that matter are verbs of vision: look, see, watch, observe. Gaze. Behold. Witness. The eye is our master, and the eye worships light. That which makes light is good, that which takes it is to be feared. We have taken it from you, but we will give it back again. Make of that what you will.

God—if you will forgive such sweeping pronouncements so early in our acquaintance—is an eye.

It would be better if you would consent to disrobe. Skin is the most intimate and perfect of screens. But having come from so many ports and climes, we do not expect your taboos concerning modesty to match up perfectly with ours—why, thank you, miss, you are most kind. And sir, we are greatly obliged. The matron seems to be having some trouble with her costume; if you could assist her, young lady? Thank you. You have all proven yourselves wonderfully gracious and liberal-minded. You are an audience we do not deserve. Perhaps it is a relief after the heat to shed silk and leathers? Nevertheless, we are thoroughly impressed. We shall endeavour to make ourselves equally naked, equally bare, equally vulnerable to iris and pupil, whose bites are ever so much fiercer than teeth.

The clatter and whirr of the projectors pick up like wind across a long desert. Look down. You can see a woman with dark hair and unhappy eyes moving silently on your bellies, your breasts, your thighs, your feet. Upside down, shorn of colour, flickering. Bent and cut up by the curves of your bodies and the age of the film. You see her as you see anyone in this world: distorted, warped, reflected, refracted, contorted, mutilated by time.

Perhaps you recognize the scene. It was once a famous film, after all. She was once a famous woman. I hear you say her name, sir—but this is our show, pray allow us to reveal things in our own time.

Observe: It is daytime in the movie on your chest. The crew is setting up the morning's shoot. The director of photography, a great, broad-chested fellow with a smart moustache, shaves in a mirror nailed to a cacao-tree. The looking glass hangs at a rakish angle, half-sunk into furry black bark. You will know by the tree that he stands upon the surface of Venus, not far from the sea. It is late summer. A spot of rain glimmers on the lens.

Yes, my dear fellow, you know his name, too. You are just awfully clever.

The DP uses a straight razor inlaid with a scrimshaw of fossilized kelp. You will find it along the east wall. Do not be afraid; it has not dreamed of sharpness since its profligate youth. The blade belonged to his grandfather, a merchant sailor who played the bassoon—a most impractical instrument for a seaman, but how the old man loved his pipe! The scrimshaw shows a sea serpent, each scale lovingly etched, as round as fingernails. The director of photography is shirtless, his skin as dark as unshot film, his face angular and broad. He catches a glimpse of the woman in his mirror and whirls round to catch her up. He kisses her with a resounding smack you cannot hear, smearing shaving cream on her face. She laughs noiselessly and punches his arm; he recoils in mock agony. It is a pleasant scene. Some phantom discontentment pops like a flashbulb in her eyes and obliterates itself into love.

Observe: It is evening in the movie on your legs. A small boy, head bent, dressed in the uniform of a callowhale diver, walks in small, tight circles in what was once the centre of a village called Adonis. The houses and outbuildings look as though they have been gored with great horns: lacerated, burst open. Long, squalid lashings of what appears to be white paint spatter the ruins. But it is not paint. Adonis, the lost city, destroyed, obliterated, without reason, without warning. A mystery that pulled a woman across the stars and down into its scarlet seas. The boy does not look up as the camera watches him. He does not see himself being seen by the film crew, by the audiences to come, by us. He does not see his echo; he does not hear his projection. He simply turns and turns and turns, over and over. The corrupted film skips and jumps; the boy seems to leap through his circuit, flashing in and out of sight. Clouds drift down in long, indistinct spirals. Celluloid transforms the brutal orange of the Venusian sun into a blinding white nova. Beyond him, pearlescent islands hump up out of the foamy sea of Qadesh: callowhales, a whole pod, silent, unmoving, pale.

Now. Gaze, behold, witness: A third projector judders on, seeing but unseen, hidden in the curtains. It fires its beam at the laughing couple, the shaving cream, the razor that once belonged to a bassoon-loving grandfather. Image over image over flesh. The woman seems to step out of her lover's arms and into a ballroom, becoming suddenly a pouting, sour-faced little girl practically drowning in the stiff lace and crinoline of one of those old Gothics we love so well— would you care to name it, sir? You know so much; I will not believe for a moment you do not recognize The Spectre of Mare Nubium, *the marvellously morbid masterwork that earned its director, Percival Unck, his first Academy Award. Your fine chest sports the classic ballroom sequence, wherein the blood-soaked villain receives her much-deserved comeuppance. The little girl can be seen crouching miserably near the rice-wine fountain, chewing her fingers and spitting the nails at the whirling dancers. The grand dresses of the waltzing ghosts pass over her face like veils.*

Please, ladies and gentlemen! Your protestations destroy the dark quiet of our little universe. I can see you leap quite out of your skin. You must be prepared for these interruptions, invasions, intersections. They are necessary. They are the exhalations of the dead. Humans do not proceed in an orderly fashion from one scene to the next. Memory lies underneath happenstance; hope and dread sprawl on top. Our days and nights are their endless orgies.

Now, listen: Our phonograph scratches up a man's voice and a small girl's, the very girl who at this moment is flickering silver and black on your thighs, sinking her face into balled fists under the murderous Clarena Schirm's banquet table.

"How many beginnings can a story have, Daddy?"

The man chuckles. It is a nice chuckle, tobacco-velvet, a chuckle that says: Oh, the questions my kid asks!

"As many as you can eat, my lamb. But only one ending. Or maybe it's the other way around: one beginning but a whole Easter basket of endings."

"Papa, don't be silly," the child admonishes in a voice accustomed to getting its way. "A story has to start somewhere. And then it has to end somewhere. That's the whole point. That's how it is in real life."

The man laughs again. You like his laugh. I like his laugh. We cannot help but feel well disposed toward a man with a laugh like that, even though it is not really his, but a laugh he learned at university, copied meticulously from his favourite screenwriting professor as you and I might copy from our neighbour during an exam.

"But that's not how it is in real life, Rinny. Real life is all beginnings. Days, weeks, children, journeys, marriages, inventions. Even a murder is the beginning of a criminal. Perhaps even a spree. Everything is prologue. Every story has a stutter. It just keeps starting and starting until you decide to shut the camera off. Half the time you don't even realise that what you're choosing for breakfast is the beginning of a story that won't pan out till you're sixty and staring at the pastry that made you a widower. No, love, in real life you can get all the way to death and never have finished one single story. Or never even get one so much as half-begun."

"Papa, you're babbling. Ada says you have to stop that. She says you're full of hot air."

"I'm full of many things, I'm sure. Very well, you do so love rules! I shall make some up for you on the spot, so that my little

moppet is not forced to wander the world in a soup of stories without laws. A tale may have exactly three beginnings: one for the audience, one for the artist, and one for the poor bastard who has to live in it."

A bright cascade of giggles splashes out over the crackle of the phonograph. The child lowers her voice to a whisper: "I like it when you swear."

And at that moment the child leaps out of the phantasmal throng of dancing ghosts, out of the frame, out of The Spectres of Mare Nubium, *and shimmers into the shape of the Venusian boy, his serious expression so like hers, turning in endless circles on a grey lawn.*

Her name is Severin Unck. She is ten years old. She is talking to her father, Percy.

She is dead. Almost certainly dead. Nearly conclusively dead. She is, at the very least, not answering her telephone.

Welcome. This beginning is your beginning. We have saved it specially for you. Shall we?

Oh, Those Scandalous Stars!

Places, Everyone!, 3rd **July 1919**

Editor's Note

My darlings, if only I could have brought you all with me!
Just gathered you up in my arms out of your parlours and
kitchens, still in your aprons and overcoats, and spirited you
to the glittering premiere of Percival Unck's latest thrilling
picture, *Hope Has No Master*! How I would have loved to
play Father Christmas and appear on the cobalt carpet with
a sackful of my readers—nay, my *friends*—so that you could
see the brilliant and the beautiful for yourselves, spilling
out of their long cream-coloured limousines, cars clean and
bright and glittering as though they'd just passed through
a storm of diamonds instead of our lowly lunar raindrops.

Well, if *I* am not Father Christmas, who is? Gather
round! The beard is quite real, I assure you. Here is an
orange for each of you girls and a plum for each of you boys!
Watch me string up the stars for you like lights on a tree,
each one prettier than the last.

***Limelight*, 12th October 1947**

My hungry gossip-hounds, today there can be no happy
games of fetch between us. I come to you hat in hand to

report the doings of the day, but I take no pleasure in it. My hat is black, and I know that yours is, too.

I personally attended the strange funeral of Severin Lamartine Unck, born 1914, aged but thirty-one (if the sublight transits are all rounded down, as one ought to do for a lady) and passed out of our hard, bright sphere too soon. Whatever the truth, her gravestone will forever read thirty-one, and thirty-one she will, in all likelihood, remain. Her filmography stands tragically firm at a scant five: *Self-Portrait with Saturn*; *The Famine Queen of Phobos*; *And the Sea Remembered, Suddenly*; *The Sleeping Peacock*; and her final, deeply upsetting work, *The Radiant Car Thy Sparrows Drew*.

A sea of black greeted your humble whisper-collector as the empty coffin was interred in the marble halls of the newest edifice in Tsukuyomi Cemetery, the hastily built Unck family mausoleum. Poor Percy must have thought he would have more time to see to such affairs, or that his daughter herself would attend to them for his own eternal rest.

We assembled as if for a shoot . . . which of course it was, in a manner of speaking. Extras, dramatic faces, chosen professional mourners to round out the big crowd scene. Black, black everywhere. We did not know whether or not to cry—what was to be our cue, our script? What sort of Unck flick had hired us on: the father's, or the daughter's?

Now look there, children—Maud Locksley and her dashing companion, Wadsworth Shevchenko, fresh from the set of his sure-to-enthral historical epic, *Cross of Stone*. Maud ravishes as always in a sleek strapless number that rustles silver in the popping lights. When she turns, flashes of the palest pink feathers flutter beneath the hem. A slim triangle of dyed crocodile scales soars up to a daring rosette of amethyst and devilish croc teeth at the point of the gown's plunging, bare back. How she smirks over her rounded shoulder! The smirk that cost a thousand contracts, if you know what I mean, and I think you do. Wadsworth's charcoal arm never leaves her waist, his trim, severe Eichendorff suit revealing its own surprise as the power couple pose: The tails of his tuxedo descend into a weave of raven feathers, stiffly, glossily pointing earthward. Our coal-tressed leading man finishes it all off with an onyx lapel pin in the shape of a lunar peony. I'm certain we can all envy Maud Locksley her journey home—save that a little bird informs your humble Father Christmas that Master Shevchenko's burning gaze strays ever so occasionally from her charms to those of his co-star, Dante de Vere. But we know better than to listen to little birds, don't we?

We suppose she is dead, though none of us can be sure. She is not *here*, though she is not *there*, either, so far as anyone can tell. What transpired that awful autumn on those far Venusian shores? What happened to her? Did she share the horrid fate of the ruined village, the very one she sought to uncover and explain? We cannot know. We know only that we will see her no more, and that, my loyal readers, must break every heart in two.

We all came together Saturday last to pretend we know what happened and can feel certain about burying her. The seven ex-Unckwives and erstwhile stepmothers of the young Severin stood at his side, their beautiful faces drawn in the refined sort of grief only those who have trained since birth to live upon the screen can produce, reflecting our feeling back to us like lunar emotions, softer and more silver, colder and more delicate.

And would I shock anyone if I nodded my head toward an eighth statuesque figure who had been standing a fair way off, a black veil shielding her face from any eyes like mine that might guess at some maternal similarity to the vanished documentarian in the angle of her nose or the heft of her hair? To that very filmmaker whose fairy-tale coffin, all empty crystal and plush red pillow (with no head pressing the velvet, no feet beneath the shroud), decorated with ivory sparrow wings and onyx myrtle boughs, lay before us, prayed over by all the radiant men Severin ever loved.

I do believe she would have loathed that coffin.

But tear your eyes from the twin comets of Locksley and Shevchenko and look upon the real stars of the evening! Percival Unck and his *devastatingly* adorable daughter, Severin. Not quite five years old, she runs boldly onto the carpet, laughing, her black curls bouncing, the tiny bustle of her red velvet Barbauld dress stitched with rough garnet chips that do not *glitter* so much as *burn* against her childish waist. She'll be a beauty one day if her father has a thing to do with it. She reaches back and beckons for him. He is, as always, shy and bemused, wearing a positively *scrumptious* red suit to match his girl. Notice the ivory-plated Venusian myrtle flower tucked into his lapel—perhaps hinting to us as to the setting of his next masterpiece! Unck adjusts his scarlet-tinted glasses and follows his daughter, the long tails of his own late-season Eichendorff fluttering with sparrow feathers dyed a spectacular orange. (I, for one, am positively enchanted with the new avian direction in men's fashion this season. I expect I'll be putting in for my own double-breasted parrot suit soon enough!) Little Severin dances up the aisle, reaching into her silk purse to throw real Venusian tamarind blossoms before her, a little goddess managing handily her own worship. Her giggles and her smile track into a dozen microphones and cameras, certain to be pored over by yours truly *and* yours truly's competition for evidence of the child's mysterious mother—which starlet, which studio head's wife, which socialite's untoward Saturday night gave us this disarmingly impish companion to Tinseltown's greatest director?

Severin's long-time lover, the cinematographer Erasmo St. John, was present and accounted for, shockingly thinned down from his once-prizefighter physique. His winnowed hand clutched the fingers of that boy we have all begged to interview, even for a minute or two—that child brought back from Adonis in Severin's place, the creature we here in Tinseltown must face instead of our old friend. As of the writing of this column the child has not yet shown any ability to speak whatever. What frustration for our little community, for whom speaking is a necessity of life. We could sooner stop breathing than stop telling our life stories—and yet he says nothing, and St. John will not compel him.

Having reported a lifetime ago upon the premiere of *The Red Beast of Saturn*, when old Percy first appeared with a little bundle wrapped in graphite-coloured silk swaddling designed by Foscolo, I hold the decidedly odd position of having documented most of the famous documenter's life. But I am afraid that this old woman must draw her account of that wretched soul to a close early, being overcome by the whole business. Would that it had unfolded in some other way, some way which did not conclude in a rainy Saturday and a hollow glass box.

I adjourn. Though it is my custom to close by inviting you all to share the empty seat in my box, that seat must be reserved for the dead tonight. Look up at that persistent little limelight in the evening sky: Venus, who alone knows the secrets we poor chattering monkeys covet so.

Halfrid H
Editor-in-chief

I have my own thoughts on the provenance of Severin Unck, my darlings, but I'll never tell. Any Father Christmas worth his holly holds something back for next year.

It's five minutes to curtain, the lights are low, and I must find my seat. I remain slavishly yours,

Algernon B
Editor-in-chief

PART ONE

THE WHITE PAGES

My soul burns to speak of strange bodies transformed!
O gods in heaven, you ardent lovers of mutation,
become the breath inside me
and draw up my song, untroubled, unbroken,
from the first beginnings of the world
to this very moment and this very day.

—Ovid, *Metamorphoses*

For an actress to be a success she must have the face of
Venus, the brains of Minerva, the grace of Terpsichore,
the memory of Macaulay, the figure of Juno, and the hide
of a rhinoceros.

—Ethel Barrymore

The Radiant Car Thy Sparrows Drew
(Oxblood Films, dir. Severin Unck, 1946)

SC1 EXT. RED SQUARE, MOSCOW—DAY 1 LATE AFTERNOON [12 JUNE, 1944]

[Open on the pristine streets of sunny Moscow, lined with popsicle-carts, jugglers, dazzled tourists. The streetlamps are garlanded with lime-blossoms, sunflowers, carnations. The joyful throng crowds in fierce and thick; the camera follows as they burst into Red Square. The splendid ice-cream towers of the Kremlin beam down benignly. The elderly TSAR NICHOLAS II, his still-lovely wife, and their five children, hale in their glittering sashes, wave down at the cannoneers standing at attention on the firing pad at the 1944 Worlds' Fair. The launch site is festooned with crepe and swinging summer lanterns, framed by banners wishing luck and safe travel in English, Russian, Chinese, German, Spanish, and Arabic.]

SEVERIN UNCK and her CREW wave jerkily as confetti sticks to their sleek skullcaps and glistening breathing apparatuses. Her smile is immaculate, practiced, the smile of the honest young woman of the hopeful future. Her copper-finned helmet gleams at her feet. SEVERIN wears feminine clothing with visible discomfort and only for this shot, which she intends, in the final edit, to be ironic and wry: She is performing herself, not performing herself in order to tell a story about something else entirely. The curl of her lip betrays, to anyone who knows her, her utter disdain of the bizarre, flare-skirted swimming-cum-trapeze-artist costume that so titillates the crowd. The wind flutters the black silk around her hips. She tucks a mahogany case—which surely must contain George, her favourite camera—smartly under one arm. All of her crewmen strap canisters of film, a few steamer trunks of food, oxygen tanks, and other minor accoutrements to their broad backs. The real meat of the expedition, supplies and matériel meticulously planned, acquired, logged, and collected, was loaded into the cargo bays overnight. What Severin and her crew carry, they carry for the camera, for the film being shot of this film being shot.

The cannon practically throbs with light: a late-model Wernyhora design, filigreed, etched with forest motifs that curl and leaf like spring ice breaking. The brilliant, massive nose of the Venusian capsule *Clamshell* rests snugly in the cannon's silvery mouth. The metal beast towers over Saint Basil's, casting a monstrous shadow. Most of its size is devoted to propulsion. The living space within is surprisingly small. That etched silver forest will be jettisoned halfway to Venus, destined to drift alone into the endless black. But for now, the *Clamshell* dwarfs any earthly palace built for the glory of man or god.

They are a small circus: the strongmen, the clowns, the lion tamer, the magician, and the trapeze artist poised on her platform, arm crooked in an evocative half-moon, toes pointed into the void.

CUT TO: INT. *Clamshell* cantina, NIGHT 21:00 ERASMO ST. JOHN and MAXIMO VARELA pour vodka for the CREW and laugh uproariously:::**FILM DAMAGED, FOOTAGE UNAVAILABLE SKIP DAMAGED AREA SKIPPING SKIPPING ERROR SEE ARCHIVIST FOR ASSISTANCE**]

From the Personal Reels of
Percival Alfred Unck

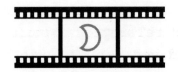

[A camera is on. The screen is black, for the camera is skewed toward the wall, a clandestine attempt to capture the child without her knowing she is being recorded. Occasionally, flickers of silver interrupt the darkness—echoes from a screen showing more lively activity somewhere behind the device that picks up the following quiet conversation.]

PERCIVAL UNCK
Now, in any film it is important that you know who is telling the story, and to whom they are telling it. Even if no one on-screen talks about it, the director must know, and the writer, too. Now, who is telling this story?

SEVERIN UNCK
Daddy is telling the story!

PERCIVAL
[laughing] Well, Daddy made the movie, but Daddy is not telling the story. Look at the

characters and how they speak to each other. Look at how the film begins, how the very first scenes shape everything else. Now, who is telling the story?

[There is a long silence.]

SEVERIN

The camera is telling the story. It's watching everything, and you can't lie to it, or it will know.

PERCIVAL

My girl is so clever! No, the camera witnesses the story and records it, but it is outside the story. Like a very tiny god with one big, dark eye. Baby girl, look at the lovers, and the villain, and the doting father, and the soldiers, and the ghosts. Which one of them is the authority? Who controls how the story is told? And who is the audience, for whom all these wonderful things are meant?

[Another long silence follows. There is a rustling, as of a little girl twisting her lace skirts while she tries to work out an answer.]

SEVERIN

They are all telling the story to me.

Preproduction Meeting,
The Deep Blue Devil [working title]
(Tranquillity Studios, 1959, dir. Percival Unck)

Audio recorded for reference by Vincenza Mako, screenwriter

PERCIVAL UNCK: If you want to know about the beginnings of things, you have to talk to the dead.

I know how that sounds. The dead should do endings. Surely that's their squat. In the space after the story, they're kings and queens, ruling with bony hands, pulling epilogues, last acts, climaxes, pulling *finality* from declining action like spinsters at black wheels.

I wouldn't know. I've always been aces at endings. At the *Fin* I'm like a ball player, balanced hips over knees, brandishing my bat, pointing to the outfield, pointing like I've been doing from the first word spoken, the first frame shot, at the revelation I intended to hit all along. Lean into the last scene; you can hear the whiff and the crack of my swing. If anything, I've always been *too* eager to get to the ending. I'll throw the haunted, wild-eyed gamine from her tower too soon, slaughter a soliloquizing retinue complete with bicyclists and bears five minutes in. Endings are lush and lascivious, Vince; they call to me. All spread out on satin inevitabilities, waiting, beckoning, promising impossibly, obscenely elegant solutions—if you've been a good lad and dressed the house just so, for its comfort, for its *arousal.* All the rest of the nonsense a story requires is just a long seduction of the ending. You throw out murders and reversals and heroes and detectives and spies, juggle love affairs and near escapes and standoffs with marvellous guns, kidnappings and sorcery and comic relief and gravediggers and princesses and albino dragons, and it's all just to lure an ending into your bed. The right ending can't resist a spread like that. She sidles up like she's lived there all along, sleepy-eyed, hair a fright, asking the antihero for coffee and be quick about it, wouldn't you? There's a love.

But I'm rubbish at beginnings. Listen to that mess. My metaphors all rumpled about my ankles. So I talk to the dead. They're the only ones who can see the whole story. All they've got is story. *Look,* say the ghosts, *she was doomed all along because of how it began. You watched her to death. She started disappearing as soon as she was born. Just to get away from you. No one could have gotten out of this thing alive. Not with Acts I-V stacked against them like that. If Hamlet couldn't swing it, what hope did* she *ever have?*

Anyway, nobody bothers with *real* beginnings anymore. We stopped making up stories about the creation of the world ages ago. But the deadest of the dead—the ancient, toga-tugging, sheep-fucking, olive-gobbling, laurel-spangled dead—*they* rattled on about nothing else. Gardens and clay and the Sky slinging back a nebula or two for courage then slicking back his hair to make nice with the Earth. They had it right. It's downright dishonest to begin with anything but the Creation of the Known Universe, and a tale that ends before the destruction of all and sundry is a damnable lie. By fire? Well, that's too obvious. And floods always look amateurish. Maybe it just winks out. Cut. Print.

Point is, the Greeks had their heads on straight: If you're going to bother beginning at all, you have to throw up a believable theory of origin or it's got no anchor. No *root*. Why four seasons? Why seasons at all? Why just the one moon? Why green trees and red roses and not the other way round? Why death and time and is there such a thing as fate, and what, percentage-wise, is the efficacy of human sacrifice? You have to answer those questions before anyone comes on stage, you know. In even the littlest story about a . . . let's say a housewife in an aqua-blue print dress and matching apron making a roast, only she's planning to kill herself later, obviously, or maybe her husband—otherwise why should we care one soggy whit about the vagaries of beef at temperature? At any rate, someone's got to die. That's why she's wearing aqua. Blue invariably means death. Even in poor lost Millicent's kitchen—yes, Vince, her name is *clearly* Millicent, do try to keep up! Before she even pricks the meat to slide the garlic in, it's all been arranged for her. Does death do its thing, in this universe? Yes. Time, in Millicent World? Progressing one second per second, twenty-four and seven and three hundred–odd. Seasons: four. The moon: intact, in orbit, in phase. Green elm, red peony. Seventeen per cent sacrificial success rate under ideal conditions, results not peer reviewed. And of course in stories there is always fate. It goes by the name of foreshadowing and it is the emperor of everybody. Given all these parameters, husband Humphrey should be dead by dessert. See? It's only that the answers in most stories are boring because they are supplied by the real world rather than—well, something better. Something more stimulating. Sit down with the Greeks and the Romans, and the boring answers get more interesting. Seasons because a girl and a crocus. Death because a girl and an apple. The moon because a girl keeps driving her daft chariot into the sea.

It's all down to girls, one way or another.

[indistinct]

All right, all right, I'm boring you. I'm babbling. I haven't made up my mind about this one yet. I don't even know how to go about making up my mind. I would rather *not* have death. I would rather that. Time is terribly tawdry, as well. And let's see what we can do about that percentage.

Let us begin properly. This is what I'm thinking: She came from nowhere. She came from the sea. She came from the dark. The Earth fucked the Sky and made a hundred children—or maybe just nine. Mercury, Venus, Mars, the whole ragtag family. And the nine had their own kids: Phobos, Triton, Io, Charon, all the brats. Maybe we can do this like we used to do, way back when. You know I can never quit Vaudeville. Toga up the main cast as the planets and the moons: rings around Saturn's head; Venus dripping wet; Mars in a cowboy getup; Neptune, I don't know, up on strings like the levitators, maybe? Stupid on af-yun, all heroin eyes and running makeup. Stand them in tableaux against a spangly cloth backdrop. Then they can start killing each other. It'll be Shakespearian. Barking big knives. Buckets of blood. Blood and callowmilk.

So the little bastards stab the Sky to death and throw the spangles into the sea, and they turn into the title, and that's where she comes from. Out of the words and the water. She can rise up on a clamshell naked and covered with blood and milk. That's what birth looks like, after all. Naked, with a myrtle branch in one hand and a camera in the other.

I have no ideas for casting. Someone new. I don't want anyone whose face has been someone else. I'll have to call Richard. He'll find somebody fresh off the rocket who looks like her. He always knows what I want. So, whoever she is, she'll look through the camera in her hand at the camera in my hand. The waves hit her and wash her clean. Mostly clean. Leave a mark on her face. Like a wound. Presto: Birth of Venus.

[indistinct]

Yes. Severin's birth, too. No difference.

But that's the last time we use her name, Vince. What's our rule? You can't name the subject. You can't say the word *death* in a murder mystery after the body gets discovered; no more than you can say *love* in a romantic flick until the end, until it's a bullet firing, the bullet you've had on deck since the scene-one-take-one clapper smacked its lips. You *circle* it. You *stalk* it. But you don't call it out.

MAKO: But everyone will know who it's meant to be. What's the point of being coy?

UNCK: Coyness is what makes it art, darling. Otherwise ... otherwise it's nothing but a funeral.

[long pause] We'll call her something else. Hell, I named her once, I can do it again. Something bombastic, something mythic, something Venusian. All the names have to come back to Venus in the end. I remember what you said when we were writing *Rocketship Banshee*—we went up to that cabin on the Sea of Fertility and trotted out our old dance, writing movies instead of fucking. Two rooms, two typewriters, the blue cassia forests, moon-daisies by the door. We swam naked in the bitter silver sea and you floated on your back under the Earthlight with water running off your colloidal blue breasts and said: *Names aren't loners, they're connected, even in real life. You name your kids for someone dead or what you hope they will become or what you wish you were and your parents did the same to you and that big, glittering net of names tells the story of the whole world. Names are load-bearing struts. Names are destiny.* You wouldn't just let me name our hero John and his demon bride Molly.

MAKO: This is different.

UNCK: We'll call her Ares. I gave her a boy's name the first time around, so why not this time? It's perfect. Ares went and shagged Venus when he should have stuck to what he was good at, which was fighting with anyone who'd put up half a fist. Good, right? Yeah. Yeah.

MAKO: Let her have her name, Percy. Let everyone have her own name. She'd hate you for changing it. You know that.

UNCK: [Clears his throat several times. His voice quavers.] I don't want to. I don't want to write it at the top of every page. I don't want to have to say it. Every day. All day. I don't want to have to call some nobody actress by my daughter's name.

MAKO: Too bad. It's my script, too. I'm not your secretary. Her name is Severin. You don't get to turn her into one of our demon brides.

[Sounds of typewriter keys and cigarettes extinguishing, lighting, smoke exhaling.]

UNCK: Fine. Fine. You win. Severin bloody Unck forever and ever amen.

Back to it. Once we've got the world created—Sky, Earth, clamshell—we move on to more important business. The Plot at Hand. We switch scenes entirely. I want to go full noir: neon fritzing signs reflected in rainy streets on Luna. Unless it shouldn't be Luna. Could do somewhere more interesting. They get vicious storms on Uranus. Wrath of God–type stuff. We shot something in Te Deum once, didn't we? What was it? *Thief of Light*? *The Oberon Assassin*? Christ, I can never remember. We've made too many movies, you and I. Or too few. Always too few. Too many to have any meaning, too few to say what we meant. But TD is a spectacular city, really. All those coloured towers—bioluminescent, you know—thick as a fat man's fingers, stubbing up pink and purple and hot green to the stars. Cheap as hell, too. Pubs everywhere like mushrooms in the morning. Good gravity, at least in the winter.

MAKO: If you insist on shooting on location, at a minimum we'll need permits for Neptune, Saturn, Jupiter. We're fine for principal photography on Luna, obviously. Venus?

UNCK: Oh, Vince, I don't know. I don't know if I can. Isn't there somewhere on the Moon we can dress for Venus? We have enough seas. I'll hose down half the globe if it means I don't have to go to Venus. Or we could try Earth. Glum old Earth. Moscow, maybe. Or Chicago. Could try Australia, but the red tape is absolutely frightful. Melbourne, perhaps. I can't stand Sydney. We almost did *Hope Has No Master* down there, remember? Looks quite a bit like the older parts of Mars. Then again, Mars actually gave us a better deal, when you figure in the tax incentives. Guan Yu is a fabulous town. You can see Mons Olympus from every balcony.

MAKO: But ultimately, we want a city. Deep in a city. Noir has to have a city. And a detective. I presume we're talking about Anchises.

UNCK: I know, I know. Who else could it be? If we don't produce him pretty quickly, everyone'll just be waiting for his entrance. We're telling a story everyone already knows. We gotta outrace their memory.

MAKO: I think he's living back on Venus, now. Shouldn't be too hard to find him, if we want the man himself.

UNCK: *Christ*, no, he's not gonna play himself! I'm not a masochist. Let him rot in those stinking swamps. I'll make him better than he ever was. Our great detective . . . and he's an amnesiac. Looking for his memory. Piecing his life together— and he can't do that without finding *her*. It writes itself. He hunts down the story, and he *is* the story. Get him a trench coat and a hat with a brim so sharp it'll cut the night. A revolver strapped to his hip, something big and mean looking. Fucking *never* stop raining on him. If I see a dry patch on that lantern jaw, so help me. We can even afford a voice-over if we want it.

[indistinct]

UNCK: Well, I don't particularly give a shit, Vince. Where's your obsession with authenticity now? Severin made talkies. It practically *has* to have sound.

MAKO: [long sigh] I'll talk to Freddy. So . . . our man needs a love interest. Someone more mysterious than he is. Long legs, long hair, long gazes. If you don't put someone on-screen who loves him, the audience won't know they're supposed to.

UNCK: Yes, now you're talking. A proper dame, in stockings and a dress tighter than a close-up shot. Smoky, broken eyes. Not the innocent kind, though. A fatale. As if I know how to make any other kind of heroine. You'd think after all these years I'd be able to manage one Ophelia amidst all of my Lady Macs. But no. It's just not in me.

MAKO: You know, I don't think we have to go to Venus at all. Our detective will know he needs to go, he'll *know* it's waiting up there, just sitting on the answers he wants like a stinking orange dragon, but he won't be able to face the idea of it. Of those red shores. Of the sound of the whales. Of going home. [wry laughter] Of course, you know Severin would hate every second of it.

UNCK: [long pause] She's not here. She started out like a heroine in one of my films. Why should she end up as anything else?

The Deep Blue Devil:
Come Find Me

Case Log: 14 December, 1961

It was closing in on midnight, the kind of midnight you only get on Uranus after a three-day bender. Ultramarine fog reeking of ethanol and neon and some passing whore's rosewater. Snow piled up like bodies in the street. Twenty-seven moons lighting up what oughta be a respectable witching hour so you can't help but see yourself staring back in every slick glowpink skyscraper. And the rings, always the rings, slashing down the sky, slashing down the storm, spitting shadows at the fella humping his carcass down Caroline Street, hat yanked down over his bloodshot eyes, coat hugged tight, shoes that need shining and a soul that needs taking in hand.

That'd be me. Anchises St. John, private nothing.

You can look at yourself everywhere you turn in Te Deum. The whole city is your shaving glass. Stare yourself down, scrunch up your eyes, and drag a dull blade down your cheek. The wall of the pub next to me flushed leek-green and I saw those sickly rings slicing across the skyline, disappearing through my neck and punching out again, a pure white shiv. I hear they used to make a big fuss over the light in Italy, painters and that crowd. Well, I've been to Italy, and the old girl's got nothing to teach

Uranus. A leprechaun would get a headache out here. It's the algae that does it. Algae in the ice, in the dirt, in the glass, in the big black dichroic swell of King George's Sea. They didn't build Te Deum, nor Herschel City, nor Harlequin. Didn't have to. They *grew* these stained-glass slum-gardens like mushrooms on a dead log. Salted the sea with a confetti of exotic hydrocarbons and up they sprung: unpredictable, enormous, disorganized— unless you dig an anemone's sense of feng shui. That's all they are. Anemones as hard as a man and as big as his ego. They only look like casinos or banks or dancehalls. Just the littlest bit alive, but nothing to lose sleep over.

If you have any sleep to lose. I like the idea of sleep, myself. Sounds like a nice place to visit.

So there I was, on Caroline Street, the hairiest street in the rowdiest city on the snowball. A good place to get forgotten. I was unshaved, unwashed, unslept, unwell, profoundly unsober, and had thus achieved all my aims in life. I had on the only suit I still owned under my jacket, a conservative raisin-coloured number with a chartreuse tie. And gloves, always gloves, even if the cold didn't slap me around like a whining brat, always gloves. I have a trunk of leather gloves lined with fleece and hydrostatic furpack. Yeah, leather. My only luxury. None of that brownfalse rubbish they say is just as good. Made special on Mars, where you gotta bat away steers like bottle flies. I need them thick, but they're never thick enough.

It was a suit fit for a job interview, though I hadn't let one of those get near me in years. I didn't think I could manage a conversation longer than *How much?* anyway. I can't stomach a man telling me what to do and when to do it. That cog got banged up good in me. The one that lets normal folks say, *Yes, sir; right away, sir,* and mean it. And then get the business done for the sirs of the world, right away, on the double-quick.

And yet. I wasn't on Caroline Street to scare up a woman or to sell my cufflinks for a lump of af-yun or put the last of my emergency protein fund on the ammonite races. I was calling on a million quid. A job. Gainful employment. A gig particularly suited to my extremely specific talents and *Historia Calamitatum*. If you lined up all the soul-choking jobs a body ever dreamed up, neat as a chorus line and twice as hungry, this'd be about the last dame I'd wanna take round the floor. And yet.

Being on time is a filthy habit practised only by roosters and retirees. Frankly, the roosters can't even get their heads on straight round here. The sun, such as it is, comes up every seventeen hours on Uranus. It's hard on the poultry. Still, I probably woulda made it, despite all my efforts to black out before the hour struck Cinderella, if the Astor hadn't put up a midnight show. One of those weird, off-putting studio talkies from back in the bad old days when Edison ruled the nickelodeon universe with a celluloid fist. We get a lot of that stuff out here. This is the end of the line for movie prints. It takes ten years to get them out to Uranus and once they make landfall they tend to stick. Just kind of swirl around the theatres like water down a drain till the reels break or someone steals them. If you're looking for a flick that no one's seen hide of for a good long howl, there's probably one kicking round some freezer case in a Uranian cellar. Who knows where they dug this one up?

The Astor marquee came ghosting up out of the blue brume, sickly topaz pop-bulbs and black block letters bearded with ice.

Self-Portrait with Saturn.

Well, fuck me sideways.

I didn't wanna buy a ticket. For one thing, I've seen it. Boy howdy, have I seen it. For another, my petty cash was feeling particularly petty that night. There's probably a third thing. I didn't want a ticket. I sure as hell didn't want the booth jockey to smell my breath and wrinkle her pretty little pierced nose like her opinion kept the lights on. I didn't wanna sit fifth row centre in a chair whose springs would leave red half-moons on my arse by the end of that self-indulgently long barely-a-movie. I *did* want the cheap pus-yellow port wine they make up on Miranda out of callowmilk, freeze-dried coca, grapes that once sneezed in the general direction of France, and whatever else is lying around the floor for flavour. Popcorn alone won't pay the rent on Caroline Street. I did want to sit in the clammy warmth of that god-awful cathedral-arched candy-cane decoglass theatre, under the headless, broken saltrock cherubs and breadcoral mermaids holding up the sconces on the wall, the threadbare peacock curtain, the greened brass EXIT sign.

And I did want to see her.

I didn't want to *watch* her. But I wanted to *see* her. The way you want to see an old friend, or an ex-lover you hope is miserable without you. Fix her coffee and listen to her troubles, make concerned faces and sympathetic mooing noises in all the right places while she gets bitter and hot as the coffee. But all the while you're sizzling with excitement; your heart's a champagne burn. Her sorrow tastes fantastic. It's a sorrow for savouring, and when she wants to spend her despair in your bed, you'll say no, and that'll taste fantastic, too.

That's why I slunk into my seat instead of showing up where I shoulda been. Rigorously ignoring the five or ten other sets of eyeballs in that dank cave of a theatre. Barely able to get my yammering heart or my pickled gut under control. Leaning forward like she'd notice me if I got far enough in her face. Like she was a schoolteacher who'd choose somebody out of the shiny row of brats spelling furiously for her pleasure and love the kid who had the right answer best of all. Except, I didn't have it. Nobody did. But nobody felt bad about that the way I did.

Nobody was supposed to know how to spell "Venus" but me.

I stopped breathing when the lights went down. Gripping the arms of my seat like the paws on a claw-foot tub, my nails going right down into the damp wood. The breadcoral broads up on the wall leered down, acting out the birth of the Titans, I think, their rough carrot-coloured arms full of lights and tiny monsters with tails and feathers and snouts. Two rows up a fella took off his hat. A head already moved rhythmically up and down in his lap. Before the credits! Have a little class!

She came on-screen eyes first. The sight of her irises slammed into me like a pair of heart attacks. I felt the port wine come up, harsh sulphur bile in the back of my throat. I smelled a storm of phantoms: cacao-fern, burnt coconut bark, the terrible copper-sugar whip of a faraway sea. My wrists throbbed. The opening music jangled in my ears, a nauseating player piano going fifteen rounds with my one working eardrum. Her face: fifty feet high.

She is a planet. She is the sun. She is the only woman in the world. She is so young. She is adjusting the camera in a self-indulgent little bit of metafilm that always made me embarrassed for her. I hate her and I am hard and I am sick and I adore her and I want to fuck her and I want to tear her apart and I want to save her and I want her to tell me it's all okay and I am ten years old again and nothing bad has happened yet. I turned to the empty seat next to me and threw up onto the floor of the Astor, a milky, mewling splash of stomach juices and Miranda's best, my head moving rhythmically up and down. No one cared. It was for someone else to clean up.

I couldn't stand looking at her anymore. I used to do nothing else. I lived to stare at her. I worked enough to eat enough to look at her. Every image; any image. All of them. And there were always so many to choose from. I could sit down to a banquet of her and gorge myself. On some nights I might even have started with *Self-Portrait*—it's such a rookie's flick, a young wine, untried, raw, too afraid of the palate to use it well. But then I'd pull back, pace myself, nibble on her cameos in her old man's films: a little baby in an interplanetary stagecoach beset by pirates, a cherub devil besetting a nun's big, bright soul. A quick salad of red carpets and Percy's home movies before gobbling down another of her features. Always keeping Venus for last, always putting off *Radiant Car* as long as possible, always dreading that first savage moment when she and I shared the stage. Not yet, not yet. First a soup course of interviews and newsreels—I always liked to end with the last interview.

You've seen it. Who hasn't seen it?

The sacrificial not-even-close-to-a-virgin laughing in a soft grey chair, wearing long silk trousers and a dark scrap of Tritonic fabric flung over her shoulders. It hides her breasts, binds them down something breathless, but shows her belly, and she's just so *languid*, so unconcerned, gesturing with a cigarette in a long black holder. A party wheels around her. Hartford Crane kisses her hand while the Grenadine sisters dance in shimmering sheaths nearby. Torn-out ransom letters of her talk flash on-screen between the dancers and the champagne like cut sequins spilling all over the floor as the night grows wild and thick.

It's her eulogy. She gave it herself and no one's ever managed better. Recorded on sound equipment that must have cost more than the house she drank in, sewn together to make a good monologue from whatever she said before Annabelle August collapsed into her lap in a tangled heap of long limbs and giggles and blue pearls and she lost interest in anything else.

I know her pearls were blue, though the film shows only smooth grey. Sometimes the things I know are of no use at all.

Oh, I'm not famous. Don't laugh! I'm not being disingenuous. I have money, and my father is famous, but that's not the same thing as being famous, and that isn't the same thing as being good, or being good at anything. That's just people knowing your name and what you wore on Tuesday. I didn't deserve any of that. It was pure chance that I was born in that place and at that certain time— and, unbelievable! Really, all those mothers! I think it needs a rewrite or two to make it relatable. I've tried to make good on that wholly unfair premise. But I haven't yet. Famine Queen, you say—sure—and The Sea. *Yes, those are certainly films I made. But they're nothing. Journeyman stuff. I took a camera along while I saw the solar system. No better than half the lens freaks are doing, and worse than some. This one, though. When I think about* Radiant Car, *my heart hurts. Like the movie is already done and showing inside me, projecting onto the inside of my skin, flickering on the white screens of my bones. As long as I don't fuck it up. As long as I don't, then maybe, when I've come back and we all know what happened out there in Adonis, when I can sit in this chair and tell you about everything I saw, everything I felt, what the seas of Venus smelled like—well, then maybe we can talk about fame. Because to me, famous is only worth shit if you've earned it through the work of your hands, and I haven't earned anything yet. I feel like I can almost touch the edge of goodness. But not yet, not yet. Come find me in two years. Maybe then I'll be worthy of you.*

I loved to hear her say those words. *Come find me in two years.* Half a year's shooting, plus transit to and from and post-production back home. I watched with my face so close to hers, waiting for her to say she's nothing yet. She's nothing yet because she hasn't met me. Just a rich, beautiful girl—and there she is, saying flat out that she's not worthy of me or even good. Her words taste like whiskey and oh, how the bouquet improves when you play them back over a long shot of her rocket disappearing in the sky, becoming a punctuation mark in that last, sad sentence.

Her flicks packed the nickelodeons and wrapped the streets three times round. Weeks before her movies opened, buskers and salesmen would camp out on the thoroughfares beside every theatre, selling genuine cells she touched with her own hand and replica spangled cages from *Self-Portrait,* sized just right to hold a gravity-challenged male of Saturnine extraction. Why? Why all that crass excitement? I still can't figure it out. Her father was

Percival Unck, a brooding, notorious director in his time. Made a heap of sweaty gothic dramas full of wraith-like heroines with black, bruised eyes and mouths hanging open in horror or orgiastic transcendence or both. Her mother was probably one of those ever-transcendent actresses, though which one it was, the man kept to himself. Each Unck leading lady became, by association and binding contract, the poor kid's mother. You can see in her flickering, dust-scratched face the echoes of a half-dozen fleeting, hopeful actresses, some still famous, some easily forgotten except in the odd mood flashing across their daughter's lean features, her cryptic glances, her scornful, knowing grin.

She washed her hands of Daddy sometime between *Famine Queen* and *The Sleeping Peacock*. Her film debut in *The Spectres of Mare Nubium* is charming, if you go for the cute kid shtick. During the famous ballroom sequence where the decadent dowager Clarena Schirm is beset with the ghosts of her victims, Severin can be seen picking at the pearls on her bonnet and rubbing at her makeup. The legend goes that when the great man tried to stick eyeshadow on his girl and convince her to pretend to be a Schirm relation while a hungry shade—a young Maud Locksley, no less—swooped down upon the innocent child, she looked up exasperatedly and said, "Papa. This is silly! I want only to be myself!"

And so she would be, only herself, forever and always. As soon as she could work the crank on a camera by her lonesome, she set about recording "the really real and actual world" (age seven) or "the genuine and righteous world of the true tale" (age twenty-one) and declaring her father's beloved ghosts and devils "a load of double-exposure drivel." Her second documentary, *The Famine Queen of Phobos*, brought that blasted little colony's food riots to harsh light and earned her a Lumière medal, a prize Papa would never get his paws on. Maybe that was it. She told the truth once or twice, and she told it with a bleeding head and a broken arm: Old Mummy Earth is a mean drunk, and she doesn't look after her babies too well.

When asked if his daughter's fury in the face of fiction ever got to him, Unck smiled in his raffish, canine way and said, "The lens, my good man, does not discriminate between the real and the unreal."

Of her final film, *The Radiant Car Thy Sparrows Drew*, only four sequences remain. They're all badly damaged. Everybody copies them, cuts them up and spits them out again into endless anaemic tell-all docs I wouldn't wipe my feet on. The originals continue to putrefy in some museum in Chicago. More people than you'd think go there to watch them rot. I did. It was comforting. You plonked your head against the cool wall on a soft pink Midwestern evening that seems impossible when you're freezing to death on Uranus. She flashes before your eyes: a sprite, a fairy at the end of a long, dark tunnel, smiling, waving, crawling into the mouth of the cannon capsule with the ease of a natural performer.

Sometimes folk recognize me, even this far out, from the old newsreels, though I never gave interviews and the lawyers haven't let anybody show my face since '51. I don't like looking at myself on-screen. It's what you call existentially upsetting: I am here and I am there. But I can't chase down all the images of myself.

Here's the short of it: A handful of people survived Unck's Venus expedition, and I'm one of them. I don't remember everything, and not everything I remember is important. My life, my life proper, began when a woman with short black hair and a leather aviator's cap and coat crouched down in front of me and asked my name. The lost boy, the turning boy. I came back, and she didn't.

Don't think I've forgiven myself for that.

Now I watch. I've watched everything. I can't stop watching.

Waiting for the docs to show me just a little of her face; show her laughing; show her when she was a child, her arms stretched up, asking her father to lift her onto his shoulders, away from the chaos of adult feet and canes and slippers dancing to Mickey Hull's latest 'dustrial-Charleston rag. Show me anything of hers. I'm as bad as any of them, begging to stare at her corpse for just one more moment—or, if not her corpse, the places where she once stood and stands no more. Tell me, invisible voice-over, voice of god and memory, tell me everything I already know. Tell me my life.

But her face was a slow poison to me. I knew it, I knew it, and I tucked in anyway, starving for her narrow, monkish, poreless cheeks, her eyes huge and sly and as black as her hair.

I can't even say her name. She doesn't have a name. She is *she*. She is *her*. She possesses the pronoun so completely that no one else can touch it. There is only one *her* in the great stinking gas giant of my heart, fifty feet high. She is a giantess. I am no one. Well, not "no one." I am Anchises St. John. But I am no one's *him*.

Do you know what she does first in *Self-Portrait*? She smiles. She fucking *smiles*. And then she laughs. A sweet, wry little self-deprecating laugh. Like she's embarrassed to be taking up so much space in the shot. Like she has stage fright. But she wasn't. She didn't. Nothing embarrassed her. Maybe she had stage fright when her ma first put a tit in her mouth, but never a day since. *Off*stage fright, maybe. She never knew what to do with herself if the camera wasn't running. But the laugh *says* she's embarrassed. The smile tells us she has butterflies. *Oh, isn't it a funny damn racket, to be in the flickies? Who, me? This old thing? I'm so nervous! Who needs a drink?*

I haven't earned anything yet.

Come find me in two years.

Her smile yawns up over me, black and white and enormous—and I knew, as only a man who's stared at it until he ralphed into his own lap can know—entirely fake. It's a good one, though. One of my favourites of hers. Full of the feral thrill that surrounded All Things Venus back then. People couldn't get enough of that shitty little burg—the one world that made all the others possible. But it's *their* smile, not hers. Look at her, *look* at her, don't you see? She's going to Venus. She smiles like people smile when they're obsessed with Venus. It's a smile like a trailer for the real thing.

But no, it's too soon for that. I was drunk. I hadn't slept in three days. When I think of *her* I see all her movies, all her faces, at the same time. Stacked up into orbit. But you can't see what I see. I see the Venus smile, but it's not there yet. This one's a baby version of that nine-thousand-watt grin. It's Face #212: Intrepid Girl Reporter. She hadn't been to Venus yet. *Venus always felt so obvious,* she told me under the hot, wet stars of Adonis, when she didn't think I could hear her. In *Self-Portrait with Saturn,* Venus was four movies and nine years away. Up there, she's just a kid. Twenty-one. Sleeps like a dragonfly so she never misses a thing. Lovers like a revolving door. Drinks like she's allergic to water. She's barely a person yet. The girl in that decrepit print with a cigarette burn in the middle of her forehead like the mark of Cain and film scratches all down her cheeks doesn't even know that *Self-Portrait* will be a hit. Better than a hit. It'll make her name. *Her* name. Not her old man's.

These're things I know about her. These're things everyone knows about her. It's not fair that I should know as much as anyone who cares to pick up a magazine. I should know more. I should know it all. But you begin where you begin, and hope—even if hope is a pickpocket with both fists full—to go, somehow, further and higher.

Well, I began with her. And she began on-screen.

I hunt for likenesses between us. For places where, laid over one another, our topographies would match. Capital to capital. River to river. There aren't many. I try to make more, but she's done, finished, finite, and I am not.

And what about me? I don't remember a damn thing before the age of ten. A man is nothing but memory, and by that count I was born on a burnt grass shore with a woman grabbing my wrist so hard she bruised me, a neat line of her four fingers on my skin, over my pulse, over my heart. A flash of light: *fiat* fucking *lux*. The smoky, acidic smell of the sea. Hot, pollen-drunk wind. A whirr and a clatter. I've been recorded since I was born. So has she. That great black eye got us good. I was born the minute I was noticed.

Before that there's just a calm pre-credits wipe of darkness, nothing into nothing. There's footage of my entrance; there's footage of her exit. We're each missing the other half. I only know my parents' names because people who oughta know wrote them down for me. Her father sat astride her life. His name is her name. What luxury.

The fifty-foot woman winks. To no one. To me. To the hatless man and his orally-fixated buddy. To the Astor and Te Deum and the mermaids with their miniature Titans. But really to a solemn goatee'd bellhop in a blue cap who dutifully dropped the needle on an old phonograph so that we could all hear her deep yet somehow nasal voice echo loudly—too loud, too loud—in the theatre.

It hurt our ears. Everyone winced, straightened up. Hatless got his jollies *interruptus*. We all hated it. We all squirmed.

Nobody makes talkies anymore.

I could stand her face, but her voice did me to pieces. I heard her say the first words of her first movie and her first words to me all at once; and I've taken punches, I've taken gut stabs, but I couldn't take that.

I used to look up at night and dream of the solar system.

Hey, little guy. It's good now. It's fine now. I'm here. My name's Severin. You can call me Rinny if you like that better.

I stumbled out of the Astor and onto Caroline Street, into the blue fog and the smell and the wet, snowed-in trash. Into the bells bonging out my missed midnight appointment. Coughing, crying like a damned widow, wiping sour, half-digested port wine slime from my mouth. The glowglass alley pulsed grape to apricot. Juliet and Titania, coupla old crescent hags, judged me from the heavens. Umbriel sloshed up slowly under the girls, the lights of Wunda coming on across its blasted moonface. All those moons. The sky over Uranus always looked like a bloody traffic jam to me. Venus doesn't have any moons. The sky is unbroken. Perfect. A sky that can't look back.

Tears froze on my face. Very unmanly. But of the things I've lost, manliness left first and easiest.

Radiant Car's a horror flick, is what it is. An old Gothic screamer with tits just barely kept in check by veils and corsets and the rating system. A girl went into the dark and met a monster there. So simple. So easy to fill the seats with that kind of thing.

So easy to empty them with the truth.

I wasn't even allowed to enjoy my misery. Caroline Street gagged on the mobs getting riled up for All-Clear. Nothing but elbows and eyeshadow. A car pulled up alongside me, a gorgeous red Talbot that would part the seas anywhere else, but the All-Clear has no respect for vehicles. See, old buddy Uranus, he got a day as short as your mama's skirt. Humans don't like it. Keeping a seventeen-hour day jitters you up like bad cocaine. Feels like you've got engines behind your eyes burning out your fluids. Like you carried the sun with you all this way, and lord but the old bitch hates being ignored. At this distance, she's not much more than a foggy streetlight through the snow and the fumes. Jupiter's bigger and badder and brighter. But the lady does like things done her way. Thing of it is, seven hours is just too big a gap to be able to make it up with a nice Martian nap at 12:01 Greenwich. You notice seven hours when they don't come home from the bar. So they built us a fake day out of the outworld twilight that goes on forever. Ignore that little splatter of phlegm in the sky; the glowglass will tell the hours: bright in the morning, dim in the evening. If you know what's good for you, you let your neon tenement tuck you in with a cup of warm shut-your-mouth at 2100 sharp. These All-Clear kids, though. They sleep the short sleep. In their clock-addled heads, they've gone Uranian. They keep the seventeen-hour day, sped up, cat-napping, caffeine-surfing, cramming their living and sleeping and joyful noise into a horrid squeezebox. And at 1700, that no-man's time in which their midnight ticks over while the rest of the world grinds home to supper, they begin their dalliance with the Uranian clock. They're all dead asleep by the time most of TD is tucking into the evening's drink, and up again for work and wickedness when everybody's babies are snoozing away the lightless night. The All-Clear rings out at midnight proper, midnight mean time, and in their dawn and our dead of nothing, they have their church. God is in the overlap, they say.

And when the All-Clear sounds, Bedlam would call it madness. They dance this no-skill-required rabbit-jumping dance and shove stimulants up their noses, down their throats, in their arms, under their tongues, anywhere a fix will fit. They wear big glittery fish-fin masks dripping with snowmelt and those wizened little glass pearls that fall out of the sky in the gorgeous, higrav spring monsoons. Rainpearls. Or so I hear. I arrived in winter, and it'll be another twenty years before I see the crocus shrimp mass on King George's Sea.

I tried the All-Clear when I first got here. You always gotta try the local madness once. It gave me a heart murmur. There's an awful little pantomime right before it ends. Like one of those old Punch and Judy shows. The whole thing is pretty low-rent, but religion usually is. Takes some piss-poor manners to worship a planet. It's already doing everything it can for you.

I didn't want any part of their hallelujah, or, for that matter, anything the long, lurid, teardrop-shaped Talbot had to offer. I was nowhere near far gone enough for whoring, and I had no scratch for purchasing distraction. I turned up my collar. Houndstooth light stung my eyes like snow. I made a sharp left onto Tethys Road. A dark spit of nothing, is Tethys. All back doors, no front. Strictly corridor action, running from Caroline Street to Epimetheus 'Vard. But that bastard car ground on in after me over the snow. Its headlights swung round, pink whips against my back. I knew the drill: Sooner or later they'd get bored with lumbering after me in first gear and step on it, swing wide, roll down the window, and out would come the girl with rouge on her face and eyes practically spinning a merry-go-round with af-yun and King George's Fumes. She'd offer to buy me or sell herself for the men in the backseat. I've lived in Te Deum for seventeen months of winter. It is a *fuck* of a long block I've been around.

That's about how it happened. Before I could disappear into the All-Clear crowds on Epi 'Vard, the Talbot swung out in front and cut me off. Just sat there glowing like a hot coal. So dark a red as to be black, so bright a black as to be red. Steam coming off the cherry hood, fog on the smoky windows. Christ, it had to be so warm in there. Warm enough to sleep. Warm enough to lay down naked with that long leather bench seat—leather from a *cow*, not squeaky brownfalse imitation—under your bum. The driver kept the engine running. Mocking me. Even in this snap I bet you could fry a ham on that hood. Raise a Miranda pig in the boot, let it run wild in the acreage of the backseat, slaughter it in the passenger side, and fry it up on the hood.

The window stayed shut. The door swung open and a pair of

long, long legs slid out. Legs like a pilgrimage. Silver stockings, pumpkin pumps, suit green as the salads I haven't seen in years. Her scarf was a scrap of silk the same colour as the Talbot, disappearing down her cleavage—which, I'm happy to report, was both substantial and on display. The dame didn't even get out. She leaned her elbows on her knees and plunked her sweet little face down into her hands. She was tall, but delicately built, like a moth. She had rouge on, but not a slut brand. The expensive stuff. The kind that comes in colours with names. The kind that comes from *home*. From Earth, where you can make anything as easy as tripping and falling. Lipstick to match her shoes. Eyelashes as long as my thumb, tipped in a soft fuchsia fringe. Nails to match her big violet eyes. I bet she had that shade done up special—the nails or the eyes; I wouldn't know which. A classy piece by any measure. She smelled like accounts receivable. She looked like old money. The kind of money that can ship a Talbot all the way to the outer planets without chipping the paint.

"You're late," the dame said. Big, rolling voice. An American voice: round, hard, flat, open as Sioux country and twice as dry. Interesting.

"Not 'late' if I never planned on showing up," I replied. My voice was not big, nor did it roll. My voice cracked. It crumbled. It shook. I never had what you'd call a leading man's timbre. My voice starts coming apart as soon as it leaves my mug.

Lady pouted. Small baby-bird lips in her broad, curved face. Maybe some Chinese mixed in with the Sioux. Maybe not. Not too much call for knowing the American gene spread on the snowball.

"Now why would you want to hurt my feelings like that? And after my employer has been so generous with you. Anyone in TD would skip their rocket home for the tiniest hope of the faintest ghost of a meeting like the one you're booked down for."

She blinked demurely. The furry fuchsia petals on the ends of her eyelashes kissed her cheekbones. It was a gesture designed to unman. Lucky for me that job got done long before she came along. But this girl did have other weapons. Smells fired out of the cabin with precision, hit me with both barrels: cigar smoke and oily brown liquor and, Christ redeemed, *bread*. High-end labels on all counts. No callowmilk mix-ins, just applewood casks and tobacco fields in the sun. And wheat. I couldn't believe it—couldn't even understand it. There just isn't money like that. It doesn't exist. Drug money, mineral money, whore money, sure. But not bread money. Not here.

You can't grow grain on Uranus. Point of fact, grain is a hard call all over. Grain guzzles sun; accept no substitutes. Venus, Neptune, and parts of Uranus do rice. The road to heaven is paved with rice. Rice isn't picky, doesn't play favourites, will go home with anyone if they've got water and light in the fridge, though she mutates if you look at her funny. Uranian rice is electric blue with a black bran, the longest of long grain. Tannic tea-ish aftertaste that'll pucker your face. Official name is *Capilli Regis Filiae Sophiae*. Princess Sophia's Hair. With a name like that, you know there's nothing but groundbound idiots in charge back home on Earth. They'd name their own shits after a princess if they could. We call it rice, for fuck's sake. Saturn has rhea: carefully bred lavender corn. It's not half bad. But then, anything Uranus can do, Saturn can do better. Bigger rings, more moons, deeper mines, food that'll grow without a guy getting down on his knees to beg. Mars, being a bitch of many talents, can do you quinoa, amaranth, even a stunted barley in a good year, but no wheat. Mercury's got fuck-all, and who'd bother trying on Jupiter? Probably half the moons get by on hybrids. Pluto, our nearest buddy, the mad wife in the attic of the solar system, has a night-blooming lily called infanta. (See? Even the Yanks love a princess.) Big, blowsy white flowers with a nutritional mug shot not unlike a coconut: fat, sugar, carbs, calcium. When the first ship landed, all they saw were the lilies, covering the whole planet. Turned toward the spittle-sun like radio antennae. Landed in a field of them like Santa Claus in the snow.

I've never eaten one. I'd like to, before I close out my accounts. I've heard they taste like honey and coffee and your mother's own milk. But Plutonians don't export. Not so much as a fart aimed down-system. The youngest kid never has to share their toys.

You think about food a lot when you don't have any. The parts of your brain that used to think about getting ahead in the world, about doing wrong to those who need it, about art or fucking, they just get burnt out, 'til they can't do anything but grind on the thought that if I lived on Saturn I could have corn.

Here you get loaves of midnight-green lichen scraped off the bottom of King George's Sea, mashed up with callowmilk and Sophie's Shits and morels. Cubed for your barest sustenance. Collect your weekly allowance at your local Depot. Oh, I know morels sound like the better quarter of that mess, but they're not really morels, just what we call the powder-blue mushrooms that grow on the lee side of the luminescent towers. Come up by the million at sunrise; taste like your grandma's worst perfume; rich in all-important vitamin D, vitamin C, and Queen Sugar; and ever so slightly hallucinogenic.

Fuck morels and fuck vitamin C, too. The bitch had *bread*. Real bread. With a crust and a soft middle. And it was *hot*. It had had carnal relations with an oven on the recent.

My stomach, recently vacated, made its preferences known. It wasn't a fair fight and the American lady knew it. *Come, dog. Heel. Good boys get treats.* She reached back and pulled out a knob of something wrapped in wax paper. She didn't say a thing— didn't have to. Just peeled back the red wax wrapper corner by corner with her perfect purple nails. Slow like, so I could hear it coming away from the creamy lump of heaven within.

Butter.

"Get in the car," the dame said, and it would knock your head back how fast I did what I was told.

Good dog. Sit up. Shake a paw.

Newsreel

PROMOTIONAL MATERIAL INCLUDED WITH ORIGINAL TRAILER REELS OF THE RADIANT CAR THY SPARROWS DREW; *WITHDRAWN IN FINAL PRINTS*

TITLE CARD

The Road to Heaven is Paved With Prithvi Brand Concentrated Callowmilk—You Can't Leave Home Without It!

[Male voice-over, a rich, deep, and reassuring voice, but not authoritative—an after-dinner voice, merely sharing its knowledge among friends.]

VOICE-OVER

What can you do without Prithvi Brand Callowmilk? Nothing.

[Stock footage of Venus beaches, palms waving like vacation posters under a brilliant sun.]

Hand-harvested on the lush, scarlet shores of Venus, the most precious bounty of the universe arrives at every supper table courtesy of your friends at Prithvi Deep-Sea Holdings Incorporated.

[Shot of a thick mahogany table groaning with

an array of PDSH products: glass pitchers of foamy callowmilk, porcelain dishes of callowbutter, china bowls of ice cream, rinds of callowcheese enrobed in gleaming wax. A happy, portly family greets each other at the evening meal, all smiles after a long day of honest labour. They join hands to say grace. Transition to another family, this time on Venus, in a traditional cacao-wood hut, divers' helmets visible in the background. The same PDSH largesse blesses this table, the same contented smiles, the same bright-eyed, attractive children.]

Our divers, carefully selected for their strength and daring, begin by seeking out the most majestic and fertile of the great callowhales in the furthest deeps of the Sea of Qadesh. They tirelessly search out the fattest fishies with the richest colours and the longest fronds, heavy with the sweetest milk available. Like knights tangling with the dragons of old, Prithvi divers pierce the most promising balloons with their gleaming spiles, draining that exquisite cream into instant-sealing amphorae, locking in freshness so that not a whiff of vapour is lost.

[A diver in a finned copper helmet battles the immense, seaweed-like fronds of a callowhale. The perilous electrified ferns fall all around her like a forest, like Sleeping Beauty's briars, until she thrusts her spile into a greenish gas bladder as if tapping into a maple tree to catch the syrup.]

Don't worry, kids! The whales don't feel a

thing, any more than you do when a strand of your hair falls out and wafts away on the wind. Once the milk arrives on shore, it enters our clean and modern processing stations.

[Footage of assembly lines and bottling machines; workers smile and wave at the camera.]

Prithvi Holdings cares about sustainability. Our facilities are wholly integrated with Venusian village life, providing safe, reliable employment and a number of enrichment programs that make life on Venus a breeze. Happy workers make premium products!

Take young master Willem Greenaway.

[A fresh-faced young man with wide-set eyes shakes hands with the foreman of the Hedylogos sector plant. The boy wears a Sunday suit. He is well fed and tall, with excellent posture.]

Only sixteen and already possessed of a lifetime of applicable skills! When his tour on Venus is finished, he will be able to choose his homestead from any planet or moon—and, no doubt, his wife from any of the solar system's most eligible ladies.

[Willem's steely, stalwart stare takes in the crashing Sea of Qadesh, the massive callowhales floating like islands offshore.]

Yes, his work is dangerous, but young Willem knows that without his service and the devotion of everyone at Prithvi, from the lowest milkmaid to the fleet-fingered shipping agent to every last shareholder, there could be no saloons on Mars, no cruises on Neptune, no movies on the

Moon. Willem Greenaway and those like him are truly the backbone of all the worlds. And Prithvi makes it possible.

[A young, buxom mother with well-muscled arms sets a platter of pint jars brimming with milk in front of her crowd of five ruddy-cheeked children. She holds the dish before her ample breasts— a wonderful substitute and improvement on their bounty—and smiles beatifically, the vision of responsible motherhood.]

And now, Prithvi Brand Concentrated Callowmilk has a new, better-tasting formula!

[The children, all taller than average and without blemishes or birthmarks, clamour for their mother's milk. She gives them what they want and settles into a hickory rocking chair with her newborn—and a bottle of Prithvi Brand Callowrich Infant Formula.]

Fortified with a secret blend of spices and vitamins, callowmilk products don't just taste good, they taste *better* than dairy products, more wholesome, richer, cleaner, and better for you! We know you care about your family's health—and so do we.

[A nutritional graph shows briefly, the bars of the chart represented by cartoon callowhales with cheery grins and spouts of water bursting from friendly blowholes in varying, informational heights.]

Just one serving of Prithvi products at every meal provides a wallop of protein, fat, immuno-boosters, ultra-calcium, and plain, old-fashioned deliciousness. In recent taste tests, mothers preferred Prithvi milk over our competitors nearly two to one. Those are numbers we can be proud of. And it doesn't stop at the supper table!

[An array of PDSH products flashes before the camera in new, redesigned packaging.]

Our callowmilk proves itself over and over, as a foodstuff, industrial lubricant, fuel additive, fertility aid, antibiotic, anaesthesia, base for many indoor and outdoor paints, recreational hallucinogen, and coal substitute. When dried and moulded, it produces excellent building materials and its proteins provide fibre for the most fashionable fabrics. And, of course, callowmilk is the only source for the all-important bone density supplement and radioactivity prophylactic, without which humanity would still be bound to one lonely planet.

[The buxom mother tucks her children into bed one by one, finishing with the baby in its bassinet. Her face shows infinite love and careful concern.]

Yes, Prithvi Brand Concentrated Callowmilk truly is the stuff of life. We take our duty as stewards of this priceless substance seriously. You can taste our commitment in every sip.

[A bottle of classic Prithvi Callowmilk on a black starfield, the label showing the same genial, comic callowhale blowing a fountain of milk out of its grinning blue head.]

Prithvi Brand Concentrated Callowmilk: You can't leave home without it. See your local recruiter for information about lucrative opportunities in Prithvi's Offshore Operations Sector!

From the Personal Reels of
Percival Alfred Unck

SEVERIN UNCK

Daddy, why won't the movies talk to me?

[PERCIVAL UNCK laughs and crouches down next to his dark-haired gamine child. His beard is thin along his jawbone. She pats the silk projection screen with her hands, imploring it to speak.]

PERCIVAL UNCK

Do you remember Uncle Freddy, from the Christmas party?

SEVERIN

He gave me a wind-up pony.

PERCIVAL

Yes. Well. Uncle Freddy has enough money to buy all the wind-up ponies you can think of, because his grandfather invented the moving picture camera and several other devilishly useful gadgets, plus a few things he didn't really invent but told everyone he did anyway, including a machine that could record sound and make the movies talk.

[SEVERIN lights up, as though she expects that now her father will reveal to her a world of speaking movies she had heretofore been denied.]

PERCIVAL

Oh, my wee small baroness, don't look at me that way.

[He takes his daughter in his arms. Her dress crinkles loudly as the petticoat brushes the microphone.]

PERCIVAL

Baby girl, do you remember the bandit in *Thief of Light*? How he wanted to keep everything locked away in his great lonely house, the crown jewels and the Miraculous Machine and Mina Ivy most of all?

SEVERIN

Yes, Papa. He was bad. And he had a mask.

PERCIVAL

Well, Uncle Freddy is like that. Only the crown jewels are audio patents, and the Miraculous Machine is a stack of colour film patents, and Mina Ivy is a world where a girl in a movie could sing to you in a red dress.

Self-Portrait with Saturn

(Tranquillity Studios, 1936, dir. Severin Unck)

(ACCOMPANYING MATERIAL: RECORD 1, SIDE 1, COMMENCE 0:37)

SC1 INT. LOCATION #3 NAVIGATIONAL CABIN—DAY 483 AFTERNOON [3 SEPTEMBER, 1935]

[FADE IN: Pilot's nave of the good ship *Stone in Swaddling Clothes*, 1600 hours. Six hanging lanterns are tuned to low afternoon. Portholes show the glittering ice flow of the Orient Express speeding before and behind: Earth's affectionate nickname for the steady, stalwart currents and eddies of ether and frozen debris cradling the *Swaddling Clothes* in advantageous gravitational tracks and the kind of acceleration no engine could muster. Jupiter shines ahead: Grand Central Station. There the long silver craft will loop around and lurch forward with renewed, breakneck momentum, the final leg to Saturn little more than a controlled fall from Jupiter's great height. But the giant planet is still small, no bigger than a lonely cellar light bulb in the distance. Readouts display all well. Lights pulse on and off, slow and steady, the heartbeat of the ship.

SEVERIN UNCK curls up in the plush astronomer's chair with a globe of cider to suck and a knob of af-yun palmed in her large hand. A casual habit now, but one she will never quite kick. She chews tiny peels of it as she talks, carving them free with a dark fingernail. Most prefer to smoke it, but the fumes would interfere with the instruments. She wears a pearl-grey sari; her eyes sport heavy black shadow and liner thick as a zebra stripe. Her short hair has gone frizzy from the static charge in her cabin and she looks tired. Tired but excited. Scrupulously maintained shipboard muscles show in her arms, her stomach, and the stony calves she dangles over the arm of the chair. Exercise on Earth and exercise in transit do not make the same bodies. SEVERIN has spent half her life in the sky. There is a *longness* to her, a hyper-Vitruvian extension anyone would recognize. Her skin is the odd blue of all natives of Earth's Moon, the natural result of long-term exposure to the colloidal silver present in the entire lunar water supply. It appears on black and white film as the distinct soft charcoal grey sported by every star and starlet since the first ingénue took a bow with the Earth rising behind her.

Nine months on the ice road this time. Only another fortnight to go. Nine months with the same twenty-seven souls: her seven-member skeleton film crew and the twenty-strong mummers' troupe SEVERIN hoofed to Saturn as a show of goodwill to the locals. Entertainment is as dear as bread on the outer planets.

Her delivery is natural and thoughtful, as though she has just pulled up that velvet chair to have a chat with us. Almost out of frame, a multicoloured script rests on the floor of the nave. The original draft pages are white; new scenes and major edits are a range of colours: blue, red, green, gold, pink, lavender. On film, they all flatten to silver and black. She turns the pages with a casual, dangling toe. It's a subtle movement, but it's there. It has a rhythm. A little dance between her body and the script. Whatever we are about to hear, however casual it sounds, none of it is unplanned, unedited, or unrewritten from the first earnest pause to the last well of tears.

SEVERIN adjusts George's aperture. Her face comes very close to the camera—we can see the bags under her eyes and the first lines starting at the corners of her lids. For a moment, it is possible to imagine what she will look like as an old woman. Satisfied, she slots a sound cylinder into place and rests her feet against the long-distance radio. The film fuzzes and judders with the motion of the ship as Severin records the opening monologue of her first and perhaps most personal film.

SEVERIN smiles.]

SEVERIN

I used to look up at night and dream of the solar system. I know, I know—who didn't? But your
own dreams always seem so special, so terribly
yours, until you grow up and figure out they're
just like everyone else's. How perfect and beautiful and silent and dead each planet hung in my
heart! All nine names, written in squiggly, shaky
handwriting, glowing inside me.

[FADE to a series of drawings. They are the
works of a child, but an exceptional child, who
might make something of herself someday. The
beginnings of an understanding of chiaroscuro, a
hard handle on perspective. A male hand turns each
drawing aside. It wears a wedding ring, but on the
wrong hand. The child's planets go by in school-
house order: Mercury, Venus, Earth, the Moon, Mars
and the asteroids, Jupiter, Saturn, Uranus, Neptune, Pluto. Forests stick out from the surface of
the Moon like sunbeams; flowers ring Pluto like a
doll's curls. Susanoo-no-Mikoto, the eternal hur-
ricane, glowers red on the face of Jupiter. The
crayon strokes slash so deep they almost rip
through the paper. Venus is pink and green and
ringed with a hoop of whales joined tail to tail,
a kindergartner's idea of whales: big tails shaped
like wide lowercase m's, flumes spouting merrily
from blowholes, jolly grins with disconcertingly
human teeth.]

SEVERIN (V.O.)

I imagined them all empty and waiting for me,
gorgeous, radiant playground worlds: the red

plains of Mars, Neptune's engorged oceans, still pools in the jungles of Venus, Pluto's lilies shining violet and white. They turned in the dark without sound, like a movie. No one lived there; no one could. When *I* stepped on them I would be the first, a pioneer-girl with a whip and a gun, like Vespertine Hyperia in the old radio dramas.

That notion lasted longer than it should have. When my father took me to Mercury for principal photography on *The Hermit of Trismegistus*, I reasoned that Mars still held herself pure for me. When he bundled Maud Locksley to Mars for *Atom Riders of Ma'adim*, I knew that Saturn, at least, would cast her rings around me and hold me close. When I got to the outer planets for the first time, well, no one even looked out the windows to see ringrise anymore. Someone snapped off a picture of me standing in the observation car and crying like an idiot. I've still got it pasted on the inside of George's case. I look at it sometimes, try to *really* look. To remember everything I hoped the solar system would be. Self-portrait with Saturn. The photographer sold a copy of that miserable snapshot to *Limelight* and I hated myself for forgetting that I have never been unwatched, unwitnessed, unrecorded in my whole life.

[CUT BACK to SEVERIN, sipping from a cider globe. She looks out the porthole and speaks in profile. Dollops of ice cascade past. They look like stars, more like stars than the stars themselves. The camera can barely pick up those dim stellar pinpricks washed out by the greater light of the ship and a million glassy cold shards.]

SEVERIN

This is how you learn to see: You put together a crew. No one can see a damn thing clearly with only two eyes. Pilot, lighting designer, director of photography, production assistant, sound engineer, astronomer, local guide. You pay Mr Edison through gritted teeth and try to recover your finances by launch. You choose good kids, strong and a little gullible and intrepid as Argonauts. You check their references and they're just as bright and perfect as stained glass. You get them all in a tin can together, set the clock for nine months transit on a favourable orbital window, and pour out the last real bourbon you'll see for a year. Settle in for a long sail in the dark. And the first thing your kids do when the cameras are off and our big dumb blue mama is drifting away in the portholes is lean in close with eager puppy eyes and say: *Come on, Severin, you can tell us now—who's your mother, really?*

But it doesn't matter, that's what the rags don't get. And my crew does read the rags, sucks them down like sweets.

Let me tell you something terrifying, instead.

When I was seven, I saw Mary Pellam in *The Seduction of Madame Mortimer*—do you remember that series? Madame Mortimer, lady detective, having lost an eye on Uranus in *The Saturnine Solution*, finally meets her match in the dashing person of the master criminal Kilkenny, known to me as Igor Lasky, actor, Lothario at large, and frequent occupant of our liquor cabinet and back bedroom. Oh, how I loved those murder flicks! And Madame Mortimer best of all, with her bouncing blond curls and cruel laugh and hidden pistols and leaps of pristine logic. Madame always got her man. This was after Clotilde Charbonneau left us *quite* bereft and ran off with Clarence Feng, darling of the Red Westerns. Papa and I were both disconsolate. And I looked at my father and I pointed at the screen and I said: *I want* her *for my new mother.*

And he got her for me.

It took almost a year of gentle, insistent courting to seduce Madame Mortimer for my personal use. But Mary Pellam moved in by Christmas and had taught me to shoot like a bandit queen by Easter. The night after my father put a ring on her finger I sat up quite late, thinking very seriously about what had just occurred. I could ask for anything and receive it. Even people. Even a mother. I had a terrible power. I could easily become a monster like Kilkenny. Monstrous in my appetites, and each of them satisfied without end. I was reasonably certain I didn't have a choice in the matter. I'd never seen a movie about someone with power who turned out nicely. If you have something, well, you've got to use it. I cried myself to sleep that night. I had been given a destiny, and that destiny was to be a villain, when all I wanted was to be Madame Mortimer.

Mary Pellam was a good mum. She taught me the

Four Laws of Acting, which she had made up over gimlets at the Tithonus Savoy one afternoon so she could make a little scratch teaching between MM features.

[SEVERIN breaks into a glossy imitation of Mary Pellam's crisp Oxford accent.]

No one will listen to a word you say if you don't gin up a System of some sort. Everyone loves a System. Laws, Rules, Keys. You can sell Laws. You can't sell, "Just be good at this for God's sake; I'll need a drink if you're going to keep on like that." If there's a System to follow, that means it's easy—why, patting up a good strawberry tart is a harder job than acting! If only we had known all along! Jolly good we've got you to set us straight, Mary. Offer up a System and everyone relaxes.

Mother Mary's been retired for a while now, so I won't be stepping on her side gig if I reveal her secrets. Miss Pellam's Four Immutable, Immaculate, Ingenious, Imitable Laws of Acting:

1. *Show up on time.*

2. *Bring your own makeup.*

3. *If you're going to sleep with someone on set, make sure it's the director.*

4. *Remember that the expressions and vocal patterns you are committing to film will become synecdoches. That's a big word for a little mouth like yours, Rinny. It means something little that stands in for something big. Your smile will stand in for all human happiness. Your tears will be a model for everyone else's sadness. Wives will copy your red nose, your shaking voice, the shape of your aghast mouth when they beg their husbands not*

to abandon them. Rakes will arch their eyebrows the way you do, grin just like you, tip their hat at your hat's angle, and, with the weapons you give them, they will seduce the folk of their choice with ease. The more successful your film, the wider these synecdoches will spread. You have a responsibility to the people who will repeat your lines, wink your winks, imitate your laughter without knowing they are imitating anything. This is the secret power that actors hold. It is almost like being a god. We create what it is to be human when we stand fifty feet tall on a silk screen.

So you'd better be good at it, for God's sake.

Mary Pellam was pretty as a playbill and hard as a hammer, but she was a philosopher, too. I used to stand next to her in the upstairs bath and we'd practice our faces in the mirror.

Determined. Betrayed. In Love. Awed by the Numinous.

She had 769 faces in the bank, she said, and was working on Number 770. She kept a little notebook with a green velvet cover that had all her Systems inside. But she wouldn't write in a face until she had it deep down, locked up and loaded into the bones of her face. As I was only little, I couldn't be expected to have so many, but no time like the present! If I applied myself, I might have as many as twenty under my belt by the time school started in the fall. *Try Number 123, Attentive Reporter. Or Number 419, I Know Whodunit but I Won't Say Yet, No Sir. And Number 42, Is That for Me?, useful for class birthday parties and being asked to jump rope with the*

*bigger girls. Don't think school isn't a movie
set, kid. It's the most cutthroat location you'll
find 'til you work for your father. You'll be com-
peting for roles and you won't even know what they
are, or when auditions are over and you're stuck
with what you've got. I'd shoot for Professional
Understudy. That way you can move from clique to
clique undetected. Play chess until you can beat
the club champion—but don't move in for the kill.
Let her have her pride. Move on and learn how to
outqueen the queen bee.*

Pretend you're Madame Mortimer, she told me.
*Perfect your disguise case and you can go any-
where.*

I remember touching her green velvet notebook. It had a brass lock on the side. I thought
it must contain everything you could ever need
to know about being alive. I was sure Mary had
a System for anybody I wanted to be somewhere in
that book.

She and my father weren't well matched, though.
That's what happens when you let your kid pick
your wife. He's lucky I didn't pick the dinosaur
from *Attack of the Cryptolizards*, a B-flick my
Uncle Gaspard made on the cheap and I loved like
most children love their blankets.

Obviously, Gaspard Almstedt wasn't really my uncle. He was Ada Lop's agent's lover, which made him
family. Eventually, Madame Mortimer packed up her
things and moved on to her next case, citing a
need to hunt down Number 771 on Neptune, where the
gravity changed the whole muscle sequence of smiling. In her wake, my father fell hard for Ms Lop.

Ada Lop, born Adelaida Loparyova, got her start in the business as a ballerina, although she was never one of the pink and rose-scented set. [Footage of Ada Lop's performance with the Bolshoi plays beneath SEVERIN'S words.] Instead she tore her tulle to pieces at the culmination of *Giselle* and streaked her body with ugly black paint like blood. She kept the paint in little packets sewn into her leotard until the moment at hand. The first time, this was rebellion on her part—a statement about the stagnation of the ballet world, performing the same handful of very pretty but stultifying shows on a long loop—but it caused such a storm that she was compelled by her directors to repeat it night after night, to increasing and passionate crowds. She repeated it until she hated it. Until the tears were real. Until her body revolted and developed an allergy to the pigment in her leotard, and she retired up to the Moon and onto the screen, as so many dancers did in those early days. It is now simply part of the ballet. You'd be hard pressed to find a *Giselle* mounted anywhere outside of Nekyia that does not conclude with a young woman doing serious damage to her costume. The Plutonians are all decadents, anyway: the planet of the lotus-eaters.

On the first morning of her new life as my third mother, still in her bridal nightgown, with her long hair falling down her back like black paint, Ada made me breakfast. Hard-boiled egg, bitter greens, Saturnine corncakes, and a thin, almost translucent slice of pink pork from the rooftop farms in Tithonus. She even let me have coffee. She poured it into a cup meant for one of my old dolls, then poured herself a much bigger cup. We both got cream, I got sugar, and Ada Lop looked at me with those famous gigantic dark eyes and asked me what kind of mother I wanted her to be. She was very frank that way. She just asked things and expected straight answers, even when they were inhuman, unrealistic, performative questions. She performed even her most intimate conversations. As if we were recording all the time. I suppose we were, which is probably why Ada lasted so long in our house. No one in the world talked out loud like Ada talked. Not even people in plays. It's too hard to write. Embarrassing to everyone else, but nothing embarrassed Ada.

[SEVERIN'S voice deepens, a cigarette-voice, feathery and Slavic.]

What does love look like to you? What do you think a mother is?

I was ten and a half. I was ten and a half and she was asking me for stage directions. I said, rather churlishly: *A mother is whatever a father isn't. She's a detective. She's a bandit. She knows 770 faces. A mother is a person who leaves.*

Honestly, Ada Lop was the best interviewer I ever met. She got you off your guard. She asked things nobody asked. You never got to know her, but she'd get every last drop out of you and in her cup. I always wear her wedding ring when I interview somebody. It has a black amber stone in it with a golden flaw, like an eye. And she did exactly as I asked. Whatever my father failed to do, she picked up; taught me how to fix a cannon and do my own taxes and do a perfect plié and that to perform, to *really* perform, you have to make yourself ugly at some point. *Nothing real is pretty*, she said. *Only a doll is pretty. And a pretty doll drinks out of a tiny cup forever. A woman wants a big cup.*

There's a fairy tale where all the good fairies come to bless a princess and give her something she needs. Beauty, a good singing voice, manners, skill at maths. But they forget to invite one fairy and so she curses the girl to die young and a whole heap of nonsense follows on—I don't really care about the rest of it, it's a just lot of overwrought handwringing about who marries who.

Point is, I didn't have twelve fairies, but I guess I had seven.

[SEVERIN leans into the lens conspiratorially, inviting anyone and everyone into her confidence. Smoke curls around her face.]

I'm thinking of actually putting this stuff in the final cut. Everyone wants to know about my mothers, so why not lay it all out? But then I'd have to start over. From the beginning, because the beginning is where the end gets born. I suppose I could edit it back together so it looks like I started with Clotilde, which means starting with myself, with that morning and that doorstep and that ridiculous blanket. But that wouldn't be *honest*. That wouldn't be real. That would give you the idea that a life is a simple thing to tell, that it's obvious where to start—BIRTH—and even more obvious where to stop—DEATH. Fade from black to black. I won't have it. I won't be one of the hundreds telling you that being alive flows like a story you write consciously, deliberately, full of linear narrative, foreshadowing, repetition, motifs. The emotional beats come down where they should, last as long as they should, end when they should, and that *should* come from somewhere real and natural, not from the tyranny of the theatre, the utter hegemony of fiction. Why, isn't living *easy*? Isn't it *grand*? As easy as reading out loud.

No.

If I slice it all up and stitch it back together, you might not understand what I've been trying to say all my life: that any story is a lie cunningly told to hide the real world from the poor bastards who live in it. I can't. I can't tell you that lie. That's Dad's game, and I've been sick of playing it since I was four.

If I fixed it so time goes the way you expect, you might come away thinking I know what the hell I'm doing.

So. Act One, Scene One. Arriving shortly after Scene Two but well before the swelling Overture. We'll get to the trumpets and the timpani when this big bullet fires into Jupiter orbit.

[SEVERIN rolls her eyes in disgust and runs her hand through bobbed hair full of split ends and static, scratching the back of her head, bashful. She pulls her knees up under her chin and watches the camera watching her. She peels a slice of af-yun from her ball and places it on her tongue like a Eucharist. A shower of ice shimmers outside the porthole ringing her head: a saint's corona. The rest of her words play over exterior shots of the ice road intercut with old footage in which she is just leaving the frame: ice crystals; a girl running out the door of a soundstage; snowy seeds and pebbles; the back of her head as she burrows into a heap of costumes; frozen boulders, colliding and breaking apart, fracturing, bursting, tumbling through the dark. The *Swaddling Clothes* had to be kitted out pre-launch: fore, aft, two starboard and two portside cameras, each globed in a protective plasto-crystal lantern. The lantern warps the image slightly, fisheyes it so that we seem to see as we do when just waking: blurry at the edges, soft with frost and dust, only the centre of vision perfectly, painfully clear.

The flotsam dissolves to show their passage through the asteroid belt, never an easy slalom. Other ships pass by in the Orient Express, the ice road, the traffic jam of heaven, nearly clipping the corners of the swift, silent reef around them, sometimes just barrelling through and hoping for the best, streaming on undaunted, with dents buckling their hulls.]

SEVERIN (V.O.)

God, when I record sound, I feel so *alive*. I feel excited about my work. I feel like Ada Lop when she first crushed a hundred little capsules of black paint against her breast. I feel ugly. I feel real. My voice is raspy and kicks around a low tenor from the af-yun. The dryness of our recycled air kicks it down a note or two from true and makes it squeak when it should flow on. It's not a leading lady's voice.

But it's mine.

And fuck Uncle Freddy if he thinks he can keep me quiet.

Well, once upon a time I was a baby. Everybody was, but no one *remembers* themselves as babies. There is some line in the sand, some pole vault of sentience over which we suddenly begin to learn the trick of memory. It's not innate—I don't think so, at least. I think if you left a baby alone it would grow up on the crest of *now*, experiencing time like a lion: only this instant, only the hunt and the blood and the cubs and the mating and the long savannah full of prey. Nothing comes before you sink your teeth into skin and meat and marrow. Nothing will come after. Everything is always happening for the first time.

But what baby ever got left alone?

Not me, if that's what you're thinking.

I hate talking about how I was born. Obviously I don't remember it. It's a story that's been told to me. We all start out with this lie. Our parents tell us the story of our beginning and they have total control of it. Over the years they change it—they know they've changed it, and *we* know they've changed it, but we just let them. They massage the details to reflect who we are now, so that there will be a sense to it: *You are* this *because* that. We gave you a blanket with birdies on it and now you're a pilot, how lovely!

All so that we think of ourselves as being in...not just a story, but a *good* story. One written by someone in full command of their craft. Someone who abides by the contract with the audience, even if the audience is us. Everyone loves a System. Everyone relaxes.

In my case, this is the literal truth. I have been an audience to my own life. I can verify most of the events because I have watched them happen on film. I am told that the first time I saw my father without a camera held up to his eye I shrieked with terror and confusion and would not be consoled. His camera was his household god: Clara, an Edison Model B II handheld 35 mm, painted pearl-white with silver inlay and a walnut tripod. Even when more elegant, lighter, less cumbersome cameras flooded the market, old Percy just took Clara's guts and transplanted them into a new, sleeker casing, or vice versa. These days there's probably nothing left of the original girl but a bit of glass and polish, but it's still Clara to him. The only woman he was ever faithful to.

I began my life as a character in my father's films. It's mortifying, really. I appeared one morning as if from nothing. A spontaneous child. A mystery afoot! The commencement of plot! I was, in point of fact, dropped in a literal basket on the actual doorstep of one Percival Unck. A note tied round my neck with a black velvet ribbon, wrapped in swaddling clothes of pewter-coloured satin. Even the wicker basket was silver. And I was, too—I had been prepared to meet my father. My dark hair and dark eyes needed no help, but the rest of me had been painted as well: my blue skin tinted as white as death, my lips stained black with greasepaint, even my tiny fingers daubed as pale as a mime. I entered real life as monochromatic as a movie. And as archly, humiliatingly Gothic. I have been assured that the doorbell rang at the stroke of midnight and that there was a thunderstorm.

This was, naturally, by design. I wonder: if my absconding mother had not framed the scene just so, might old Percy have stuck me in an orphanage and never given the little gurgling wastrel at his feet another thought? I wonder if I'd rather that.

My mother vanished, as the genre requires her to do. She also would have been painted and dressed in shades of black and white and grey. Otherwise she'd never have gotten past the gate. Those were the days of Virago Studios. The rules were strict. No exceptions.

[Archival footage of the construction of Virago Studios, the soundstages, the colourisation barns, the set builders setting up shops like medieval blacksmiths.]

It was more a city than a studio lot. Virago is one of Artemis's names, because heaven forbid anything on the Moon not get named after Artemis. Or Chang-e or Hathor or Selene. It means a maiden who behaves like a man. [SEVERIN grins impishly.] Maybe I was too hasty about foreshadowing. He built it far enough away from the Big Four's territory that it felt safe, a place of his own outside sparkling, noisy, filthy, gorgeous Tithonus—Grasshopper City, my home and yet never home for a moment. Far enough for peace but not so far that anything Papa did at Virago would not be breathlessly reported upon. Lord, it was so much easier then. All money was new money, land was cheaper than beer, and you could build Versailles for a tenner. So he did. A city of sets and scenes and great glass greenhouses dressed to stand in for Mars in winter, Ganymede during Carnivale, Venus before we landed there. Our own house was formerly the mansion set for *The Gods Alone Delight in Thunder*. If you turned the wrong way, you'd run smack into a false wall, a staircase that went to nowhere, a painted window instead of a real one.

Back then it seemed so important to cover up the fact that living on the Moon turned us all blue as gumdrops. Who wants to watch a movie where no one looks like them? So in the early days they caked on the greasepaint like clowns so that everyone on Earth could rest easy knowing life offworld was just like life at home. Nothing weird out there, lovies, finish your tea! But Percy took it a step further. That's all he ever does: go a step further, more ridiculous, more difficult, more absurd. So the Law of Virago was simple: No Colour.

Colours show up strangely on black-and-white film. You can't be sure what that magenta bustle will look like on the final print. So Virago lived in black and white. And grey and silver and jet and charcoal. The makeup never came off.

I was four before the sight of scarlet ceased to utterly paralyze me. I'd go stock-still with horror. The red could *see* me. It could *get* me. Of course I saw myself without makeup in the morning and the evening, but it didn't help. I thought I was the only blue girl in the world and had to be covered up for the shame of it. If I opened my mouth, everyone would know that the red was already inside me. I was the very carefullest girl in Virago. No one would guess my secret.

I've never seen the note. That does seem odd to me. Of all the artefacts of my life, that one is surely the most important. I assume it shared the rather tawdry information that my father had gotten some hopeful little fool of an actress in trouble and wouldn't he kindly do something about it; thank you, regards, sincerely. Perhaps some appropriate evidence of my provenance, as if my face—even then nearly identical to Percy's sloping, lupine, dissolute mug—was not as good as a birth certificate. Perhaps some little pillow-joke they shared. Perhaps a name for my father to ignore.

I should like to see my mother's handwriting. I should like that.

Vince found me. Vince brought me in out of the dark and the wet. Vincenza Mako, who never slept with my father but outpaced all the women who did by miles: She wrote his movies, every one. What's the point of screwing somebody once you've gotten that close? It's . . . redundant. Vince brought me in, kissed my forehead, read the note, and made the decision before Percy got downstairs.

She opened her dress to hold me against her hot, greasepainted skin, out of the cold. I couldn't stop shivering, but I didn't cry.

[The footage of SEVERIN'S discovery in Virago plays under her narration.]

And Percival Unck, unable to stop being Percival Unck for even a single moment, made her do it all over again. Get the shot. It didn't happen if it didn't happen on film. No matter what else happens—hell and the resurrection and dinosaurs and comets—get the shot. He made poor Vince take me back out into the screeching storm and the rolling clouds and *never you mind the rain and the lightning, just leave her there until I can get Clara and at least one good overhead light going. Yes, fine. Shut the door. We'll add in the doorbell cue later.*

It all happened again. This time, Percy opened the door to find the abandoned orphan daughter he had never known existed. [PERCIVAL raises his hand to his mouth. His eyes fill with tears.] Percy looked into Clara's big black eye with an exquisite expression of shock, wonder, fear, and cautious, not-quite-believing joy. Percy gathered the shivering black-and-white bundle into his arms with a father's instinctual protective gesture. [PERCIVAL brushes a stray tuft of dark hair from his daughter's brow.] Then Percy, his own Byronic, Stygian hair plastered across his forehead by the deluge, gave one last gaze out into the street and the wind as if to say, *By golly, the world is so terribly full of unlikely magic,* before closing the door to the great house and opening the door to a new life. [A slow, tender, terribly vulnerable smile blossoms on the face of Percival Unck. He shakes his head. The rain pours down. He shuts a heavy door on the storm, bringing an innocent within.]

This is the version I've seen. I have watched it over and over. It is beautiful. It is right. It is full of hope for the future. It is perfect. It is a *whopper* of a lie.

Percy had to find me a mother right quick. It was the casting decision of a lifetime, as all the papers speculated wildly. He couldn't raise that wee poppet all by himself, the poor man! A child needs a woman's tender hands! And he could have his choice. Who wouldn't leap at the chance to slot herself into that family portrait, to cradle the beautiful baby, to rest her hand possessively upon the elbow of the great man? A role had been written, the costumes made, the sets impeccable . . . he only needed a leading lady. Oh, but isn't that always the trouble, though? An actress who can be nymph enough to interest the patriarch; mother enough to comfort the child; genius enough to build a kid from scratch to be that most elusive of creatures, the *useful* and *interesting* adult; fairy godmother enough to make the thousand magical woods and towers and castles of childhood appear at a snap of her fingers? File your headshots with the secretary, please. Form a line to your left.

But Clotilde? Clotilde wasn't an actress. His first choice, and she couldn't have delivered a line with conviction if God in Heaven cried action. Clotilde was no topless tart of Ilium. But she made a fine Airy Spirit, to say aye and thank him for his commands.

Clotilde Charbonneau is a box of photographs in my mind. She was gone before I started school and I recall her in bursts, flashes, frames, stills. Moments exploding in the recesses of my brain like lightning effects. I remember Clotilde's furs. I remember Clotilde's fingers. I remember Clotilde's soft, throaty French consonants. I remember Clotilde's hair, falling around me like the trees of a dark and secret forest. Hair like mine. Excepting Mary Pellam, Percy was always careful to make certain my mothers looked like me, could plausibly be mistaken for sharing my blood. They all had black hair, big dark eyes, and cheekbones like statues. He made sure I was never an alien; always a native in a nation where all the women looked like sisters.

When I think of Clotilde Charbonneau I am surrounded by blackness, by softness. She loved furs, and my father was delighted with an obsession he could so easily satisfy. Otter, stoat, mink, fox, sable, rabbit. Wilder still—Martian beaver, Ganymedean woodmonk, Uranian glacierfox. All black, infinite and uncountable shades of black. I remember closing my fists in her furs as though she were an animal and I were her cub. I must have seen her without her furs at some point, some pale slip of a thing beneath her panther skin, but I cannot recollect it.

But her fingers—oh, yes, the fingers of Clotilde Charbonneau! In all the monochrome kingdom of Virago, Clotilde's fingers were rainbows. She couldn't help it; she wore the silver paint we all did, but by the end of the day it always rubbed away and her colours showed through: saffron and rose and moss and robin's egg and lilac and lemon.

Miss Clotilde was a colourist, see. Percy had *scads* of them; a whole army, really. Squirreled away in a great grey barn hand-colouring every frame of whatever opus he could not bear to realize in black and white alone. They are strange beasts, those prints. Their colours lie on top of the image like fitful lovers, unable to quite sink into the impermeable silver world of my father's heart. The vampires from *The Abduction of Proserpine* soaked in wriggling red. Peachy-golden quivering angels in *Trismegistus*, their vapour trails ghosting green. Clotilde's fingers were saturated in those poisonous inks. All the water on Mars couldn't out that damned spot. She began wearing gloves when she moved in (black, obviously), but I saw her secrets when she put me to bed, for a child needs human touch and not leather, no matter how fine.

So after all the Moon's most eligible ingénues had eaten Percival Unck's cake and sipped his tea and exclaimed over the very special beauty and intelligence and character of his daughter, he pulled a twenty-two-year-old colourgirl out of his barn, put ermine on her back, and sat her in a nursery that spangled and glittered like New

Year's Eve, every surface covered in silver and glass and white and shimmer. Because she was the best painter he'd ever met. Because she liked to drink and swear, even though she looked like the kind of girl who never would. And because she told him that she'd never see a single one of his movies in a theatre, for she'd seen them all already, flowing, frame by frame beneath her hands, and she liked the stories she made up in her head better than anything the dialogue cards could say. *Fill her in like a new frame,* Percy whispered to her. *Make her red and green and peachy-golden. Trace the woman she'll be around the child she is like indigo round grey. Make her leap off the screen in better colours than the real world has ever met.*

Clotilde eventually tired of inking Uncks, both celluloid and flesh, in anonymity. I can't blame her. She left us after *The Majestic Mystery of Mr Bergamot* premiered. I cannot imagine what an iron-sided soul she must have had to be the first to leave my father. To tell him *no.* The last words she said to me in that mirror-ball nursery weren't even her own words, but they're the only ones I remember her saying to me. It was a quote from *Mr Bergamot.*

[SEVERIN'S voice goes soft and tired, vanishing down into Clotilde's Marseilles accent.] *Buck up, baby blowfish. Just puff up bigger than your sadness and scare it right off. That's the only way to live in the awful old ocean.*

Funny thing about Clotilde. She remarried—didn't even take long to manage it. To a Battersea backdrop artist indentured to Oxblood Films. Practically every forest and starscape and lonely moor you've ever seen were his, excepting the ones done by her after she signed on to his contract. His name was Felix St. John.

[SEVERIN extends her hand offscreen and pulls ERASMO ST. JOHN toward her. He perches delicately on the arm of the navigator's chair, incongruously graceful for a man of his size. He kisses her; they grin at each other.]

ERASMO

Which mum are you on?

SEVERIN

I'd only just got through ours. But I already did Mary and Ada. It's a little jumbled at this point.

ERASMO

Ah, then it's Amal next, is it? Number Four.

SEVERIN

Queen of the Tigers. I'm impressed you remember.

ERASMO

[He reaches out, tucks her hair behind her ear.] I know your life story cold. It's like the twelve days of Christmas. Five golden rings, four calling birds, three French hens, two turtledoves, and Amal Zahara the Tiger Queen.

SEVERIN

She was the animal wrangler on *The Virgin of Venus*. Almost as tall as you.

ERASMO

You first saw her leading six tigers to the set, dressed as a squid-princess so that she could direct the animals without seeming out of place in the shot. She had on a crown of tentacles and stars. The alpha tiger was called Gloucester.

SEVERIN

I was twelve. She let me ride him home. He had fur like a chimney brush and he licked my face all over.

ERASMO

Your father loved her selfishly for once—for himself, for herself—and they were happy. The tigers moved in. She refused to dye their fur. They were a constant, cheeky orange eyesore in Virago.

SEVERIN

Ravens, too. And parrots who could all say one line of Chekhov each, but nothing else. A brace of black bears; four peacocks; two pythons; an albino deer; a komodo dragon; several lynx; seven ponies; and a tame, elderly kangaroo.

ERASMO

They all had something wrong with them. The albino deer, the aged kangaroo, one of the bears was missing an eye . . . Which one?

> SEVERIN

Gonzalo. Trinculo had had his hind foot mashed in a trap.

> ERASMO

The peacocks were deaf. The pythons had eczema. Half the ravens had broken wings and the other half couldn't stop imitating babies crying. Gloucester had a stomach condition and could only eat meat ground up to slurry and mixed with milk, which Amal fed him by hand three times a day.

> SEVERIN

The komodo dragon—Andromache—seemed all right at first. The only one of the lot fitted out for life in this world. But she fixated on Percy. Wouldn't leave him alone. Insisted on sleeping with the pair of them every night or else she'd put up this terrible hue and cry, keening like a broken trumpet till they relented.

> ERASMO

You tried to learn that cry.

> SEVERIN

But they wouldn't let *me* sleep with them.

> ERASMO

Amal collected broken beasts.

> SEVERIN

So naturally she collected us. The tigers slept

in my room when they weren't working. When I had
tea parties, only tigers were invited.

ERASMO

Amal was the first person in your life who
didn't slather you with attention.

SEVERIN

[laughing] Hey.

ERASMO

Hey yourself. Not even six tigers could give you
enough attention to let you rest easy. Hey, let's
talk about you a little more, and then we can address the issue of whether or not the world re-
volves directly around Severin Unck. I like Amal.
I've never met her, but I like her. She had her
zoo and she was in love with Percy and she treated
you a little better than the deaf peacocks but not
quite as well as Gloucester the tiger. You didn't
need your meat slurried, after all. There're whole
weeks when you were that age where there's no film
of you at all.

SEVERIN

Don't let Percy hear you say that.

ERASMO

I like thinking about a version of you that
doesn't look for a camera all the time.

SEVERIN

Amal said once that I needed her tigers more

than I needed a mother. That I had all the wild-
ness of a plate of cheese. And a little tiger
shit was good for a girl who lived in a fairy
tale.

ERASMO

[His smile is enormous, frank, warm.] I can be a
tiger if you want. What big teeth I've got.

SEVERIN

[ignoring him] She left anyway. One of the
younger tigers, Cortez, bit off most of her hand
when they were doing *The Jupiter Circus*. She
was putting the bellhop's hat on him and he
just took it off at the wrist. *No matter how you
think you know a beast*, she said in hospital,
no matter how much love you've spent on him . . .
then she waggled her stump. But she had an extra-
wide bed brought into her room so that Cortez
could lie next to her while she recovered. He
rested his big old head in her lap and never
moved from her side. She slept with her good arm
around his scruff. Percy didn't come to visit
once. I suppose a twelve-year-old can't begin
to guess what goes on inside a marriage, most
especially a marriage primarily concerned with
lenses and the half-tamed. But when Amal got her
clean bill of health she went to her chalet on
Mount Ampère and sent for the rest of her animals.

ERASMO

Except two.

SEVERIN

Except Gloucester. I found him sprawled on my bed with his belly ready for scratching and a note round his neck that had instructions for his slurry on one side and on the other: *No matter how much love you've spent.*

ERASMO

And?

SEVERIN

[laughs softly] And Andromache. I bet she was sprawled on Percy's bed, too, cooing and flicking her tongue at the pillows. Sometimes I think Amal was having a last joke at his expense. Percy complained about Andromache noon and night, but he grudgingly gave her soft-boiled eggs at breakfast when she came nosing at his bathrobe and called her a hell-bitch just like he called me sweetheart. I caught him rubbing her nose just once, and he looked ashamed of himself. But really, I think Andromache would have lain down and died if she'd been parted from her Percival. I think Amal left a lizard in lieu of a wife.

ERASMO

And then Faustine.

SEVERIN

[Her eyes take on a faraway, clouded expression. She chews on the inside of her cheek.] And then Faustine, my fifth mother. She only lasted a year. Opera singer. She started out a soprano, but she was an alto by the end. Chest like a barrel of bourbon. Everyone adored her. She was like laughter turned into a person.

ERASMO

And a baleen addict.

SEVERIN

Well, who isn't? [SEVERIN peels a rind of af-yun with her fingernail and sucks on it ruefully.] But Faustine grew up on *Venus*. I'd never met anyone who'd been born on Venus. I thought she was magic. A real life Vespertine Hyperia come to live in my house and lie on my bed and tell me tales of pirates on the callowseas. Her parents were divers, then homesteaders. She floated in callowmilk in utero—literally. Her mother tapped a huge lode on one of the outer whales when she was six months along. We think it's in everything here, but on Venus . . . on Venus it *is* everything.

ERASMO

Baleen, though . . .

SEVERIN

I know. A lady can smoke her af-yun on the steps of the Actaeon and still be called a swan in girl's clothing, a gift to man and the stage. It's delicate, pure callowmilk, nothing added but a little cacao-butter, a little ergot, a little cocaine. A drawing-room vice. Baleen is the whore's luncheon. Have you ever seen a piece of baleen? When you're married to my father you can afford the best. She had it brought in on a jade tray every morning. On a piece of black lace. It looks like a white piano key. About that long, about that thick. It snaps like cold chocolate. Smells like Monday laundry. Raw callowmilk protein cut with soya, industrial bleach, sugar cane, a dash of oleander, a whiff of boric acid, and a healthy lashing of heroin.

ERASMO

She gave it to you.

SEVERIN

Well, of course she did. I was fourteen. Do you have any idea what a fourteen-year-old girl will do to be loved? I wasn't any kind of innocent at fourteen—she didn't corrupt me. If you could pour it down your throat or stick it up your nose, I had managed to get my hands on it and give it a go. Percy didn't care. *Experience*, he said. *Experience is the only reason and the only master.* I asked Faustine one afternoon what Venus was like. She put a stick of baleen in my hand and said *it's like this, baby girl.* I ate it and curled up into my tiger and went to Venus with my mother.

ERASMO

And what was it like?

SEVERIN

It was like being inside a star. Like a star turning on inside of you. And then Faustine sang and that was like a star, too. A blue one sizzling down the dark alongside the red star of me. I remember she sang the opening aria from *Her Last Nocturne* and I saw the night sky pour out of her mouth. Every time I went to hear her sing afterward, even months afterward, I saw the same thing. Blackness and stars flooding her mouth and splashing onto the boards in great gouts. Galaxies and the void dripping off her chin. Her teeth burning. I told her about it on a night in December and she whispered: *I know it, baby. I see it, too. That's my insides coming out. Sometimes I see it so clear I pull back my feet to keep my shoes clean. But that's what it looks like when you're doin' okay up there. Maybe you'll do okay someday and I'll get to see your guts blown out. That'd be nice. Wouldn't that be nice?* And then she put her head in my lap and died. Miss Faustine had so much baleen in her stomach that it backed up her works and she was poisoned to death by her own fluids.

[SEVERIN and ERASMO are quiet for several seconds. The displays tick on, lights faithfully flickering like candles.]

Araceli Garrastazu came after that. The femme fatale, Mary Pellam's opposite—the perfect witch-seductress for my father's every overwrought phantasmagoria. I barely knew her. I was running with whatever wolves would have me by then. The colours of Tithonus beat grey Virago every time. I didn't want to act, but I slept with producers anyway; Gloucester and I danced on the carousel boats every weekend with my father's rivals and I took girls and boys to my cabin on endless ugly promises of introducing them to Percy: *Yes, of course, darling, he's just dying to find the next big thing and you're so lovely. You're devastatingly talented. You're perfect. You're perfect.* Until that horror show with Thaddeus Irigaray. That turned off my faucet, I can tell you. And by then Araceli was off to reinvent herself on the radio. [SEVERIN strokes her throat with her hand, a throttling, effacing gesture.] We're almost done, aren't we? Lumen's left. Lumen's my mother now, lucky number seven. She's the reason I've got a boatload of circus with me. I love her. I love Lumen Molnar for everything she is not. I love her because she is nothing like me. I love her because she has never been to Venus. I love her because she has only one face. I love her because she is at this moment having supper in the cantina with Maximo and Mariana and Augustine and Gloucester. Because she came with me. Come with me, and I'll love you until Jupiter burns out and the callowhales speak.

[SEVERIN clutches ERASMO'S arm. Her nails dig in. But she speaks to the camera.]

Do you want to know the truth about my mother? She was wonderful. She was kind. She never left me. She tucked me in at night and woke me in the morning. She played with me every day and she never missed a recital or a bedtime story.

Her name was Clara.

She could hold just under 150 meters of film at a time.

Oh, Those Scandalous Stars!

***Limelight*, 20th February 1933**
Editor's Note: The Iron Hand of Edison
A simple rule, enforced simply:

Movies don't talk.

But whose rule is this? What Moses came down from the mount with such a thing engraved upon his personal stone?

Surely, our current state could not have been the shining future meant by those early masters of light and sound. It is Edison's rule, enforced not by the Burning Bush but by Lawyers Burning for Their Fees. The name of Edison has become synonymous with the dastardliest of business practices, the most crushing arrogance. It stains the whole family, from Thomas Alva, who collected patents like baseball cards, to Our Present Edison, who continues such draconian strategies that he has, single-handedly, retarded the progress of motion picture technology by fifty years.

Your humble host has taken out editorials of this sort before. My readers must forbear. Given the upcoming Worlds' Fair in the glorious metropolis of Guan Yu, overlooking the glittering shores of Yellowknife Bay on our dear sister planet of Mars, the very first to be hosted offworld, what better time can there be for Mr Franklin R.

Edison (Freddy to his friends) to release his patents' vice grip on reel, recording, and exhibition equipment and allow talking pictures to run wild and free? That is, after all, the natural state of technology. And so it was, once upon a time. Before the right to speak, the privilege of the voice, became the property of one man, to give and take away as he pleases.

Places, Everyone!, 14th April, 1933
Editor's Note

In the beginning was the Word and the Word was with God and the Word was God. That's how the song goes. It does not go, *In the beginning was the Word and the Word was with the Patent Office and the Word could only be afforded by God.* In the early days, for a brief moment, the wealthiest of studios and directors—and of course, governments— could afford the exorbitant fees demanded by Edison and his descendants for the use and exhibition of films. For a dim, glimmering moment, the great epics of Worley and Dufresne crackled with orchestras and soliloquies. But it did not last.

One must praise the independents, who simply ignored Edison and continued to make beautiful silent movies, more advanced and complex and heartbreaking than any throwaway studio talkie stinking up the summertime. I remember it: how slowly, then less slowly, sound ebbed away. Sooner rather than later, for an actor to talk on-screen became the mark of the Sellout—someone with deep enough pockets to pay Edison's blood price. No True Artist, no Work of Quality, no Real Film would be caught dead making that kind of obnoxious noise. And bit by bit, the Big Boys on the Moon copied the starving artists so that they could convince the public of their Authenticity, their Great Aesthetic Merit, so that they could butter their bread on both sides. We are the People's Entertainment! Bang, Smash, Yell, Crescendo! No, wait! We are Radical, Envelope-Pushing Artists! Hush, Hush, Soft Now. Win awards, stuff cannons with cash, bask in acclaim—and, hell, it saves money not having to deal with the devil in a back room, dithering over the price of a microphone.

And thus we find ourselves in an upside-down land where the technology exists, works beautifully, has even advanced—for no Edison can keep his hands to himself for long—but no fashionable soul would be caught dead using it. Men stand astride our world and call out: STOP. The System Works. They ask that everything stay the same forever, for Sameness is Profitable. Our Man Freddy E still bleeds filmmakers for exhibition rights, and we may all look the other way while he rolls piggily in his piles of lucre. Time passes, and we become accustomed to the status quo. Theatre Speaks, Vaudeville Sings, Radio Yammers Away Nonstop, but the movie hall is quiet as a church. Time passes, and audiences drink in this Truth with their mother's milk. I have seen with my own eyes the recoil of audiences when faced with some flickie that sliced up its producers' hearts at Edison's golden table for the right to let poor Hamlet ask his famous question instead of staring dumbly at a plaster skull and waiting for the title card to do his job for him. Today's moviegoer will get up and leave, convinced he has been swindled, rather than listen to a human voice.

What could it cost Friend Freddy to, quite simply, let us speak?

And yet, and yet. There is beauty in silence. I do not

believe a film like Saul Amsel's *Bring Me the Heart of Titan* would have been made in a world where every film chattered on to its contentment. What of *The Moon of Arden*? *The Last Cannoneer*? If I were to turn back the clock and pluck Fred Edison from his ill-gotten celluloid throne, I should lose these reels which wrapped my heart three times round. He has bound us to Prometheus's rock—but have we not made friends with the eagle? Have we not learned to love life without our livers?

The Worlds' Fair is a time of brotherhood and goodwill. It is an expression of Progress and Marvels of Modernity.

Let me put it baldly: Mr Edison, get out of the way.

Halfrid H
Editor-in-Chief

I am not willing to relinquish the rare and rough magic of our silent movie halls. They are silent as a church, yes. Because they *are* churches. Yet I am no less willing to never hear the dreary Dane fail to decide his own fate. For him, the question will ever remain: To be or not to be? For us, it is: To speak or not to speak?

I myself can put nothing baldly, for I feel quite hirsute on the matter, tangled, knotted. But I will say: Mr Edison, you have exiled us to an uncanny country of the mind. We cannot love you for it.

Algernon B
Editor-in-Chief

Look Down

Look down.

Across the stage of your skin. The graceful proscenium of your clavicle, your shoulder, the long bones of your arms. The apron of your gentle belly. The skene of your skull, where all the gods and machines hide away, awaiting their cues, clanking away in their cases, puffing smoke and longing. Look down; something is happening on your navel, your omphalos, your knotted core of the world. You cannot feel the light playing over your skin, but you prickle with gooseflesh anyway. Light has no personal temperature. But your body knows instinctively that light is cold. The idea of light, the narrative of light. Light will chill you blue. The trickster hemispheres of your brain insist that the flickering images do have weight; they press on you like greyscale fingers, corpse fingers, angelic fingers, unworlded hands. The touch of images alters you— it must, it cannot help but. And more than touch you, these pictures, these maps of illumination enter you. Photons collide with flesh; most reflect, some penetrate. You carry them inside you. You carry them away and far.

You feel them, though they cannot be felt. You shiver, though there is no cold. You take them inside you, though they asked no permission.

It feels like breath. A breath spent long ago, arriving only now.

Severin's face dissolves into another. This one is more beautiful. Anyone would admit that. It possesses the pressed-moth-like quality of a person born, through sheer chance, with precisely the face that her era prized. It's too delicate and arch for our modern tastes. Too crafted, too distinctly feminine to suit our current rage for the androgyne. The small, sullen, Christmas-bow mouth. The immense, slightly wounded eyes. The pale hair curled like a statue of Apollo, crowded close in to her heart-shaped head. The perfect and somehow vaguely perverse jut of jaw. Her eyebrows spring high, high, high, like parentheses over the sentence of her face—a sentence that goes, "Love me, and I will laugh for you, and if you can make me laugh, my laughter will, quite simply, ransom the whole of the world from death."

This is Mary Pellam. The Moon's Sweetheart. Ingénue for Hire. Seventeen years of age, in her first significant role: Clementine Salt, heiress with a pistol in her petticoat. Meet Me On Ganymede *(dir. Hester Jimenez-Stern, Capricorn Studios, 1908), in which Miss Pellam appears on-screen for a scant four minutes, one and one half of which she spends shut into a stasis cask, banging on the glass with her fists like a Snow White who hasn't read the script. But she quite makes off with the picture. She will work steadily but not spectacularly in the maiden mill after* Ganymede, *her look too innocent for villainess roles, too cherubic for the fallen woman. In distress and out, she remains an upstaged damsel until wrinkles sign her resignation letter. Only then does her career really crack off. With a Hamburg hat and an eye patch she will become Madame Mortimer, greatest detective on nine worlds. With a shot through the eye of a villain she enters our concerns.*

Mary's smile is a spotlight—whomever it lands upon becomes brighter, becomes more real.

It lands upon us.

The Ingénue's Handbook

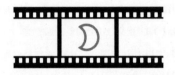

Begun 20 August, 1908, Quarter to Three in the Afternoon
By Mary Alexandra Pellam (Age 17)
Grasshopper City, Luna

I have come to the Moon to make my fortune!

Good Lord, isn't that what all the girls say? And the boys and the richies and the paupers and the grifters and the *real damn artistes* and the homesteaders and the silver panners and the writers and the vaudeville has-beens and the bank men and the gangsters and the patrons—oh the patrons! You be sure to call them *patrons*, missy, while they're patting your knee and sweating through your skirt—the old perverts and the young ones, too. A chickie hates to be cliché, but the minute you set foot up here, on this rock that's nothing but one big studio set, you figure out right quick that clichés sign your checks and tuck you in at night. Come on up to wardrobe, honey, we've got a belt-sander to take care of any originality you might not have checked at customs. No problem.

I didn't need much work, truth be told. I could've come off a showroom floor. The Latest and Greatest Model, Shined and Sheared and Shipped First Class, Perfectly Engineered and

Industrially Lathed to Factory Specs! Get One Now, Before the 1909s Come In!

That's me. I'm not ashamed of it. It gives me a good giggle. I am the Girl. I barely need a name. Every audition is a room full of rose-faced cupid fodder, and they all look just like me, talk just like me. They've suffered just the way I have: enough to give the eyes a knowing slant, but not enough to ruin the complexion. And they all came to the Moon as freight, just like me.

Check my credentials if you have a care: Born Oxford, England, Earth, eighteen and ninety-one. Mama was a mama but she did something artistic-like so you can be sure I come by my ambitions honestly. Mine painted. She covered canvases with portraits of the prize roses in her garden, large and small, red and pink and coral and puce like shades of lipstick. Wild and tea and heirloom. Desperate, weeping things, they were. I'll tell you something: when you see a Pellam rose blossom in close-up, three metres by three metres, it looks like a mauve monster. It looks like a mouth set to gulp you whole. Papa was a professor of linguistics. Helped to write the dictionary, did Pellam Senior. Gaze upon my childhood, O ye curious: I was built out of roses and etymologies.

Obviously I ran away to Camden Town just as soon as my nicely turned calves could carry me. No more dinners with those lurid leviathan gullets staring at my peas and potatoes with pointedly erect stamens. No more Greek origins of simple household words and *I say, we've started in on the J's this year and you know what that means: Jackals and Juggernauts and Jungles! Deriving respectively, of course, from the Sanskrit roots* srgalah, *"the howler,"* jagat-natha, *"the lord of the world,"* and jangala, *which, oddly enough, signifies "aridity."* Couldn't you just scream?

I could. Because when you draw a *really* rotten lot in life, you stick it out, make your best, tighten your belt. But when your draw is just a *touch* irritating, just a *squidge* confining, well, you hightail it and right quick. I'd have been good and goddamned if I was going to end up painting roses like my life depended on it in some snivelling doctoral candidate's hut. Oh, but you didn't *stay* in Camden! Not if you could help it. Not if you were a Girl Like Me.

No, in those days—and by those days I mean these days, and by these days I mean all the days to come—it was the heavens or nothing at all. If you had a brain to rub against a lust for something better than shabby old Earth and her crabby old empires, you were saving up for a rocket or already long gone. It was fifty years on from the great train robbery perpetrated by Master Conrad Xavier Wernyhora and his big sister Miss Carlotta Xanthea, a couple of Australian-born Polish kittens run off from the Hobsons Bay rail yards with spare parts, lunch, and a working knowledge of engineering to set off their little cherry bomb in Hawaii, where the equator loves us and wants us to be happy. I used to draw pictures of that first fabulous ship in my schoolbooks. The *Tree of Knowledge*, shot out of a bloody circus cannon, a snug capsule with their handprints on it in gold paint. It carried Conrad and Carlotta all the way up here to the Moon, crashlanding through a genteel sort of gravity into . . . well, just about where I sit, where the Savoy in Tithonus now stands, with the silver-choked shores of Mare Nubium in sight.

It's a fair bit nicer now, with pistachio meringues, a nice pot of white-tips, and a waiter with a rear that I daresay won't quit. Although I've not developed a taste for creaming my tea with callowmilk yet, I'm sad to report. It's just not *right*. Milk shouldn't taste like much of anything but vague thickness and sweetness. Callowmilk has a spice to it. A *tang*. I expect I shall learn to savour it soon enough. I need it, after all. We all do. Slaves of Venus where the callowhales lie silent offshore and ooze. Without callowmilk we couldn't stay. It's a matter of density, see. Skip the cream in our tea and our bones would go as light as hat-straw within a year or two and we'd keel over with a sad Irish slide whistle. So I stir and stir and stir and it still tastes positively beastly.

Once upon a time I played Conrad and Carlotta with the neighbour boy, the son of a lowly junior lecturer in astronomy and therefore utterly delicious with the *frisson* of slumming it. I do not imagine Conrad and Carlotta did half the things in their capsule that I did in the peach trees with . . . oh, what was his name? Lucius. Or Lawrence. Lawrence! From the Latin *Laurentius*, meaning from the city of Laurentum, near Rome.

Well, I missed the first big rush. One always does. The good bit is forever one generation back. But I'm not such a latecomer that I escaped the sense of being *historical*. Here I sit, writing in my little green book while I gnaw over whether or not I can afford a bowl of the monkfish soup to insulate my belly against the fact that I've (finally!) gotten a part in the new Stern flick but not been paid yet. I know, I just *know*, that my little diary will be read by somebody someday, and not just to divine how to get me in the sack. It'll be read because I'm an actress in the early days of cinema and the somewhat later days of interplanetary immigration. I don't have to do a thing to be interesting! Did she or did she not have the monkfish soup? Did the thyme taste like the thyme she knew back home? (Or the scrubbly stuff we call thyme even though it's lunar native and in no sense of the word thyme. Though, for that matter, it wouldn't be monkfish either, but we call our local long scaly bastards with their razor snouts and six vestigial legs monkfish because the Savoy, good sir, does *not* serve moon-monster soup!) Did the flavour make her think of innocent days in the manger of man?

Not especially, no.

But we all keep diaries. We all scribble and babble. Because we know the future is watching everything and taking its own notes.

So I shall tell you, Mister Future, all about Conrad and Carlotta, just in case you get careless and misplace them along the way.

I was saying I missed the first big rush, wasn't I, Mister Future? By the time I made my entrance, all the planets had their bustling baby shantytowns, each and every one with a flag slapped on it. You weren't anybody at the imperial picnic if you didn't have a planet. Moons, though lovely, just lovely, are consolation prizes. Sino-Russian Mars. Saturn split between Germany and Austria-Hungary. French Neptune. American Pluto. Spanish Mercury. Ottoman Jupiter. All present and accounted for—except Venus. Nobody owns that Bessie because everyone needs her. The path to the stars is paved with treaties. If I wanted to stay English, I had my pick of the Moon or Uranus or a sea of satellites. But I didn't see it as a choice. Only the Moon for the likes of me! Who wants to freeze on Uranus where there's no paparazzi at all?

I hoarded my little walnuts like a good squirrel, sitting for advertisements and doing the occasional shimmy on some appalling stage. I'll have you know I was the face of Dr Goddard's Premium Disinfectant *and* Little Diamond Brand Refined Sugar in the same fortnight. And that very fortnight I did my evening shifts at the Blue Elephant Theatre, playing Ariel in an all-female, mostly nude production of *The Tempest*. The glitter stuck to my nipples something vicious. Stained them green for a month after the coppers shut us down on indecency charges. *Fair enough,* I said then, and I say now. I drank too much and ate too little, got in a spell of trouble with a stage manager and had it taken care of; put something up my nose and something in a pipe, but that's what was done. Preparations for a better role. I tried to get plum work. I did try. Turned out for Mr Wilde and Mr Ibsen's affairs, lined up round the block to be seen for the opportunity to cough offstage in Chekhov. But the bold truth is that nothing on your person earns as well as tits earn, and only after I did a spell as a cheesecake bacchante (I got to carry Pentheus's head three nights out of five—four if Susanna had a boyfriend that month) did I have my egg.

I lined up in Kensington Gardens with the crowds. Passed by the statue of Peter Pan and reached up my hand to pat him as thousands have done. Millions now, I suppose. Built but the year before and already his foot is near worn away. Second star to the right, my lad. Right-o. Carpetbags and cold-weather rags and the afternoon sun like a sickly porridge glooping over the lindens. The cannon towered over me. I went terribly quiet inside, as you do when you're little and your father looms over you and you don't know yet whether he means to praise or scold. I went up on a boat called the *Topless Towers of Ilium*, which made me smirk. I looked round and saw a sea of flappers—flappers!—heaps of girls with bleached hair and dance shoes and carmine lips. All of us piling in for a day's flight in cramped quarters with a lot of men who will be happy to tell you they're directors, kid, you just sit right here by me. It was like an audition. An audition for a whole world, to see if the Moon would accept us and let us in or turn us out after a spin as an extra in a crowd scene and a starring role on a hotel bed with a producer in a top hat testing your range with his prick.

Oh, the wide universe needs us all, great and small, to fill her up and make her good, make her ripe, make her full and teeming. There are no small stories, only short ones. But the Moon . . . the Moon is where they make *movies*. And the Moon is a heartless bitch. She only needs a few. She wants fewer than that. She sits up there, high and mighty as you please, on her starry director's chair and she ticks off the weak on a clipboard stained with ingénues' tears. The Moon cares nothing for our cute little troubles. She ate a thousand girls for lunch yesterday, and she was hungry again in an hour. She barely even looks at us.

But I only have eyes for her.

So here I am. I've a room—not at the Savoy, goodness, perish the thought! I've the room they assigned me at Princess Alice's Landing, at the top of a three-floor boarding house on Endymion Road, back end of Grasshopper City. Five girls to a room. And our wardrobes count as a sixth tenant, for not a one of us earns her keep anywhere but before the lens and on the boards. Callista's Virgin Queen getup takes the whole rear corner, and all our cats live under the skirt. But I save my little shillings for luncheons at the Savoy so that I can feel *grand*. So that I can feel like I'm somebody going somewhere. So I can read Algernon B dishing gossip and maybe spy with my little eye old Wadsy Shevchenko canoodling with a prop boy. So Søren Blom can find me if he's scouring the cafes for an Ionian duchess who might just look like me, or if that dashing darling Percival Unck comes looking for a new heroine to drop into a bucket of ghosts. So I can watch the summer Earth at half-wax going down over the froth of Mare Nubium and the candy-coloured streetlights come on in a long bright wave over my city.

My city! Tithonus, jewel of the Moon, Queen Slattern of the Alleyways, Grasshopper City, my home! I stepped off the *Topless Towers of Ilium* and took in her round blueglass spires and filth-fat holes and opium gardens and botanical dens and the wicker-coral palaces barely keeping the moss at bay like I was taking the first breath of my whole life. I was in love. I was a new bride. If I'd had a penny left over I'd have grabbed the first whore I saw and had her right there against the side of the Actaeon, just to have the city inside me and my hands on its heat. Nickelodeons every four steps, but those four steps also hoisted up grand theatres like castles, studio gates like St. Peter's, peep shows and brothels and dance halls coming up like posies in every which spot between. They even built a Globe, so achingly, throbbingly familiar out there on this new West End, looking like an ice queen's personal gladiatorial arena, blueglass and silver and scrimshaw.

I am going to play them all.

Oh, I thought I'd be sensible about it. *Don't pan for gold*, says the wise man. *Sell pans.* I'd learn cameras, I thought. Inside and out. I could do it. Find work as an assistant to an assistant to an assistant. As long as I could be near the movies, I'd've won. Maybe someone would catch a glimpse of me taking light readings, notice the way the Earthlight caught my profile. Maybe not. Manage your expectations, Mary! But oh, I took one look at Grasshopper City, at the Globe and the Actaeon and the Savoy, and I knew it would never do. I don't give a fig how a camera works, just as long as it works on me.

No, I am going to play them all. I intend to step on-stage as Ariel with my dress *on*. I shall pose just so at the Actaeon's emerald double door at my own premiere, name above the title, all in lights, all in red, like a rose, like a mouth, all in. I shall absolutely *murder* Wilde and Ibsen and Chekhov; I shall eat Claudius's heart in the marketplace, I shall pine for the love of Robin Hood. All of them, all of them. Men's parts, too. Hamlet in high heels, and don't you *dare* forget my name! I will hunch my back as Dickie III until I am quite literally blue in the face. I will make the Moon love me if I have to spike her drink and knock her on the head to do it.

And I *am* turning blue. It thrills me to my toes! I would say I'm a shade between powder and sky so far. I shall be quite sapphire by Christmas, I expect.

Granted, it's not going *so* well on the working front. I ran around like a perfect fool during the slaughter of the suitors in Dorian Blister's *Odyssey* last year. My bathwater ran pink with fake blood. Even after I seemed squeakingly clean, the bubbles said I still had a bit of Telemachus on me somewhere. But the camera lingered on me for a half second longer than the other handmaids, and I had a *particularly* good expression of horror on. Then, I was a dead body in *The Mercury Equation*. Strangled in a short dress. Big black finger marks on my neck. (Pssst: The prodigal son did it). And a fairy in *The Fair Folk Abroad*, which if you ask my opinion was an absolute coke-addled *mess*. Just a great wad of big paper flowers and suspension wires and pukingly sweet orchestral nonsense, along with half a circus's worth of animals that'd had rum poured in their water bowls the morning before their scenes so they'd stagger docilely across the sound-stage instead of ripping Titania's face off. You can see a panther passed out cold on the horn of plenty in the second scene.

I've learned it's important to have a name. Fairy #3 is a losing game. At least let me be Mustardseed in the credits, Mister! It won't cost you anything. I do so long to graduate from being a number to being a name. Dead Girl #2. Handmaid #6. I celebrated with one of my four flatmates (Regina Farago—you'll see her in that big splashy Napoleonic flick next year: built like a giraffe, tall and brown and possessing that clumsiness that looks like grace when you've got legs like hers) and a bucketful of gin when I was cast as Faun #1 in *The Thrice-Haunted Forests of Triton*. Moving up in the world! Yesterday #6, today #1!

But now I've a character with a proper name! Signed the contract *Mary Pellam* with a big flourish. Maybe something will come of it. Probably not. But I've got years to make my go.

Today I'm Clementine Salt.

More important, Miss Clem is my ticket to a studio contract. Oh, the Grail, the chalice, the font of prosperity! Locked away in the castle perilous and just *sloshing* with fine print! I do so dream of selling myself to a studio. For a tidy sum, of course—Dr Pellam didn't raise a fool. I positively *wriggle* with the thought of some big meaty boss closing his clobbering hand over mine and guiding a gold pen across glossy pages. Sign here and we'll make you immortal, little missy. And they'll own you for just as long. A pretty unicorn in a pretty zoo. What to eat; who to breed with; shows at seven, nine, and eleven.

Look at me, I'm growing a proper lunar coat of cynicism.

The fact is, a unicorn cage is the safest place to be. And I want to be safe. I *have* to be safe. And to be safe I need protection. These studios prowl the Moon like little emperors bouncing on great stupid beasts. They've carved up the place between them like England and France and Austria-Hungary and Russia.

They've put on actual wars!

You won't hear a breath of it back home, no sir. But it's happened. They've all the costumes and props and explosives for any battle in history, after all. Why let it go to waste just because no one is making a war flick this week? Tithonus is divided into territories: the north belongs to Capricorn, the south to Tranquillity, the east to Plantagenet Pictures, the west to Oxblood Films. The rest of Luna is carved up the same way, minus a few independent strongholds here and there. Virago, Wainscot, Artemisia. Woe betide the soul who crosses lines! Little wee emperors with ivory crowns jousting on rhinoceroses. Only, what actually happens is that Oxblood swipes Maud Locksley from Plantagenet and Simon Laszlo storms their backlot—which is more or less the whole west end up to Coriander Street—with a hundred actors who think they are re-enacting the betrayals of the Duke of Burgundy until their bullets actually blow the heads off the "loyal French peasants" and Miss Locksley gets a shell-shocked escort home and a month locked up in Laszlo's house with her head stuck in a bushel of af-yun before she can pull herself together enough to stand on her mark.

Oh, the money on the Moon is English—you can see Vickie's sour old kisser on the bills. But no one is under one single illusion as to who runs this joint. You take sides if you're smart. Offer up your loyalty, 'cause it's all you've got to trade.

Trouble is, most times, when you go looking to sell your soul, nobody's buying.

I picked up this little notebook at the shop round the corner from the Huntress, which is a whorehouse, but quite a good one. If I'm ever in a bad way, I'll hope to get hired on there. You get breakfast brought on a tray and don't have to start work 'til four. I mean to record in it Things I Know. There is such an awful lot to know up here. I suppose I thought the Moon would be like London, only bigger and less expensive. I'm quite certain that was the idea. But just like everywhere else, it only took about five seconds for folk to notice that Earth is very, very far away.

The first supper rush is coming on. My tea's gone cold. There is already a foxtrot tinkling away in Imperatrix Square: garlands of pale green callowlanterns swinging in the sea wind, heels clapping on the cobblestones like an audience, girls with short hair laughing at boys with feathers in their lapels. Perhaps I shall join them later. I am a fair dancer. Not superb, but fair. I am always honest about my capabilities. I am very pretty, though my prettiness lacks depth and therefore misses beauty by a hair. I have an extremely expressive face that I can contort at will. I am short, but I have a serviceable chest and practically perfect calves. For stage work I have a rich voice which carries well, though it is somewhat deeper than the fashion. I can alter it somewhat. I can pass for an American or a Frenchwoman, and I am working on a Muscovite lilt. Perhaps at twenty I shall be a superb dancer. Perhaps at thirty I shall be beautiful. Anything is possible.

My waiter has taken pity upon me and brought me a plate of walnuts and cheese and thus won my heart entire. Yes, my lad, I shall marry you. I *shall.*

Very well, Mary, very well! Get to it!

As of today, the Twentieth of August in the Year of Our Lord Nineteen Hundred and Eight, I believe the following to be Immutable Lunar Laws:

1. A woman has but eight roles open to her: ingénue, mother, witch, detective, nun, whore, queen, and corpse.

2. Sooner or later, someone's gonna own you, kid. Call yourself Queen of the May if you get a say in whom.

3. You have no pride. If you have it, misplace it. Under your mattress, in someone else's cupboard. It'll do you no favours.

4. That person you are when the camera's having its way? That's not you. That's a Looking Glass Girl. She lives on the other side of the lens. She's better than you are—prettier, more graceful, walks more properly, sparkles when she ought to, blushes when she ought to, fades to black before anyone gets bored. And better things happen to her than the sad little teas and flophouse fleas that happen to you. Love that Looking Glass Girl. Love her hard and love her true. Make obeisance; say your Aves. She is your personal god, and you'll chase her for the rest of your life.

Ship's Manifest,
Small Commercial Craft *Clamshell*

Owner-of-Record: Oxblood Films/ Franklin R. Edison
Port-of-Call: Tithonus, Luna, United Kingdom
Built: 1940, Copernicus Ironworks
Manufacturer: Wernyhora Motors, Inc. (Subsidiary: J.P. Morgan & Company)
Model: Cerigo VI (Inner System Restricted Permit #NK55781432F00QWP)
Occupancy: 35
Tonnage: 5,771
Length: 425 ft.
Beam: 56 ft.
Propulsion: Ourania Class Cannon, Ford Quad-Firing Orbital Slugs, Carnegie Diesel-Balloon Braking, Foldback Magnetrisse Sails
Carriage Decks: Bridge, Crew Berths, Cantina, Observation, Passenger Berths, Radio Room, Darkroom, Cargo Bay, Engine Hold, Fire Room, Ballast
Preflight Condition: No Malfunctions. Kitchen Equipment, Data Transmission, and Interior Communication System Scheduled for Maintenance Upon Return to Dry Dock
Examined by: Piotr Krupin, Arkady Lagounov, Ekaterina Bogomolova, Depot Noviy Kitezh, Moscow, 11.6.44

Great Railway Merger Expected 2100 12.6.44, Anadyomene Junction, Switch 9.6.4.2

Film Crew:
Severin Unck: Director
Cristabel Ossina: 1st Assistant Director
Erasmo St. John: Director of Photography
Horace St. John: Cameraman
Maximo Varela: Lighting Master
Mariana Alfric: Sound Engineer
Santiago Zhang: Best Boy
Konrad and Franco Sallandar: Craft Services

Support:
Anastaas Dajo: Pilot (Inner System Transit Authority
    Certified 1919, Hesperides Medal 1924)
Griet Van Rooyen: Navigator (Junior Cartographer, British
    Railways, Corps of Engineers Special Commendation
    1942 for Work on the Venus-Mercury Toll Artery)
Isaac Deerfoot: Conductor (M.S. Massachusetts Institute of
    Technology, 1938, Junior Conductor, Mohawk and
    Hudson Railway, Mars-Asteroid Corridor 1939–1942)
Ghanim Boulos: Signalman
Balazs Almassy: Security
Dr Margareta Nantakarn: Surgeon (Edinburgh School
    of Medicine, 1922, Specialization in Epidemiology.
    Offworld Residency: Mercury, Trismegistus, St. Talaria's
    Children's Hospital, 1925)
Aylin Novalis: Venus Liaison (White Peony Station)
Henry Lamb, Simon Poole, Jaromil Kysely: Stewards
    (Contracted from Tithonus Savoy, Term of
    Contract 29.5.44-8.8.46)
William Kaur: Sanitation Engineer

Carolyne Derrick: Wire Walker
Arlo Covington, C.P.A.: Oxblood Oversight
Mr Tobias: Ship's Cat (Abyssinian, six years old, missing left
ear)

Materiel:
1200 pounds beef
700 pounds mutton
775 pounds tinned beef
600 pounds veal, pork, sausage (beef-fennel, hot lamb-za'atar,
chicken-tarragon)
1500 pounds chicken
250 tins preserved fruit
250 tins Dundee marmalade (orange, lemon, blood orange,
muskbulb), Crosse & Blackwell jam (strawberry-
peppercorn, gooseberry-port, cloudberry-champagne,
Martian goji-serrano) and chutney (mango, cranberry,
lunar coconut, Triton mint-miseryrose)
250 bottles pickles and sauces: Branston, Serapis Peppers,
Nergal Morels, C&B Walnuts, HP Sauce, Hermeneus
Fancy Catsup, Caloris Basin Hot Mustard, Worcestershire,
Mount Penglai Soy Sauce, Tethys' Tail Fish Sauce, Io's Best
Sweet Chili Sauce, McCollick's Bird Pepper Sauce, Lyle's
Golden Syrup, Chinkiang Black Vinegar, Tethys' Tail
Shrimp Paste, Celestial Moose Maple Syrup (grade B),
Rose's Lime Juice. 65 bottles reserved for onsite sale/barter.
370 pounds Nereid roe (Interplanetary Quarantine cleared
2.5.44, Exotic Foodstuff Record #777121Ne, see attached
form. Reserved for sale/barter in tot.)
250 pounds coffee
200 pounds tea
100 pounds potted fish (anchovy, salmon, herring,
monkminnow)

900 pounds moist sugar (350 pounds reserved for sale/barter)

300 pounds lump sugar (100 pounds reserved for sale/barter)

660 pounds salt (200 pounds reserved for sale/barter)

510 pounds black pepper (200 pounds reserved for sale/barter)

825 pounds butter (various grades)

2 tonnes potatoes

1 tonne other vegetables

400 chickens, ducks, moonquail (live, egg-laying, to be bartered/sold upon landing in White Peony Station; buyer secured)

1.25 tonnes lard

78 barrels wheat flour

56 barrels rhea flour (Interplanetary Quarantine cleared 9.6.44, Exotic Foodstuff Record #413066Sa, see attached form)

40 barrels Phlegyas flour (Interplanetary Quarantine cleared 9.6.44, Exotic Foodstuff Record #900142Ma, see attached form)

7564 gallons fresh water

250 gallons callowmilk (Promotional Consideration Provided: 125 gallons Hathor Brand, 125 gallons Prithvi Brand)

21 quarts Prithvi ice cream (chocolate, vanilla, fig-pistachio, blueberry cider, black caramel, green-tea pink pecan, sweet potato, Saturn's Bounty, Ionian Fire Tart, Quandong Ripple, Phobos Macadamia Surprise, Morning on Ganymede. Reserved for landing)

21 bottles Domain Aphros champagne (reserved for landing)

16 cosmetic cases (Provided by Elizabeth Arden, Fifty Daughters. Unused supply to be sold/bartered before departure)

27 cases perfume (Provided by Chanel, Madame Zed, Saturnalia, reserved for sale/barter in tot.)

4 Underwood typewriters
50 reams paper
46,500 feet Eastman 35 mm film
3 dollies (custom + collapsible tracks)
10 Pharos lenses, various lengths
3 cases Jotunn brand batteries
2 Aitnaios generators
2 jib cranes
3 tripods
5 Eastman light meters
4 Edison microphones + sleeves
4 cases flares
Assorted gels, lights, blackwrap, filters, tape, mixer, recorder, boom, cables
3 cases clamps
2 Edison Model G III handheld 35 mm camera
2 Edison Model B II handheld 35 mm camera
3 diving suits
1800 m. breathing tubes, various sizes

(Primary funding provided by Oxblood Films, Inc. Secondary funding provided by Prithvi Dairy Products, Hathor Brand Callowmilk, Crosse & Blackwell, Redrose Deep Mars Mining Corp., Chanel, Carnegie Steel Company, Lumen Molnar.)

I Left My Sugar Standing in the Rain

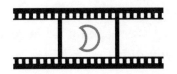

Transcript from 1946 debriefing interview with Erasmo St. John, property of Oxblood Films, all rights reserved. Security clearance required.

CYTHERA BRASS: Begin recording. Session one, day one. The time is eight-fifteen in the morning on Tuesday, January third, 1946, at the Oxblood Industrial Park, 1770 Endymion Road, North Yemaya, Luna. I, Cythera Brass, Chief Security Officer for Oxblood Films, Ltd., am the sole conductor of this final postproduction interview. Would you please state your full name, age, and place of birth for the record?

ERASMO: Erasmo Leonard St. John. Thirty, Guan Yu, Mars.

CYTHERA: Am I then to assume you hold dual citizenship?

ERASMO: I believe my Chinese citizenship can best be described as "lapsed." Why? Will I need to call down to an embassy for lunch? Or are you just wondering who might find my incarceration irritating?

CYTHERA: You are hardly incarcerated, Mr St. John. Don't be absurd. And your last employment?

ERASMO: Director of Photography on *The Radiant Car Thy Sparrows Drew.*

CYTHERA: [sound of a ballpoint pen clicking] All right, then. Are you ready to begin, Mr St. John?

ERASMO: Nope.

CYTHERA: I think we've been exceedingly patient. It's been nearly seven months. If you prefer, we can provide you with materials and you can prepare a written statement, but either way, we see no reason to delay further.

ERASMO: Then why bother asking if I'm ready? You've decided I'm ready. And you didn't even bring me a cup of tea. Some interrogation this is.

CYTHERA: This is not an interrogation. This is a standard debriefing conducted by the studio at the conclusion of all off-Moon shoots.

ERASMO: I've worked on . . . twelve? No, fourteen Oxblood pictures. I've been debriefed 'til I can brief no more and I don't think I've ever talked to a swot over the age of twenty. Debriefing is intern's work. The CSO wouldn't shine her shoes with a DP's report.

CYTHERA: [intercom crackling] Would you bring two espressos, Jane? And some toast with butter. Thank you. And yet, you still decline legal representation.

ERASMO: Oh, entirely. And I asked for tea.

CYTHERA: Mr St. John, you are entitled to access the full resources of our legal department, as an employee of the studio. These resources are both substantial and free of charge. Given the circumstances, I highly recommend you use them.

ERASMO: [short, sharp, quite humourless laugh] It strikes me as more than a little backward to allow a gaggle of Oxblood suits to look after my interests when, at the moment, you lot are the only ones accusing me of anything.

CYTHERA: I don't know what accusations you're referring to. This is just a conversation between colleagues. It doesn't have to be anything more stressful or unpleasant than that.

Everyone else has already given their statements and gone home.

ERASMO: Then you already know more than I could possibly tell you. How about I get my own tea down at the Savoy and never have to look at your fucking face again?

CYTHERA: Don't you *want* to go home, Mr St. John?

ERASMO: I couldn't possibly give less of a shit.

CYTHERA: There's no need for belligerence, Mr St. John. Let's start with something easy.

ERASMO: [laughs]

CYTHERA: You were involved in a romantic relationship with Severin Unck, correct?

ERASMO: You're right, that is easy. Yes. Please do not use the past tense, or I shall have to start swearing again.

CYTHERA: When did this relationship commence?

ERASMO: Officially? Christmas . . . um . . . 1937. At the *Phobos* wrap party. Unofficially, I met her when I was ten and she was twelve. Felix—that's my father—contracted on *Atom Riders*. Mum was off working on some Blom flick. They never worked on the same film at the same time. People felt uncomfortable with a black man and his white wife just walking about, holding hands, laughing, other assorted sins against civilization. So I was helping Dad paint the flats for the shadow rodeo scene, shading depth on the radioactive lassos when Rinny wandered over to me. I saw her shadow on my shadows before I ever saw her. She said: *Gosh, that's just splendid! I feel as though they're about to leap out and snatch me round the neck!* And that was it for me. The rest of us just took a while to catch up.

CYTHERA: Very romantic. Did you ever have similar trouble when you and Severin worked on the same projects? On *Radiant Car*?

ERASMO: If we did, it didn't matter. Come now, you know better. The director can do as they like. My parents were just set painters. Instantly expendable, if a producer happened to glance at them and get a crick in his soul.

CYTHERA: [amused snort] So you and Unck were together from 1937 through to 1944, is that right?

ERASMO: We broke up for a while on the way back from Neptune. There was another girl, a levitator. Rin was crazy about her, too. That was the problem, I guess. We both strayed. Took most of a trip across the solar system to spackle over it. That, and Rin didn't want to get married. You can't blame her, given her history. Then we split again when she was doing preproduction for *Radiant Car*. I thought she was being pigheaded, refusing to go into the shoot with an open mind. It wasn't like *Self-Portrait* or *And the Sea*, which were personal and confessional, or even like *Phobos* and *The Sleeping Peacock*, where we were in the right place at the right time and filmed what was happening; the food riots or the proxy war on Io. *Radiant Car* was supposed to be almost . . . journalism. We were seeking answers. And if you think you've already got all the answers before you start investigating, you . . . alter what you find. You miss things. Ignore things. I told Rinny Bart Worley wanted me on *Let Them Eat Death*, his big French Revolution epic. Would have been a good gig for me, a huge production like that. But she gave in for once. Maybe she shouldn't have. We would have patched it up anyway. Being apart never really stuck.

CYTHERA: But you would describe your relationship as stable during the Venus expedition?

ERASMO: As stable as we ever were. We're not . . . easy people, either of us. We're both selfish and stubborn and want our own way all the time, every time. We fought. We'd start laughing in the middle of the fight. Then pick up the argument a week later like we hadn't even taken a breath.

CYTHERA: [clears throat] Are you sure you want to say that you and your girlfriend were having problems when her where-abouts are in question?

ERASMO: What the hell does that mean? We fought about what to have for breakfast. Who'd left their washing all over the trailer and thus was the bigger pig. The shooting schedule. Whether she or I or everyone on Venus was drinking too much. Normal couple things! Are you insinuating that I did something to her?

CYTHERA: I'm not insinuating anything, Mr St. John. I think we're getting ahead of ourselves. Let's go back to easy questions. What was your crew compliment at launch?

ERASMO: Oh, fuck off. You know all this. Eight attached to *Radiant Car*, ten support staff.

CYTHERA: And upon return?

ERASMO: I don't know, what does your expense report say?

CYTHERA: Please, Mr St. John.

ERASMO: Well, I think that depends how you count. How is Santiago doing these days?

CYTHERA: [clears throat] I have been instructed not to discuss that with you, Mr St. John.

ERASMO: Of course. Fine. We got back on the *Clamshell* in White Peony Station light one director, one sound engineer, one idiot, one cameraman, and heavy one kid. Happy?

CYTHERA: And for the record, how do you account for the discrepancy?

ERASMO: Are you joking?

CYTHERA: I am not. Let's take them one by one. Mariana Alfric, your sound engineer?

ERASMO: [shakes his head] Dead. We buried her in the village cemetery.

CYTHERA: Arlo Covington, the Oxblood representative?

ERASMO: Emphatically dead. Most likely, almost certainly, probably dead.

CYTHERA: Horace St. John, your cameraman? You knew him well, is that right?

ERASMO: He's my cousin, yes. Dead . . . ish. I don't know. We had to leave him.

CYTHERA: And Severin Unck, the director?

ERASMO: [unresponsive]

CYTHERA: Well, we'll get to that. Can you take me through the landing and establishment of base camp? In your own words.

ERASMO: [long pause] [When he speaks again, it is in a whisper.] When I shut my eyes I see the film we meant to make. It was something elegant. Something accessible but still stylized, beautiful, satisfying. We saw a mystery in Adonis—the village that vanished. The movie would be like one of those wonderful scenes at the end of a Madame Mortimer flick, where she tells a room full of suspicious types how it all went down and you feel . . . you feel like you were groping around in the dark and your hand finally found a light switch. And the light comes on and it's such a relief to see that those awful, frightening shapes in the shadows were just boxes of old clothes and a chest of drawers and a staircase. Our movie was meant to be a light switched on. It was our baby. We'd flip the switch and show how two hundred people could up and disappear in a night and leave nothing but wreckage. There was a solution, obviously. We just had to find it.

CYTHERA: The lighting master, Mr Varela, has indicated that a rough edit was completed at some point? Is this true?

ERASMO: Don't. Don't talk to me about Max. I don't want to hear his name. Yes. We had enough footage for a feature. (Well, I say enough. You never have enough.) Not enough to make *Radiant Car* the way we'd broken it coming home from Enki. But enough for *something*. Cristabel and I worked on it in the *Clamshell* darkroom, cutting like Fates. Putting her together again. It was good in there, in the darkroom.

Cristabel and I didn't have to look at each other. Didn't have to look at anyone else. Shadows and red light and little Anchises sitting in the corner not making a peep. Just looking at us and listening to us playing back the sound of screaming in the wind. If we stopped working, we'd have to look at everyone else. At Maximo and Santiago staring at nothing and Aylin and the Sallandars, at the crew who'd been gambling and drinking and swimming their brunches off in White Peony and were too polite to ask what happened. Their *politeness* just wrecked me. The only one of the lot who even seemed to care where the hell Severin went was the ship's cat. Mr Tobias kept yowling and clawing up her berth. Just kept looking for her.

If not for Maximo, I'd have come home with a movie and you wouldn't give two dry shits who died. Because the story's better if people died for it. Disaster sends ticket sales through the roof. It's a better mystery, a better *story*, if it hurt to make it. If not for Max, I'd just load up a reel and I wouldn't have to try to say all this with words like a caveman poking at a rock wall with a damned stick.

I wonder . . . I wonder if I'd have been able to forget if it had happened somewhere else. If Horace had gotten torn up by a slickboar on Ganymede. If Arlo had drowned on a Nereid hunt off Enki. If an Edison man had shot Mari in a Tithonus back alley. If I didn't have to drink Severin's death every day, if I didn't need that whale slime just to keep puttering along. I imagine other deaths for her quite a bit, you know. Uranian influenza. Trampled in the Phobos food riots. Strangled by a mad Belt miner. It's a morbid hobby. It keeps me going. But a death is a death. It's a thing you can't get around. It just sits there like a fat arsehole in black pyjamas, eats all your food, drinks all your wine, and demands you call it mister for the privilege. I could handle a death. I could live with a death.

Cook for both of us. Clean up after it. Pay its way. But I don't get that luxury.

CYTHERA: The landing, Mr St. John.

ERASMO: I know. I know you want a simple accounting. Put it to bed, Raz. But the thing is, you already have the simple accounting. You know what happened. I know it. That's not the mystery. You ask me to take you through it as though you don't already have fourteen versions typed up neatly on your desk. As if it's not public record. The facts are easy. See? I'll do them standing on my head. I can recite them like a poem. Anything is a poem if you say it often enough. My poem goes: *I loved a girl and she left me.* You know that one?

CYTHERA: [sounds of china clinking, spoons knocking against cups, knives scraping against bread] Shut the door when you leave, Jane. We'll take lunch at one o'clock. Now, back to the landing . . . ?

ERASMO: [long pause] We landed in White Peony Station on the seventeenth of November, 1944.

CYTHERA: Earth time.

ERASMO: Yes. We kept to the home clock throughout. I won't be giving you any headaches with a November sixteenth that lasts a year. We weren't staying; no need to synchronize our watches with the local time in Wonderland. November sixteenth means autumn, and on Venus autumn means permanent dusk. No dawn 'til spring. Our rendezvous with our liaison, Aylin Novalis, at the Waldorf on Idun Avenue, went off fine.

    Principal photography commenced on the seventeenth—interviews, man-on-the-street stuff with every crazy person who thought that Adonis had been taken by aliens, or God, or Hathor Callowmilk Corporation, or that the villagers had succumbed to religious mania and killed themselves at the climax of some orgiastic cannibalistic ritual coinciding with the

Venus-Mercury alignment. The utter bullshit we heard, Miss Brass, I cannot begin to tell you. Every shade and flavour.

We spent three nights in the hotel—the ship's crew, too. Everything was beautiful, though mostly broken and very damp. Some of the ceiling tiles had fallen down into the lobby. I remember the pink stone columns out front were all sort of pockmarked from the salt air. They looked like an old man's skin. Even inside, there was pale white moss everywhere like velvet, on the chairs, on the bar, on the walls, on the beds. I think we checked in on a Tuesday. Like today. I suppose that makes it an anniversary. I'll expect cake with lunch, Miss Brass. And a candle.

Anyway, on our last night in White Peony Station, everyone got out one last pretty thing to wear before we all had to start living in our hiking kit and waterproof socks. We all drank a great deal and gorged on ice cream like a gang of kids after school. Even Arlo seemed to have a good time. He kept trying to remember these dumb jokes, but he couldn't get them right. *So there's this mummy snake and this baby snake and the mummy snake says, "Honey, I just bit myself!" No, wait, the baby snake says, "Mumsy, are we poisonous?" Wait, shit . . .*

The ceiling dripped onto the plastic tubs we'd hauled over a hundred thousand kilometres, and before I finished my Quandong Ripple my spoon had grown a little fur of moss on it as well. Mariana and Cristabel sang "I Left My Sugar Standing in the Rain" up at a big mouldy baby grand while Aylin played, and pretty well, too. Crissy wore silver sequins. Mariana had a lavender flower in her hair. Maximo fired back with "It Never Rains on Venus" in his old rye-whiskey baritone, and you'd have thought no one in that shabby hotel bar had ever realised the irony of that tune before, the way we laughed while the chandeliers leaked onto our heads. They all tried to get

Rinny to sing, but they took the wrong tack. I know my girl. She'll sing you the moon—no kid raised in a theatre can turn down applause any more than they can turn down a meal. But Van Rooyen—that was our navigator—wanted to hear "Callisto Lullaby." Too bad, Roo! That's from *Thief of Light* and Severin would rather take an ice pick to the eye than do anything even the littlest bit Percy-adjacent, so she demurred. I don't think I ever saw her demur before. It was interesting. Didn't look quite right on her.

That was the worst Waldorf from Mercury to Pluto, but it felt like the most exciting place we could possibly be. Just us, the old crew. Except Cristabel, who we nabbed right out of film school, before anyone else could snap her up, and Franco, who was barely in long pants, we'd all been together since Saturn. We'd all fucked one another and cried over one another and gotten right with one another again. Maximo taught me how to juggle. I taught Santiago how to play the squeezebox and order a cocktail in eleven languages. Mariana and Severin swam together every morning at dawn in any town with so much as a puddle. Just the two of them, their arms flashing up in the mist, two dark heads like seals heading out to sea.

I can't imagine many of us slept much that night. I heard Maximo and Mariana going at it already when Rinny and me stumbled by their door on the way to ours. I found out later that Crissy had a thing going with the signalman, Ghanim. That fellow was handsome as a statue and talked like a book, which made him candy for our little AD.

She told me about it in the darkroom while we watched some handheld stuff from that first night. We saw Carolyne (she was our wire walker) and Horace snuggling by the fountain—big brass Aphrodite, who else. We hadn't even known they were an item till that moment. We watched ourselves jumping around drunk and grinning for the camera.

And we smiled at ourselves smiling, Crissy and me. Our first smiles since it happened. A camera collects secrets. It collects people and holds them prisoner forever. And that's when Cristabel told me about Ghanim and how he quoted Chaucer to her—in Middle English, no less—while they made love, all glottal stops and breathy German consonants, and how she couldn't look at him now because if she looked he'd come to her quarters, and if he came, he'd ask, and if he asked, she couldn't answer, so that was that over, she guessed.

Severin and I had Room 35. I remember it had this huge fuck-off mirror, half-frosted over with moss and dried rain, and I watched Severin in it while she straddled me on our sticky, lichen-y bed in a black kimono; drank the most bog-awful grappa that has ever touched my lips; and sang "Callisto Lullaby" for me. Just for me. This is what you want to hear, right? Details? We kissed half the night—we could have kissed for England, her and me. We could kiss so long we'd forget to fuck. We didn't forget that night, and I'm glad. We listened to Idun Avenue and the drunks singing "Flower of Scotland" and "La Marseillaise" and some Chinese one we didn't know, listened to the shops closing up, to the rattling percussion of pachinko parlour doors opening and shutting, to trucks peeling down the road too fast, to little curls and wisps and crumbs of music floating out of dance halls, to the constant trickle of rain into the gutters and grates and sloughs and potholes, to last call. We talked about the things you talk about when it's two a.m. and you're naked and you've known the person you're naked with so long you could draw their face blind in the dark. About Clotilde, which other people always found strange, but never troubled us. We weren't related. Aren't. Her father married half the Moon and fucked the other half senseless. She'd have to go pretty far to find someone whose mum had never stopped round for supper.

Clotilde connected us, from the beginning, like a story with foreshadowing. We talked about being children on the Moon, about the hole-in-the-wall curry place with the turquoise tureens in the Plantagenet Quarter back home, about the night on Phobos when we finally got together and how good it was. We both wore black and red, because we couldn't live without dressing the set first. I tasted funny to her at first, and she thought maybe it wouldn't last. A person has to taste right if you're gonna stick around. I joked that she just didn't like the taste of an honest man. I'd made that joke many times. It wasn't even a joke anymore so much as a refrain. And then she said: *You're not that honest,* because that's the next line.

You know the first time we said *I love you* it got all banged up? She took a beating in that warehouse in Kallisti Square. I was patching her up in an emergency medical bay. Blood everywhere, both of us faint from hunger and adrenaline. One of her teeth didn't look like it was going to make it. I tied my shirt around her head to soak up the worst of it. She said: "He kicked me right in the face," at just the same second as I said, "I love you." She laughed and she kissed me. The Kallisti water tower exploded. And after that, we always said "I love you right in the face." And bit by bit, that's how a couple gets pounded together out of two busted people.

Christ, there are things I miss and there are things I miss, but I can hear her voice now just as clearly as when the rain fell through our talking and the moss closed in as quiet and soft as falling asleep.

Am I making you uncomfortable?

CYTHERA: You're certainly a very . . . frank man.

ERASMO: Good. Good. That makes me happy. I want to keep going, if I can make you squirm. If I can make you embarrassed to listen to me, because you should be.

I woke up like a shot at four in the morning. Severin was

snoring away next to me. Only she didn't quite snore. She made a sound with her jaw like a click, and then a sigh, and then a little soft choke. The first time I heard it I thought she was dying. Anyway. You know how sometimes you wake up and you're certain as the grave that's it for you and sleep? That's how it was. So I got up and went down to the lounge. A proper hotel lounge never shuts, and I made sure the Waldorf was a proper hotel when Logistics was booking everything. I went down to the lounge. I wanted a pink lady. They're my favourite. Do you have a favourite?

CYTHERA: Bourbon neat.

ERASMO: [laughs] That's because you're a terrible person. It's my opinion that you should never order anything "neat" at a bar. Pour yourself a couple of shots at home for free—there's no skill in it. Let the nice bartender-man strut his stuff a little! Me, I love pink ladies. I order them on every planet, on every tiny bootheel of a moon. A pink lady is never the same twice. Did you know, on Neptune they make them with saltwater? Disgusting, but wonderful. It's all wonderful. I mean that. Everything, every place. Even salty grenadine. So I got down to the lounge and my cousin Horace was sitting up at the bar with my drink already ordered for me. We've always been like that. When we had sleepovers as children, we always had nightmares at the same time, or had to get up to pee at the same time.

The lounge had a wizened little gramophone wheezing its way through something called "Over the Rainbow." I'd never heard it before. Horace pushed my drink over my way and said, "It would appear the Venusian recipe is a vague stab at gin, which they make out of all this white moss; grenadine which comes from xochipilli fruit and has nothing whatever to do with pomegranates besides being red; frothed callow-cream; and a spritz of grapefruit, which is, shockingly, actual grapefruit." Horace favoured pisco sours. Rinny was just starting to see my ineffable wisdom. She'd taken to chasing down gimlet variations.

It wasn't half bad. Spicy. A little musty. We drank for a while and watched the twilight outside. The autumn light on Venus is a big gift wrapped up in a bow for a DP. A year of magic hours. No waiting for that perfect four-thirty p.m. sunlight. Venus is forgiving. The shoot can run as late or early as it wants, and you'll still have the light.

I asked Horace, "Have any theories? Before we get started. My money's on psycho axe-murdering diver. Chops everybody up and feeds them to the eels."

Horace smiled. Two things about Horace smiling: It's the only time you can really see the little scar on his cheek where I pranged him with a pub dart when he was eight, and when he's smiling, he looks more like my dad than I do.

"Aliens," he said. "Stands to reason we'd find some, sooner or later. I mean, other than the whales. They don't count. They don't *do* anything. I mean proper aliens that walk and talk and complain about the weather. Aliens, or Canada. That whole sector is contested. Could have been a tactical thing ordered by Ottawa. Peasants won't move? Easier to wipe them out than try to have a civilized talk about it."

And then we got this idea into our heads that we'd go for a run before everyone else got up. We didn't have the right shoes for it but we jogged the whole length of Idun Avenue, down to the estuaries. We stuck our feet in the red water. His feet smelled horrible. Always did.

CYTHERA: I think we're getting a bit far afield.

ERASMO: So what? You said, "in my own words." These are them. You take what I give you or you get nothing.

Fine. I'll speed up the reel. No fraternal waterfront breakfast for you.

Aylin Novalis met us at the Pothos docks at 0900 with four gondolas. She had to have been as hungover as the rest of us, but she never looked it. Even at the end, Aylin never looked tired or shaken. She was a better actress than anybody I ever met. Scrubbed and shined and ready to go, that was Aylin. Born and raised on Venus, Aizen-Myo Sector. She'd been a guide for ten years. The best. If you woke her up in the dead of night I bet she'd have her work shoes on under the covers. Her hair was up in a pretty little knotted ponytail that looked complicated to fix but really wasn't. I saw her do it at camp later on. She looked for all the world like a schoolteacher ready to take us all on a field trip to the aquarium. *Look at all the lovely fish! Let's see how many different kinds we can count! One, two, three—don't touch the glass, George . . .*

We loaded up the gondolas. Land travel is useless on Venus—it's all mud and silt. It took them forever to get the few cities there are to stand up straight enough to take a road. But the water goes everywhere. The gondolas weren't anything of the sort—I assume they're named after some hoary old Venusian/Venetian pun, but they're just industrial swamp boats with pontoons and outboard engines and absurd little flourished prows like someone's gonna pop out from under the tarp and start singing "*O Sole Mio.*"

Really, it all went fine. We montaged right past it in the first cut. Battened everything down, said goodbye to the *Clamshell* kids, except the doc, Margareta, who came with us in case of . . . injuries. The rest of them were pleased as punch at the prospect of six months' debauchery in White Peony without us. We set off by 1000. Took nine days in the waterways to get to Adonis, which is due south of White Peony Station on the backside of nowhere. We came out through the Suadela Delta just clotted with dark pink silt. The pontoons looked like fairy floss. The cacao-trees canopied us, all full of blue-throated glowworms as long as my forearm. I gather they're quite predatory toward the local fauna but uninterested in humans. I took stills; Horace got some establishing shots, some bits of Severin smiling, of Aylin consulting our maps and permits.

I should say that contrary to what I've heard on the radio down here, the whole area around Adonis was totally quarantined, no different than Enyo or Proserpine or any other run-of-the-mill disaster site. We had a pile of permissions the size of a baby hippo. Because of Venus's unique political situation, our passports and visas looked like a Parade of Nations. That little world belongs to everyone and no one. Too precious to be claimed. Severin recorded a voice-over to play through some of those boring establishing shots.

When she came shining from the sea, all the gods desired her greatly, and strove one against the other for possession of her. But Jupiter the Lightning-Father knew that to give her hand to any among the Olympians would only cause war unending in the quiet of his halls, and so no one was allowed to station enough personnel or resources to effect a manned quarantine or repair or dispose of much of anything; nor, even if they could, would any of them agree upon the rights of one officer to shit before another on Venusian soil; and thus quarantine on Venus means little more than a sign saying GO AWAY *in as many languages as can be shouted out before the Honourable Representative Whoever from the Republic of Nothing finishes her drink.*

We built our camp on the freshwater delta before attempting Adonis. Minimum safe distance. Aylin had secured us what amounted to a portable town, all military surplus. Collapsible barracks with solid roofs to keep the rain out and foldout floors to keep the equipment and our feet from sinking in the mud. A mess tent, a command centre, fire braziers, a chemical toilet, the works. Horace, Cristabel, Santiago, and Mariana set about testing all the equipment to make sure it had survived the trip. The Sallandars got dinner started—hardtack, 'tryx stew, tinned peas.

It started the next morning. Everything went tits up right away. We took one of the gondolas into Adonis proper. We saw everything just like you've seen it. It was so much like the stories and stills we'd seen that walking through the place felt like being in a movie that was already made. The hotel looked like an earthquake had hit it. The old carousel, smashed into a twisted junk heap studded with horses' eyes.

And there he was, centre stage. It was like glimpsing a celebrity at a café. Anchises, just walking around the memorial like it was nothing, a morning constitutional, and in a moment he'd ask for orange juice and eggs. Only he wasn't Anchises yet, he was . . . an artefact. Like a weathervane. Or a church bell. Part of the town. Evidence.

We spent the afternoon setting up lighting for the sequence where Rin makes contact with him. And, you know, sometimes I think the only difference between Severin and her dad is that he lived through things first and then reshot them to get them right, while she hung back until everything was perfect, *then* called action. Couldn't live through a thing until the camera was rolling.

[coughing] I need a break.

CYTHERA: If we could just get through your first encounter with the auditory phenomena . . .

ERASMO: I. Need. A. Break.

How Many Miles to Babylon?:
Episode 764

Airdate: 1 June, 1943
Announcer: Henry R. Choudhary
Vespertine Hyperia: Violet El-Hashem
Tybault Gayan: Alain Mbengue
The Invisible Hussar: Zachariah von Leipold
Doctor Gruel: Benedict Sol
Guest Star: Araceli Garrastazu as the Finnish Fury

ANNOUNCER: Good Evening, Listeners, if it is indeed Evening where you are. Gather in, pour yourself a cup of something nice, and sit back for another instalment of the solar system's favourite tale of adventure, romance, and intrigue on *How Many Miles to Babylon?* Celebrating our thirtieth year on the waves, *Babylon* is a joint production of the United/Universal All-Worlds Wireless Broadcom Network (New York, Shanghai, Tithonus) and BBC Radio, recorded at Atlas Studios, London.

This evening's programme is brought to you, as always, by Uzume Brand Soap, milled pure and clean with soothing oils, invigorating herbs, and wild alpine flowers plucked fresh from the gentle fields of Europa. Additional promotional consideration provided by Hathor Co. Premium Callowmilk,

Diver Owned and Operated since 1876; Red Chamber Specialty Teas, Bringing the Bounty of Titan Home; the East Indian Trading Company; and Edison Teleradio Corp.

Previously on *How Many Miles to Babylon?*: Our pioneer heroine, Vespertine Hyperia, having been taken captive by Venetian bandito-magicians in the Venusian pirate paradise of Port Erishkegal, was bound by unbreakable chains to the volcanic glass spire of Namtar Tower! The dastardly king of the banditos, Doctor Gruel, determined to make sweet Vespertine his bride, strapped her into his wicked Cartesian Splitting Machine, causing her to forget not only her beloved, Tybault Gayan, but her own twin brother, the great inventor Valentino. Valentino staged a daring rescue, soaring through the Venusian mists on his miraculous mechanical musk ox Braggadocio. Listeners gasped as Vespertine turned her face away from her own kin! They leaned in close when Braggadocio begged her with his tinny tongue to come and live with Valentino in his big belly and sail through the skies, safely home to Earth, where Tybault waited with the longing of a thousand hearts. And when she would not answer, the whole system wept.

VESPERTINE: [sounds of whistling wind and clanking metal] Begone, deceiver! I *shall* marry Doctor Gruel at the stroke of dawn! He is my one true love! How I adore his warty chin and heavy fists! I grow faint at the thought of his hunchback; I dream of nothing but his scarred and hairy brow! I will never love another for all my days! [long, mournful groan over clanking engine parts]

ANNOUNCER: Meanwhile, we find our stalwart hero, Tybault, having defeated a band of mercenaries and black alchemists bent on inciting war with Austria at any cost, recovering from his grievous wounds in a mysterious hospital, attended by buxom masked nurses and a physician revealed last week to be none other than his sworn enemy: the Invisible Hussar!

THE INVISIBLE HUSSAR: [music cue #3: minor key crescendo 2] Yes, it is *I*! None other could vanquish the Hero of the Crimea! And these masked beauties are my sisters, the Ninja-Nuns of Nanking! They thirst for the blood of good men. I really don't know how long I can hold them back. But first, you must witness the magnitude of your defeat! Behold, this is not a hospital, but my ship! [sounds of howling space winds] You have slept soundly, my old foe, with the help of my sisters' potions. We will soon rendezvous with my comrades—Doctor Gruel and his band of banditos! [music cue #4: minor key crescendo 6]

ANNOUNCER: Will Tybault escape the clutches of his nemesis? Can the Ninja-Nuns of Nanking resist their terrible bloodlust? Will Vespertine marry the devious Doctor Gruel or will her loyal lover reach her in time? Who *is* the Invisible Hussar? Will these long-suffering sweethearts—one untamed spirit enamoured of the stars; one true man, devoted to King, Country, and Mother Earth—find each other at last, or will they yearn on in vain? Find out now!

Come with me to the rough-and-tumble worlds of Venus and Earth in the early days of the Diaspora, a fantastical journey into that special place in the heart where history meets the imagination, hard science meets flights of fancy, love leads the way, and the impossible becomes—for a moment—true, on . . . *How Many Miles to Babylon?*

[theme music]

From the Personal Reels of
Percival Alfred Unck

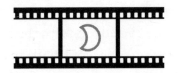

[SEVERIN UNCK walks hand in hand with CLOTILDE CHARBONNEAU down Usagi Avenue in Tithonus. Christmas lanterns glitter all around them. The Actaeon Theatre is visible behind them, searchlights swinging wildly over the night sky. CLOTILDE and SEVERIN are bundled in thick coats. Identical furs frame their faces. PERCIVAL UNCK walks backward down the street, filming them as steadily as his camera Clara will allow. SEVERIN sucks the filling from a street vendor's *blin*. CLOTILDE'S face is sullen. She scratches at ruby earrings. She will leave them within a month.]

PERCIVAL
How did you like the picture, pumpkin?

SEVERIN
I'm not a pumpkin!

CLOTILDE
Are so. If we put a candle in your head you'd be a jack-o'-lantern.

SEVERIN

Ew! There's no room in my head for a candle, Mama.

PERCIVAL

All right, you are definitely not a pumpkin, and we will definitely not put any candles in your head or make a tart out of you or turn you into a coach at midnight. Now, did you like your papa's movie? He made it just for you, his first one for children.

SEVERIN

[long pause] No.

PERCIVAL

But you were so wonderful in it, darling! Didn't you have fun filming your little bit? Isn't it nice to see yourself on that big giant screen?

SEVERIN

[bursts into tears] I'm sorry, Papa! But there just aren't such things as octopuses that talk or wear spectacles and spats in real life. It's only Uncle Talmadge in a suit with sequins stuck on him. I shall never meet a talking octopus like Mr Bergamot, never, never! [Tears roll down SEVERIN's cheeks and into her *blin*. She dries her face on one furry sleeve, sniffing in the cold.] It's just a lot of silliness.

The Deep Blue Devil:
The Dame in Question

Case Log: 14 December, 1961

"Mr St. John, my name is Cythera Brass," said the dame in question, shaking my hand like an adman while the Talbot drove itself calm as you please through a particularly obnoxious All-Clear mob and into the money-gargling heart of the Te Deum business district.

She let me eat. She let me drink. I feel about the same describing that as I do describing a quality fuck. It's private, you pervert, take a hike. What I do with my gullet is my business. I mumbled my name back at Cythera Brass. I don't care to say it too often. I barely live in that name. Hangs on me like someone else's coat. It's a name with too much room in it for a chap like me. Too famous, too fancy, too much chance of someone looking me up and down and belching out the dreaded: *Oh, you're* him. But Miss Brass, she already knew who I was. She wouldn't've come to scarf me up if I wasn't who I was, so she and I, we could just sit tight, each knowing what we knew. Except she had me at a disadvantage, as I didn't know a blessed thing about her. I hate that. Goes against my nature. I'm a hoarder of information.

"You American?" I asked her. Slugged back more of her bourbon.

She nodded; barely moved her chin, but it was a nod. "Seneca."

Right. Sure. I'd thought Sioux, but hell, Americans all sound the same to me. "I went to the Nation once, when I was a kid. Toured the League halls and grounds. Shook hands with a coupla judges. Liked it better than the States, myself."

"Mmmm," answered that long-legged dame, without taking her eyes off a fish-masked fella jumping around outside the limousine like a particularly unnecessary exclamation point.

"I'm nothing, me. Don't even know what ball I got myself born on. Spent time on Venus, obviously. Good long spate on the Moon, which was miserable as a year of Lent. Just about everywhere else, too. If you count up all the orbits on which I've hung my hat, I've been a subject of four different Crowns; a citizen of China, France, and Argentina; and a serf on Io—which I think technically made me Italian—but only for a month."

Look at me. Hoarder of information, spilling my worthless biography to a lady just because her pretty bronze knees looked like a premonition of kingdom come. I didn't have to say anything. I coulda soaked up the Talbot and the quiet and the drink. Cythera Brass had it all in a file somewhere anyway. She was the kind of broad whose job it was to keep files. To keep the secrets in a straight line and working toward payday. And still, I sat there on leather the colour of chicken fat trying to get her to *like* me.

"Listen," I said. The slick of her booze greased my head. "I know it's a lot of money and I'm broke. But I don't want the job. I've got no gut for travelling anymore, and I just don't *care* about what you care about. I don't want to know. I'm not curious. You'd think I would be, yeah? But I'm not. I'm good. I am right with the Lord my God on this. Frankly, I don't like to work at all when I can avoid it. I came here to stick it out. Just plunk down in the snow and ride out the long year. Should be enough. Eighty-four Earth years for each natural year out here on the snowball.

Maybe I got it in me to see it through to spring. Maybe summer'll gimme a lick and a slap. Summer on Uranus. That'd be something. But maybe not. I'm not fussed if it's not in the cards. Look—" I grabbed her hand suddenly, panicked. I don't know why I did it. She looked down at my paw like a Sasquatch with the clap had gotten ahold of her. "Look, you might call it sixty years or fifty or, given my habits, twenty, but the way Uranus sees it, big-picture-wise, I got less than a year to live. And I find that just *peachy*, Cyth. I find that *comforting*. I need that comfort. I don't want it fucked by running around with aims or ambitions or plans beyond my next fifteen rounds with sleep. Don't you take my year from me, Miss Brass. It's mine."

The Talbot swung tight into a plaza. I was meant to meet my contact at the Tartarus Diner: not a dive, but not a proper sort of place, either. Clearly we had bypassed Tartarus and headed straight for HQ. Frozen fountains. Tall statue of a naked girl with her arms glued to her sides and her head thrown back so her body looked like a rocket ship. Ice junking up her feet like afterburn.

Melancholia.

The most expensive address in Te Deum—well, one of. Melancholia. There's four of them, naturally, the Towers. The Humours: Sanguina, Cholera, Phlegma, Melancholia. Four fluorescent high-rises spiking TD like birthday candles. Twisted-up unicorn horns studded with bosses. Bosses run things. The rest of us get run. It's the only rank that matters these days. You can dress it up as baronies or boyars or caliphates, but that's just sticking lace and ribbons on a dinosaur and hoping he'll take you to town. Is you a boss or isn't you? That's about the size of it.

I'd been inside Cholera once, for a game of quoits and an unhappy little blowjob. The walls were soft. Like lungs.

"It's not me, Mr St. John," Cythera Brass said in that wide-open voice. She poured herself out of the Talbot and came round to open my door—downright gentlemanly, this Iroquois maid. "You made your year. If it were up to me I'd let you lie in it."

A bubble lift strung us up through Melancholia's lavender spine. Up above the blue stink of Uranus's cigar smoke. Through a dormant patch of glowglass I saw black sky and stars. Hard and bright as bullet holes. No moons. Something in my bones righted up. My body knows that's how a sky should dress. It poured over me like a hot shower.

The lift bonged out the penthouse, and Cythera Brass, not a molecule out of place, walked crisply out onto a huge checkerboard floor. Her heels smacked kisses on the glass squares. An office, big as a ballroom. Low buttressed ceilings crisscrossed with liquid glowglass patterns, tangerine into candy cane into St. Elmo's Fire. At one end of the room sat a long black desk with a green lamp on it. A personal long-distance radio setup occupied substantial real estate in the north corner. Windows ate up the whole back wall, opening onto Epi 'Vard, way down below this hundred-story nest. Over the windows hung a painting—a glowglass painting. I'd never heard of anyone who could control glowglass well enough to do something like that. I gawked at it. The colours slid and ran: a lady with no clothes and long peacock-coloured hair. She didn't use it to cover up, either, the way ladies in paintings like to do. She just stood there, bold naked, looking down at a bloody-bright man with more muscles than pride. He knelt rosily at her saffron feet, offering her a long coppery belt stuck all over with jewels: Hephaestus presenting the girdle to Aphrodite. When she wore that belt, not even the gods could keep it in their trousers. The gems swirled, oozing through every colour, every possible colour. And then, just for a moment, they weren't gems. They were planets. They were moons. Then they oozed back into garnets and emeralds and opals. I felt sick. Coloursick. Uranian vertigo.

A figure turned toward me, hidden in the shadows of the far

right side of the room. I focused on it. It wore brown. Grey. Black. My eyes held on for dear life to that drab spot in the darkness.

"That will be all, Cythera. Thank you," the figure said. A woman's voice. Easy bull's-eye: Hungarian by way of Saturn. Not just Saturn, but Enuma Elish. My old instincts rubbed their cricket legs together to spite me. An upper-crust capital madam—but her consonants were a little too practiced. She wasn't born to it, I reckoned. "You can wait outside."

Miss Enuma Elish emerged. Shaved head. Short, hard, squared off, a boss like a shotgun. I'd have called her a gymnastic fifty, but living out here ages you fast. Guessing gets pointless. She was wrapped up tight as a mummy, but I could see the thick quality of her suit. It practically *flexed* at me. Three silver clamps up the ridge of each ear. A tiny speck of rainpearl in each nostril. *Huh*, creaked my crickets, waving their antennae. *She's All-Clear. Top of the world, dripping money, not a dumb kid or a junkie, but All-Clear, nonetheless.*

The boss kept mum. She moved some papers around on her coffin of a desk. *It must kill her not to be down there with the crowds,* I thought.

I took that away from her. By not showing up.

"I just told your girl," I said. My voice skittered out over the glass floor. "I told her. I don't want the gig. It doesn't matter what the price tag is. I don't want it. So why don't you go down there and be with your kin? An hour left. That's ages."

The boss gave me a look that clearly communicated how ignorant I was on every possible topic. "This is not a negotiation, Mr St. John. The commission is as follows: In exchange for a sum of nine hundred thousand pounds sterling plus expenses, you will investigate the disappearance of and uncover the current whereabouts—"

"Lady, it's not a negotiation because I don't want the shit you're peddling! Save your breath!"

"—the current whereabouts, if any, of Severin Unck, a young woman who disappeared some eighteen years ago near the village of Adonis, on the White Peony archipelago in the northern hemisphere of Venus, which falls into something of a grey area between the Chinese and Canadian sectors."

"*Don't you think I know that?*" I hissed. I well and truly hated her now. That's all it takes. Say the word. Any one of them: Adonis. White Peony. Severin Unck. How could this shaved bitch say her name? Fuck her for saying it. I hadn't said it in three years and it was mine to say more than anyone's.

The boss circled round her desk, coming to lean against its heavy frame. She tented her fingers. Her face caught the harlequin lights. Her cheekbones had unbelievable angles, like a martyr's statue. "I am quite certain that you do, Mr St. John. I, and the interests I represent, feel you are uniquely situated to carry out our investigation. I will be clear: We expect success. We expect *resounding* success. We expect—I will be plain—a body. We are open as to its state. Alive or dead, partitioned or whole. Aware or . . . well . . . whatever one might consider to be the opposite of awareness. That gives you a fairly wide playing field."

"That's fucking grotesque, but as I won't be doing it, I'll let it slide."

She chuckled. Her hushed Saturnine vowels cajoled; her Hungarian consonants sneered. "But who else? Who else could we find on any world, under any rock, who knows the subject so intimately? Who would be so motivated to uncover the truth as Anchises St. John, the orphan of Adonis, the boy who saw it all? The boy with the hands that sing?" She grabbed for my gloved hands, faster than my filed-down neurons could answer. Her skin was cold, even through the leather. I snatched my fists away.

The boss frowned. She stepped back, rocking on her heels, a prizefighter. Round one wasn't going her way, but she'd played this ring before. She spat her words at me, rat-a-tat. "You have no memory before the age of ten. Your parents are recorded as Peitho and Erzulie Kephus on the 1940 Venusian census—Ottoman subjects, taxes delinquent by quite a bit and for quite a while. But they might as well be characters in a novel for all the connection you feel to them. You don't use the name they gave you. Severin saddled you with that clunker of a first name the day you met. Your surname is your adopted father's. You spent your teenage years on Luna—but not in Tithonus, in Ibis. A pleasant enough seaside town, but more importantly, one with a renowned hospital specializing in—"

"Stop."

"The Deformed, Insane, and Infirm. St. Nepthys, was it? I believe Ibis also has a charming amusement park with a rollicking good roller coaster. And *bumper cars*. How nice for you! Who wouldn't grow up into a fine young man given such idyllic circumstances? A splendid estate overlooking the Sea of Serenity. The very eyeball of the man on the moon. Toys and books and good, nourishing, *Earth*-grown food. Even an outpatient program! Ah, but you didn't do well at St. Nepthys, did you? Well, who could? Nurses can be such a *bother*."

"Stop."

"So you ran away from your hospital and your guardian and the bumper cars and that steadfast little rollercoaster. And where did you land first? Come now, surely you remember."

My face burned. The drinks I'd gulped down in the Talbot were in a hurry to come back up.

"Stop it. Just stop it."

"Oh, but I'm sure you know better than me, Mr St. John. Where was it? Mars? No, no, that was later, after you dried out— the first time, anyway. What was your first stop?"

I gritted my teeth.

"Mercury. Trismegistus."

"Oh, that's *right*. The hacienda. Now, was that your first suicide attempt, or did we miss one back at old St. Neppie's?"

"Enough."

"Tell me, Mr St. John, what exactly *is* a callowhale?"

A man can only hear so much of his own history before he cries uncle. And that was my uncle, right there.

"That's me, then," I said cheerily, lifting my hat as I walked away from her. *Fast but don't flee,* I thought. *Fleeing doesn't look good on anyone.* I shot over my shoulder: "You have a nice morning, madam. I'll see you in hell."

"Mr St. John, get back here this instant or I'll have you breaking your ribs in a titanium mine by glassup." I froze. If you'd seen the inside of a Uranian mine, you'd freeze, too. "And I'll find a foreman with a particularly oppressive home life to look after you." She softened her voice, but not by much. "Don't be an idiot. We will pay you more money than you've seen in your life. We will supply you with food. Drink. Transportation. The drug or drugs of your choice. Companionship, if you fancy it, though I'd recommend a bath first. A personal, dedicated radio unit so you never have to bother with Depot queues again—which is worth nearly half what we're paying you to begin with. Cythera will go with you, of course—we are not fools. You need a governess. But, I promise, you can do this job fat, drunk, high, and fucked senseless, and afterward you can sleep with a security blanket made of money. Or you can do any number of less stimulating jobs digging out the marine tunnels or hauling sewage or mining the most poisonous thing I can think of this week. But you will leave my office employed."

God, I just wanted to leave. *Just let me leave.* "Jesus, woman, *why*? I am as useless as a sack of nothing, you can see that. Your secretary, or whatever Miss Brass out there is, could see it."

"Because I know you can do it with a needle in your arm and a fifth in your fist. You were a private eye on Callisto for seven years.

It's the longest you ever stayed put. You were good at it. You don't like being good at things; it makes you stand out. But you couldn't help being good at it. You tried to fail and for once you didn't. But I guess regular meals and an apartment where the heat stayed on were too much for you, kiddo. We're not offering any of that. We're offering what you do want: enough money and vice to drink yourself to death in comfort after you've done with us."

"Who is *us*? Who are the 'interests you represent'? For that matter, who are you? What do I call you?"

The boss smiled, the smile of a boss who knew she'd won. It was a sick fucking smirk. "My name is irrelevant to you personally. You can call me Melancholia when you need to call me anything, which I do not expect to be often. Nor should it concern you who I represent. Do your job; get paid."

"Not good enough." Not good enough for *her*. Not if I had to hunt her down like a dog after a fox. I wanted to know who was up on the horses.

Melancholia sighed. She looked out the window at the blue froth of the All-Clear. Her sharp nose stood starkly against the bleeding colours. "Only four sequences of *The Radiant Car Thy Sparrow Drew* survived whatever happened, and they are quite badly damaged. I'm sure you've seen them. I represent a consortium of business interests loosely gathered under the tent of Oxblood Films. Oxblood underwrote all but one of Ms Unck's movies. We own *Radiant Car*. We paid for it. In a very real sense, we own *her*. And we must insist upon recovering our property. Undiscovered footage may not even be out of the question."

"It is."

The boss shrugged. "If you say so. We will accept a body in lieu of a print. Either of these things would be beyond value as far as we are concerned."

"I don't get it. If you've seen the footage, if you've seen those *scraps*, then you've seen how it ends. You've seen her just . . .

whoosh. Vanish. You want me to pull a body out of a hat? How about a rabbit, too?"

"If you like." Melancholia shook her shaved head. "I don't understand you. At this very moment, every conceivable resource lies in your hands to solve the central mystery of your whole wretched life. We thought you'd be . . . driven to succeed. We thought you'd be relieved."

I looked up helplessly at the glowglass painting, that sad sack of a man tying his coppermelt belt of planets no mortal or god could resist round the waist of a cunt who'd use it every chance she got.

"It was a nice idea," I said.

"What was?"

"On Uranus, a year is a life. Eighty-four years. Born in the winter, young in the springtime, still going strong in the summer, old in the autumn. It's the only planet where you can do that. It's perfect. It's beautiful. It's downright *artistic*. God*dammit*."

"This is everything we have on her," Melancholia said quietly. She put her hand on a stack of files. Impressive enough, I guess. Thorough. But it looked pathetic to me. "I assume you don't need any film archives. I don't think we could add anything to your collection." I don't blush. Never have. But if I did, I think the sore, just-punched feeling I had then would have done it.

"Probably not."

"There's a cannon leaving once the All-Clear sounds." Of course—she wouldn't arrange business during services. "It'll take you to Pluto. One of the *Clamshell*'s crewmembers is living there; in some state of dissolution, we understand. He is going by a false name, rarely finds himself lucid, wants merely to be left alone. You two should find much in common. It's all in the file. You'll have plenty of reading time on the road." Melancholia paused. Ran her hand over her bald monk-head. "Come on," my boss whispered. She put her fingers round my wrist, avoiding the glove. "Didn't you ever want to know how the story ended?"

I took the file. I got into the lift with Cythera Brass. She looked so smug I could have popped her one. As the bubble doors slid shut, I heard the crackle of that radio rig coming on. The first breathless lines of this month's instalment of *How Many Miles to Babylon?*, a wireless soap loved by everyone but me, wound down after us, chasing us through Melancholia Tower.

Oh, Vespertine, I will find you, even on the onyx towers of Erishkegal! Do not lose hope! One more night and we will be together at last . . . Alas, the nights on Venus are as long as years . . .

There's nothing the rich don't skim off the top.

All-Clear

The morning's Uranus is chosen by lot. He wears a funhouse-mirror version of the Imperial Crown, but where the Black Prince's Ruby and Lizzie One's best pearls ring the original, his glows with brazen electric bulbs: stars, winking on and off. He dons a coat of furpack and rain slicker blackfalse which reeks of the sweat of other Uranuses and their blood. Faces have been drawn onto the 'false in chalk and oil: Titans and gods in stick figures. Anonymous hands clamp a white collar round his throat: rings.

Uranus is joyful. His congregation throws blue paint onto his face. It drips down onto his cheeks, beads on his eyelashes. He puts his arms out, beckoning magnanimously—it is always smooth and sure, this motion. Uranus, every Uranus, has seen it done many times before it falls to him to perform.

Women and men come to him. Twenty-seven. Titania and Oberon and Puck wear shimmery greenfalse and brambles in their hair. Ariel and Umbriel, long silver veils and wild red leotards beneath. The maidens, then: great Miranda clothed in sails, Juliet strapped with golden daggers, Cordelia and Ophelia, Cressida and Portia, Desdemona and Bianca all dance painfully *en pointe*, their mad hair loose and long. Prospero strides with staff and book. Little children play the small moons: Belinda, Sycorax, Ferdinand, Setebos, Stephano, Mab, Trinculo, Francisco, Margaret, Rosalind, Caliban, Perdita, gamboling behind him like medieval dancers after Death. A toddling Cupid fires an empty amber bow over and over at everyone he sees. Uranus, ringed by his moons, his harem, his family.

The satellites throw garlands of rainpearls, dried crocus shrimp, morels, and the wild rubicund varuna flower that grows on the snowdunes of King George's Sea, Oceana Telchine, the Fury's Pond, and Herschellina, the vast dark waters of this world.

Titania steps out of the dance, though her stepping out is part of the dance and not separate from it. Her fairy crown flickers with shards of glowglass. Her green gown, cut like clinging leaves, shows the same crude sketching as Uranus's raincoat: the great canyons of the moon Titania; the thriving farms and mining cities spreading over her hip, her breast, her back. She offers her hand to Uranus; he presses it to his cheek. She is lush and fertile; he is the god of air and cold. She bows to him, he to her. They dance, not in the cavorting, half-extemporized orgy of the other moons, but formally, as folk danced back home before these two—whoever they may be tonight or on other nights—shut their eyes and fired themselves at the reaches of the heavens. They are careful; they hold each other stiff and far apart, their feet precise. He leads, she follows. Uranus speaks in a slurry, the local mine-and-dice argot: a sing-song stew fashioned out of the Queen's English, Manchurian, Russian, Punjabi, French, and anything else, picked up like toys, gnawed, shaken, held to the ear.

URANUS TO TITANIA: *Aye-o, me larkhee, difujin moya, me mademoibelle, je lay on me side for thee, tbye, sur-la-vous. Scamp me round, q'est que yes?*

TITANIA TO URANUS: *Oye sohneya, me bolshy hazy ta. Je spin thee round-rosie, je never fall down.*

URANUS: *Gander all these melly platypups we made with us! Ain't us proud. Ain't us trop-gros Grand Papa.*

TITANIA: *Akara-thee lie on me full, heavy nicht on heavy vert. Thee dole me stars, je dole thee 'ren.*

URANUS: *'Fess now, quoi ren do Moonmama and Grand Papa love plus-most?*

ALL: *Uranian 'ren! 'Ren quoi turn aback on dodder-Ertha. Aye-o me babba! We are no earthserfs. Titans we are, nowforever.*

URANUS: *Est thee lonely, difujin moya? Est thee lonely, me ren? Out in the noir and the shiver?*

TITANIA: *Longside all these coeurs a-beat? Never.*

ALL: *Never again.*

PART TWO

❀ ❀ ❀ ❀ ❀

THE BLUE PAGES

The camera is much more than a recording apparatus, it is a
medium via which messages reach us from another world.

—Orson Welles

Many cities of men the traveller saw, and learned
the turnings of their streets and of their minds.
Many sufferings he learned as well,
drifting heartsick upon the endless open sea,
striving to keep his life within his breast
and bear his comrades home.
But he could not lift their stars from their shoulders,
not even with his whole strength.
Recklessness destroyed them all,
those blind fools who in madness
devoured the Cattle of the Sun—
and so it was that bright god removed from them
their homecoming.

—Homer, *The Odyssey*

The Radiant Car Thy Sparrows Drew
(Oxblood films, dir. Severin Unck)

SC2 EXT. ADONIS—DAY 6 POST PLANETFALL 23:14
[30 NOVEMBER, 1944]
[EXT. Former site of the Village of Adonis, on the Shores of the Sea of Qadesh, Night.

SEVERIN UNCK and her CREW have lit the cracked braziers of the village; this is the only light source, but it is ample. Callowbrick flames flicker ghostlike over what was once the centre of town, Ahab Square—whose name provides a neat indicator of the general humour to be found in callowhale villages such as this, all over Venus. The ruins of Adonis's dwellings and public buildings are visible as tall shadows, unsettling shapes, no longer recognizable as human habitation, their angles stove inward and burst open to become the shattered bones of a place once living. Lashes of a milky substance splash foliage, ruins, beach, roads. A light rain falls.

Dead Adonis, laid out in state on the beachhead, possessed of one single mourner. The great ocean provides a score for this starlit landfall. In the old days a Foley boy would thrash rushes against the floor of the theatre to simulate the colossal, dusky red tide of the Sea of Qadesh, the great waterway that flows through all the corners of Venus, having no beginning and no end. The audience would squint in the dark, trying to see some sense of scarlet in the monochrome waves, emerald in the undulating cacao-ferns. The black silk balloon of the *Clamshell*'s amphibious dinghy crinkles and billows lightly on the strand.

SEVERIN steps into frame, into the diffident, limping light, her bobbed hair sweat-curled in the wilting wind. She has thrown the exhibition costume into an offscreen campfire and is clothed now in her accustomed trousers and black aviator's jacket.

Other shapes move with busy intensity as the CREW sets up camp. SEVERIN holds her hand out like she would to a horse or a dog—walking carefully, quietly—but she does not walk toward a horse or a dog. SEVERIN looks uncertainly over her shoulder at the long snarl of sea behind them—and at ERASMO ST. JOHN, temporarily trusted with the care and feeding of George. He says something to her offscreen—he must, because she cocks her head as though considering a riddle and says something back to him. Her mouth moves, but the microphones have not been set up yet. Her lips make words the audience can never quite read.

A SMALL BOY walks in circles around the stub of what was once a Divers Memorial. All such villages have a Memorial: a cairn of diving bells bolted together on a pedestal in the town square, one for each diver who perished fast to a whale, lost

in pursuit of the precious pale gold of callowmilk. Adonis's monument has its bells no longer,
vanished with the population, but the pedestal
remains. The boy stares down as he turns and
turns, endlessly. His hands flicker and blur as
if he is signing something, or writing on phantom paper. He wears an adult's diving costume,
its brass bell attached firmly round his neck.
Its folds and grommets drag against him, slow him
down.

SEVERIN calls to him. He does not flinch or
stop. He does not look up. The camera watches
him. SEVERIN watches him. Slowly, the CREW cease
their activity and turn their gazes to the child.
The footage crackles into life as the sound
equipment comes online. SEVERIN squats down on
her heels in a friendly, schoolteacherly fashion,
still holding out her hand, beckoning. She tilts
her head in an *aw, come on* gesture. Two kids in
a garden. One wants to play. The other does not.]

SEVERIN

Hey, little guy... it's okay now. It's fine now.
I'm here. My name's Severin. You can call me
Rinny if you like that better.

[The BOY simply turns and turns and turns,
over and over. His huge diving bell casts a
shadow like a black spotlight. The film is damaged. It has always been damaged. It was damaged
in the dailies. No one has ever seen it uncor-
roded. The BOY seems to leap forward and backward
round the ruined Memorial, jumping in and out of
reality as the print cuts in and out, in and out.

CUT TO: EXT. ADONIS, DAY. 07:45: MARIANA ALFRIC
is screaming, clutching her hand to her breast
**FILM DAMAGED FOOTAGE SPLICE CORRODED SKIP AF-
FECTED AREA SKIPPING SKIPPING UNABLE TO COMPEN-
SATE ERROR 143 SEE ARCHIVIST FOR ASSISTANCE**]

Production Meeting,
~~The Deep Blue Devil~~
The Man in the Malachite Mask
(Tranquillity Studios, 1960, dir. Percival Unck)

Audio Recorded for Reference by Vincenza Mako

MAKO: No, no, Percy, listen to me. It's not working.

All right, it's *working*, but it's not *right*. The noir setup has a certain energy, I agree, but it sits pretty heavy on the action. Though I like making Cyth Brass a secretary. We should keep that. She'll probably sue us for defamation. But we said we'd give him a love interest, not a probation officer! And what are we going to do when we get to Venus? And we do have to get to Venus, I promise. You can dawdle all you like, but it's there in the middle of the story, throwing its gravity around, warping everything toward it. The point is, what kind of hard-boiled finale did you mean to stick on it? Shootout at Adonis? Breathless bullets and betrayal and a fedora on her grave? Is that what you think happened? That she's buried in a swamp somewhere with a hole in her head? If you go with noir, you're building in a certain expectation of violence. Of death.

PERCIVAL UNCK: Varela has said she's dead all along.

MAKO: And Erasmo has said she isn't. You said you'd rather not have death, but you're stuffing it in from all sides. And . . . Severin's outside the scope of the story. She can't help it. That's all a script like that will let her be. An object on a mantle that has to go off by the third act. A gun that must be fired. She's not a person, the way you've got it set up, with your broads and bitches and dark streets at the edge of space. She's just a goal.

UNCK: Not a goal, Vince. A Grail.

MAKO: Sure. Fine, *Percival*. A Grail. Very clever. Very subtle. But a Grail isn't an alive thing. It has no blood but the blood of another; it has no life but the life it grants. Its job is to sit there and . . . be a Grail. To be sought. That doesn't sound like anyone we know. And, frankly, it's all a bit pedestrian for you. For us. I think you're holding back. I know I am. Because . . . because we think she'd want us to. To double down on the kind of stories *she* liked to tell. Really, how different is your Te Deum from the actual digs? Barely a streak of grime out of place. It's just . . . events that could really happen taking place in a real city. That's not you. That's not me. That's *her*.

UNCK: But it did really happen. In a real city. Just not *that* city.

MAKO: When has that ever slowed us down? We put vampires in *The Abduction of Proserpine*! That was a real thing that happened in a real city. And Proserpine is a real city that really disappeared off the map of Pluto, I think it's fair to point out, not so different from Adonis. We shovelled in vampires by the coven and we didn't even blink. We just ordered up a vat of fake blood and started stitching capes.

[Unck laughs, a laugh that is half a grunt.]

Listen, I have an idea brewing. It's just a little shift, really. In perspective. In framing. Because noir isn't really a new thing at all. It's just a fairy tale with guns. Your hardscrabble detective is nothing more than a noble knight with a cigarette and a disease where his heart should be. He talks prettier, that's all. He's no less idealistic—there're good women and bad women, good jobs and bad jobs. Justice and truth are always worth seeking. He pulls his fedora down like the visor on a suit of armour. He serves his lord faithfully whether he wants to or not. And he is in thrall to the idea of a woman. It's just that in detective stories, women are usually dead before the curtain goes up. In fairy tales, they're usually alive. Fairy tales are about survival. That's *all* they're about. The princess lives to get married in the last act. The detective solves the woman; the knight saves her.

And really, *really*, when you put a fairy tale together with grime and despair and industrial angst you get the Gothic, and that's where we live, Percy. That's *our* house. So why don't we lose the trench coat and pick up a black cloak. Turn the Byronic all the way up. An ancestral curse, a mad lord, a brooding castle. Obsession, desire, secrets. It's all already there. And a ghost. Because the truth is . . . the truth is, this is all a ghost story. It always has been. We're pouring out a bowl of blood on the banks of the Styx, asking her to drink it and speak.

UNCK: That's . . . not bad.

MAKO: I know, dummy. It's my idea. Of course it's not bad. We've already sent him to Pluto. It's perfect. Nothing darker and more mysterious than that blasted place. For all anyone ever hears out of Pluto these days, it might as well be Hades itself. A whole planet that's nothing more than the haunted mansion on the hill. Lights in the dark. Sounds in the night.

Percy . . . we owe her our best, not just our most polite. You and I, we're no good at telling a story straight. It won't come off right. Like a dog reciting a sonnet. Impressive, but how much better to let him howl? So, look. She's . . . she's captive in a black palace of a thousand rooms. Imprisoned by a terrible master. Behind briars, Sleeping Beauty in black lipstick. No one has seen her for years. She's a legend, a whisper in the taverns and the alleyways.

UNCK: And a stranger comes to town.

MAKO: A stranger with a hidden past. An unnatural secret. A concealed deformity?

UNCK: And a curse, Vince. You've got to have a curse. It's the accessory the fashionable antihero cannot go without. How about . . . when asked, he must always tell the truth. It's not even much of a leap from the detective who must deliver the truth to his bosses. We've still got all the Pluto sets from *Proserpine*. And the Bertilak woods from *Sir Gawain on Ganymede*.

MAKO: And Varela slots right in. He was always hip deep in a phantasmagoria anyway. You want to look that liar in the eye? Let's do it. Maximo Varela did actually run off to Pluto when Oxblood turned him loose.

UNCK: And the end, Vince?

MAKO: How do all Gothics end? With magic. And with revenge.

~~The Deep Blue Devil~~
The Man in the Malachite Mask:
My Sin

20 February, 1962. Early morning. *Obolus* cantina.

During the whole of that frozen, dark transit through the glittering, howling autumnal moorlands of the trans-Neptunian wastes, as the ice road hung thin and ragged as funereal curtains beyond the portholes, I had been keeping studiously to myself within the confines of our slim vessel as it passed through that singularly lonesome expanse of darkness and, whilst the blue and ghostly shades of morning at the edge of civilization roused the passengers, drew within sight of the melancholy face of Pluto.

Breakfast brought an oppressive gloom down upon my spirit. Soft-boiled eggs oozed a golden ichor of loneliness onto my spoon; the buttered rolls spoke only of the further torment of my being. Failure swirled in the milky depths of my tea and the bacon I devoured was the bacon of grief.

"There is naught on Pluto but magicians, Americans, and the mad," rasped the old woman who had settled in beside me in the *Obolus* cantina, a lavishly appointed, elegant space filled topful with the intolerably irritating chime of cutlery and soft whisperings. She needn't have troubled me; there was room enough for her to encamp at a table of her own and gum at her crumpets whilst leaving me in peace. I despised her for failing to do so and turned up the corner of my greatcoat against any further conversation. It is always damnably cold on these ships. At the evening receptions, the décolletages of all the earnest and well-meaning ladies prickle with gooseflesh and the throats of the paler girls sheen a trembling, vampiric blue. The crone with whom I unwillingly shared my morning meal, however, did not worry herself with the chill. She wore red and violet, and she had pinned in her white hair black silk calla lilies with long, viridescent stamens thrusting suggestively upward, as though her head were a radio array tuned every direction at once. She smelled sour—but then, so did I. So did the blue-necked ladies dancing in their rosettes and pink damask. Everyone reeks after six months on the Orient Express. There is no hiding our animal nature out here on the ice road. Crone, maiden, paladin, my own unhappy self: not a one of us smells better than a week-dead lion on the veldt.

"Is that so?" I groused at her, nose plunged deep into my tea, praying for her to return to the counter for more of today's pastry (sugared gardenias in a glazed puff globe), more of today's jam (fig-candleberry), more of anything but my attention. My own flaky globe and pot of jam sat unmolested before me—how quickly I had forgotten my previous starvations, privations, depredations, and come to that unimaginable point wherein I refused the obscenely precious food supplied by our invisible, unmentionable hosts at Oxblood Films. The price of my breakfast, which only increased with every day further distant from any place where a gardenia or a candleberry could grow, could purchase a small estate in the less fashionable bands of the Kuiper Belt, yet I could hardly taste it. The past coated my tongue and robbed the present from me—and yet I own no nobility on that account. Give me a little bacon and milk and I become, inevitably, a decadent like all the rest of them.

I wondered what use our hosts could have for this doddering

old woman, what favour she had done or would do them, to earn passage. I had grudgingly reached first-name terms with most of the other passengers, but for six months, this baggage of a woman had declined to share her name with anyone at all. Perhaps she had once been a starlet. Perhaps I would recognize her younger self, if presented with evidence of those lilies in red hair thick as blood and life. Her voice had that old-fashioned, hard-edged showman's twang, that affected, too-bright accent of the Nation of Theatre, as though all plays came from a single strange planet where you could pick up, without meaning to, the local dialect. That voice had no relation to her broken body, to the lump in her back or the long, sad draperies of her skin. Her voice was a wholly separate being, one flush and good and bright and subtle. She was all voice. In the dark, I might have worshipped her.

"Oh yes," she said, crunching a sugared gardenia between her shockingly white teeth. An addict, then. Af-yun turns the teeth a lambent, unsettling, inhuman white, so white it edges into lavender, into a colour as clean as death. That's what comes of eating the muck scraped off of Venus's underside, of breathing the stars' putrescence.

I will not say my teeth are brown.

"The question is," the crone chortled in that surprisingly rich, full, clotted-cream voice, spilling bits of flower and pastry down the front of her red gown, "which one are you? *I'm* American, which doesn't bode well for you, I'm afraid. Well, I'm American now, in any event. Morocco never treated me as well as I deserved, so I saw no reason to stand by my man. Pluto is the end of everything. Last Chance Gulch. For me, that spells home."

I made a noise in my throat that could be interpreted as agreement, rebuttal, amusement, disgust, or commiseration—I have perfected this noise. I consider it vital, for rarely do I wish to say anything to another person which a well-timed grunt cannot replace.

My tormentor, however, wheedled on as though I had clasped her to my chest and implored her to speak, speak now, speak forever, speak until the sun gutters and the snow road melts! "But you are a young man. Only the young are so rude and unpleasant. There's no fortune to be made on Pluto, if that's your mind. Someone ought to have told you."

"I have business."

"With whom? The buffalo?"

I sighed and fixed her with a black gaze. I have perfected that gaze also—it is necessary in Te Deum and elsewhere. If you cannot wither a man with your eyes you will be withered by his fists. Yet my best back-alley glare did not move that ridiculous soul whom I by now had to admit had become my breakfast companion. "With Maximo Varela, if you insist on prying into my affairs. Though it has been indicated to me that he is no longer going by that name."

The woman snorted. Even her snort had melody. Incredulity shaped itself upon her face. "That . . . that he is not."

"We are to be met at the Depot by his daughters and escorted safely to his house, though neither the house, nor the daughters, nor the Depot, nor the meeting are any concern of yours."

Her rheumy eyes swam with dark mirth. "Poor lamb," she crooned, and patted my hand in a grandmotherly fashion. "What a pity we wasted this voyage in not knowing one another. I might have told you tales. I might have told your fortune. I might have told you to yourself. People used to listen to me, oh how they used to listen! Hung on every word. I made gold out of horseshit in my day, my boy. Imagine what I could have done with you."

I, naturally, did not share her sentiment. We would disembark at midnight tomorrow and already my feet itched for earth, my heart for silence, for the surcease of the endless thrum of engines in the walls, the constant hum and rumble that maddened me, made my blood ricochet up and down my spine, no less than the equally endless need for the smallest of talk shared between the few rarefied passengers, all of us avoiding the plain fact of the ghastly waste of this ship, its food and fuel and polish spent on sixteen nervous, uncertain souls.

"If you have information on Varela, I will certainly hear it," I allowed, knowing I might as well accept my defeat. I would be her creature until lunch service, and probably dinner, too. She would never let me be.

The crone with the bronzed voice looked out the bolted port-hole at the growing spheres of Pluto and Charon, opals hanging in the stony blackness, clouds like hands clutching their few, scattered continents, clutching warmth, clutching life. When she spoke, the pitch of her voice plucked at my sinews. It was as familiar as my own shadow, yet I could not, *could not* recall where I had heard it before. Its rhythms changed, peaked, rolled—and I felt as though my mother were telling me a tale before bedtime, though I have no memory of my mother and would not know her if she called my name from the depths of hell.

"Once upon a time, a man, weary of both body and soul, shipwrecked upon a faraway isle. This isle dwelt in the midst of an endless, wine-dark sea whose depths were strewn with stars and horned leviathans and secrets kept by unguessable fathoms—and upon this isle it was always night. This man possessed in his heart and his hands the power to command light and force it to follow his will, but this power no longer comforted him, for he had once been charged with the protection of a maid both good and beautiful, and had lost her. But the whispers of the world said that he had done more than lose her, that he had killed her with his own hand. In shame, this man threw his name, the name of a man who could cast an innocent girl into darkness, underfoot and trampled upon it. From the moment his foot touched the sweet-smelling shores of that faraway isle, he called himself Prospero, a name so famous he could bury himself within it. He put upon his head a jester's crown and on his feet the belled dancing shoes of a fool, and spoke only madness to any who came before him, begging him to perform his old feats of light and shadow. Yet even this did not bring him the oblivion he craved, the anonymity of the guilty or the rest of the defeated. The more absurd his speech, the more frenzied his dance, the more he behaved like a jungle creature in a man's skin, the more he found himself sought after by the folk of Pluto, for whom amusement is the only currency.

On that lawless carnival isle, the castle of Prospero became a constant Saturnalia, a house on a high icy hill where unholy lights flashed and burst through the permanent night of that world of phantasms. Even to breathe the air of those halls was to become intoxicated. To light a single lantern was to invite ghosts and will-o'-the-wisps and sirens from every gable and eave. Into this miasma the man thought he could finally disappear. But word reached the great Emperor of the shadowy isle that wonders unheard-of were afoot in the house of Prospero, a house which was quickly becoming a kingdom unto itself. The Emperor donned a mask, the face of a black coatl whose tongue dripped with nightrubies, and went to the revels to see for himself. What he saw there no man can say, yet when he emerged, he had made Prospero his only heir, and placed the coatl crown on that poor magician's grieving head.

"This is the isle toward which our pretty silver ship flies, for whose sake our golden sails catch the sun's good wishes and bear us both across the starry, frozen wasteland between our former lives and the End of All. And the man I speak of is Maximo Varela: Prospero, the Mad King of Pluto. I wish you your fill of him—you will have it, I'm sure, and more."

The old woman looked back to me and laughed like a young girl. A flush rode high on her cheeks. She clapped her hands, applauding herself. "I reckon I'm as good as I ever was, don't you? Give me a script; I'll eat you alive and you'll love every moment. Now clear off and quit bothering an old woman at her breakfast."

I returned to my quarters in a consternation of curiosity and black dread. I felt, far beneath the polished green floorboards, the fragrant Ganymedean banyan with its glinting golden grain, the pneumatic array gasping into life, the intimate suckle of gravity cupping the *Obolus* and drawing it down, down into its long well. Very soon my work would have to begin, truly begin, rather than remaining comfortably far off, like a suit in a closet with all its attendant discomfort, ready to be worn sometime soon, but not today.

The smell of our staterooms flowed over me: sweat, skin, stale breath, lavender, talc, shoe polish, typewriter ribbons, last week's peach-xochipilli preserves left uncovered on a night table. Above and below it all, penetrating every surface, every linen and lantern glass, was that perfume I had grown to both loathe and long for, Madame Zed's latest vicious, stinking, delicious golden bottle: My Sin. It smelled like a forest of fallen women.

I looked down at the shape of Cythera Brass, the source of My Sin, in the emerald sheets of her bunk. She wore that witch's unguent so often I was convinced that even her marrow would stink of its musk and spice. From her alone I had never smelled—from Uranus past Neptune's unhinged orbit—even the slightest noxious emanation. Any foulness of air in our quarters belonged to myself alone. I smelled only My Sin on her, only that alien wood where a creature like her might cut her teeth. My warden, my minder, my leash. Her long, lovely limbs lost in sleep—but not so lost that she did not wrap her arms around her shoulders, her head sunk in her chest, guarding and girding herself even in dreaming. I despised her: for her orderliness, her efficiency, her beauty, her imperturbable calm, her—quite correct—disdain of my person, her loyalties, and her constant reminder that I was being tolerated only for the work I could perform. All aboard presumed her my wife, for she kept closer to me than any lover, always at my elbow, my side, practically barracked in my waistcoat pocket. I had risen inhumanly early in order to escape her company at breakfast—but one can never escape the quiet, implacable hell of company.

I did, in a moment of extreme and regrettable sobriety, try to kiss Cythera at the little Christmas ball held in the starboard conservatory. Shards of the ice road swirled and banged beyond panes of submarine glass overhead. Pine boughs hung festively all about—though of course not actual pine. Our yuletide green had been knitted out of jute and wire and shredded dresses by the Udolpho triplets, those wanton Martian contortionists and—as I had discovered—wanted counterfeiters, from Guan Yu. Each of the nine women aboard had donated a green gown to the effort. We whirled away under Cythera's lime spangled flapper-fringes, Harper Ibbott's hunting cloak, every girl's bright emerald and olive hoopskirts cut and ruched into garlands. We were a strange lot, the *Obolus* cargo, some famous, most not, all vibrating with the things we did not tell each other. Cythera seemed happy for once, in a long, ghost-grey sigh of a dress, assaying a Charleston, singing carols. True to the word of our mutual masters, Miss Brass had brought along a steamer of intoxicants and exotics that would turn a pirate into a teetotaller, but in those early days I had hatched the comical notion that I would do my job *well*. I spent my nights reading and rereading the histories and reports provided by Oxblood, staring at photographs as though my gaze could set them ablaze; coming close, I thought, to connections that danced just beyond the reach of my deprived, shrivelled brain, which had thrived on liquor, opiates, and hallucinogens. I could see her, I could *see* Severin, big and dark as a heart, at the nexus of some glowing web whose edges I was so close to touching.

Alas, that is the danger of sobriety. Everything seems possible.

At midnight on Christmas, with the disc of distant, turquoise Uranus like a tiny crescent moon above us, I slung my arm around the waist of Cythera Brass and kissed her. It was a good kiss, one of my best. We are the same height, but our noses did not clash, nor our foreheads collide. The scent of My Sin drenched my fingers, my eyelids, my mouth. I thought perhaps I had impressed her with my dedication to the work, that though we had been forced into sharing a certain chain of events, we might find warmth—indeed, even strength—in each other.

Those long limbs went to stone in my arms. When I withdrew, her face crackled with contempt. "I am not a perk of your position, Mr St. John," she said, with the finality of the grave. "Do not mistake me for an opium pipe."

And that was the utter terminus of any camaraderie or goodwill between us.

Yes, I despised her. But I am a strange creature. I am strange even to myself. There is no specialness in my ashen feelings toward Miss Brass. I despise myself as well, and all my works. It does no good. No matter how I practice my despising, I remain Anchises, and my works keep working.

"Wake up," I barked, and though I did not mean to bark, I was not sorry. "We make Charon orbit in ten hours."

She stirred beneath those soft green linens. My Sin filled the air.

I spoke more softly, then. I doubt she heard me. "By the way, I think I just had breakfast with Violet El-Hashem."

21 February, 1962. Noon (thereabouts). Pluto, High Orbit.

Shall we have trumpets? Shall we have banners? Shall we have garlands and chords and bursts of coloured flame to announce our presence, descending in a slow angelic spiral from high

Plutonian orbit down, down, down into the fields of pale flowers that soften the face of that little lonely world and her twin?

Perhaps a little trumpeting. Perhaps a little flame.

Night is Pluto's native crop. I thought myself darkness's man, but I had never even kissed her cheek until the sun set on that flower-choked world. Night poured itself down my throat. Night was my wine and my meat. Night wed me and bedded me, widowed me and murdered me and resurrected me whole a thousand times over with each hour. I saw before me, in that selfsame hall that had boasted our Christmas ball, beyond the veins of frost forking through the glass panes, a carousel hanging in space. Severin never came here. The one world she missed in all her profligate travels. At last, I shall have something she did not.

I will warn you now, Reader: Pluto is a place too mad for metaphor. What is there can only be what it is: a world far gone, decayed from the moment of its birth, lost in the unfathomable tides of these black rivers, so far from the sun that is our heart that it is, quite plainly, a place of delirium and dissolution.

It is a bestiary of the grotesque.

It is a Jacobean horror-hall.

It is a brothel of the undead.

It is so beautiful.

Welcome to America, to the Grand Experiment's last light bulb, left burning long after the household has locked up and fled.

Your Friend Pluto!
(Patriot Films, 1921)

[VISUAL DAMAGED, UNSUITABLE FOR VIEWING.]

VOICE-OVER

Welcome to the American sector!

Feast your eyes on glorious Pluto, her wild frontier, her high standard of living, her rugged, hardworking citizens, her purple mountains majesty! Ride the mighty buffalo! Marvel at the bustling industry of the great cities of Jizo and Ascalaphus! Climb the peaks of Mt. Orcus and Mt. Chernobog!

Congratulations! You have chosen to stake a claim on *your* corner of the bountiful Plutonian pampas and start a new life here on the Little Free World. Out here, the old empires fear to tread! On Pluto a man can make his own fate and no one will trouble him to get on his knees and kiss a crown.

A joint venture of Uncle Sam and the Iroquois League, Pluto and Charon are a wholly self-sufficient binary system—we gotta be! Our unbeatable location requires a special kind of soul: an enterprising, fearless, burly, bootstrap-pulling sort of man with a high tolerance for cold and work ethic to beat a Puritan senseless. We here on Pluto are delighted to welcome you into our family. We only take the best, and you have been specially chosen for one of our provisional citizenship programs, entitled to benefits and privileges that remain the envy of the nine worlds. Please refer to your complimentary deep-freeze rated pocket-size Constitutions for a full accounting of these rights—as well as inspiration, comfort, and the sense of profound well-being conferred by the presence of that most exceptional document.

No matter your nation of origin, you are now a part of the great American project—and if that doesn't make you proud, I don't know what will! In its short time on the interplanetary stage, Pluto has produced, abetted, or sheltered first-class poets like Miss Dickinson and Mr Frost, inventors such as Mr Tesla and Mr Marconi, titans of industry and politics with names as grand as Morgan, Rockefeller, and the great Emperor Norton II, as well as architects by the bushel who have put the streetscapes of Vienna and Venice to shame. Now you can stand tall among their number and make your mark on this miraculous planet.

Now that you and Pluto have made a proper acquaintance, you'll find in your intake portfolio a region assignment, dependent on your skills and background, as well as where folks are needed most. Are you bound for the ivory waves of blossoms on Pluto Actual, or the lucrative mines of Charon? Or perhaps you're headed for the fashionable districts and urban excitement of Styx, the

Great Bridge! Homesteads are available in all three regions; assignments may be revisited every five years.

Whatever your destiny, Citizen, a life like no other awaits you!

Each new Plutonian citizen is furnished with sufficient materiel for the construction of a dwelling, a sturdy and reliable Bunyan Brand Heating System with a free backup generator, seeding for a fast-fertilizing infanta crop, two shotguns, and basic-model breathing masks for the whole family. The rest is up to you! The extraordinary properties of the unique infanta blossom mean that no soul on Pluto will go hungry—easy to grow and easy to harvest, each flower provides a complete nutritional profile, save for folate, riboflavin, Vitamin A, and iron. Our scientists are discovering new and useful qualities of this wonderful species day by day! Don't eat them all at once!

Now, a day on Pluto comes out to a week back home, and a year lasts about two hundred and forty-eight Earth years, but lucky for you, good old corn-fed Frank McCoy, John Smoke Johnson, and the crew of the *Red Jacket* made worldfall smack in the middle of spring—a twenty-year span we call the Rose of May. We won't see winter in our lifetimes, no sir. And now that summer is on the horizon, it's a perfect time to put down roots. Summer on Pluto is a balmy life indeed—and there's a whole lifetime of summer for your pleasure. The lagoons of Tawiskaron call to bathing beauties and fishermen alike; watching the magnificent Sunday Sunsets from the balconies of Mormo will take your breath away. Nowhere in the solar system is a world more blessed, more genteel, with a richer portion of God's bounty. No more must man labour under the Union Jack or the Red Hammer, Vienna's long arm, or Nanjing's watchful gaze. In point of fact, the passage of the Sun between Earth and Pluto some years back means that those lace-cuffed dinosaurs aren't watching much of anything but their afternoon tea. We won't be getting word from the Old Worlds until round about the year 2112, so sit back, relax, pour yourself a whiskey and ice, and blow them a real nice kiss.

Please note that Proserpine and her environs are off-limits to all non-police personnel. The incident there is considered concluded by all involved, and no outbuildings or further items of interest remain. All relevant structures have been subsequently dismantled, recycled into building materials, and used in nearly every Plutonian city as a gesture of solidarity and collective mourning. We declare openly our hostility to treasure hunters, occultists, and other bandits who come to raid our sweet, peaceful land for purely imaginary secrets. There is no mystery; colonies fail. Seek that mother of the Plutonian experiment in the ironworks of Mormo, in the bricks of Niflheim, in the roof tiles of Elysium, in the spires of Tawiskaron and the cobblestones of Lamentation, in the great citadels and their deep foundations.

We are all Proserpine.

We ask that you respect the personal tragedy of that city's loss as you would the widowhood of a dear grandmother—the lady would prefer not to discuss it, and it behoves us all to abide by her wishes.

Trespassers will be shot on sight.

Yes, we all pull together here on Pluto. Be a good neighbour and you'll have good neighbours. Please report weekly to your local Depot for callowmilk and vitamin supplements, work assignments, and other sundry entertainments.

You can be anyone on Pluto. The possibilities are endless.

~~The Deep Blue Devil~~
The Man in the Malachite Mask:
Totentanz

February 21, 1962. 4:34 p.m.

Pluto is such a small place. When you dance with the gas giants, you become accustomed to vastness. But this is a doll's world. We circled the pale planet like a raven round a mouse scurrying over a grey and blasted heath. Down, down into the wishing well of its gravity, gravity like a handshake between Pluto and Charon, those dark, sullen twins, forever bound, waltzing without end on the edge of known space. Neither of them much bigger than Africa, wearing their tawdry bracelets of glaciers and black, brittle land—land covered in fields of infanta flowers so bright and broad I could see them as we spiralled off the ice road: swathes of light, faintly violet, faintly lime. I imagined that if I floated outside of the *Obolus*, I would have been able to smell them, their perfume permeating the empty void like a nervous lady announcing her presence.

I will tell you what I saw in my descent, for I have seen no photograph of it nor any film, only sound stages peopled with half-witted guesses, fancies far too sensible to match the original. Cythera stood by me at the porthole, each of us in our own way policing our faces so that the wonder we felt made no mark upon our cheeks. Pluto and Charon in a verdant jungle embrace:

between them grew vines as thick and long and mighty as the Mississippi river, great lily-lime leaves opening, curling toward the distant star of the sun like grasping hands wider than Lake Erie. And upon them unspeakable blossoms, petals of lavender tallow, infanta greater than ships, obscene chrysanthemums pointing like radio antennae in every direction. Those mighty Mississip-vines lashed round both planets in a suckling clutch, so enmeshed that I could not say whose earth they grew in, just that whoever's plant it was loved the other world so much that it could not let it go. And the Styx, the bridge of flowers! Towers and spires in Boschean number and Escherean style, torqued and corkscrewed by the currents of gravity and pollen that pooled between Pluto and Charon, their angles all out of proportion, sinuous, unreal, a hanging garden of architecture, upside down and right side up and protruding in every possible direction like broken, arthritic hands. Coloured lights glowed in warped windows. Tunnels of some sort of taffy-like glass ran like flying buttresses between the gnarled edifices. The braided bridge twisted like the very double helix of life, and on it life seemed to bristle, to boom. I felt sick. My breakfast moved in me no less than gravity.

"'When I looked upon that new world, splendid in every way and in every way terrible, I looked upon a tiger with stars falling from his striped tongue. I looked and saw my true bridegroom—but would it also be my grave?'"

So said the crone, who appeared silently beside us as if she ran on wheels and not flight-swollen feet. I knew those words. Everyone knew them: episode one, series one, broadcast March 1914.

"It's bad taste to quote yourself, Violet," I said, certain now in my guess. She merely snorted as that Plutonian Babylon rose up to envelop us. "The new Vespertine is shit," I added, with the barest twitch of a smile. I took her hand in mind and kissed it as our engines roared into undeniable red life, braking into the thin atmosphere, skidding into the tiger feet first, eyes open.

24 February, 1962. Midnight. Setebos Hall.

This is how one becomes temporarily American: stuff yourself into the uttermost depths of the best cold-weather gear you've managed to borrow and hoard, hold your documentation before you like a knight's shield—*Yes, Officer, a bear and phoenix rampant indicates that I summered on Mars three years past; four panthers passant mark my sabbatical on Callisto; this single whale embowed shows me Venus-born. My passport is my troth; you may find upon it all my soul displayed.* Queue in the most disorderly fashion you can manage, always remembering to yell when you could just as easily whisper. Intrude upon the privacy of the gentleman beside you while he tries to enter the pleasant meditative trance any citizen of the Empire craves upon taking a number and waiting his turn in the embrace of bureaucracy. Ask him his name at least three times, his business, his romantic history, his dreams and hopes and failures, his favourite way of preparing beef when he can get it, how many bones he has broken, whether he prefers men or women or Proteans, if he has any plans for supper, and how many times he has seen *The Abduction of Proserpine.* Before allowing him to answer any of these questions, interrupt with your own chronicle of longings and losses and boeuf bourguignon. As you move through the queue and the queue moves through you, you will pass through little nations without number: Here, a lady in an atrocious plaid cloche has managed to get a tuba through the weight restrictions; a throng presses round her, throws her coins and bread, and, by god, she can make a tuba sound as mournful and subtle as it was never intended. A slim lad with a choirboy voice warbles extemporized lyrics to her weird, sad, lovely, bleating horn. There, six or eight travellers in white furs and sealskin wallop on their trunks with drummers' hands, hooting in rhythm and grinning. Though it is February, a family sings Christmas carols in a pretty, uneven harmony, then switches to the alphabet song and multiplication mnemonics, anything to pass the time and keep the little ones pleasant. And when your number is finally called, you show your worth, plead your case, watch a short informational film, and don your mask.

Everyone wears masks here. It is a Plutonian necessity, eminently practical, and, in the space of minutes, my own became dearer to me than a lover. They say the wind on Earth can steal your breath, but such phrases are quaint antiquities now. The mask is a semipermeable heat shield, cycling the warmth of your breath back into useful service, oxygenating the thin air, keeping the sensitive airways safe from the worst of the vicious Stygian cold. All one needs is a callowfibre mesh, a hypoallergenic liner, a secure strap, a simple filter, and flat-disc heating unit.

Naturally, Pluto has turned simple necessity into a seething mass of carnival masks to make any midnight masquerade blush.

In the receiving station alone I saw minotaurs with topaz-spangled horns, ravens beneath cascades of night feathers, leopards, maenads, stained-glass butterfly wings framing dark eyes behind turquoise panes, elephants with muralled ears and bladed tusks, gilded and tricorned *bauta*, onyx *moretta* painted with phosphorescent trailing vines, silver-lipped *volta* with sapphire teardrops at the corners of the eyes. My eyes became drunk as the Depot reeled with colour and frost, with sound and epileptic glittering.

I chose my own mask from a hawker hoisting dozens of them on long black poles like ears of dried corn. My contrary nature, riled by the odious flamboyance of the American stew around me, fixed on the simplest one I could see—plain white with a thin black mouth and pinholes of red in the knife-sharp hollows of the cheeks. It would suffice. Cythera selected a sun-queen's mask, golden rays and copper peacock feathers arrayed around a burnished, rounded face engraved with a detailed map of the

Virgilian underworld. A cloisonné Lethe sliced across the patrician bridge of her new nose.

When she lifted her new face from its hook, I saw another lying beneath it. I startled at it as though it were my own face, and I knew that against its dark beauty my contrariness had already crumbled. It was a plague doctor's mask, black, a beak so thick and long it would cover half my chest. Bubbles of green glass cupped the eye sockets; in threads of tiny emeralds the *Totentanz*—the old Germanic dance of death—whirled around the shaft of that long hooked mouth, the savagely angular cheekbones, as if a mask could starve. A sparkling green pope skipped after a king spun after a peasant leapt after a child in malachite rags gambolled after a maiden whose long ultramarine hair rippled and ran along the edges of the mask's face; all cavorting, careening, capering after Death, who jigged upon the brow, partnered in own his dance with his scythe, his leg lifted in a flamenco stride, his bone hands clapping the beat of a human heart as it sped or slowed to nothing. A fan of stark shear-blades gave the mask a brutal tiara. I put my fingers against its slick lightless face, the shimmer of the prancing child, his little arms straining toward the maiden dancing out of reach before him; but she did not spare a single glance backward, her green, living breast surging forward, forward, her arms open, taut, eager, stretching toward Death, her eyes shining only for Him.

"Hundred bucks, one-eighty for both," said the mask-seller.

Safe inside that emerald *Totentanz* I swam within the rhotic rumble of the Depot: the sound of clothes moving against the people inside them; the bell-toll of station announcements; the luggage porters' shabby uniforms; the beggar children asking not for coins but for news of Earth, some sugary morsel of life back home to scurry away with to some hovel and pore over with a pervert's concentration.

Our escorts were, of course, unforgivably late, which I suppose one must expect when they are sent by a fellow who calls himself a Mad King, but it was no less irritating for being supposed. What use is it to detail the hours spent waiting? At six o'clock in the evening a klaxon sounded and the whole of the Depot surged to one side—*How Many Miles to Babylon?* was coming through on the public antenna, as clear as it was going to get, come one, come all. Sit together, draw close, Vespertine is in trouble again and it feels like being alive. I saw Violet El-Hashem, my ancient shipmate, position a chair so that she could watch the Plutonians gathering at the radio, to see her audience in the flesh for the first time. An old episode, either repeated or new to this furthest of the outer planets. Or perhaps arranged by her studio so that she could have this moment in the cold while plastic cups of cider went round the throng. I felt a bizarre, unwanted pang of missing her; I put it away like an old handkerchief.

Madame Brass, a shark in woman's skin, unable to hold herself still and do nothing, even for a moment, questioned any passersby too slow to escape her: *We are for Setebos Hall, is there a road, a public conveyance? At what hour do the trains stop running?* I let her. I excel at doing nothing. It is, you might say, my hobby. But she got no satisfaction from the parade of masked Plutonians. A man in a creased and beastly blood-red boar mask shook his head and held up his hands. *Do not ask—better yet, do not go.* A flatiron-chinned copper *bauta* with a frozen tricorne of split pomegranates begged off: *No one goes there unless summoned. If you have not been summoned, thank your stars and keep your head down.* A woman in a wine-dark *moretta* with the circles of heaven painted on it and a body so lovely that you could see her shape even under her pillowed snowsuit actually crossed herself.

Our small talk was too small to relate. Cythera Brass and I had long ago exhausted our stores of acceptable conversation, but our interpersonal cisterns had been briefly topped off by the landing, disembarkation, the tuba and the masks, the finding of fault with Americans and their goings-on, and the unloading of our mysterious cargo, which turned out to be mail: impossibly precious on the outer planets and yet impossibly quotidian. *My* post is worth all the diamonds in antique Africa; *yours* is scrap for the furnace grate. I care nothing for some Venusian bastard sending money to the bottom of the solar barrel or a Martian mother complaining about her daughter's choice in men, in career, in dress, in every little thing—oh, but she tucked in her recipe for lime pie! Well, then! I still do not care.

In film, even in *realité* such as Severin's, these sorts of human intermissions are happily elided with jump-cuts or montages. Action to action, point of interest to point of interest, that's the way! In life they must be suffered, wallowed in. We waited into the night, sitting on our suitcases like refugees, not daring to leave the rendezvous point even to forage for a prepacked lichen-slab meal.

Our escorts arrived just after midnight. You will think I am joking when I say that we were collected by stagecoach. Stagecoach! After the Talbot limousine in Te Deum and the absurdly posh appointments of the *Obolus*, I was spoiled. It is easy to become spoiled—a little taste, a little ease, a little shaft of light let in and suddenly nothing is good unless it bests the last luxury. And now we were meant to travel as though the last hundred years had never occurred, as though this was that wretched preflight America of raccoon hats and pony expresses. Was this a colony or an amusement park full of animatronic Americans and roller coasters shaped like the Rocky Mountains? A stagecoach—and not *just* that, but a *buffalo-drawn* stagecoach, driven by twin girls with livid dyed-purple hair, uncut black rubies binding their chests like bandoliers, and identical fuchsia masks stippled with wild gold fairy tattoos and mouths painted in the shapes of orange starfish.

The buffalo were my first experience with the Plutonian sense of humour. I had seen vast herds of buffalo in my youthful travels to America—woolly and prodigiously bigheaded, -horned, and -hoofed. These animals that dragged their mistresses' coach behind them were in no sense buffalo, though the girls insisted on calling them that. They were, as best I can describe them, sleek blue lizards the size of cougars, their glassy night-eyes bulging like fish, their silver tongues lolling and lashing like whips, their three tails held curled and upright like scorpions, tipped in strange silver bulbs. They bore wild strips of honey-coloured fur running the lengths of their spines and six swinging mammalian breasts, each black nippled and heavy with milk that dribbled in magenta trails behind them like oil leaking from an engine.

Everyone calls them buffalo, in fact. They run wild over the whole of both planets, native fauna, their hoots and howls unnervingly wolf-like on the Plutonian moors. They are domesticable, barely, and I have heard it said that like parrots, the smartest of them can mimic human speech. Their meat, which I was to sample rather sooner than I liked, is somewhat softer than beef but not so sweet as chicken and has a peculiar, almost floral aftertaste. It did not agree with me and my indigestion was fierce— but I get ahead of myself. Four of these "buffalo" stood bridled to the black stagecoach. Two green callowlanterns hung from its roof, illuminating the constant night of Pluto.

The daughters of Prospero introduced themselves as Boatswain and Mariner; the buffalo as Sarah, Sally, Susie, and Prune. They told us sternly to keep the windows shut tight and not to trouble them with our problems, and handed us long goose-down coats (I shudder to think what Plutonian geese look like) to fit over our already thick, quilted, furred travelling clothes. Once inside it all I felt quite like a stuffed caterpillar. Boatswain (I think) assured us that the journey was not long, not long at all. The two of them repeated some phrases over and over, as though they could not quite believe they'd actually spoken. *Eat, eat, eat,* they said. *Not long, not long at all. Quiet now, quiet, quiet.* We ate. We kept quiet. Into our hands they pressed infanta flowers, petals heavy as eyelids, white-violet and wet with juice and pollen. I held mine gingerly, all my old longing to taste the thing pooling in my mouth, waiting and wanting. Offworld, no amount of money could purchase even one of these blooms, not even Oxblood money. The Americans would not part with them, even if the delicate flowers could survive transit. I devoured mine ravenously; I tore it with my teeth. It shredded like lacework, turning to sweet ash on my tongue, evaporating like fairy floss. It did not taste like honey or coffee or mother's milk. It tasted nothing like I had heard. I cannot even compare it to another taste—it was its own. I can only compare it nonsensically: It tasted like a shade of white near blue; it tasted like the idea of pearls; it tasted like a memory nearly grasped but lost at the last moment.

The journey—which, in truth, took us through to dawn—unfolded over a long, flat countryside. Infanta blossomed everywhere, their perfume flooding through the mouths of our masks, stomping upon and drowning the last of My Sin with velvet shoes. I took deep, gulping breaths. The scent was so sweet I felt I was not inhaling it but *eating* it and gaining sustenance, but it left an aftertaste of unsettling, dank musk. Yet I drank and drank of the air and felt so drunk as to fall down flat. The fields of blossoms gave an illusion of fertility—what land could be lonely that gave birth to such wild and splendid things? And yet, as the hours drew on, their sameness began to look like *meanness,* a paucity of imagination in the core of the planet itself.

As the morning crept in, we watched the carnival bridge between Pluto and its moon brighten in the sky, a harlequin umbilicus. Its light haloed and twisted in the freezing air, brightening the hills around us. The slabs of ice, the long black cliffs falling off into shallows, the glassy seas took on that same rainbow halo, that prism-corona, rimmed in shimmering St. Elmo's fire. That mad bridge called Styx was their sun, its waxing and dimming cutting a rough day and night out of the single black cloth provided by this miserly world. The long cries of untamed buffalo echoed on the pampas and the ruffs of our own mounts rippled in reply, each individual bristle glowing with its own savage colour. Though the carriage possessed a curling horn through which we might have spoken to the twins, asked after all that we saw, silence was strictly observed until the great house reared into view.

Cythera, in a rare unguarded moment, had fallen asleep and allowed her head to droop, ever so lightly and hesitantly, onto my shoulder. Infanta juice dribbled off her chin and dried on her collarbone, like a fingerprint, faintly shuddering with phosphorescence. I stared at it for a moment. The mark writhed and bubbled in my vision, a sweet, painless acid burning into her body, altering her, filling her with light. And then, as the carriage pranged upon an outcropping of black rock, the light on Cythera's skin guttered out and became once again no more than crusted sap and spittle. I roused her then to see what waited for us like an open mouth: a house alive, a house beating against the ancient glaciers like Hades' own pulse, a house no more a house than those four cerulean lizards were buffalo.

My pupils contracted with pugilistic force. Within a crystal dome as wide and high as Vesuvius, a volcano of light released its heart's blood in gouts and arterial sprays. Like a terrible wedding cake, it rose in tiers of porphyries and agate and deep red wood. The castle began with elephants: a ring of carved stone beasts, their trunks raised, tusks displayed, legs fused together to make a glimmering wall of violet rock. Cathedral windows rose from their heads; candlelight and shadows moved within them. Above the windows rose green stone griffins, their paws outstretched, their haunches flowing into one another, delicate balconies hanging from their chests. Up and up it went, in rings of black unicorns thrusting their horns into the air like spiked ramparts, red polished wood bears, and weathered grey walruses. The whole structure was crowned with a small ring of smoky quartz girls sitting with their legs kicking out over the great menagerie, laughing in stone, their crystal chins in their crystal hands. Within their circle a Ferris wheel turned, empty but lit, an absurd diadem for that maddened and maddening place. Light dripped from every crease in the rock, the wood, the glass.

I was dazzled. I covered my face with my hands.

"Home," said a voice, and the voice belonged to one of the buffalo. Her feathers ruffled in the black wind.

In that haze we entered Setebos Hall, the castle of Prospero, through the bodies of the elephants, dragged and prodded by Mariner and Boatswain, their masks catching and exploding every candelabra's exhalation until their faces seemed to become stars. Even within the crystal dome they did not remove those masks, whether due to some Yankee affectation or personal deformity or local custom, I shall hazard no guess. I cannot begin to recount the stairs and hallways we sped down and through—they streamed by in a rich, jagged blur. Wild laughter and music echoed from deep within the hall, but the passageways we ran along were utterly empty.

Now that I am closed into my bedchamber, surrounded by deep ochre silks and curtains and writing with ink of that same sunrise shade, I recall only the throne room. I can call it only that. In our headlong flight we passed by a pair of open doors and looked within—we are human, we must always look. The room thronged with people, pulsed with warmth stolen from some impossible engine made to fight the awful extropy of Pluto's strict climes. Masks moved and spun like a field of un-sane flowers;

some bore not only masks on their persons but wings and tails protruding from their bodies. And how those bodies writhed, how they arched and shook! In the midst of it all, on a tall black chair tipped with garnet pomegranates and silk asphodel and cascades of ribbons, sat a man who wore a mask made to look precisely like a human face. Not his own—not the face of Maximo Varela, for I know now it was none other than he—but the face of Severin Unck, moulded in resin and satin and paint, as perfect as the first moment I saw her, brow as clear, colour as bright, pride as pointed in those high, high cheeks.

My flower-fattened belly lurched in horror and fascination; my skull seemed to *wriggle* within my skin. The body beneath the mask was a man's—lithe, healthful, ageless, and beautiful, but male, dressed in a magician's motley colours, a tunic tight at the waist and thigh, blossoming at the shoulders. The black hair that fringed the mask was longer than Severin had ever worn it, cascading in curls as thick as any Juliet's on any stage, a savage woman's hair, a Medusa's, a lion's. Bubbles of music popped and frothed around me. He rose from his throne. A youth and a maid, lying sprawled at his feet, trailed their hands after him, willing him to stay. Severin's face floated to me, moving through dancers and prowlers and pipers and hounds. As if no other soul in that place existed, the Mad King of Pluto took me into his arms, crushing me to him, whispering into my ear in a deep voice I knew out of the depths of my memory—a rough voice, a fragile voice, the wrong voice, not hers at all, but bearing the words I had so yearned to hear her say:

Anchises, Anchises, you've come home.

From the Personal Reels of
Percival Alfred Unck

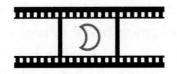

[SEVERIN UNCK stands amid a tangle of cables on the set of *The Abduction of Proserpine*. Vampire extras mill around her, touching up their makeup, chatting, taking their teeth out to smoke. She is very small, perhaps four or five. She wears a black dress with a black bow and black stockings. Her face is painted deathly white. She looks up at a demonic ice dragon with sword whiskers and icicle teeth, a massive puppet managed by the renowned TALMADGE BRACE and his team. She does not see her Uncle Madge pulling on the puppet's works. It towers over her. She stares at its tinfoil eyes intently, quietly, hands clasped behind her back. She rocks up on her toes.]

SEVERIN

Did you eat that big old city all up?
[The ice dragon nods solemnly. His lines creak.]

SEVERIN

What a bad thing you are. You ought to be punished.

[The ice dragon nods again. TALMADGE works his
lines and pulleys just out of frame, slumping the
creature's snow-puff shoulders in deep shame. He
can barely suppress his amusement.]

SEVERIN

Why did you do it? If you were really so keen,
I should think you'd have waited till the city
fattened up a bit. It couldn't have filled you
up! It was only little.

[TALMADGE cannot answer; the beast will never
have a voice, so he had no reason to devise one
to match its vast crinoline body.]

SEVERIN

Daddy says the settlers dug too deep and woke
the ancient heart of Pluto. But you have wet glue
on your nose, so I don't think you are the ancient heart of Pluto.

[The ice dragon shakes with TALMADGE'S silent
laughter. Severin reaches up and wipes away the
glue with her thumb. She whispers into the puppet's huge, glitter-spackled nostril.]

SEVERIN

I forgive you. I get hungry, too.

And the Sea Remembered, Suddenly
(Oxblood Films, 1941, dir. Severin Unck)

(ACCOMPANYING MATERIAL: RECORD 8, SIDE 1, COMMENCE 0:12)

SC1 INT. LOCATION #19 NEPTUNE/ENKI—STORM
OBSERVATION DECK, DAY 671. NIGHT
[29 NOVEMBER, 1939]
[FADE IN on a balcony crusted with salt and electric green coral. Its coils and floral motifs and columns recall the balustrades of New Orleans. Rust-bound lanterns hang on long, Marleyesque chains, casting white-blue light onto the churning cobalt sea that covers the whole of the unspeakably vast surface of Neptune. A semipermeable glass bell encloses the balcony; rain spatters onto the crystal and rolls down, but wisps of marine wind are allowed through—nothing, however, compared to the gales outside, which would murder any human in their path in the space of a thunderclap. The soft, grinding, gentle rumbling of Enki moving through its equatorial circuit underlines every spoken word.]

SEVERIN UNCK

The city of Enki is also a ship, perhaps the greatest ship ever sailed. She circumnavigates her planet once a decade, following a lugubrious echo of the Gulf Stream that flows more or less true, avoiding with grace the white and squalling knot of the mother storm from which all the other cyclones of this world descend. This balcony and thousands like it blister the exterior walls of the Neptunian capital. Whatever else occurs in this city—whatever work, whatever ambition, whatever decadence—its souls always return to these lookouts: a pilgrimage, a comforting hearth, a night watch. They come to see the storm. To stare it down. Whether for an hour or eight—or, in the cases of some old-timers, every moment not spent sleeping or eating—Enki-siders are drawn to this primeval sight of their world contorted, writhing in her constant oceanic distress, to bear witness to the eternal maelstrom that is the ancient heart of Neptune.

[All the camera can see is blue. Monstrous waves lash an indigo sky oppressed by clouds. Whitecaps crest and shatter; shadows of kelp forests the size of Asia skitter and dance. But there is no scale, can be no scale, because there is no land in sight. It could be the Pacific; it could be Lake Geneva. But it is neither. Only when a fishing vessel drifts into frame and, a moment later, the body of some unphylumed leviathan breaks the surface off its portside, geysering the sea into the methane-rich air, is there a moment of sickening understanding. There are

cities on Earth smaller than that barnacled beryl-
ine beast.]

SEVERIN (V.O)

Enki is a nomad; she follows the tide. There
are, of course, other ships on this sea: Manannan, Snegurochka, Ys, Lyonesse, Sequana. But Enki
dwarfs them all.

[SEVERIN rests her hand on the balcony rail.
Coral crinkles and drifts away under her fingers.
She looks exhausted—dark rings around her eyes, a
thinness to her skin.]

SEVERIN

Silence is the rarest commodity in Enki. The
ear never rests; the engines that roar life into
the city call and answer, call and answer, without ceasing.

And yet, from home? Nothing. Though nominally a
French colony, Neptune will pass behind the sun
tonight, disappearing from radio contact with
Earth for an estimated seventy-two years. The
voices will stop. The only news will come from
lonely ships creeping through the black on the
longest of roads. They will not hear any rumbling
of war, any rattling of Viennese sabres or English
guns. If the government in Paris changes once
again, they will learn too late for it to matter
much. No one will know whether Tybault will defeat
the Invisible Hussar this time, or whether Doctor
Gruel will succeed at last in making Vespertine
his bride and his victim. It will all happen
without us.

I say *us*. There is, of course, a passenger liner leaving before the lines go dark. A last chance to jump ship for civilization. The truth is, I have not yet decided whether I will be on it. My crew is going home. Tickets in their breast pockets, cabins reserved, champagne already chilling in silver buckets below polished portholes. Mariana, Amandine, Max, Margareta, Santiago, Horace, Konrad. Even my Raz has tired of kicking snowballs around on the frozen arse-end of the universe.

But me? Me, I don't know. I find myself at the end of this journey I mapped out after the death of dear Uncle Thaddeus—how many uncles have I had? I think every man on the moon has been my fuddy old uncle at one time or another. I suppose it has all been a funeral march to outlast the dreams of Hades. Saturn back to Mars and out again to Neptune. And I do not know if I am done. There is always somewhere further to go. Until there isn't.

[PAN LEFT to the warmly lit interior of Enki's starboard hull. Women in dresses with iridescent hoopskirts wide enough to conceal small armies raise their hands to the glass; rain drives down across their dry palms. The women, men, and children all wear shades of blue and green, sea shades, full-fathom colours, the turquoise of each rosette, the emerald of each brooch painted onto the film frame by frame, as Virago Studios did in the old days, as Clotilde Charbonneau did. The clothes were chosen for the evening's celebration: old-fashioned, seventy years out of date, dug out of grandmothers' trousseaus and costume trunks, just as their own clothes, made new to-day, will be seventy years past *la mode* when Earth comes round again. Chandeliers dangle like seabirds and music can be heard, harpsichords and strings and drums made tinny by the thick-ness of glass.]

SEVERIN (V.O.)

Tonight, Enki is dancing. Before Tritonrise, I will dance as well. This is not a night to stay in, curled up with a pipe and a book and a snif-ter. This is the end of the world, but the begin-ning of the world, as well. This is Cinderella's ball. And at midnight, Neptune will flee her Prince into the gloaming, leaving the nameless, lonesome shoe of her last broadcasts abandoned on the steps of the stars.

And what broadcasts: They have killed a Nereid, and she was full of roe.

[DISSOLVE TO a fishing vessel, approximately the size of the Isle of Wight, crawling with thousands of Nereid-men, the broad-muscled, ice-bearded career hunters who have tracked and killed the creature being hauled on board with cranes and hydraulic lifts.]

They may never catch another in their life-times, but for them this once is enough. They are Ahabs without rancour, living for the chase, men and women whose hearts quicken only at the eardrum-shattering bassoon song of their prey.

[The storm batters them mercilessly; still the fishermen heave and ho as the dark mass of the

Nereid rolls, obscenely, onto the decks. CUT TO: the flensing plain, a white expanse of artificial sand and salt crystals on Enki's lower levels. Despite her size, the Nereid looks bereft and helpless in the blazing lights, naked and abandoned by whatever god rules these dragons. She is quite dead. She is icthyosauran: a long neck ending in two heads, each covered in sea detritus and pink Neptunian lampreys, her four eyes blue, lifeless, but strangely primate-like in that cetacean head. The black-green body, the myriad flippers, the vestigial legs, the orange sailfin, the tail tapering for an imperial mile. Her bulk swallows the lens. The image jiggles with the slightly uncanny effect of coloured paints hovering over the black and white footage, never quite sinking through. The Nereid-men open their catch with equipment meant for industrial forestry—just a small gash at first, they can manage no more. But from this gash the deluge comes, magenta roe, quivering, each egg as big as a dancing girl, tumbling like awful Easter eggs across the flensing floor. The Nereid-men cheer; tears course down their cheeks amongst the ruby muck of countless unborn calves. CUT TO SEVERIN.]

SEVERIN

The Nereid-men have made their fortune tonight. The Nereid has lost hers. And if Paris or London or Nanjing expresses concern for the conservation of these astonishing animals—for all xenofauna—after tonight, it will not be heard.

[CUT FROM the Nereid-men sharpening long

knives to a YOUNG BOY cleaning his pocketknife. He empties his pockets, counts his coins, then counts again.]

There are no rules at the end of the world. Everything is permitted. [SEVERIN smiles with one side of her mouth.] The people of Enki have spent weeks painstakingly hammering out the rules for a ritual of rulelessness. Parliamentary procedure was decorously observed. [SEVERIN produces a beautifully typeset broadsheet. She reads out its contents.] *The final official broadcast from Paris will play until orbit silences it at approximately forty-six minutes past midnight. For a period of not more than seventy-two minutes afterward—one for each year the Earth will slip beyond notice—law and order shall be suspended. Post-hoc prosecutions will blind themselves to all incidents save the most egregious crimes of murder and rape, grievous harm to Enki or her essential mechanisms, or injury to children. To this end, firearms must be turned over to the constabulary, as ballistics are, at best, unpredictable bedfellows. Rank shall not be enforced or acknowledged. Stores of food and alcohol shall be open to the public. All other contraband will fall under the discretion of its purveyors, and the council certainly knows nothing about the identity or location of such persons. Those not wishing to partake in the festivities may enclose themselves in the southern sphere of the city, whose gates will close at twenty minutes to midnight and not reopen until morning under any circumstances.*

The list goes on.

It is not yet nine in the evening. The public announcement system pulses a warm and comforting stream of French. They have read us a bit of Molière and Voltaire, some Victor Hugo, some Chrétien de Troyes, a bit of Apollinaire and Balzac. They have sung us "La Marseillaise" seven times, by my count. They have exhorted us to remember the ideals of the French Republic and the glory of Jeanne d'Arc, Charlemagne, the Sun King.

[A MAN'S VOICE crackles over the shot of SEVERIN on the balcony.]

RADIO FRANÇAISE

Rappeler qui vous êtes. N'oubliez pas d'où vous venez. Nous ne vous oublierons pas. Nous vous attendons pour vous. Terre est votre maison pour toujours. La France est toujours votre mère. Le Soleil est encore Roi sur tout . . . Remember who you are. Don't forget where you come from. We will not forget you. We will be waiting for you. Earth is always your home. France is always your mother. The Sun is still King over all.

SEVERIN

I recognize the voice: Giraud Lourdes, who fell off the Moon, as they say. Monsieur Lourdes failed so utterly on-screen that he suffered a most modern form of professional disgrace—he returned to Earth. And then became Chaunticleer, the voice of *Radio Française*, reading the news each morning and telling his tall tales every Wednesday night.

He is a bigger man than his sweet, soft voice

might suggest. A thick red moustache. A preference for purple cravats. A weakness for women, poetry, and marzipan. These are the things that make up the beginnings of a person. But for me he is only those things. I met him just two or three times as a child and I remember nothing else. And now I can add to that list that his is the voice Paris chose to sing Neptune to sleep, for it is easier for Paris to pretend that they will go to sleep for seventy years than face the fact that when they come back into the fold, they will be no more French than England. So Giraud uses his seductive vowels to plead with a planet to behave itself while the cat's away, to freeze itself in time, to lie still, to change not. He sings it, he recites it. The violins of a Berlioz concerto whisper: *Hush now, my far-off children. Prick your fingers on the spindle of our voice. Be the kingdom that fell asleep for a hundred years and woke unchanged.*

But who knows what wild things Sleeping Beauty dreamt of while waiting to awake?

[CUT TO: SEVERIN, ERASMO ST. JOHN, and AMANDINE NGUYEN recline on black-and-white chaises, watching the party flicker and move within the oily, distorted storm glass separating the observation balcony from the interior of Enki proper. AMANDINE belongs to a levitator cult based on the tiny moon of Halimede, where the wind hardly blows at all. She is a titanium sculptor; she practices a sexual variant of Samayika meditation. Her hair is lashed with traditional leather whips that hang down around her face like wires or liquorice. Her skin is dyed green, as is the custom on Halimede.

The gravity of Neptune does not allow her to practice her faith here. She seems to stretch upward slightly with every movement, as though her body remembers its home, where it floats instead of merely sitting. SEVERIN drinks clay cups of creamy saltbeer with the levitator. ERASMO nurses a pink lady that looks rather orange. The lights of Enki turn their faces into a play of shadows.]

                    AMANDINE
  I have sometimes wondered if we will make it.

                     SEVERIN
  What do you mean?

                    AMANDINE
  [She shrugs.] Perhaps when Earth peeks around the Sun again Enki will be gone. Lyonesse, too, and Manannan. Halimede might become a ghost moon. Or maybe we will all just . . . float. Like the Flying Dutchman, skeleton ships following the current forever, with only spirits as cargo. It has happened before. Places have vanished. Proserpine. Enyo. Adonis, now. We send up cities like fireworks, but there is a tax, I think. The empty worlds we expand to fill . . . sometimes the emptiness takes something back. To keep the books balanced, maybe.

                     SEVERIN
  Colonies fail. It happens.

ERASMO

You know better than that. Colonies fail because crops fail, or supply ships don't come in time, or some *Babylon*-fanatic fancies himself a warlord and straps on bandoliers. Proserpine didn't fail. It was *ripped to pieces*. The foundations of the houses shattered. A thousand people vanished. It's been twenty years and nothing *grows* there, not even infanta.

AMANDINE

I've heard it was worse than that.

SEVERIN

Stop it, both of you. [She moves her hands as if to clear the fact of Proserpine out of their little oceanic bubble like cigarette smoke.] You haven't the first idea what does or doesn't grow on Pluto. You're just telling slumber party stories. Besides, what planet is there without a mysteriously vanished colony to pull in the tourist cash? Slap up a couple of alien runes on a burned-out doorframe and people will stream in from every corner of space. Might as well call them all New Roanoke and have done with it.

[SEVERIN loads a lump of af-yun into her netted atomizer. ERASMO takes a pink lady from a tray of sweets and quaffables, raises it to his lips and manages to frown around the cocktail glass's rim. SEVERIN'S voice begins, unconsciously, to pick up the shy, breathy Halimede accent of her companion, mirroring without noticing, her lunar syllables disappearing beneath the Francophone sea of the Neptunian dialect.]

We like these stories because they aren't really stories about losing things. They're stories about finding them. Because everything gets found, sooner or later. Everything gets remembered. Eventually, somebody did find Proserpine, and took it all apart, and put it back together to make new cities on Pluto and Charon. It comforts us, tells us there are no lost children anywhere, not really. Not even cities. It's all just Atlantis in another dress.

[SEVERIN looks out at the storm. Foam spatters across the glass bell.] Atlantis, that great floating city where humans got so beautiful and so wise, so strong and so *able* that they invented civilization. Invented being alive, in the sense of plumbing and temples with friezes and taxation and clay laws and hecatombs and public sporting events. And the sea took it back, if that is how you want to tell it, how you want it to be told *to* you, because, well . . . because humans feel uneasy in tales without punishment. No good thing can last forever, because people are terrible and we have this feeling, we all have this *feeling*, that if not for that essential terribleness we could have gotten further by now. Done better. Done more. We have failed collectively since Plato first choked on an olive. So it's no surprise when we fail individually—when we shirk duty, when we hate our parents, when we run away, when we get drunk every night, when we lose love . . . when we lose love. Because by all rights we should be living in the crystal palaces of Atlantis or in the Tower of Babel's penthouse apartments, right? Comparatively, our private blunders are insignificant. Just part of the general pattern of human awfulness. We map our little disasters onto a beautiful picture of a great one, so that there's continuity. So that there's balance. We fail because we always fail. It's not our fault. For evidence, see the paradise we lack.

But there never *was* any Atlantis, my darlings. Nor Babel, nor Shangri-La. There *was* Santorini and the Visigoths and the Great Vowel Shift, but you wouldn't have liked living in ancient Santorini one little bit. And Proserpine failed because it's bloody hard to farm anything but flowers on Pluto, and quakes can crack up anywhere there's a crust and a core.

AMANDINE

But you admit that cities have vanished. And there are no stories of finding the people, only the wreckage.

SEVERIN

I do admit that. If it makes you happy.

AMANDINE

But not totally vanished. Something is always left behind. The ruins, yes, the loss, that horrid fluid splashed everywhere—but something else, too. It happens in the space of a night. Three times now. Radio silence, then a city cut out of the very earth. And in its place . . . something new. I have heard that in Proserpine it was a voice. If you go there, if you stand where those people must have stood, under the twilit sky, you can hear a voice. A woman's voice.

SEVERIN

[She arches an eyebrow.] Yes. I've seen the movie, you know.

ERASMO

But Percy got it from somewhere. He didn't make it up. Vince brought in the dragons and the vampires and all that, but Percy wanted to make that movie because the story was floating around already. I heard it on the backlots. I've heard it everywhere. A voice repeating one word.

ERASMO AND AMANDINE

Kansas.

SEVERIN

But no one is allowed to actually enter Proserpine. How would anyone know that there's a voice saying that? Or saying anything? It's nonsense, anyway. What the hell is a Kansas?

ERASMO

In Enyo, on Mars . . . oh Rinny, don't look at me like that! What better night could there be to share ghost stories round a fire? And what better fire than a city lit up to celebrate going into the dark? Weird things *do* happen, you know. Not everything in the universe is *cinema verité*!

SEVERIN

You're not really going to tell a ghost story, are you? Maybe I'll go see how the Neptunian Crime Spree Hour of Fun is shaping up.

ERASMO

Shush. You don't get a vote. So. Enyo was a Martian trading post near the Chinese-Russian border—surrounded by kangaroo ranches and brothels and dice halls and mining stakes. Good times for all! And in one night—gone. Windows smashed, buildings shattered, as though someone pulled them up by the roofs and dropped them. Callowmilk, or something like it, splashed twenty feet high, like blood spatter or graffiti. No bodies. No blood. But something else.

[ERASMO stops. He pinches SEVERIN'S knee and grins sidelong at her.] Want me to stop? [She says nothing. Her lips part slightly.] Very well. Let the record show Miss Unck wants to hear a ghost story. This one even less reliable than the voice shouting *Kansas* at the outer reaches of space. I have heard it said—only a few times, but I've heard it—that in the centre of town where the pump used to be, the Martian constables found a reel. A movie reel. Just sitting in the dust, covered in milk.

SEVERIN

And? What was on it?

AMANDINE

I've heard about the reel, too. People say a thousand things. It's the destruction of the town. Or it's some print of a porno the miners loved. A woman crying. Forty minutes of blackness. Worse. Better. Who can know? Who has the reel now? No one even claims to have seen it, only heard from someone who met someone in a Depot queue who had a family friend in Martian salvage and demolition. Enyo is the sort of thing you thrill about late at night, when shadows feel like electricity on your skin.

But then there's Adonis. Adonis is different.

[ERASMO drinks his pink lady; he lets AMANDINE take the story.]

It wasn't a trading post or a farm town. It wasn't just getting started. It was a whole colony—gone. Divers mostly, like most settlements on Venus. Slaves to the great callowhales, like the rest of us. But in Adonis they built a lovely hotel and carousel for the tourists who came to get their catharsis revved up as the divers risked their lives to milk our benevolent, recalcitrant mothers in their eternal hibernation. I have heard it was a good place. A sweet village on the shores of the Qadesh, plaited grease-weed roofs and doors hammered from the chunks of raw copper you can just walk around and pick up off the Venusian beaches. They lived; they ate the local cacao; and they shot, once or twice a year, a leathery 'tryx from the sky, enough to keep them all in fat and protein for months. There's good life to be had on Venus. I almost went there instead of Halimede.

But in the end, I wanted to fly. Maybe, if I had not flown, I would have found my way to Adonis and helped build the carousel. Then I would have been stuck. Because, just like Enyo and Proserpine, one day—pop! All gone. Houses, stairs, meat-smoking racks, diving bells.

[SEVERIN drinks her saltbeer. You can see her thinking, some new and massive idea taking shape behind her eyes. ERASMO chews on the crust of a crab-heart trifle, mesmerized by AMANDINE'S voice. AMANDINE casts her eyes downward within the equine blinders knotted to her head.]

All gone except for the something new. Only this time, it's not a reel and it's not a voice. It's a little boy, left behind. They say he's still there. I've heard it on the radio, so it's as true as anything is. He's stuck, somehow, in the middle of where the village used to be, just walking around in circles. Around and around, like a skip on a phonograph. They can't get him to talk. He doesn't eat or drink. He never even stops to sleep. He's just . . . there. He's been there a year already. Like a projection. But flesh.

ERASMO

What do you think happened, Amandine? Don't listen to Rin, just . . . what do *you* think?

AMANDINE

[She is quiet for a long moment.] I think we are all suckling at a teat we do not understand. We need callowmilk. We cannot live without it. We cannot inhabit these worlds without it. But we made a bargain without thinking, because the benefits seemed to be endless and the cost nothing but a few divers, a few accidents—what's that next to what we stood to gain? My god, it was *nothing*, nothing at all. All these empty worlds could be ours—no one living there, no one to make us feel ashamed. Not like the New World, with its inconvenient millions. A true frontier, without moral qualms. You must admit how compelling that is. Whole planets just waiting there for us, gardens already planted and producing. A little gravity wobble this way or that; a slightly unpleasant tang to the air; oh, perhaps we can't have as much hot buttered corn on the cob as we'd like—but they were so *ready* for us. Edens full of animals and plants, but no *folk*.

Except the callowhales. We don't even know what they are, not really. Oh, I went to school. I've seen the diagrams. But those are only guesses! No one has autopsied one—or even killed one. It cannot even be definitively said whether they are animal or vegetable matter. The first settlers assumed they were barren islands. Huge masses lying there motionless in the water, their surfaces milky, motley, the occasional swirl of chemical blue or gold sizzling through their depths. But as soon as we figured out how unbelievably useful they were, we decided they didn't matter. Not like *we* mattered. Beneath the waterline they were calm, perhaps even dead leviathans—*Taninim*, said neo-Hasidic bounty hunters; some sort of proto-pliosaur, said the research corps. The cattle of the sun. Their fins lay flush against their flanks, horned and barbed. Their eyes stayed perpetually shut—*hibernating*, said the scientific cotillion. *Dreaming*, said the rest of us.

And some divers claim to have heard them sing— or at least that's the word they give to the un- predictable vibrations that occasionally shiver through the fern-antennae. Like sonar, those shivers are fatal to any living thing caught up in them. Unlike sonar, the unfortunates are in- stantly vaporised into their constituent atoms. Yet the divers say that from a safe distance, their echoes brush against the skin in strange and intimate patterns, like music, like lovemak- ing. The divers cannot look at the camera when they speak of these things, as though the camera is the eye of God and by not meeting His gaze, they may preserve their virtue. *The vibrations are the colour of need*, they whisper.

Of course, no one works as a callowdiver for- ever. We aren't built for it. The Qadesh or the callowhales or maybe just Venus itself, the whole world; something does us in. Everyone goes milk- mad eventually, a kind of silky, delicate delirium that just unzips us, long and slow, until we fall down babbling about the colour of need. We say the callowhales are not alive like we are alive. But I say: Where there is milk, there is mating, isn't there? What is milk *for*, if not to nurture a new generation, a new world? We have never seen a callowhale calf, yet the mothers endlessly "nurse." What do they nurture, out there in their red sea? And what do they mate with? It would have to be something big. The size of a city, maybe . . .

[The indistinct crackle of the radio broadcast from home suddenly spikes in volume—*Au revoir, mes enfants! À la prochaine fois! Bonsoir! Bonsoir! À bientôt!*—then cuts abruptly to silence. Within Enki, the lights go dark.]

AMANDINE

Welcome to the end of the world.

Look at Her Face

Look at her face. It is your face. She is the mask you wear. Look, and you can see the film she wants to make being born across her features. Across your features. It has not happened yet; it doesn't even have a title. It is less than a full idea. But it is there in her set chin and her narrowed eyes. She frowns sourly in black and white, and her disapproval of such fancies—her father's fancies: disappeared heroines and eldritch locations where something terrible has surely occurred—shows in the wrinkle of her brow, the tapping of her fingernails against the atomizer as bubbling storms lap their glass cupola and armoured penance-fish nose the flotation arrays, their jaw-lanterns flashing.

Where there is milk, there is mating, isn't there? There are children. *The ghost-voice of Amandine comes over the phonograph as the final shot of* And the Sea Remembered, Suddenly *flickers silver-dark and the floating Neptunian pleasure domes recede. Everyone knew where Severin was bound next, long before principal photography ever began. You could see it on her face. To Venus, and Adonis; to the little village rich in milk and children that vanished two decades after its founding, while the callowhales watched offshore, impassive, unperturbed. You would have gone, too. You would have yearned to go. Chasing after an ending to a story already in progress. An ending means there is order in the* universe, there is a purpose to events. There is a reason to do things, an answer to be found, a solution key at the back of the book that maps to the problems posed. Find one ending, a real ending, and the universe is redeemed, ransomed from death— but death can never be that ending. It is a cheat, a quick shock, but no story truly ends with a death. A death only begs more questions, more tales.

Across your ribs her ship speeds over the ice road as fast as it can go. You almost want to cheer it on—but it speeds toward cessation, toward negation, toward sound and darkness and a final, awful image flickering in the depths.

But you can see her thinking, see her new film, her last film, taking shape behind her eyes.

They are documentaries, yes. They are also confessional poems. She is her father's girl, though she would rather no one guess.

Severin asked the great question: Where did Adonis go in death? The old tales know an answer. But it can never be her answer. We offer it anyway.

Adonis returned to his mother: the Queen of the Dark, the Queen of the Otherworld, the Queen of the Final Cut.

The Miranda Affair
(Capricorn Studios, 1931, dir. Thaddeus Irigaray)

Cast:
Mary Pellam: Madame Mortimer
Annabelle August: Wilhelmina Wildheart
Igor Lasky: Kilkenny
Jacinta La Bianca: Yolanda Brun
Barnaby Sky: Laszlo Barque
Arthur Kindly: Harold Yellowboy
Giovanni Assisi: Dante de Vere
Helena Harlow: Maud Locksley
Father Patrick: Hartford Crane

[INT. The observation carriage of the good ship *Pocketful of Rye*, barrelling down the icy, starry tracks of the Orient Express. Ferns and chaises and brandy and cigarettes in gold cases. Io looms overhead, volcanoes glowering, electric cities glittering and blinking. The *Pocketful of Rye* is thundering through Grand Central Station, the heart of the Jupiter System, a thick knot of gravitational whirlpools thrusting the ship toward beautiful and dangerous Miranda, moon of a thousand seductions.

Little do her passengers know that KILKENNY, master criminal and assassin at large, hides on board! MADAME MORTIMER, lady detective—fresh off of her latest victory over the forces of anarchy and corruption in THE CASE OF THE DISAPPEARING DESPERADO—has taken a private car on the *Rye* with her loyal companion, the heiress WILHELMINA WILDHEART, hoping for a little rest and relaxation.

In the lounge we find our players: FATHER PATRICK, a missionary with a dark past and a secret to protect, bound for Herschel City; HELENA HARLOW, wealthy owner of Blue Eden, a notorious Te Deum brothel; ARTHUR KINDLY, a veteran of the Martian wars, headed for retirement and the good life in the outer system; BARNABY SKY, a dashing playboy with vicious gambling debts; and JACINTA LABIANCA, a Mercurial horse breeder with a man on the side.

GIOVANNI ASSISI, interstellar coffee baron, lies face down on a Turkish rug with a Psementhean bridal knife in his back. Madame Mortimer stands over him with her hand on the pommel of her pistol.]

MADAME MORTIMER
Oh, I do love a spot of murder with my tea!

JACINTA LABIANCA
What a thing to say! Poor Mr Assisi!

MADAME MORTIMER

Poor, indeed! Didn't you hear? Typhoons took out his Venusian plantations. The man was just desperate for a wife to top up his coffers—he's been canoodling with half the ship, really scraping the bottom of the blueblood barrel. He'd have been knocking at Father Patrick's door before long. It would seem someone has spared him the embarrassment. Well! The cards are dealt! [She claps her hands sharply.] Place your bets, ladies and gentleman. We have a murderer on the ship and I intend to flush him out. And not only on the ship—I have reason to believe the murderer is *in this very room*!

[All gasp.]

Wilhelmina, darling, would you be so kind as to stand guard by the carriage door? Thank you. I'm afraid I can't allow any of you to leave just yet. Everything we need to solve this sordid little mess is right here at our fingertips, if only we are keen enough to *see*, *grasp*, and *act*! Confusion spreads out from a corpse like blood. The further one gets from the body, the harder it is to see the truth. Mr Assisi's death is a *fact*—everything else is mere supposition.

Let us hew to the facts. Firstly, Giovanni Assisi is dead. Secondly, he lost his fortune. Thirdly, he recently divorced his wife, the long-suffering nurse Annalisa Assisi, leaving her with seven children on Ganymede. Fourthly, he has been carrying on an affair with Miss LaBianca—I'm sorry, my dear, but how many women wear a Venusian coffee flower in their lapel? It's a hideous plant. Besides, you reek of his aftershave.

JACINTA LABIANCA

I'm sure I have no idea what you're talking about! I have an aunt on Venus!

MADAME MORTIMER

Don't worry, dear, he meant to break it off with you before we made planetfall. Your . . . bank accounts . . . aren't nearly large enough for his tastes. And, fifthly, I'm afraid, he was a frequent customer of Miss Harlow's, and he paid her a great deal of money while we were docked in orbit waiting for our acceleration window. Clearing a bill? Perhaps. A creature of prodigious appetites, our man Giovanni! Next, I believe our young Master Sky owed the deceased a rather large poker debt? He needed you to pay up, and quickly, but you couldn't, could you, Barney?

BARNABY SKY

How the devil would you know that?

MADAME MORTIMER

Oh, it's perfectly obvious. You aren't in the least upset by his death! Our unhappy friend here positively adored cards and played with everyone on board—except you. He wouldn't come near you, and when you dealt in to a table he got up to leave. And Father Patrick—tsk tsk, Father! One of those seven children is not an Assisi, isn't that right? Annalisa is a noble beauty and a pure soul, it's true. But when Papa Johnny here showed Willy and me his lovely family portrait, I couldn't help but notice that one of the little angels—Lucia, was it?—looked *ever* so much like you.

FATHER PATRICK
That's a damnable lie!

MADAME MORTIMER
Oh, I think not. But that's the *marvellous* thing about a murder—it brings everything out in the open. All the dark places just scrubbed with sunshine and flung wide for all to see. A sudden and unexpected crime sharpens the soul wonderfully.

[KILKENNY has been sitting in a chair facing the quiet hearth all the while. He is smoking a pipe, wearing a pinstripe suit and a rakish hat.]

KILKENNY
Well put, Miss Mortimer. I quite agree.

WILHELMINA WILDHEART
Kilkenny!

MADAME MORTIMER
Good morning, sir! I trust you slept well in the cargo bay? You missed stormrise—the great red eye is especially beautiful this time of year.

KILKENNY

I expect I shall see it again. Some small sacrifices must be made in the pursuit of one's ambitions. I've seen a few rainstorms in my time.
And how is your sister, Miss Mortimer? I do so
miss Emily at Christmastime.

[MADAME MORTIMER'S face flushes angrily; her
hand tightens on her pistol.]

MADAME MORTIMER

You know perfectly well how she is. And if you
were a decent man, you'd tell me where you buried her!

The Ingénue's Handbook

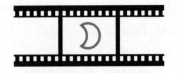

13 January, 1930, Half Past Three in the Afternoon
The Savoy, Grasshopper City, Luna

I've been prancing about in front of a camera for—Heavens!—twenty-two years now, so kindly invest the following statement with grave and dignified Authority.

I love wrap parties more than just about anything else in the world.

Oh, it's lovely to plan, and lovely to work, but *having* worked is ever so much better. And dancing yourself silly in pearls knowing you don't have a thing to do tomorrow is best of all! The fine and the fatigued positively *sparkle* with the frantic fizz of having pulled it off despite the odds—you can't help being light on your feet with all that weight off your shoulders. It's the party at the end of the world—the quick, fantastic world you've all made together, a world that now exists only on a heap of black tape in a tin can. Oh, well! On to the next one! And the funny, impish magic of a wrap party is that everyone still has scraps of their characters hanging off them like Salome's veils, fluttering, fading, but not quite finished tangling the tongue and tripping the feet. You're not in Wonderland anymore, but you positively reek of rabbit. It's a secret, rollicking room where everything is still half make-believe. That scamp can't stop walking like Robin Hood; that *other* fellow isn't done trying to seduce you like Heathcliff; those two prizefighters might come to blows tonight because they haven't quite scrubbed off Cain or Abel; and oh, *gracious*, the mischief you'll get up to while your heart's half Maid Marian, a squidge Cathy, a wee bit Madame Mortimer—but then, I never *completely* shed MM. I've been her almost as long as I've lived on the Moon, which is to say almost as long as I've been alive. Before the Moon, it hardly counts as living. Madame Maxine Mortimer has thoroughly rubbed off all over me. Why, just the other day, Betty Raleigh's black pearls went missing from her dressing room and I'd locked all the doors and started interrogating suspects before I came to my senses.

Poor Betts. Her insides are nothing but sunshine and bunny tails, but she's had a devil of a time lately. It's *intensely* trying. Hartford Crane gave her those pearls right before he ran off with Yolanda Brun. The gossip rags are just full of their sopping laundry, and while Yolanda loads up her supper plate with the attention, sweet innocent Betty can hardly squeak for shame. Cheat first and cheat often, Betts, that way you're never stuck cleaning up after your husband's midnight snacks.

Thus we circle the point, miss it, put our car in reverse, and come round to it again, and the point is this: *The Miranda Affair* is in the can, along with the last, rather wobbly, decade. It'll be Thad's last talkie—the tide's against us. Receipts go up the moment I shut my mouth. I've always liked my voice. It's a pity MM will have to save the day with wild gesticulations, but what the people want, the people will have!

Well, never mind! The wrap party is TONIGHT. And no smoky speakeasy for our rarefied carousing, no sir! Banish silence! Tear up the title cards! My darling maestro Thaddeus has thrown us all such a treat: it's to take place aboard his yacht on the Sea of Tranquillity! The *Achelois* is a grand, wasteful, brilliant beast of a thing—it's got its own ballroom, a ninepins alley, a wine cellar fit for a bevy of Roman emperors, and Thad makes sure there's fresh violets and a dash of snuff in everyone's staterooms.

Or so my darling Regina tells me. This will be my maiden voyage. The yacht used to belong to Jefferson Dufresne, back when he was the King of the Historicals at Plantagenet Pictures and everyone licked his boots for the chance to fart on Bosworth Field. So Regina, my old flatmate (gosh, it feels like a thousand years ago that I had to split the rent!), got to go after she played Empress Josephine in his great big Frenchie flop. *Quelle* injustice! That I should have to wait until I am nearly forty, when she got to go at nineteen!

They'll paddle us all about for a few days, and I don't doubt we'll all turn up on Monday with Earth-tans and hickeys. Boats practically *require* debauchery—why, nothing that happens aboard ship really *matters*! It's a little bubble, floating free away from the world. A weak and idle theme, no more yielding but . . . blah blah blah. Slap that together with the divine nonsense of a wrap party and I'll be surprised if I survive the weekend.

I plan to wear my best Plutonian buffalo fur, a ruby tiara, and not a lick else. Though at the moment I am looking *quite* respectable in my ecru suit and a hat with just two skinny old feathers in it. I only have this drab thing for meetings with my agent and tribulations at traffic court . . . bless me, but I am as clumsy as clown shoes in an automobile! But today I shall (probably) not be admonished for speeding on the Hyperion Speedway—for goodness' sake, why call it a speedway if you aren't meant to floor it? Today I have a perfectly ladylike luncheon date with my erstwhile stepdaughter. I'm not certain when my private little teas at the Savoy became teas for two, but I'm ever so glad they did. It's occasionally refreshing to simply sit with someone who has known you a long while and still thinks you're worth a damn. I suppose that's why people have children in the first place. It's hard to scare up such a thing, otherwise.

I do miss old Percy sometimes. Thad invited him along on the yacht, so I may rescind that statement by Sunday night. I wonder if he'll bring a date—other than Clara? The better question is, who *won't* be there? Even that bitter mongoose of a man from *Places, Everyone!* will get his fresh violets and snuff. I suspect Thaddeus let his secretary make the guest list. It's chock-a-block with people who've nothing to do with *Miranda*. It's a wrap party for *my* film. I do not see why *both* my ex-husbands should be in attendance, except that the girl who does her nails while I take my meetings thought that it would be *scrumptious* to see all her favourites in one spot! The Edisons are coming as well, boorish Freddy and Penelope, that fretful slip of a wife he's got.

She wasn't always, you know. When I met her, she was Penny Catarain, a brilliant lit fuse of a girl. A techie, good enough to get hired even with a mountain of boys ahead of her. She always gave the impression of having accidentally wandered in from a mad scientist's conference, and felt rather desperate to get back. She worked sound on my first big studio talkie, before speaking in a flick became the equivalent of farting at a dinner party. Penny made my voice sound like a crystal fountain. But I suppose being married to an *utter* pig will wear a soul down to the nub. I shall make certain to get her good and sauced on the *Achelois*. I'll get Mrs Edison dancing if I have to put firecrackers in her slippers.

I got Penelope alone once at the Capricorn/Plantagenet Studios treaty signing. You can't really call it a merger when Plantagenet invaded—with a squadron of soldiers, three biplanes, and one, albeit very old and crotchety, Chinese tank—Capricorn's backlots in order to liberate two leading men and a stack of prints being held in a vault. Those boys were nothing but an excuse, anyway, a cover to make Mr P look like the injured party. Plantagenet's real objective was to force Cap to "sell" the rights to their marquee characters Marvin the Mongoose, the Arachnid, and Vickie VaVoom for less than I pay for stockings. I took a bullet in the shoulder over a cartoon rodent. But so it goes on the mad old Moon. I heal like a champion.

It was a jollier evening than you might expect: pink paper lanterns, extras dressed up as Marvin and Vickie signing autographs, plenty of champagne and saxophones. Penelope wore blue, I recall. We jawed about the good old days, and she got that look on again, like she'd only slipped away from her fellow mad scientists for lunch and really had to be getting back.

I took her arm. "Honey, does he beat you?"

Mrs Edison looked quite stunned. "No! Christ, what a thing to ask."

"Then what is it? You always look like you want to lay down and become one with the floor."

I didn't expect an answer. I felt certain she would walk away, head high, and never speak to me again. But instead she shrugged and whispered, "He doesn't let me work."

People think Percy's a vicious bear, too, but he's not so bad. Husbands come a lot worse than mine. I often thought Percy had his head on the right way round, anyhow. It's only what you print to film that sticks, in the end. That's what people will see forever, not your silly, flawed memories and inelegant bumbling after happiness. The power of the final cut is what you want—and if you can make it all a little better, a little brighter, a little more symmetrical, and a touch more mysterious, well, why not do it, after all? So what if I had to do a couple of Christmas mornings over again so the light on my face looked nicer, or Sevvy could summon up a little more joy over those woolly socks? I've seen the film: those Christmases were glorious. Nowadays, I can only really remember them the way they looked when Percy played them back to us. It's not the worst thing in the world, to only remember the best version of yourself.

But it *is* unsettling to see a child do three or four takes of Yuletide ecstasy without batting an eye, I must say.

Still, I did love him. He never minded if I wore my pyjamas for a week and didn't brush my hair. That's a good quality in a man. Maybe the best a girl can hope for, considering. And, by Jove, he loves that child. Did you know you can fall in love with the way a man loves someone else? It sounds all zigzagged, but it's true. Love takes so much *effort*. You have to get up ever so early in the morning to really love someone properly.

I don't suppose I shall have a daughter of my own now. I'm not fussed over it. It was on the to-do list, but you know to-do lists. They get longer and longer until you might as well just carve the last items on your tombstone.

Do the dishes.

Pick up gown from the cleaners.

Sign contract.

Perish.

Oh bollocks, I forgot: Have children.

Cue that sad trombone. Besides, I'm rather off marriage at the moment. First Percy, then poor Nigel Lapine—what a disaster! Remind me, my darling, loyal diary, to never again marry a man who makes love with his socks on. I don't care how his slapstick flickies make me laugh! Diary, you must stand firm! Nigel told me I ought to quit the pictures and make babies, so I told him he ought to quit my house and make a movie with more depth than getting kicked in the balls, and I'm not the teensiest bit sorry. Comedians have no sense of humour.

Thaddeus asked me to marry him, of course. The same day that he told me *Miranda* had been greenlit. He does it every time he offers me a new Madame Mortimer picture, comes sailing into my parlour with a part in one hand and a ring in the other. I always take the part, but leave the ring. Saints and ministers of grace! It would seem only directors can love a girl like me. I told the scoundrel not to be absurd. He doesn't mean it. He's never so much as kissed me, and he never will. Thad is the Moon's uncle, every starlet's confessor—but never their lover. Perhaps I shall just say yes one day. That would shock the red out of his hair! But then I might have to go through with it, and I'd rather have a half-barrel of spinach than a husband at the moment.

For that matter, I'm rather off men these days, full stop. I suppose that would make me perfect for Thaddeus. Perhaps that's why he's forever asking me. He knows I won't spill his plate of beans and he won't spill mine. We are each quite safe in the company of the other. After all, everyone needs a secret to stick in their lapel.

Perhaps I shall invite Sevvy on our little cruise. It would do her good, poor lamb. Being a teenager is always trying, for them and for everyone else, but she cannot seem to get into the rhythm of the thing. I've tried to tell her she doesn't have to go into the industry. There's every other thing out there, and a lot of it doesn't require our sort of genteel schizophrenia. She's just burning up with ambition, but the poor bunny's got nowhere to put it. I don't think the Patented Pellam System for Prevailing Over the Perils of Pubescence would be of much help.

1. Stop speaking to your parents
2. Run away from your planet
3. Take off your clothes as often as possible, but only while reciting Shakespeare (and being paid scale)
4. Buy a cat
5. Drink your milk
6. Mug your destiny in an alley and punch it until it gives you what you want

See? What use is that rot to my girl? I don't think I will invite her. It's hard enough to grow up without having to watch adults act like fools and monsters all the time. And it's hard enough being a fool and a monster without a knock-kneed kid spitting responsibility into your drink.

Aha! Speak of the devil and she arrives, desperate for a proper hug.

16 January, 1930, Two in the Morning . . . Or Is It Three?
The Butterfly Room, Aboard the Achelois, *Sea of*
   Tranquillity

Come on, Mary, sober up! If you don't write it down, you won't remember it, and if you don't remember it, somebody's going to get away with murder and you'll never even know who. It's only a spot of gin, girl. Give yourself a couple of good slaps and steady your damned course.

Thaddeus Irigaray is dead!

God forgive me, I think Percy killed him.

How Many Miles to Babylon?:
Episode 1

Airdate: 24 March, 1914
Announcer: **Henry R. Choudhary**
Vespertine Hyperia: **Violet El-Hashem**
Tybault Gayan: **Alain Mbengue**
The Invisible Hussar: **Zachariah von Leipold**
Doctor Gruel: **Benedict Sol**
Guest Star: **Wadsworth Shevchenko as the Maroon Marauder**

ANNOUNCER: Good Evening, Listeners, if it is indeed Evening
where you are. BBC Radio is proud to present to you a Sunday
night drama you won't soon forget. We'll see you here every
week at seven in the evening for rollicking stories of derring-
do and breathless excitement. Journey back to the early days
of planetary settlement. Join the brave men and women of the
Pioneer Age as they explore a Venus untouched by man!
Gather in, pour yourself a cup of something nice, and sit back
for the first thrilling instalment of the solar system's newest
tale of adventure, romance, and intrigue on *How Many Miles
to Babylon?*

   Babylon is a joint production of the United/Universal All-
Worlds Wireless Broadcom Network (New York, Shanghai,
Tithonus) and BBC Radio, recorded at Atlas Studios, London.

This evening's programme is brought to you by Idun's Apples Cosmetics, makers of fine soaps, hair oils, cold creams, lip rouges, and foundations, prepared lovingly from a secret blend of soothing botanicals, exotic scents, and ambergris from the finest Venusian sources. Additional promotional consideration provided by Prithvi Deep Sea Holdings Cooperative, a Family Company; Branston Pickle; Kerykeion Premium Coffees, Roasted on Mercury, Served at Your Table; the East Indian Trading Company; and Edison Teleradio Corp.

[Cue wind effects, hollow, haunting, wild breezes echoing through space. Fade into electronic background noise, beeps #445, 23, 71, and 101.]

TYBAULT: Oh, Vespertine, heart of my heart! When you open the door of this stalwart rocket which has been home and hearth to us for so long, we will behold the surface of a virgin world! Who knows what we may find on the shores of watery Venus? What marvels, what perils?

VESPERTINE: They will be *our* marvels, my beloved, *our* perils! We will make a new home, hewn from the tree of our love!

[Door creak #6, footsteps #11 and 12.]

VESPERTINE: [aside] When I looked upon that new world, splendid in every way and in every way terrible, I looked upon a tiger with stars falling from his striped tongue. I looked and saw my true bridegroom—but would it also be my grave?

TYBAULT: A sea as red as a rose garden stretches out before us— but what are those strange shapes on the horizon? We shall investigate on the morrow! Ah, how marvellously the cacao-trees soar into the rosy sky! I shall build you a house of these fine planks. How rich the violet fruit on every bough! We will never starve, my darling!

DOCTOR GRUEL: But perhaps you will BURN!

VESPERTINE: Oh no! Who are you, masked sir?

DOCTOR GRUEL: I am Doctor Gruel, and Venus is mine! I am

the Wizard of the Whales! I command their awesome power and ride upon their backs as on a pirate galleon! I will allow no man to dwell upon this Eden planet but me and mine!

TYBAULT: I warn you, Doctor Gruel, I am a strong man—I am not without powers of my own! And I am but the first. More ships follow behind in a great silver wave!

DOCTOR GRUEL: And my banditos and I will DESTROY THEM ALL! AH HA HA HA HA!

His Master's Voice

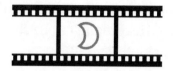

CYTHERA BRASS: Are you ready to start again?

ERASMO: I don't know why you ask that when you've already begun recording. Obviously, we have started, whether I like it or not. Is it in a handbook somewhere?

CYTHERA: Actually, yes.

ERASMO: I would love to see that handbook.

CYTHERA: Perhaps after we finish here. Begin session two, day one. Let's roll it back a little. How would you describe the general mood that first night at the Adonis base camp? Before you ventured into the village itself. December first, 1944.

ERASMO: Let me ask you something. Have you ever worked on a movie?

CYTHERA: [short laugh] I *am* the Chief Security Officer of the biggest film studio on the Moon.

ERASMO: I know that. But have you ever worked on a movie? As a script girl or a gopher or a rigger or a costumer, or, hell, even as an actress? Actually been part of a crew, not just signed checks and kept out riffraff and called in tactical strikes on Plantagenet lots.

CYTHERA: As a matter of fact, I have.

ERASMO: Oh?

CYTHERA: *Cross of Stone.* 1919.

ERASMO: I love that flick.

CYTHERA: I was one of Queen Matilda's handmaidens. You can only see me in the background of one shot.

ERASMO: I knew you looked familiar.

CYTHERA: Don't be absurd. You couldn't possibly remember.

ERASMO: Cyth, my love, it is my job to see the smallest details of a film. You wore that ridiculous headdress with two points on it like antelope horns. You tore your veil halfway through the scene but kept your game face on quite admirably.

My point is, if you've worked on a movie, you know what it's like, the night before you start filming on location. There's an energy bouncing all around like balloons fizzing out. Everyone needs their sleep but no one wants to be the first to go. We just wanted to wallow in that wonderful moment before everything started, because in that moment, we all believed the movie was perfect. All we had to do was go and get it. No one had fucked up a shot or wasted film or started giggling in the middle of a line yet.

So what was the mood? What did we do? We actually sat around an actual campfire and told stories. Arlo tried to tell a joke again. [pause] Did you know him?

CYTHERA: I did.

ERASMO: Did you ever manage to hear him tell a whole joke all the way through?

CYTHERA: [laughs softly] Once. But it was a really short one.

ERASMO: Tell me.

CYTHERA: It was at a company picnic out by the Sea of Serenity. We played cricket against Plantagenet—it's not all tactical strikes, as you so bluntly put it. Arlo and I were both hopeless. You'd think the Australian would've put up a better show than me. The Seneca nation has never had a team and never will. But Arlo made me look aces. After we lost, we were lying on the grass and he turned to me and said: *So, two fish are floating in a tank and one turns to the other and says, 'Hey, do you know how to drive this thing?'* I think I actually applauded.

ERASMO: Good for him. Well, he kept on at the one about the mummy snake and the baby snake, but it was no go. The weather was calm; no storm clouds. We ate bacon sandwiches with hot mustard and roasted sausages over the fire. Aylin Novalis, our guide, asked Mariana about growing up on Mercury. Aylin had never been, which shocked me. Mercury is practically right next door! So Mariana told her all about it.

"I was born in Nefertem, a small town not far from Trismegistus in the Tropic of Gemini, the temperate zone between the hot side of the planet and the cold side. My parents raised dragons. Most everyone in Nefertem did."

"It's my lifelong ambition to see one of those up close," our best boy Santiago said. Now, as far as I can tell, everything imaginable was Santiago Zhang's lifelong ambition. Did you eat real camel once? He'd practically leap into the air and tell you it was his lifelong ambition to eat real camel. Pilot a ship the whole length of the Orient Express? By god, it was Iggy's lifelong damned ambition to shoot a rocket down the ice road like a billiard ball.

Mariana said, "Go to a damn zoo sometime, Iggy." Everybody laughed. She told us what they looked like, the native Mercurial beasties. Komodo dragons crossed with zebras crossed with otters, with the personality of a drunken granddad set in his ways. Have you seen one?

CYTHERA: I have a hacienda on Mercury. They taste marvellous with a béarnaise sauce.

ERASMO: Aren't you a delight? [sounds of swallowing, a water glass being set down roughly] I bet you never rode one, though. Mari did, when she was little. She wasn't supposed to, but she made her parents save one from the slaughterhouse so she could have a pet. She rode it around the ranch and called it Sancho Panza. Taught herself to sing leaning against Sancho Panza's back and singing nursery songs with dragon slipped in to all the lyrics. *Twinkle, twinkle little dragon, won't you come and pull my wagon. Up above the world so high, Sancho Panza in the sky . . .*

Mari had such a pretty voice. But girls who can sing tenor don't get a lot of work. It's soprano or bust. So she hired on with Edison Corp. Learned the tech so she could help other people sing.

"What happened to Sancho Panza?" Cristabel asked her.

"Same thing that happened to half of them in the twenties," Mari said, and you could tell she was still a little heartbroken over it. "Who knew a dragon could get whooping cough?"

After that, Cristabel got to talking about cloud surfing on Titan when she was young. The clouds on Titan get so heavy sometimes that you can hop out of a glider and surf them all the way down to the surface. Crissy never saw a blue sky until she was thirteen! She still wears sunglasses all the time. Her eyes never got strong enough for sunlight without cloud cover to diffuse it. Even the Venusian twilight was too much. She loves film, I think, because it makes everything look silver and soft again, like it did back home. She said, "The clouds fold over you like your mother tucking you into the biggest, softest bed in the world."

CYTHERA: And how would you describe Mr Varela that night? Happy? Distracted? Did he socialize with the others?

ERASMO: Sure. I suppose.

CYTHERA: Do you remember anything in particular before . . .

[papers shuffling] quarter of two in the morning? That was when it started, wasn't it?

ERASMO: What you have to understand about Max is that he's a technician with a leading man's soul. He's Henry V, but his England is electricity. If Aylin had asked him about his childhood, he'd have regaled us for hours—and we'd have been totally absorbed, because he was wonderful, really magnetic. But he had to be *asked*, or he would just sulk. He grew up on Earth, you know. Only one of us who did.

CYTHERA: So did I.

ERASMO: Well, you two would have a lot to talk about. You can also tell him that if I see him again I shall drown him in a ditch.

CYTHERA: Why?

ERASMO: You were asking if Max socialized. He did, in his way. He jawed with Horace and Cristabel about lenses. He cuddled Mari while she sang about Sancho Panza and tried to slip Arlo a punch line on the sly—but old Covington didn't want any help. Oh . . . and he got into it with Dr Nantakarn. But they'd both been drinking.

CYTHERA: What did they argue about?

ERASMO: Callowhale anatomy. Max kept saying they were basically a series of balloons, just sacs of fluid, more like plants than anything we'd recognize as an animal. Retta wasn't having a bit of it. She had a theory that they're *actually* cetaceans, that if you could cut one open—God, with what? Bulldozers?—if you could cut one open you'd find something not very different than a humpback whale, just much, much bigger. She's published papers, so you can imagine how bent out of shape she got after a little of that vile moss-gin when some theatre kid started telling her callowhales are basically houseplants. Max sort of sneered that maybe we'd get lucky out here and she could be the first to autopsy one. Retta just swigged from her flask, winked at Santiago, and said, "It's my lifelong ambition."

CYTHERA: Did Varela argue with Severin that night?

ERASMO: Not that night, no.

CYTHERA: And the sounds began . . . around 0045. Correct?

ERASMO: [very quietly, imploringly] I don't want to talk about the sounds.

CYTHERA: I'm afraid you have to. They're a significant factor in all this.

ERASMO: What if I just cut to the end—this isn't a novel, I don't need to keep you in suspense.

CYTHERA: [papers shuffling] ". . . we secured the foodstuffs in lockers in case local fauna came sniffing around for crisps and bunked down around midnight. I don't really know how long it was, half an hour? Forty-five minutes? Something like that. Half an hour to forty-five minutes later I heard something. It was really, really quiet. Sort of a *scratching* sound, like somebody rubbing two pieces of burlap together. My brother Franco went outside to investigate." That's Konrad Sallandar from craft services. [more shuffling] "I went to bed before everyone else so I could study my maps and just . . . get a break from all of them. Artistic types don't really talk. They just wait for their turn to tell a story. It's amazing, but I'm an introvert. I'm not trained up for that level of social interaction. I'd say I turned my light out around 2330, Earth clock. So I was almost asleep when I heard it. It wasn't loud—not then. Just the softest noise. Like somebody breathing. Somebody with a bit of a chest cold. I remember looking at my watch, so I can definitively say I first heard it at 0043." That's Aylin Novalis. Do I need to go on?

ERASMO: No. Christ, no, please, stop.

CYTHERA: Did you hear something that night?

ERASMO: Yes.

CYTHERA: Did Severin?

ERASMO: We all heard it. I don't know what fucking time it started. I stuck my head out of the tent and I started giggling. I couldn't help it; I get the giggles when I'm nervous. Heads popped up out of all the other tents and it looked like a Whack 'Em game at the fair. Once they saw me giggling they all started in, too, and pretty soon we were rolling in the sand. We weren't scared. You hear funny things on funny planets. In the dark, in the middle of a swamp.

CYTHERA: Once you got yourselves under control, did the sound stop?

ERASMO: No.

CYTHERA: What did it sound like, to you?

ERASMO: Like a radio stuck between stations. It was diffuse, coming from everywhere at once. But it was still very, very distant. You had to shush everyone to hear it. Mariana checked her mics but everything was dark, wrapped up, A-OK. So we all went back to bed and didn't give it another thought.

CYTHERA: And the next morning?

ERASMO: Up at 0600. Toast and sausages and Venusian coffee and not a worry in the world or a sound in the sky, except those mad black birds that sing in Mandarin.

CYTHERA: And this is December second, the first day of actual filming. The day Severin made contact with the boy.

ERASMO: Anchises.

CYTHERA: That's not his name, you know.

ERASMO: It has been for a year. That's long enough to stick to his ribs.

CYTHERA: Do you want to know his legal name?

ERASMO: [surprised snort] Actually, yes. I'd like that.

CYTHERA: It's Turan Kephus.

ERASMO: [long pause] He likes Anchises.

CYTHERA: Tell me your first impressions of him.

ERASMO: I told you already—we spent most of the morning setting up cameras and lighting rigs. Horace and I set up coverage. Mari's equipment didn't seem to like the humidity—she was way behind schedule. We all kept busy . . . because if you looked at him once, you'd never stop.

CYTHERA: Walking in circles?

ERASMO: You've seen the film. But in real life it was . . . it was just awful. That poor boy. He'd been like that for years, but he still looked like a child. Like all the photos we'd collected of Adonis before the . . . event. The disaster. It was a genuinely unexplainable thing. Severin kept saying somebody must be feeding him. But I don't know. Every once in a while he would kind of . . . wink out. Like a shutter clicking. And then he'd come back, so fast you told yourself it was nothing, it was just *you* blinking, moron. Until we watched the dailies.

It got to me. I felt sick. I felt like I'd run at full speed straight into a brick wall. We'd come all the way across space to see him, and he was exactly like the stories. Exactly like the photographs. There was no new information. Everybody exaggerates; everyone embellishes. But Anchises was just so bizarre that you couldn't top him.

CYTHERA: What time did Severin make contact?

ERASMO: Around 1300, I think. The light was perfect; the light is always perfect on Venus. Max didn't think she should touch him. He said, "Just try talking first. We have all the time in the world." And Dr Nantakarn said something about trauma victims and how you couldn't predict their reactions to human touch. I wasn't really listening. Rinny was *definitely* gonna hug that kid, so I didn't consider it an important debate. Rinny didn't like *being* hugged all that much, but she was a great practitioner of hugging others. She liked to initiate the whole process. When she was younger, she said it could fix anything, if you timed a hug right and were really good at it. And she was. Really good at it.

Later, she revised that to "almost anything."

But she did try talking to him first. I don't remember what she said. Generically soothing stuff. She could be so comforting, if you really needed it. Needed her. Not if you'd just had a bad day or lost your watch or something. She didn't have a lot of pity for the little tragedies. But if you got stuck in a big one, you'd want her there to kiss it better. [clears throat] Right. So she said a few sweet nothings and then she went in for the hug, and then all hell broke loose.

CYTHERA: What particular kind of hell?

ERASMO: The kid started screaming bloody murder. I thought for a moment he was going to blink out again, to get away from Severin, but she held him still. Held him while he shrieked and shook and clawed at her. Like that girl in the story. Who holds onto Tam Lin 'til the wicked fairies have all marched by. What's her name?

CYTHERA: Janet.

ERASMO: [chair squeaks] That was quick. Under other circumstances, I think you might be an interesting person to know, Cyth. Janet. She held him like Janet, and at the same time the sound roared up again, nothing like the night before. Loud— and I mean marching band–loud. It was absolutely mechanical this time. Machine noise and voices. We didn't recognize them at first. We couldn't begin to understand words out of all that junked-up static—skipping, popping, screeching feedback, looped back on itself, the timbre fucked from top to bottom. But somewhere in there we could hear . . . voices. We were all pretty freaked out—but that kind of freaked out where you're excited and alive and so fucking curious your curiosity could punch a hole in the ground.

CYTHERA: Can we discuss the boy's hand for a moment?

ERASMO: [loud sigh] After all this time I still don't know what to say about his hand. It was disgusting, I can say that. I couldn't see it clearly, not right away. He was still hollering his head off. His eyes were absolutely wild. I saw a horse bolt during a fireworks show once. When the gauchos finally tracked her down, she was lying in a lake of her own sweat, panicked entirely out of her ability to stand on her own four legs. And her eyes, her poor eyes, looked like Anchises's eyes. Irises spinning in their whites.

Anchises held up his hand—*the* hand—to Severin like he meant to strike her, but she didn't recoil. I was so proud of her. I would have flinched. All I could think was: *He has a mouth in his hand.* But it wasn't a mouth. Later he let us all examine it as much as we liked. With gloves and masks, mind you. We didn't just shove our thumbs in. He had a gash in his palm that didn't or couldn't or wouldn't heal, and the gash was full of horrid squirming bits of flesh, like tiny tentacles, but so fine. Silky. Wet. Greenish-bronze. And alive: they moved by themselves, stretching out of him. Severin just kept telling him how everything was fine as paint. Giving him her best Face Number 124: Adoring Mother. Instead of hitting her, he touched her cheek with that ruin of a hand. It was such a tender gesture, so . . . adult. And when he touched her it all shut off. He stopped screaming and the static stopped screeching and he let her scoop him up in her arms. She carried him away from the Memorial and then Margareta conducted her examination while Rinny cradled him in her lap.

Anchises slept in our tent for the next three days. We tried to get him to talk, but he wouldn't. Just clung to Rin like she was something new to circle round. We sat by the fire singing all the songs we could think of to the kid. Maximo took him for walks and kept up this constant patter, hoping he'd do the primate thing and start trying to mimic the big monkeys.

CYTHERA: If we could step back for a moment: What steps did you take to investigate the source of the static? Did Dr Nantakarn suggest that you might have been hallucinating? It seems that all of you freely indulged in drugs and alcohol . . .

ERASMO: Oh, please. Don't patronise us. Retta heard it, too. So did Aylin, and neither of them touched a drop of anything even the slightest bit *altering*. We did what you'd expect—strip that sound equipment, son! Get into those Edison innards. But it was all fine. Mariana kept saying, "It's perfect, it's perfect."

CYTHERA: The rest of the night passed without incident?

ERASMO: Reasonably. We decided not to try to get anything out of Anchises yet. He slept like he'd died. At breakfast the next morning—

CYTHERA: This is December third?

ERASMO: Sure. Who cares? At breakfast I offered him some eggs—he wouldn't eat solid food yet, but I made him a plate just in case. Max had taken him walking on the beach earlier in the morning and the boy seemed almost cheerful. I offered him eggs and he opened his mouth and static came pouring out of it—but inside the static we heard something else.

Mariana. Screaming.

It was only a coincidence; he wasn't *making* the sound. It came from everywhere—from the sky, from the Qadesh—but he opened his mouth in time for it to look like a cue. Mariana's scream was clear as bleeding daylight, and we all knew it was hers. Mari lost it. You have to understand, she wouldn't have suffered the indignity of getting certified on Edison gear if she didn't have a delicate ear and love that mixer on her hip like a child. She screamed in harmony with herself, holding her hands over her ears, yelling over the sound of this other staticky voice we didn't recognize yet, garbled, warped, followed by a lot of audio vomit. From then on, it never stopped.

You understand, we didn't know what it was saying then. Afterward, Cristabel and I played back Mariana's tape in the studio on the *Clamshell* and cleaned it up. Only then could we get at the actual words.

CYTHERA: Which were?

ERASMO: "Now my charms are all o'erthrown, and what strength I have's mine own, which is most faint."

Billy Shakes, my dear. *The Tempest*. But it was just growling then. Growling, and that vicious, shrill screaming. It never stopped after that. None of us could sleep in that invisible static mess, listening to shredded voices coming from nowhere. It just swallowed Mari up. She spent the morning banging on her temples to make it stop. Moaning, rocking back and forth, clutching her mixer to her chest.

CYTHERA: Alfric struck the boy, correct?

ERASMO: That is so entirely, utterly irrelevant. Yes, she slapped him, that morning when I gave him a plate of eggs and he gave us the hell's loudspeaker. When it looked like the sound was coming from him, she slapped the scream off him.

CYTHERA: Was that the only time she made physical contact with him?

ERASMO: I don't know. Probably not. Maybe.

CYTHERA: Varela said he argued with Severin on the night of December second.

ERASMO: I think everyone argued with everyone on the night of December second.

CYTHERA: Do you know what they argued about?

ERASMO: She said it was nothing. She and Varela had a thing when they were kids—really, just kids. So they couldn't just disagree on what gels to use, it was always the wrong gel *and* you broke my heart a million years ago. I usually tuned it out. But Mari was still an absolute wreck and the static kept rising and falling like waves, hitting us over and over, and it wouldn't stop, it never *stopped*. Max was worried about Severin. Maybe that was it.

CYTHERA: Was there a physical altercation?

ERASMO: She wouldn't have told me if there was. I'd have slammed his face into a tree so hard he'd have had to live there. And she liked his face.

We were all on edge. Sleeping in that ghost town, in the middle of all those shattered houses and wreckage and misery, feedback sawing on our ears every minute of every hour and the sun never coming up or going down and this poor helpless kid with the monster in his hand . . . By the fourth hour, I wanted to slide out of my own skin and return to the invertebrate sea. I would've been thrilled to hit something. Anything.

You want to know how bad it was? I can sum it up for you. That night, after eight or nine hours of that horror show ripping through the air, Severin curled up next to me and hauled my arms up over her body. She was hiding in me. And do you know what she said?

CYTHERA: What?

ERASMO: Miss Severin Lamartine Unck said to me, "Baby, I'm so scared."

CYTHERA: What did you say?

ERASMO: What do you think I said? I said what you say. I said I loved her right in the face. It was just some kind of malfunction in Mari's gear: *you know how touchy all that Edison rot can be, don't worry, go to sleep, I'm right here. Not going anywhere, my love.* We sang "Down to the River to Pray" to Anchises. We always sang beautifully together, Rin and me. We sang to him and he stared up at us and his eyes didn't seem quite so horsey anymore.

I woke up late that night. Both Rin and the little bit were snoring away. Click, sigh, choke. I put my trousers on and went out to the village well—I suppose that would be the hotel lounge, wouldn't it? If Adonis had a hotel anymore. I knew Horace would be there. I sauntered up. The static sizzled madly in the air. I mimed holding a glass full of sweet pink lady and lifted it up like I was going to toast my cousin. But he didn't move. He stared straight down into the well.

"Hey, mate," I said. "You sleepwalking?"

Nothing. I grabbed his shoulder, a little roughly, but he was upsetting me with this nonsense. I yelled over the static, "Horace, wake up!"

He did. He turned to me and smiled. He looked so much like my father. I saw the scar where I'd got him with the dart all those years ago. And then he jumped into the well.

[long pause. Sounds of fingernails scratching against the table.]

It was very deep. I heard him land.

CYTHERA: Had Horace St. John shown suicidal tendencies before this? Do you have any idea why he would take his own life?

ERASMO: [ragged breathing] Stop it. I don't like you using his full name. He was just Horace. I loved him. Horace was sixteen months older than me and our fathers were brothers. Horace's mum sold hats in Grasshopper City. Horace would not abide anyone calling him Ace, and God knows I tried. Horace liked to bake. You wouldn't think a bloke like him would, but he made coronation cakes that looked like iced heaven. If you lined up everyone I'd ever met, he'd be the last one I'd pick to kill himself.

CYTHERA: And when the others found out?

ERASMO: [quiet weeping] They didn't, right away. Because Mariana woke up with one of those *mouths* in her hand where she'd slapped the kid, and she started screaming, and it was the same scream we'd heard on the static wind hours before.

So it took a while before they listened to me bawling my eyes out that Horace was dead.

CYTHERA: I know this is difficult. But I have to ask, for insurance purposes—what was Mr Covington's reaction to all this?

ERASMO: Arlo? Oh, he said the shoot was over and we were heading back to White Peony as soon as the equipment was packed.

Oh, Those Scandalous Stars!

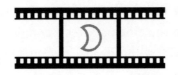

***Places, Everyone!,* 4th May, 1924**

Column #431: The Man in the Moon

Greetings and salutations, cats and kittens, darlings and dear hearts, galactic apples of my all-seeing eye! What have I got in my pockets for you this week? A little sex, a little decadence, a dash of illicit never-you-mind, a lashing of underage naughtiness? YOU BET.

Yours truly secured an invitation Saturday last to what is sure to be remembered as the shindig of the century, or at least the week: the wrap party for Percy Unck's newest flickie, *The Abduction of Proserpine*! Don't ask how I came to be in possession of my invitation (engraved in silver, naturally, on black paper—our man Unck omits no detail!) for I shall never tell.

I am your eyes and ears on the Moon—I see all and hear all! And what did I hear and see on Saturday?

Well, you already know, loyal readers, that Mr Percival Unck was turned down flat by the Americans when he tried to pop out to the nether quarters of the solar system to shoot his little Gothic trifle in the actual ruins of poor Proserpine. People are so funny about tragedies! So what did the King of the Silver Screen do? He built Pluto on the

Moon. That's right, all that hush-hush hustle and bustle out on the Endymion Flats beyond Grasshopper City, all those trucks bouncing out of the Virago lots, all that grumbling and rattling you heard from the Oxblood and Plantagenet offices? All of that was to whack us up a little Pluto of our own. Oh, it'll be gone by the time you read this—that's just how the celluloid crumbles—but it'll be alive forever up there on the cinema screen come autumn. The camera eats the world: points itself at everything, and sucks it right up into Movieland.

But on Saturday, oh, on Saturday, we all danced the Charleston on Pluto's night-drenched shores! We drank pomegranate smoke out of stained-glass snifters and wriggled into paper buffalo suits left lying all over the sailcloth glaciers like party hats. Mickey Hull himself played the evening away with his twenty-man band. Miss Mary Pellam, half out of her dress by nine p.m., brought the house down with "It Never Rains on Venus." Mickey H. belted out "I Left My Heart on Halimede," and, I tell you, there wasn't a dry eye.

But I get ahead of myself.

Our host set the soundstage up like a labyrinth—the flats and mattes arranged so that we revellers got quite lost, plunged into the mixed-up world of Unck Brand Patented Instant Pluto—Just Add Cameras! The interior walls—all painted windows with real curtains, candelabras and mantelpieces concealing the triggers to hidden stairways—stood at ninety-degree angles to broad landscapes of the frozen Plutonian tundra: wild silver-tailed buffalo prancing, Charon looming huge and sinister and shimmering with what I could only assume was enough glitter to entirely coat the island of Madagascar. Expanses of the ruined city of Proserpine had been swept aside to make room for sets of the city at its rough-and-tumble height. No one could find their way; we stumbled over each other, giggling like children at a slumber party. Tucked into every turn of the maze were caches of drink and delicacies—usually tipped over and scattered by the time I found them. But all roads led to Unck, and the winding, wriggling paths eventually emptied out into a great central stage where Talmadge Brace's gargantuan ice-dragon puppet wrapped around Mickey Hull's band and a ballroom floor the colour of blood. The red positively throbbed in my eyes after all that gentle silver and black and grey and white.

And who did I see on the dance floor but beefy Capricorn Studios golden boy Thad Irigaray putting the moves on Mary P, the current Mrs Unck! Not that the chap was doing much of a job of it. And what's this? Old Wadsy canoodling with Richard Boreal over by the vampires' chiaroscuro hideout, my my! *Quel scandale*—or it would be, if I hadn't told you all about it months ago. Our leading lady and gent, Miss Annabelle August and Mr Hartford Crane, kissed grandly in public view, but went to the bar separately, wiping their mouths with the backs of their hands. The birdies say those two kids can't stand each other, and Annie's looking to jump ship to Capricorn with Thaddy-boy—but who'd let a dove like that go? I smell a skirmish coming, so batten down the hatches and hold on to your hats.

Percy himself held court in a dashing green suit, so unusual for the monochrome mishmash of the Virago homestead! And don't think I missed the sidelong looks he dished out to that pretty little ballerina we've been seeing in the chorus lines in Grasshopper City. I miss nothing.

More troubling to my eyes was the sight of little Severin Unck, but ten years old, weaving in and out of the labyrinth with more ease than any of us, darting into the flats to sling back vodka and Callisto bourbon like a bad wee fairy child, some wastrel by-blow daughter of Puck. By midnight she could be found curled up on the massive snout of the ice-dragon puppet that features so prominently in the film, her fingers tangled in its tinfoil whiskers, stocking feet tucked up under her petticoat, a crystal af-yun atomizer clutched in her fist. She would not be the first child to go that way on our Pleasure Island in the sky, but it hurt my heart all the same.

When the rumpus wound down and the confetti had been thrown, the poor girl woke with a start and found herself alone but for myself and a few of the catering staff tidying up. She climbed up onto the face of that glitter-caked dragon, standing on her tiptoes, surrounded by the funhouse-mirror Pluto, ruins, drawing room, and glacier, and began crying plaintively: *Papa! Papa!*

And for one moment—the only moment of the whole *Proserpine* shoot, I'd wager—I felt as though I stood on Pluto in truth; right there at the end of it all in the terrible chill and emptiness of that very real and very dead city, of which all that remains is a ghostly voice crying out one word to the night, over and over, without a reply.

Algernon B
Editor-in-Chief

~~The Deep Blue Devil~~
The Man in the Malachite Mask:
The Murder of Gonzago

25 February, 1962. Half four in the morning, Setebos Hall

My hand shakes as I attempt to record the activities of the night. My lantern gutters, casting shadows like ink drops over my knuckles, my pen, my pages. There are sounds in this house . . . sounds I can scarcely begin to describe. I might call them *howlings*, and yet there is nothing in that lonely word bloody and primeval enough to encompass what my ears have been made to endure. Perhaps if I knew the Sanskrit for it, that ancient tongue of tongues, that would suffice.

I understand now that what happened in my presence in the throne room of the King of Pluto happens every night—it is a performance that repeats like a skipping phonograph, like a church bell. It was not done for my benefit; I am incidental. It does not alter; The King keeps a wooden hammer ribboned like a maypole at his side, and with this wicked gavel he punishes any improvisation or deviation with swift brutality. I saw with my own eyes a maid who mistakenly sang the word *agony* beset by hammer blows until she corrected herself, weeping: *Ago, ago, I mean ago!*

Enough, enough. Anchises, enough. There must be some comfort in relating of events, or else why has any tale been told? To salve, to soothe, that is the only purpose of language.

Cythera and I were guests of honour at supper tonight. We suspected nothing particularly untoward—at least, no more untoward than the average Tuesday on this accursed planet. We dressed accordingly, in black suits that invited no frivolous business. Even I managed to project a professional, detached air of importance, perhaps even a slight edge of intimidation. I flatter myself that I can pull off such a combination on some rare occasions. Cythera took my arm without even her usual sigh of distaste, ever-present yet almost imperceptible to anyone who had not shared quarters with her for three months, a sigh with deniability, as soft as loathing. But tonight she held it in abeyance, so I must have been in fine fettle. I closed my hand over hers and whispered:

"Cythera, you must not let your guard down around Varela. Whatever he has made of himself here, he is . . . a bad man." I sounded, even to my own ears, like a frightened child. I had been just that when I last found myself trapped in a room with Severin Unck's lighting master. Frightened of everything, but of him most particularly, of his stare, of his terrible lights in their black cases, gathered round him like the wall of a gaol.

"You've said nothing about him in your notes," answered she, pausing at the door of our conjoined quarters. "Is there something you've neglected to tell me?"

I shut my eyes. From beneath years of drink and worse, images swam upward, breaking the surface: the cantina of the *Clamshell*, people weeping, men and women yelling, a doctor with yellow hands, a pistol belonging to no one . . . smoke— Stygian, unnatural, smoke with a vicious taste—but it was a smoke without fire . . . so much light, so much *light*. And then a man's fists—Maximo's—striking me over and over, his boot crunching down onto my deformed hand . . .

I swayed on my feet. Cythera steadied me, real concern in the eyes beneath her golden mask. What a wonder. She did worry for me, after all.

"On Venus I remember nothing of him except his smell—he took more care than the others for his personal cleanliness. Even Severin smelled sour in the morning, but Varela . . . there was always a breath of soap on him. But . . . on the ship, on the ship home. He beat me; he told me to keep silent. To never speak if I could help it. And he showed me the airlock. He asked if I liked it. Every day he asked. I ran from him . . ." But there was something on Venus as well. In the photographs, in the files, in my own memory, dancing just over the precipice where my brain dared not delve.

My companion gave me a glass of her own brandy, a Callisto vintage she must have hidden away from me aboard ship; I felt my strength returning. Perhaps all the strength I've ever owned has come from a bottle, from an atomizer, from a syringe. Without them I am friendless.

"You are not a child now, Anchises. He cannot hurt you. He certainly can't hurt me. I've stared down men with more mettle than some pisspot theatre-rat, I assure you."

How kind she was to me then. I've no idea what came over her. Perhaps she was ill. If only we had known.

Boatswain and Mariner appeared, once more maddeningly silent, maddeningly masked, and led us into the dining hall. A long black table lay prepared, groaning with wonderful foods, Earth foods: glistening roast turkeys and geese, bowls of green vegetables garnished with sweet nuts and butter, steaming bread, champagne, cold cherry soup, pumpkin tarts, everything as perfect as if it were made by some St. Louis matriarch in one humble kitchen. Merrymakers already sat at table, talking, laughing, even singing, as though nothing could be the matter. We took our places at the far end of the banquet table. At the other end sat Maximo Varela, the great lighting master, the Mad King of Pluto. He wore a suit not much different from ours—yet still, too, that unsettling, uncanny Severin mask.

We ate; yet it did not satisfy. The turkey, the goose gravy, the broccoli and Brussels sprouts all tasted the same, their flavour no stronger than that of the infanta flowers: sweet, complex, but hardly a patch on a leg of lamb as I remembered it. No one spoke to us; they behaved as though we were quite invisible, reaching across us for second helpings, kicking our shins beneath the table. I searched Varela's eyes for the man in my memory, the man who had pinned my arm with one boot while he ground his other heel into my hand. But all I could see was the plastic face of Severin Unck, expressionless, unnerving.

Afterward, the company processed into a dark chamber adjoining the dining hall. Real fear moved in their eyes. The nakedness of it all unsettled our bones—naked walls, without sound, without light, yet nothing guarded. The hyena of the human heart had been loosed in the rooms of this place. I offered my hand to Cythera, but she refused it.

"It's not *your* comforting I was concerned with," I mumbled, and she gave me that old shipboard glare I knew so well.

Very well. Comfortless, we faced that lightless room, wide and long enough for draughts and echoes to play awful, invisible hosts. I could feel the movement of bodies, hear the rustle of fabrics, the soft thump of objects, but nothing had a name or a shape; nothing was yet itself. Light, finally, began as dawn begins: barely perceptible, except as an ease in the air, a redness. I could hear, suddenly, overwhelmingly, the crash and boom of ocean waves. Shadows leapt into stark existence—cretaceous shadows, of vast ferns and trunks, of tangled bush, of thorns and brambles. I felt a raindrop land on my head. I smelled ozone, moss, a storm just wandered off. Green lights like lost emeralds spattered down from the black depths of the ceiling. The silhouettes of broken ships, of broken palaces, of broken bodies came into relief. Lights the colour of drowned flesh crept in, slithering forward to meet the King as he stepped into the world of his making.

He stepped. And stepped. And turned. In a small, tight circle, round and round. He no longer wore the mask of Severin's face. Now a grotesque Green Man rode his skull, a tangle of kelp, wild orange blossoms, and cacao-bark; hanging vines and fish bones. The King turned round and round, his head down, clutching his hand to his naked chest. *No, no, no,* I whispered, shaking my head from side to side, trying to retreat, to back out of that place before the place could see me, but a wall of bodies caught me, kept me. The King spun. The heavy leaves of his mask quivered in a real wind that picked up from nowhere, swirling, clawing at my gloves as if it knew, it *knew* what it would find there.

I began to weep. I am not ashamed. Any man would.

The King stopped as suddenly as if he had been stabbed through the eye. He turned his head toward me, his body motionless. The eyes of his mask were holes gouged in the green. Two long tendrils hung down nearly to his waist. They ended in coppery globes sloshing with some terrible pale wine—and didn't I know that wine? How could I not? I clutched at Cythera Brass.

"Get me out of here," I hissed. "I cannot be here. This is cruel. Protect me. Do your job."

"Get yourself under control," she hissed back.

The King spoke: "No tale can truly begin until its author is shriven. Thus, I offer up my confession on the altar of the telling. Will you hear me? Will you do as I ask?"

I did not, could not, answer him.

"Do it!" the King of Pluto roared. He ran at me suddenly, as a lion after wounded prey, his limbs painted, streaked, splashed with black and white, stark, terrible. Pigment dripped from his biceps, his hipbones; viscous, greasy tears.

"Do it," he cried again, and sank to his ruined knees. His fern-tangled mask implored me with its empty sockets. What did his face look like? I should remember it; should remember him, Max, the man with the lanterns; should recall him as vividly as any child recalls a favourite character from some charming tale told in the wee hours of their youth. But there was nothing. My mind refused. I shook my head, held up my hands, choked back the bile churning through my body. I was all bile; I was nothing else. I did not know what he wanted from me!

"Do it," he whispered. "Forgive me. Forgive me. I killed her. Forgive me."

I stared down at the pitiful wreckage before me. Could it be this easy? As simple, as quotidian, as *quaint* as murder? He loved her, and she didn't love him; or she fired him, and he could not bear the shame; or they quarrelled, and he did not know his strength? I tried to imagine it, his choking the life from Severin, dashing her brains out on the flat rocks where my parents had laid out laundry to dry before they were clawed from the surface of the world. Perhaps . . . perhaps I saw it happen, and that is why my mind refuses to grasp those unspeakable days on the shores of the Qadesh.

"*Never*," I hissed. "I will never forgive you."

But he only laughed: high, screeching, shrill, boiling laughter that steamed away into the nothingness of that horrid vault.

Maximo Varela snapped his fingers. A campfire appeared in the centre of the room, its embers seething. Drums began, and pipes as well—hooting, owlish horns. Eight figures danced around it, naked, painted, masked: a silver man in a beaked mask with deep camera lenses over its eyes like a raccoon's bandit face; a man and a woman painted like flame and forest, her mask a clock face, his the burnt ruin of a diving bell; two men, their clothes all woven of priceless grain, a woman cyclops, her single eye a pit of blackness; an indigo man with the face of a bull and a scar like a star on his cheek; and a chalk-marked child, clutching one of his hands with the other, his mask a simple, harlequin white with two black hearts where the dimples ought to be, his mouth a heart-shaped hole. I clutched my own hand reflexively, instinctively. Beneath my glove I felt the topography of my scars; the ropy flesh; the hidden, seeping wound; the soft, sinuous writhing of *it* . . . Saints in heaven, why now? *It* had not stirred in years.

The child spun among the dancing adults, reaching up to them, to be touched by them, to be held by them, comforted. They ignored him. The women embraced; the camera-eyed man lifted a bowl of milk and poured it over himself, over the others—they lapped it from one another's skin, swallowed it, danced in its fall like pale rain. The cream beaded on their collarbones, their chests, their flat stomachs. The child sucked his fingers sullenly, crouching by the fire. Then, the woman painted like the forest cried out and vanished into the shadows.

No, no, no.

The man with the face of a bull began to choke. He clawed at his throat. His face began to swell; vomit flew from his lips and the vomit was not liquid but a torrent of light, bubbling, foaming, scarlet light. Long nails pricked at the rags of my memory. Hooks, shards. *Ah, but there is nothing there for you, Prospero. My memory is a land where everything dies.* The cyclops lurched unnaturally, his limbs jerking at hideous angles, and a blade appeared, stuck through the centre of his monstrous eye.

The King of Pluto entered the scene. He came leading a woman painted red. No—not painted red, but soaked in blood. She wore the Severin mask, but now that porcelain face was ravaged by arterial spray. Scarlet and black blood splattered over naked breasts, clotting in the hollow at the small of her back, pooled and half-dried in the valleys of her clavicle, turning her belly into a country of crimson. She was not Severin. She was *not*. That body, so blatant and unguarded, was not the body I dreamt of. Still, I looked away as though it were, as though it *could* be. The King passed her from dancer to dancer; she was tender with each of them, even—finally, finally—with the pale child. She hoisted him up, spun him in the air. He laughed, and she threw him to the ground. I lurched forward despite myself, stupidly. *He is safe, of course he is safe. It is only an act, a little mummers' nonsense to pass the time on this godforsaken world; only you needn't be so rough with him—he's only small; he is a good boy.* The boy's laughter opened a door into weeping.

The drums and pipes quickened, and so, too, the sounding sea: harder, urgent, arrhythmic. The silver man, erect as a knife, lifted bloody Severin into his arms and penetrated her, the blood running liquid down her limbs and mixing with the milk—how could there be so much blood? Where was it coming from? I thought my heart would stop. Cythera watched calmly, interested, never turning away for a moment. The music groaned, creaked, sped along its jerking, spasming path toward I knew not what; the silver man fixed his lenses on the wet, red body of his lover as though he could drink her in through those black mouths. She bounced in his arms, screaming now. The others bent in their dancing, hunched over, their arms brushing the ground, fingers contorted into hooks, claws, talons.

The Mad King of Pluto did not dance. He tore a green frond from his mask and cast it into the fire, where it became a great book, spitted on spikes, the flames licking at its spine like a beast roasting. He read from its flaming pages, and his voice echoed against the crash of invisible waves:

"Take her and spare us, take her and spare us, You who moved upon the face of the deep before the dark had any need of God. Take her and spare us. As long ago the daughter of Agamemnon was called upon to present herself to the ships moored at Aulis when the winds would not blow, so the daughter of Percival gave herself so that we might live. Agamemnon's child came in beauty like the star of the morning. Take her and spare us. The lords of men told her she was to be wed to the greatest of them, and readily she prepared herself for a soft bed garlanded with flowers, to be thus brided. Take her and spare us. But the bed was not a bed, nor were the garlands flowers. Take her and spare us. The daughter of Agamemnon lay down upon a stone altar, bound with rough ropes, and there the priest slit her throat to appease the angry moon. Take her and spare us. And from her bleeding body the winds began to sing and fly so that every man's ship found its destiny. Take her and spare us, take her and spare us. Send us home, and send her to hell."

Prospero yanked Severin down from her silver mount by her hair. For a moment, a silken, elastic moment, he danced with her. A formal dance, a waltz, her face tipped up, straining to reach his. He touched her cheek, the cheek of her mask, the cheek beneath. And then he threw her savagely against the green-lit rocks, splashing through the blood and milk and mire. Before my eyes, the remaining dancers shuddered, howled, and transformed into four red tigers and a cub, maskless and striped: *real* tigers, starving tigers.

In the pit of drums and milk they bent their heads and ate her. I saw her bones snap, I saw the marrow within, I saw her rictus of anguish, I saw the King of Pluto drink her blood, and I saw that woman die with the face of Severin fixed to her skull.

But past the moment of her red death I remember nothing, for it was then that I lost consciousness.

25 February, 1962. I know not what hour.

I have seen her. I have seen her here on Pluto, in this damned city of Prospero's, of Varela's, alive, whole, laughing.

She came to me in the ochre bedchamber—how I got there and who brought me, I cannot say. I woke in the night, flushed, trembling, the memory of that poor girl's clavicle snapping under a tiger's mouth washing my brain in blood. I clamped my hand over my mouth to keep either shouts or sickness inside, and I still could not say which would have won out. But at that instant, the pale door of my room opened and someone stole in, sneaking— though not very well—through the shadows. Her smell filled the room, her sweat, her hair oil, her breath. Severin, Severin, all the pieces of her that my mendicant memory could scrape together. She crawled in beside me, her skin cold, beyond cold, glowing blue and bloodless. She wore no mask in the dark. Her black hair, a little mussed and frizzy, framed her heart-shaped face, that face bending down over me as it did on the first moment of the miserable life I now lead.

"Move over, silly," she whispered. "I'm freezing."

And then I was holding her in my arms. She was naked. Her long, space-stretched bones, her smallish breasts pressed against my chest, her breath light against my throat. A dream, yes; it must be a dream. Impossible to conceive of anything but dreaming. But she had such weight. Such aliveness.

"Didya miss me?"

Her voice was the voice from the cinema, from the phonograph—crackling, even, as a phonograph crackles. Static poured out of her mouth.

"All I've done my whole life is miss you," I answered. I am what I am, and what I am is an answer. I must tell the truth. I can commit every sin but false witness.

"Well, isn't that nice?" She laughed, and her laugh skipped like a needle over a scratch. I stroked her hair—I could feel it, each strand, beneath my fingers.

"What happened to you? Just tell me, tell me so I can stop wondering."

"I'm right here, sweetheart. That's all that matters. I'm here."

"It's not all that matters. Everything matters. You disappeared right in front of me . . ."

Severin raised her perfect black eyebrow. "Did I? What a funny thing for a girl to do." She punched my arm playfully. "And you said you didn't remember anything."

I didn't remember. I *didn't*—until that moment, with her frozen lips nearly touching mine—remember the morning light of Venus and the jungle and the molten, brilliant water shining around her, and then through her, and then through nothing but an empty strand following down to the surf.

She took my face in her hands. "Hey now. Rest easy. It's okay now. It's fine now. I'm okay. You don't have to be so sore about it. You're a good boy. You always were a good boy. Everybody just loved you, right from the start. Like a little puppy." She looked so serious and sad, her great deep eyes full of shadows. "Just close your eyes, Anchises. Close your eyes and listen to what I say. Everybody's alive. Everybody's alive and happy and I got the shot I wanted. Just the perfect shot. It'll be shown in film school for a million years, it's *that* good. *I'm* that good, and so are you. So are all of us. There is such a thing as grace. I'm supposed to tell you that. There is such a thing as grace. Everybody's alive. Mariana and Horace and Arlo and Erasmo and Max and Aylin and you and me. What I say three times is true."

Severin moved her cold hands over my body, in the secret world of the ochre bed sheets and the unutterably Plutonian night. She stroked me, clutched me, her gestures needful and knowing. Her breath quickened. It smelled of the cacao-ferns of my village. Of Adonis.

"It's not so bad, where I am," she whispered, guiding me into her, into the ice palace of her body. "You can see so far from here. So far. I love you, Anchises. I love you. You found me, and I love you. I couldn't stay dead with an audience like you waiting for me. Clap for me, darling; clap like the curtain's coming down. Harder, harder, harder."

As I broke inside her, Severin threw back her head, laughed, and came down on my throat like a guillotine. Her small teeth pierced my skin and she drank as deeply of my body as I ever did of her image.

I woke alone. But I can still smell her on my hands.

26 February, 1962. Seven in the evening. Setebos Hall.

"Is that your answer, then?" Cythera sighed beside me, holding a cup of beef broth with more irritation than I have seen from women holding wet laundry. "Murder? Varela was what . . . a madman? Well, he's clearly that. But was he always? After all, no one accused him back then, and why wouldn't they have pinned it to his chest? How much easier for everyone if it was a massacre. Disappearances invite a lot more questions than massacres."

"He confessed it!" I coughed and sank further into my sickbed, into my dank cavern of sweat-stiff blankets. I could hardly lift my head. I put a hand to my throat: bandaged neatly. *But there had been a wound.* Who had nursed me? My head pounded meatily. I could taste nothing but stale infanta and bile in my mouth.

"Come now," she said, and I do believe there was a softening in her voice, a coaxing. I had studied the haruspicy of her tones for so long I could scry the tiniest alteration. "Be the detective we went all the way to Uranus for. With enough of those damned flowers in my system, I'd confess to assassinating Thomas À Becket with a ray gun. He'll come and see you soon. Maybe he'll gloat over getting you to faint like a maiden on her wedding night, maybe he'll blubber all over you again; but either way, you need to pull yourself together and act like you've got a job to do."

"So do you," I spat. "You're meant to protect me from assaults like that, from . . . from *depredations.* And that girl! God, the dancing girl! He killed *her,* no matter what he did or didn't do on Venus . . ."

"Did he, though? I was there. I saw what you saw. I saw more, since I didn't shriek and collapse like a startled grandmother. And I listened, it would seem, somewhat better. He told us the story of Iphigenia. But Iphigenia doesn't die in the end, you know. She's replaced with a deer at the last moment and spirited away to a temple on the other side of the world. She finds steady work and lives quietly until the day her brother and his comrade turn up, trussed and shaved for sacrifice, on the steps of the house of those distant, foreign gods—and there she is, like nothing ever happened, gathering bowls to catch their blood. You really ought to read more. People always lie, Anchises. They lie like they eat, without manners, without restraint. They love lying."

"Even you?"

"Oh, especially me. Good Lord, I work in the movie industry. Given that you'll never hear the truth out of anyone's mouth, you must listen to the lies—the specific lies they choose to tell. Prospero—Maximo—could have ginned up his little panto-mime around any story he liked. The Judgment of Paris, that has a good Venus bit. Pentheus and the Bacchae, Inanna and Ereshki-gal, anything. But he chose one where the girl only *looks* dead. Where there's a trick. Just when it looks like she'll be sawn in half and there's no helping her, the false bottom gives way on the black box and she goes somewhere else, somewhere safe."

"You're better at this than I am." I squeezed my eyes against a splitting headache. I hadn't had a drink since planetfall, nor anything to eat but infanta.

"Very true."

"Why didn't they just hire *you*?"

Cythera Brass pulled back my linens with one vicious stroke. "Because I wasn't *there*, you blubbering idiot. Now be a god-damned detective and earn your keep for once."

But for all the hardness and contempt collecting like spittle in the corners of her mouth, Cythera helped me up and bathed me in cold Plutonian water. She had already laid out a suit—and the right suit, at that. I would have worn something too formal. I would have looked like I was waiting for him. I have never been a master of the secret code of men's suits; only adept enough to know that the jacket is always saying something, the shoes and trousers always whispering, but not enough to know exactly what they're on about. Cythera had chosen a soft dawn-grey number with a plum-coloured tie—which she tied loosely, messily, an artlessness full of art. She put pomade in my hair and shaved my chin—my hands shook too much to manage it myself. Not too close a shave, but not too bad, either. She was brusque in her ministrations, but I could see her relax—this was something she knew how to do, and there is relief in doing what you're good at. Had she been married once? I suddenly wondered. I watched the business work on her like laudanum. Her face gentled when she smoothed out my suit lapels; her shoulders straightened when she touched the long razor. Perhaps she'd done this sort of thing for her boss back on Uranus, picking out shoes that communicated Melancholia's stake in the fixed game of cards that people like her are always playing. When Cythera finished, I looked like a man with better things to do than whatever he was doing at the moment; a man who'd made just a little time for you, sir, but don't push it.

And she timed it beautifully, fastening my mask in place and excusing herself to rinse the shaving cup just as Prospero, King of Pluto—or Maximo Varela, lighting master for Severin Unck—came into my ochre bedchamber and sank down beside me with the familiarity of a brother. He wore a simple *moretta* mask, black and dappled with silver stars. My *Totentanz* mask smelled of sandalwood, of the creams and oils of Cythera Brass.

Though she had left the room, there can be no question that she heard everything—of course she did.

"Anchises, my boy, how are you; are you well? Can I have

anything brought up? You are fed, you are watered? You fainted dead away—I should have known it would be too much for you. Insensitive, insensitive, crass!" He struck himself in the temple with a fist and his mask skewed, showing a sliver of his real face, a face I still could not begin to reconstruct in my mind.

"I am fine. Yes, fine, really—please don't trouble yourself. Only—what was that all about?" *Be a detective*, I thought. *Questions. It's always about the questions. Seeking the right one like an optometrist's lenses. Can you see clearly now? And now? And now?* "What I mean is, no one really turned into a tiger and ate Severin Unck, did they? Art has its limits."

"You are the only one who can understand me, Anchises," came his reply. He scratched his cheek beneath his starry mask. "You were there—you saw everything. You know my heart. Her heart. I used to take you walking along the beach in the mornings, do you remember? Every morning from the first day we met you. I recited everything I could think of, just so you could hear language again and remember how to make it yourself. Homer, Marlowe, Coleridge, Chaucer, a little Poe, a little Grimm. I managed most of *The Tempest* the day before she . . . the day before. I was proud of that. I gave you a little chocolate from craft services after every walk, so you'd associate words and sweetness. Didn't work, but it seemed important. Tell me you remember. Tell me it mattered."

I considered it. I considered telling him, *Of course. Of course I remember: "In Xanadu did Kubla Khan his stately pleasure dome decree." Yes, of course. Your voice brought me back to the country of human speech on a chariot drawn by Chaucer and Shakespeare. You saved me. Quoth Kubla Khan: Nevermore.* It would have been kind, and he looked more strung out than me on my worst day. And in camaraderie he might have told me more than he would otherwise. But I could not do it. *He killed her. This is her killer.* I felt his guilt sliding off of him like oil.

I felt that old compulsion to speak the truth surge up within me—so inconvenient, so detrimental to my vocation. "I don't remember any of it, Maximo." He flinched at the sound of his real name. "I have no memory before she grabbed me in Adonis, and after that . . . just pieces. Moments. Nothing more. My 'memory'—in the sense of a series of events that occur in order, in which there is some respect paid to cause and effect, proceeding more or less in real time—that doesn't start 'til Mars. Erasmo's house on Mount Penglai. Everything before that, the hospital on Luna, the hacienda on Mercury is . . . blurred. Scene Missing. I remember Severin's face. Her voice. I remember her laughing. I remember Mariana screaming. I remember the smell of the cacao and the red sea. Why don't you tell me what happened? That's what I'm here for."

Varela studied my face in disbelief. Our masks faced each other, revealing nothing. Clever, that. Perhaps Pluto had hit upon something essential, necessary. Now that I had one, I certainly did not want to take it off, here or anywhere.

Finally, he sighed. "I don't deal in unvarnished truths. It's the varnish that counts. That makes it true. Give me enough light and I can do anything. Make you believe anything. Ghosts, fairies, vampires: Just tell me what you want and I can make it real. Just tell me what you want and I'll make it so it happened."

He gripped my hand horribly. His nails were long. "You have no idea what I can do. I made you believe in this place. In death and tigers. I have made a *planet* believe I am their King. Look around: This is the island of the lotus-eaters, and I am the hungriest of all."

"What about the dead girl? Was there a real girl dying under all those tigers?"

The tiniest sliver of mirth crept into Varela's voice. "A magician cannot share all his tricks."

He leapt up, swung round one of the thick pillars of the bed, and slapped the wall. The room seemed to quiver with the force of his mood.

"Something has to be real, you know. Something real has to anchor the magic. Death is the realest thing there is. Death holds the rest together. You'll believe everything else if you believe in the death. Once someone *exsanguinates* in front of you, well, anything can happen. You're on the edge of your seat. The tension, the tension just *rears* up. I'm aces at deaths. Always have been." Varela struck the door with the flat of his palm and it cracked, sending up puffs of dust. "Do you know how I met Severin? I was part of her mother's circus. Lumen Molnar, I mean, the last mother. I was the magician. Prestidigitation. Knife acts, girls cut in half, disappearances. I loved my work. I went to Saturn with Lumen, me and the whole troupe—even the monkeys. And, Christ, they loved us on Saturn. We lit up every halfpenny theatre in Enuma Elish—they didn't even care what the act was, they were just so hungry for a show; so hungry. You know, a person will give up food for a good show. Push comes to shove, they'll give up their *last* food. They'll do it and they'll think they got a good bargain. That hunger goes deeper and bitterer than the need for bread. And we came sailing in just dripping with gravy. They slurped us up. Licked their fingers dry and banged the table for more." He dragged down one of the orange tapestries that covered the walls. It ripped easily, like crepe paper, and floated down to the floor. "Half the time you could see the rabbit in my trousers, but it never mattered. I've had more Saturnine girls than you've had cups of tea, boy, with more lined up round the block that I was too tired to see to. Elish would have given Severin the key to the city if they'd had one. Anything she wanted—any access, any transport, anything. Because she brought the circus, and it was better than gold. Boredom will murder you dead on the outer worlds.

"I wasn't anything until Saturn. A purveyor of cheap tricks. But I learned. I learned the lantern trade. A trick of the light, boy, just a trick of the light. Everything in creation is just a trick of the light—the only difference between heaven and hell is who's running those lights, who's got the switch, who knows the cues." Varela turned and stomped on the hearth, the night table, the lovely little secretary on which I'd written my previous entries. They crumpled like drywall and ash, no more mahogany and metal and lacquer than my own flesh. "A couple of times Severin got up there with me, played my girl in the box. She looked up at me with trust as complete as a promise. You can't even imagine. You think she's yours because she let you play the urchin in some miserable B-plot scene, but she isn't yours—you never even *knew* her; she's just a face to you. I saw that face under my hands in a box like a coffin; I saw her understand totally that I would never hurt her, that I would always protect her. And I saw that face go under a diving bell with that same expression, not a twitch of the mouth or slant of the eye different. But what she trusted wasn't me, wasn't Erasmo, wasn't Amandine or Mariana or any of us who had kept her whole on every planet we visited. No, she trusted . . . Venus. The Qadesh. Her own fucking specialness. And look what happened."

I had drawn myself up into a corner of the room near the curtained bathroom door that concealed Cythera. I could not see how to get out, past his rampage, to anywhere safer. I summoned up a whisper: "*What* happened? What *did* happen?"

"Nothing! Nothing! She was nothing, and nothing happened. Nothing is happening. Nothing is all that ever happens. You look at this place and see a palace: elephants; griffins; a Ferris wheel; lights, lights, everywhere. You look at a masked girl screaming and think she's dead. I tell you this is the island of the lotus-eaters, and it never occurs to you to stop eating the lotus." Varela overturned a plate of infanta flowers, their petals already curling brown. "You see everything in such plain terms. You and her and nothing else. I'm an extra in your story. Well, you're an extra in mine, boy. A punter picking cards out of the rigged deck I offer. The thing about a magic trick is that you have to play fair. You show the audience everything you're going to do before you do it. You tell them to their faces that you're going to lie to them. You show them the tools—see how they shine! You show them the girl—see how innocent and lovely she looks in her spangled costume! You show them the knives. You say: I am going to cut her in half and you are going to applaud. And then you keep your promise. If you're any good, the shock is worse because they knew it was coming, but no one ever *believes* a man on a stage."

Varela turned and punched through the polished ebony wall—it crackled away beneath his fist like the sugared crust on a French custard.

"Yet you believe *her.* Her! You look at her pretty little face on the screen emoting and stuttering and blushing and contemplating her rich girl's life, and you think there wasn't a script out of frame at her feet, rewritten to an inch of its life, every rewrite thatched in on coloured papers to keep it straight. Oh, are we on the red pages today, where Severin is a rebel and a champion of truth? Or blue, where she cries about her mothers for thirty minutes? Or green, where the lady who's never wanted for a thing in her life whines about how much someone else has to pay for her to speak on camera? It was a rainbow by the end, every movie she ever made. And you think it's real, that Venus was any different. That the heart of that girl wasn't always an empty goddamned soundstage, and her soul wasn't a hack-job screenplay with half the pages torn out and floating down the length of the solar system. What happened to her? The same thing that happens to any bad script: Too many people get their hands on it, trying to fix it, 'til it turns into nothing—nothing; not a trick, not a twist ending, just a girl bleeding out in a box. There's no artistry to that. You can't cram artistry into it, no matter how hard you try. She's just a dead girl."

"That's not an answer. Did you kill her? Tell me!"

He calmed himself, assessing the wreckage of the room, the torn cardboard and shattered coloured lights and crepe tapestries. I knew he was right, that he was showing me his trick, but the infanta had so addled my senses that even amid the trash heap of the ochre bedroom, everything I saw was still limned with light, with richness, an afterimage of opulence, ghosts in the architecture.

"Listen, boy—and look! Behold my beautiful assistant strapped to the wheel! Vulnerable, tender, entirely within my power! See how the light catches her jewelled bodice like a burst of starlight. We landed on Venus with no complications. Transport from the International Station to Adonis took two weeks. Before your very eyes, I shall drive five knives into her unblemished body! You see the knives are sharp; I do not deceive you—I've cut my own finger with their points: one, two, three, four, five!

"We arrived on site and set up camp. We found you on the first day of scouting. I had my light meters and she had George, but she hadn't intended to shoot anything that day. You were extremely anaemic and dehydrated. We fed you and washed you and Severin took charge of you like a pet. Now the wheel starts to spin! Her sequins dazzle! Her cries arouse! The first knife— ah, direct hit in the left shoulder! See how she bleeds!

"The angels first appeared that night. Seraphim, you understand? Not frilly angels with blousy pink wings and haloes like wedding rings. These ones had wheels full of eyes and voices like the noise of the deep. We poor fools! We thought it was equipment, feedback. All that expensive sound shit nobody needs but Severin just *insisted* on. Mariana was the only one who could make those machines heel, but even she was new to it; she'd never gotten to work with anything that high-end before. We thought the whining, the *thrumming*, that horrible, horrible vibrating, was Mariana's problem. Ignore it, ignore it, just go to sleep." He covered his face with his hands for a moment, but snapped up again, his mask barely concealing the livid excitement in his quivering body. "Observe the flight path of the second knife: I've sunk it in the right shoulder, perfectly parallel to the first—what artistry! What skill!

"But the angels came again in the morning. It wasn't feedback. The voices of seraphim are the colour of need. When their words entered me, I felt a cancer in my heart, and, at the same time, the blossoming of my body into beauty. Thrumming. Voices. Quiet at first, like when you're in a room full of people and everyone is talking constantly but you can't make out the words, just an ocean of sound. A tide, sometimes louder, sometimes softer. The third knife, ladies and gentleman, a blow to the left hip! Oh, that one hurt her, you can tell! Blood running down the inside of her beautiful thigh. See it drip onto the stage.

"On the fourth day, they woke us up in the middle of the night. 2:14 a.m., by my watch. Mariana singing. Singing, screaming. Screaming, singing. She was so beautiful; the look on her face when she heard the angels singing in her voice. How I loved her! It wouldn't stop. No one could sleep. But I loved it. I ran through the ocean surf trying to get closer—if I could only get closer! If I could get closer, I could see their faces, their eyes and their wheels. You can hear it on some of the footage, whispering in the trees. That's all an Edison mic can hear of God. They wanted us to leave, but Severin wouldn't listen. I loved her, too, for that. Something she couldn't explain was happening right in front of her. Something real. Something outside herself. I don't have a drug in my cabinet to compete with that. But she and I were the only ones talking about it. And she was convinced, *convinced* it was all due to the callowhales somehow, because she couldn't see the seraphim like I could. She couldn't understand their songs, their songs like rainbows and arrows and dying. She would just stare out to sea at those fish, those big, stupid islands like desiccated brains floating in blood. She stared. Just stared.

Like she had been paused. Ah-ha! The fourth knife, as true as the rest, into the right hip like butter, my friends! Go on, gasp! Clutch your pearls! See the rictus of pain on her face—as real as you and I! Doesn't she wear her blood pretty—like jewellery, those trickles, like strands of rubies. Nothing finer!

"We fought, the night before she and Erasmo went out on their own. Mariana was hurt by then, and I wanted to call White Peony Station for transport. I wanted to take care of my Mari. But, even more, I wanted them all to go, just *go*, so I could have the voices to myself. So I could finally *listen*, really *hear* them, in the quiet. None of them could shut up. They couldn't *open* up to the sound. The voices were deafening, by then—you just couldn't *think*, couldn't *move*. Their verbs tasted like life. The seraphim were touching us, touching me. They talked all the time, like carnival barkers advertising the known universe. Severin and I fought often—we'd been lovers, on Saturn, and you'll treat someone you've fucked far worse than someone you haven't. She screeched at me: *I have to know, I have to know. Take Mari and go if you want; I don't need you.* I hit her—she hit me back. It went like that with us, sometimes. But I pushed her. I pushed her and she fell.

You could never understand. Leave me alone with the wheels and the eyes and the heavens and your pitiful questions. Just keep your eye on the fifth knife—piercing the heart, as true and sharp as love. Stop the wheel, if you please. Get her down, now—mind the sequins. A star of knives—perfect, if I do say so myself. Now, a wave of my hand, of my wand, of the curtain of light—and abracadabra! She's perfectly well! Turn around and show the audience, honey; show them you don't have a scratch. She's fine. She's fine. See? She's fine."

Then the Mad King of Pluto bent his face to the ruined floor of his broken house and wept as though he would never again see the sun.

"Calliope the Carefree Callowhale" PSA

PROPERTY OF THE BBC LUNA, RKO, AND
CAPRICORN STUDIOS
FIRST AIRDATE: 28 FEBRUARY, 1930
VOICE-OVER: VIOLET EL-HASHEM AND ALAIN MBENGUE
[CALLIOPE THE CAREFREE CALLOWHALE dances on-
screen. She is a joyful, animated character, all
cheerful lines and unthreatening colours: a stylized whale, halfway between orca and beluga with
a little happy humpback thrown in. Her palette is
turquoise, azure, and navy blue, with big cerulean eyes framed by long lashes and purple eye
shadow. The BBC shelled out heavily to Edison
Corp. for the colour animation.

CALLIOPE bounces on her clownish tail in a
field of sunflowers and magenta begonias. A fountain of healthy, nourishing callowmilk spurts
continually from her blowhole.]

CALLIOPE

HI, KIDS! I'm Calliope the Carefree Callowhale!
I'm here to remind all you growing boys and
girls to DRINK YOUR MILK!

[MARVIN THE MONGOOSE (courtesy Capricorn Studios) marches in from the left-hand side of the frame. He wears a jaunty cap.]

CALLIOPE

Hello, Marvin! What have you been up to?

MARVIN

Nothing much, Callie! Only defeating the dastardly Crikey the Cobra with my lightning-quick fists! And I couldn't have done it without a tall glass of callowmilk for breakfast! It's got everything I need to keep me strong!

CALLIOPE

Righty-ho! Now, I've heard that some parents won't let their kids have callowmilk. They think I'm full of toxins and mutated protein strands. That hurts my feelings! [Giant tears with rainbows reflecting in their surfaces fall from her eyes.] Those meanie mumsies say I make babies come out all funny-looking! But I'm a good whale. I just want everyone to be happy and healthy! [She continues to weep. The sunflowers and begonias wilt.]

MARVIN

But Calliope, if kids don't drink their callowmilk, how will they ever have amazing adventures in space, like me?

CALLIOPE

That's just it, Marvin! They'll miss out on all

the fun! I hate seeing children not having fun with their friends, don't you?

MARVIN

Sure do!

CALLIOPE

That's why I'm asking all of you to join my club, Calliope's Kids! Just get your mum and dad to send the BBC a self-addressed stamped envelope and proof of a year's worth of callowmilk purchases and, and I'll send you a badge, colouring book, super-secret Venusian decoder ring, and this spiffy hat that will let everyone know that YOU'RE one of Calliope's Kids, my very special friends! [The flowers spring back to life. Calliope does a somersault in the air and lands in a blue ocean. Marvin salutes her from a raft. He is wearing a pirate hat, an eye patch, and a Calliope's Kids badge.]

MARVIN

And if your parents are fans of *How Many Miles to Babylon?*, just tell them to include a letter telling us their favourite character and we'll throw in a neato plush callowhale and a signed photo of the cast!

CALLIOPE

Golly! I can't think of a reason *not* to be my friend! And friends look after each other, right, Marvin?

MARVIN

Right! So let's go get that wicked old Cobra King together!

CALLIOPE

You got it! [She somersaults over MARVIN'S raft, catching the sunlight in her fins. Cue theme music, freeze frame, and fade out.]

PART THREE

THE GREEN PAGES

You have often
Begun to tell me what I am, but stopp'd
And left me to a bootless inquisition,
Concluding 'Stay: not yet.'

—Miranda from *The Tempest*, William Shakespeare

A director only makes one film in his life. Then he breaks it up and makes it again.

—Jean Renoir

The Radiant Car Thy Sparrows Drew
(Oxblood Films, dir. Severin Unck)

SC3 EXT. ADONIS, VILLAGE GREEN—DAY 13 TWILIGHT
POST-PLANETFALL 23:24 [30 NOVEMBER, 1944]

[EXT. Former site of the village of Adonis, on the shores of the Sea of Qadesh. Night. The Divers Memorial is a backlit monstrosity, bulbous and black. Wind buffets the sound and lighting equipment; lanterns swing wild, illuminating splatters of congealed white fluid drenching the site. In twenty-eight months no one has cleared the damage or removed the debris. Beams of illumination land on a series of objects, as briefly as a kiss, then leave them in darkness again: A door with an absurd number of locks—more than anyone could need—stove in. The crumpled, netted face of a diving bell. The mangled head of a carousel horse. A swath of white fabric wadded up like scrap paper—a parachute, perhaps? Tarpaulin? Broken amphorae. Pieces of roof. Broken glass. The child's slack, catatonic face. The faces of SANTIAGO ZHANG and HORACE ST. JOHN, struggling with cables and the boom mic, which dips into frame with the gusts of wind. MARIANA ALFRIC, her at-waist sound rig turning smoothly, though she has turned her back on the scene. She holds her hands over her face. Her nails are bitten raw. The mic records only wind, rendering SEVERIN'S beloved talking picture a silent film.

SEVERIN is grabbing the child's hand urgently. He begins to scream, soundlessly, held brutally still in his steps by ERASMO and MAXIMO VARELA, whose muscles bulge with what appears to be a colossal effort—keeping this single, tiny, bird-boned child from his circuit. The boy clutches his hand to his thin chest as though it is a precious possession. His only possession. The boy's eyes are as wide as an electroshock patient's, pupils blown, his whole body rigid, erect. He moves his head back and forth: *no, no, no.* It is hard to tell—the film is damaged, the light levels destroyed, patches of overexposure blossom over the footage like splashes of milk—but the boy is mouthing a word that looks like *please.* The storm eats up his voice, if he has one.

SEVERIN'S jagged hair, and occasionally her chin, swing in and out of frame as she struggles with him. She turns over the boy's hand, roughly, to show the camera what she has found there: tiny fronds growing from his skin, tendrils like ferns, seeking, wavering, wet with milk. The film jumps and shudders; the child's hand vibrates, faster, faster. **FILM DAMAGED FOOTAGE OVEREXPOSED SKIP AFFECTED AREA SKIPPING SKIPPING SKIPPING**]

Production Meeting,
~~The Deep Blue Devil~~
~~The Man in the Malachite Mask~~
Doctor Callow's Dream
(Tranquillity Studios, 1960, dir. Percival Unck)

Audio Recorded for Reference by Vincenza Mako

PERCIVAL UNCK: No, no, you're wrong, Vince. It's shit. It doesn't sit right. He's too unpleasant, too weak. He's not likeable. And that curse isn't adding anything but a stick up his arse. It just *sags*. Gothic stories will sprawl if you let them, like spilled wine. No writer should go anywhere near the Island of the Lotus-Eaters—you get stuck there. If Odysseus couldn't get quit of that place, our boy has no hope. It's got all the right pieces, but the end comes in the middle of the blasted thing. I hate it. I want to get out of my own movie. That can't be good.

   And, I just . . . I just can't do it. I can't give her an ice dragon and a vampire and smack her bottom and tell her to go play. I need something real to hold on to. She's gone. If it were enough to imagine her killed by a mad magician on the American frontier, I could have done that in my head and not bothered with a script. No. No. It can't be my story. It can't be ours.

MAKO: But it can't be hers, either. The thing about a mysterious disappearance is that it's mysterious. There's no answer that will be satisfying enough for the masses. There's no documentary to be made, no scandal to be exposed.

UNCK: I don't care. I made *The Abduction of Proserpine* already.

I'm done with that. Christ, I was a young man when *Proserpine* wrapped. You can't use the language of your youth to talk about your daughter. It doesn't work. Maybe we should go back to noir. Or something else. Or fucking *quit*. It's never taken us this long, Vince. We're the king and queen of the quick turnaround. Why can't I tell a simple story? She was born, she lived, she wanted things, she died. Yes, she died. I'm willing to admit that as a possibility. I can stage her death if that's the right ending. I can do anything for the right ending. I staged her beginning, so I can place the marks for her end.

[long pause]

MAKO: Then let it be what it always was. What it must be. A child's story. Not hers. Not ours. But his. Something terrible happened to a little boy in a beautiful place and it kept happening until a woman came from the sky to save him. Came sailing down like Isis with her arms full of roses. It's a fairy tale. A children's story. Not a funny or silly one, but one with blood and death and horror, because that's fairy tales, too. A kid got swallowed by a whale. A little Pinocchio. A little Caliban. It's all there.

And, you know, in a fairy tale, the maidens are never dead—not really. They're just sleeping.

~~The Deep Blue Devil~~
~~The Man in the Malachite Mask~~
Doctor Callow's Dream:
The Land of Milk and Desire

Once upon a time, not so long ago at all, there lived a boy whose wishes never came true. The boy was born in the Land of Milk and Desire and had never known any other country. The Land of Milk and Desire had made him into himself, and he loved it the way some children love a velvet toy with a worn-out tail.

In the Land of Milk and Desire, everything is always wet. Everywhere you might want to step has, at the least, a river running through it; or a rich, golden-blue swamp; or a sweet-green suckling bog; or a bright, rosy lake; or a deep, quiet pond; or a fragrant, iridescent bayou; or one of the many seas, which are all as red as longing. The boy grew up in a little village on the shore of one of these seas: the very biggest one, the Qadesh. He played on the beach, collecting whelks (which are not really whelks, but rather rough, smoky crystals with frilly, fragile, florescent creatures living inside) and driftwood (which is not really driftwood, but the petrified bones of wily, whopping, woolly beasts that once roamed the Land of Milk and Desire before time woke up with a sore head and started ordering everyone about) and listening to the strange yelping songs of the seals (which are not really seals, but two-horned candy-striped aquatic ungulates with whiskers as long as tusks and as fuzzy as your father's moustache). And he stared out to sea, past headlands cluttered with thick, dripping jungle that smelled like salt and cinnamon and cocoa, past the lights of the boats in the harbour, past the pink breakers and the heavy mist, and out to the long, dark shapes that floated in the deeps of the Qadesh like islands, like places you could get to and climb, explore, lie down on, and dream up at the many, many stars.

But they were not really islands, and no child born in the Land of Milk and Desire could remember a time when he or she thought they were. For in the sea of Qadesh lived the callowhales, as mysterious as they were magical. The callowhales never said a word nor came out of the water, did not sing like the seals which were not really seals, nor leave their shells behind like the whelks which were not really whelks, nor behave carelessly with their bones like the driftwood that was not really driftwood. And from the time he was so small that he did not know what a lie was, the boy had one secret, silent, singular wish—a wish so secret he never once said it out loud: to see the face of a callowhale.

Now, for a long while, the boy did not know that he had the gift of wishes that never came true. He thought himself no different than any other boy or girl in Adonis. Adonis was the name of the village he had lived in since the beginning of the world, which, in his case, was July the third, when his mother gave birth to him in a cacao-hut with three rooms, while her husband and her midwife held her hands and told her she was doing *very* well indeed. She named him Anchises, who was the lover of Venus in a very old story.

Anchises was born in the morning, which in the Land of Milk and Desire is the same thing as saying he was born in the springtime, for on that wonderful planet, a day is as long as a year. The world takes as long to move on its murky-vivid golden path round the sun as the whole of the Land of Milk and Desire takes to turn itself around, though Venus manages both of these in two-thirds of the time that Earth takes, the old dawdler. This means that the morning lasts as long as springtime and it is morning for ages and ages; until the bright, glassy, humid summer brings the afternoon; which stretches on and on into the crisp, windy autumnal twilight that seems as though it will never end—until winter brings a night as long and dark as memory.

July the third was a kind year. There was plenty of rain in the morning, and in the afternoon the cacao (which is not really cacao, but a dark, dusty, dizzyingly tall tree that gives fruits which are not really dates and nuts which are not really cashews) produced thickly, the cows (which are not really cows, but four-hearted fern-eating fire-red brutes that give good meat and have reasonably even tempers) chewed cud and grew fat, and the divers brought back many groaning amphorae of milk from the callow-hales. In the pale rosy melancholy fall of evening the children gathered so many cacao-nuts and cassowary eggs (which are not really cassowaries, but grumpy, green-blue, gobbling flightless lizard-birds with black marks on their breasts like human hands) that a Nutcake Festival was declared and held every autumn twilight thereafter. Even the interminable winter night was not so cold that anything froze, but not so warm that the plants that needed cold to thrive could not get their healthful midnight sleep.

The Nutcake Festival was the boy's favourite thing in the world—after his parents, callowhales, and chasing cassowaries until they squawked indignantly and told him he was *wicked, wicked!* in Mandarin, a language the birds had learned like parrots when the first humans arrived in the Land of Milk and Desire, on account of those first humans being Chinese. (The creatures have stubbornly refused to learn any of the other languages humans enjoy speaking, such as English and Turkish, Anchises's personal tongues, but at least it all had the enviable result that little children spoke passable Mandarin, albeit with a cassowary's clipped accent.)

At the conclusion of the Nutcake Festival of Adonis, each of the villagers chose their own glittery, painted egg and a large brown cacao-nut, still in its shell, from a great copper basket at the centre of town. Now, one of the nuts was not really a nut, but an empty shell containing a pretty little ring the same weight as a nut. Whoever drew this shell got to make a wish that was sure to come true, and also got to take home a sweetloaf and a barrel of black beer. The year Anchises was six, he chose the shell with the ring in it, and, holding up the copper ring (too big for even his fattest finger) for all to see, he quite solemnly wished that his parents should love him forever and live forever, too—which is really two wishes, but the villagers let it pass, because that is a very endearing thing to ask.

Anchises did not know yet that his wishes could not come true, that any wish he spoke out loud would echo among the stars and find no home there. And since forever is a long, long time, he did not discover this curse until long after that Nutcake Festival when the salt-sweet sea wind was so full of seal song and good promises.

And in the meantime, he kept on wishing.

The next thing that Anchises wished for was to be just like all the other children in the Land of Milk and Desire. Many children wish for something like that—not to stand out or be strange among others, lest one be left alone and abandoned when everyone else has gone home to rosy windows, to full arms and plates. Anchises wished this because other boys in his class liked to make fun of him for being dark skinned and for drawing callowhales in the margins of his books, their delicate fronds flowing all around the paragraphs in precise, complicated patterns like small labyrinths, the swollen gas bladders that bore the all-important callowmilk hanging off the corners of his lessons on the settlement of the Land of Milk and Desire by the Four Founding Nations. But as soon as the wish left Anchises's mouth, it began the work of not coming true.

He grew tall first of all the boys in his class, sitting in his desk uncomfortably like a carrot ripened too soon. And he began to grow very beautiful, with high, broad cheekbones and brooding, dark eyes, with shining hair that fell just so, no matter how hard he tried to leave it messy and uncombed. Soon the parents of the other children began to talk of him leaving the Land of Milk and Desire for some other, more civilized, more cosmopolitan, less out-of-the-way place, such as the Country of Seeing and Being Seen or the Land of Wild Rancheros, or even Home (which was not really the home of anyone Anchises knew—in fact, most of the bakers and divers and packers and dairymen he said hello to every day had never seen the place they called Home, which was really the fertile, faraway, foreign world where their grandparents and great-grandparents had been born). Surely a boy with his face could become famous if only he were living someplace where folk appreciated more refined things than milk and desire. But Anchises wished to stay in Adonis by the shores of the Qadesh forever, to be a diver like his mother and father, and to one day bring children of his own to the Nutcake Festival.

Whether he wished for big things or little things, Anchises was thwarted. When he wished for a diver's bell of his very own for Christmas, he received a bicycle with a horn and a case of terrible eczema that meant he could not even put his poor, peeling toe in the red Qadesh for the rest of the night. When a girl in his class, who wore a black ponytail and loved cassowaries so much she could hardly bring herself to speak English at all, grew sick with scarlet fever (which is not really scarlet fever, but a horrible, heedless, haemorrhagic virus that occasionally strikes delicate children in the Land of Milk and Desire), Anchises wished fervently that she should get well. He loved her a little for the softness of her voice and the thickness of her ponytail, but the girl died quickly in a lonely ward in White Peony Station, the great electric city where all the doctors lived. Anchises wept on his cacao-bark bed for days upon days, wishing to the red rafters that he could die with his friend and live in heaven with her and a hundred cassowaries and a hundred callowhales all singing together in perfect Mandarin.

But he did not die.

Anchises had begun to have suspicions. He did not speak of them, lest others think him mad. He drew his callowhale pictures and thought hard while he drew them. This is what Anchises drew when he made a picture of a callowhale:

As far as beginner naturalist's drawings go, it was not bad. It was basically accurate. Anchises always drew the top half of a whale the same way, the way he had seen them all his life. But he had no idea what the bottom half of a callowhale looked like. He had never been allowed to go diving with his mother or his father, no matter how hard he had wished it. And besides, even divers didn't really know what a callowhale looked like. They were too big to see all at once. It would be like trying to guess what South America looked like when you have only seen one cafe in Buenos Aires. But Anchises guessed anyway. He tried many times to make one that seemed *right* to him, but none of them really did. They looked like a blimp wearing a hula skirt, or a pinto bean with noodles growing out of it. They looked silly to him, and stupid. But callowhales were not silly or stupid. He knew that. He knew it, though he had no reason to know anything about them. Even the people who did know something about the vast, beautiful animals that lived in the wonderful scarlet sea couldn't seem to agree on anything about them, though Anchises felt quite certain they *were* animals, and not "great bloody meatloafs," as Mr Preakness called them, nor "overgrown Brussels sprouts," as Miss Bao insisted.

Finally, Anchises decided to try something new. He laid out a piece of fresh, new paper, the best sheet he could find, with only a few bits of cacao-seed flecking the fibre. He sharpened his pencil with his knife and made sure he had a good breakfast and a glass of orange juice by his side (which was not really orange juice, but a tangy, thready, tingly juice from a plant whose fruit is orange, but whose exterior is the size of a doctor's satchel and covered in lilac fur) in case he got thirsty. He sat at his desk, which faced the beach and the foamy Qadesh, and said, very clearly, to the surf: "I wish that I can't ever draw what a callowhale really looks like, and always make a real hash job of it."

Anchises put his pencil to his paper, and this is what he drew:

After that, Anchises put his pencil and paper away under the floorboards and only took out his bottom-half-of-a-callowhale picture to look at when everyone else had gone to bed. He never asked his mother or his father whether his drawing looked right to them. He didn't have to.

And day after day, when his chores were done and he had read all the passages required for the next day's lessons, Anchises went down to the shore near his house. He no longer collected whelk shells which were not really whelk shells, nor driftwood which was not really driftwood. He did not try to sing along with the striped seals which were not really seals. He only watched the callowhales. In his mind, he kept drawing them, over and over, their endless arms beneath the red water wrapping him up like love.

※

The boy whose wishes couldn't come true was a good child with a good heart in his good chest. Even after he discovered how to wish for the opposite of what he wanted, he did not abuse the privilege. If you play too hard with a toy, it will break. Anchises had never broken any of his toys, even when he was so small he thought his stuffed velvet turtle was a real turtle. He spent his wishes carefully, like a miser spends his coins.

He wished that his parents should have terrible draws when they dove for callowmilk—and his voice trembled when he said it, for even though he knew it would come out well, it hurt him to wish bad fortune on his family. When he overheard his father weeping in the night because he had wanted seven children for as long as he could remember—being one of seven himself, whose mother and grandmother had also had six siblings—Anchises looked out to the fiery autumn waves and wished that his mother would never have any more children ever, that he should always be an only child and never have three brothers and three sisters, which was too many, anyone would admit. And he wished—finally, guiltily—that all the children in school would hate him and call him names and beat him, that they would shun the sight of him and never ask him along with them when they went fishing after school. He shook all night afterward, terrified that the spell would work, but also terrified that it would not; sick with the conviction that, this time of all times, he had gone too far, wished for something too precious, too impossible, too princely for the magic to manage.

And the amphorae of Anchises's house swelled with callow-milk.

And the mother of Anchises swelled with twins.

And the children of Anchises's acquaintance clapped him on the shoulder; and laughed at his shy jokes; and called him Doctor Callow, because he knew even more about callowhales than the teacher did; and boy howdy did the Doctor catch more trout (which are not really trout, but skinny, skittish, scaly fish with wine-coloured fins and three bulging eyes, one of which is a false lantern-eye that lights up at night to seduce krill-which-is-not-really-krill into the creatures' wide mouths) than anybody else!

Doctor Callow found himself, suddenly, a happy child. And thus happified, he grew to the age of eight in the Land of Milk and Desire, no longer wishing for the opposite of his own desire, for he had all he could ever imagine wanting.

The Famine Queen of Phobos
(Oxblood Films, 1938, dir. Severin Unck)

(ACCOMPANYING MATERIAL: RECORD 4, SIDE 2, COMMENCE 0:09)

SC3 EXT. LOCATION #6 MARS/PHOBOS—KALLISTI SQUARE, DAY 49. AFTERNOON [5 APRIL, 1936]

[EXT. The Kallisti Square Depot on Phobos, the larger of Mars's two moons. The camera careens un-steadily; a throng of furious men and women stampede across the square, slamming bats and batons into the windows of the public distribution centre, the customs house, the cafes and warehouses. They are looking for food—they chant for food, they scream for food, they sob for it. But the distribution center has nothing. The cafes have nothing. They closed weeks ago, and the warehouses contain little but shipping labels from the last deliveries of bread and callowmilk. The people of Phobos would loot the whole city, if there was anything to loot.

Phobos is a tiny world, with poor soil and few features to lure tourists or investors. It is an industrial settlement, a halfway house between the mines of the asteroid belt and the markets of Earth. Almost all food must come from somewhere else: from Mars itself, from Earth, from the fertile Inner System. Nearby Deimos can offer little help—greener, softer, but her population still hovers precariously over stability; unable, quite, to touch down. Two months ago, the organized workers, led by Arkady Liu and Ellory Lyford, went on strike, demanding all the things workers need and management withholds: wages, shortened contracts, more doctors, more food, more protection. The response was simple: all food shipments to Phobos ceased. A year from now, very few offworlders will not know the name Arkady Liu.

SEVERIN UNCK runs with Liu's mob, searching for a place to stand and speak. She ducks through the doorway of a Prithvi Deep Sea Holdings processing facility and crouches into the shadows. She breathes heavily, a flush riding in her cheeks. She has not eaten in two days. She has had one cup of water in the last twenty-four hours. She is hiding—her equipment is worth something, even her clothes. She came to shoot something else entirely: a year of holidays, each on a different moon. An ice-cream cone of a project, contracted with Oxblood to pay for the Jupiter project she is already writing in her head.

It is Easter on Phobos. An egg might cost your life.

For the first time, SEVERIN has no script at her feet. She looks into the camera; she stutters slightly on her first words, whispering, trying to recall what she wrote for this scene the night before.]

SEVERIN

Who . . . wh . . . who. [She swallows hard, begins again.] Who owns Phobos? China settled it, Britannia Fair owns two thirds of the landmass. The East Indian Trading Company is her mother and her master. But in truth, no nation owns the heart of Phobos.

It is a familiar story: Before the Wernyhora siblings gave us our road to the stars, the colonial powers and their worst-behaved corporate children made a feast of the world, and seemed ready to slaughter each other at table for one more slice of the bloody prize. To prove which one could fit the whole world in its mouth at once. And then—what? We are still stuck at that same table, frozen in place, a portrait of the dinner party at the moment it dispersed for more exciting revels. What would be left of Europe if those hungry empires had not been distracted by a hundred new worlds? What would be left now of the Iroquois League if half the American experiment had not lost interest in Louisiana the moment Venus sashayed by? Why should the doors of wild and raucous space still read England, Russia, France, Germany, China? Ninety years on, we still cannot get free of that cannibal dinner party whose invitations hit the post before any of us were born.

[SEVERIN tries to catch her breath. Terror

shows in her eyes. The flush has drained from her cheeks. Her hands shake.]

I . . . I don't remember what I meant to say. I had something written. I don't remember. [A tremendous boom sounds somewhere off-camera; SEVERIN drops to the ground instinctively, crouching low. But she does not stop speaking.] I was born on the Moon, yet am not Lunar. I call myself English for no reason but the lion on my passport. I have never been to London. I have only set foot on Earth twice. I don't know or care what goes on down there—but Earth still owns me. Earth owns all of us. And when we try to run into the garden, just for a moment, just to see something besides the same parlours and kitchens and halls our resentful parents built, we know what happens now. Phobos knows. They will starve us. They will burn us. They will bleed us.

[Fire detonates against the building; glass flies, cutting SEVERIN'S face, her arms, knocking her hard against Prithvi Deep Sea Holdings' massive steel mineral processors. She crumples to the floor. She tries to lift herself up, but her left arm will not take the weight. She does not lift her head, but her words can be heard clearly. Blood drips from her mouth onto the cement.]

Our mother countries never stopped longing to devour everything. They never stopped hanging garlands for the party they had planned, never stopped groping to pin the tail on the manifest destiny. Back then, back before the stars, they meant to go to war over who got that pin. Today, I can't escape the feeling that their war is still coming. It'll take longer than it would have if we had stayed safe in our Earthbound beds. It may take a lot longer. It will be so much worse. But there is a script, and it will be followed.

[Men swarm into the warehouse, bashing the machinery with crowbars, with their bare hands, with streetlamps hoisted by six at a time. They do not see the camera or SEVERIN; they trample her, their boots on her cheek, her shoulder, her back. She calls out pitifully before she loses consciousness.]

ARKADY LIU

They may starve us, but we will choke them on their own wealth!

SEVERIN

Raz, help me. Fuck. I'm really hurt.

From the Personal Reels of
Percival Alfred Unck

[PERCIVAL UNCK films his daughter playing on the slopes of Mount Ampère. Blue alpine cassias twist up all around her, gnarled and stumped and prickly with translucent needles. They prefer the relative warmth of the valleys. The heights turn the endless forests of the Moon to hunched, baleful, contorted creatures. A thin scrim of snow crunches under SEVERIN UNCK'S small feet. She is dressed in her father's idea of a mountain climber's costume: lederhosen, stockings, buckled shoes, a ruffled shirt. Her long hair is ribboned into thick pigtails. Severin tries to entice her father into playing hide and seek, but though he is happy to seek her, he will not perform his part by hiding. He might miss something. Finally, the child gives up.]

SEVERIN
Daddy, you have to chase me! Don't you know anything?

PERCIVAL

Oh, I'll chase you, Rinny. I'll chase you anywhere you run! And when I find you I will chomp you to bits like a bad old wolf!

[Shrieks and giggles. SEVERIN runs behind a malevolently torsioned cassia. She peeks out again, brushing needles out of her hair.]

SEVERIN

But when you catch me and chomp me, after *that* you have to hide and I'll chase *you*! That's how you play, silly! And when I find you I'll roar like a TIGER and scare you to DEATH.

PERCIVAL

[Laughing.] Shan't! I have the camera, and whoever has the camera is King and gets to make the rules.

SEVERIN

[Leaps up, grasping at air. The image shakes as he yanks Clara up and out of reach.] Gimme! Give it to me! I want it!

The Ingénue's Handbook

January 16, 1930, Definitely Three in the Morning
The Butterfly Room, Aboard the Achelois, *Sea of*
Tranquillity

Place your bets, ladies and gentleman. We have a murderer on the ship and I intend to flush them out.

The band finished playing at the stroke of midnight. Union musicians are just awful sticklers. The heaving mass of us tottered out of the ballroom and onto the decks of the *Achelois*, a glitter-mob of prodigious proportions. The night was warm; the wind blew toward Tithonus and not from, so the scents were pleasant instead of foul: the tang of salt-silver water, the sharp whips of pine forests on shore, spilled grenadine, and a hundred kinds of perfume, from Ye Olde No. 5 to Shalimar to that just-shagged musk that has no brand name, yet could never be mistaken for anything else. Nobody had the slightest inclination toward bed, so the bash went on outside while—this is important—the stewards shut up the ballroom for cleaning. We all hung off the railings, rainbow-tinsel-barnacle people, and all was right with the world so long as the world was nothing more than that beautiful boat sailing through the beautiful dark. Then the old dance began: people paired off and vanished two by two, sometimes three by three, and the decks grew more peaceful, emptier, sleepier. I was occupied with Nigel—oh, I know, it's too dreadful, all those gorgeous glitterati and I end up sitting on the staircase talking to my ex! I felt really and truly forty for the first time. I didn't want to sneak off behind the smokestack to canoodle with one of the pretty girls from contracts or even take a stab at snaring Wilhelmina Wildheart at long last. I just wanted to talk to someone who's seen me with a runny nose and a bad cough and still thought I was all right. Nigel was always aces when I was sick. He'd pratfall by the bed and make my slippers talk like dolphins 'til I laughed, even though it made the cough worse.

Digression! No! Mary! The reason I *must* make a note of the fact that I was talking to Nigel on the staircase is to establish that:

1. I did not see Percy or Thad at all between the closing of the ballroom at midnight and twenty past one in the morning.
2. N. and I were sitting in the aft stairwell, which adjoins the south wall of the ballroom, thus . . .
3. We heard the gunshot immediately and bolted toward the grand entrance, which the stewards had opened up with a quickness, however . . .
4. A small number of people had already trampled all over the crime scene by the time I arrived.

We heard a great deal of screaming and dropping one's drinks and weeping. I ran pell-mell; the heel of my left shoe broke off, but I kept hobbling on until I swung wide round the great carved ballroom door—Thad had it brought over from Mars only last year. And I saw it all. I saw the whole ugly thing like a set dressed for shooting. Poor Thaddeus lying face down on his own ebony floor, bleeding like mad. It was ever so much more blood than in the movies. When you shoot someone on film it's just a pinprick, really, and then a little trickle of red. They slump to the floor and it's over 'til the next take. But Thad's blood gushed out all over the place. People had stepped in it. Yolanda Brun was trying to wipe some off of her green silk slingback.

I've said wrap parties obey no natural law. I'd been Madame Mortimer, at full tilt, only the week before. She roared up inside me, all pearl-handled soul and acid heart. Without a word, I walked up to one of the stewards (who'd gone about as pale as arsenic), took the key off his belt, shut and locked those grand Russian doors, and shoved a brass hat-rack through the handles for good measure.

"If I may have your attention?" I put on my biggest, most booming voice, the one that had slapped the back row in the face at the Blue Elephant Theatre back in London. I locked down my tears—*I'll cry for you later, Thaddy baby. I promise.* "Thank you. I'm afraid I can't allow any of you to leave just yet. Everything we need to solve this awful mess is right here at our fingertips. There's not a moment to be lost if we're to uncover the truth."

You'd think I'd put them all in a cage and dangled the last rump roast in the universe outside the bars, the way they behaved. Shameful. But I stood my ground, and the stewards stood with me—whether because they knew who sliced their bread or because they appreciated the need to secure the scene of a crime before all the evidence gets simply fucked away by cretins, I've no idea. It would take a day to sail back to Grasshopper City, and by that time there wouldn't be so much as a sip of evidence left for the police. I had to work quickly. For Thaddeus. He didn't need my tears just then, he needed his heroine.

I knew everyone I locked into the ballroom that night, some better, some worse: Yolanda Brun, Hartford Crane, Nigel Lapine, Freddy and Penelope Edison, Percival Unck, Algernon Bogatryov, Himura Makoto, Dante de Vere, and Maud Locksley. (I'd only met Makoto, Capricorn's newest golden boy, that night, but we'd already made plans to shoot pheasant together on the weekend.) I don't quite know what came over me in that moment, facing those people—people I had known most of my life, worked with, slept with, admired, loathed, envied, the whole handbag of human push-me-pull-you—but suddenly, watching Yolanda whine and pour club soda on her bloodstained shoe, I was positively sick to death of them all. I could have gaily tossed them all into the drink and poured myself a grapefruit juice without a wink of pity in my heart. I don't know what got into me, except Maxine Mortimer and her damnable need to solve the puzzle.

"Shut up, you puling, overstuffed veal calves," I snarled, and even though it's a line from *Doom on Deimos*, I delivered it better in 1930 than I ever did in 1925. "Have a little respect! Clear off! Give me some room!"

They flattened against the wall like school kids at a dance. I examined Thaddeus. He still had his dinner jacket on. The shot had gone through his back, straight into his heart. His cigarette still burned itself down between the fingers of his right hand. His left arm was folded under his chest. The craziest thought popped into my silly head: *His hand's gonna fall asleep that way! He'll be all pins and needles when he wakes up.* I went to disentangle him. *No!* Maxine Mortimer snapped in my head. *Don't you dare move that body, you dozy cow! The further one gets from the body, the harder it is to see the truth.* I looked quickly round the ballroom instead. What luck! The gun lay under one of the banquet tables. Kicked there? Hidden deliberately? Dropped in the turmoil of it all? I sent Makoto to retrieve it, as he and Nigel were the only ones I felt certain about. Nigel was telling me about moustache wax when the gun went off, and Mack was fresh off the rocket. He didn't know any of us well enough to care whether we lived or died, and besides, who would want something this drastic for their debut?

.22 Perun, walnut grip. Martian, I thought, but that didn't

mean anything. We'd all been to Mars. There wasn't much to do there but shoot kangaroos.

Hartford raised his hand like a little boy in class. "Mary, whoever did this probably ran off at once. Why do we have to hang about watching you play detective? We've all seen it, love. Let's be sensible: make a search party, comb the ship. Staying stuffed up in here won't help anyone."

"Hartford, if I thought you had the sense God gave a gumdrop, I'd let you 'comb the ship' to your heart's content. What, pray tell, would you be searching for? The murder weapon—" I sniffed the Perun's barrel to be sure; indeed, freshly fired. "—is here. The body is here. The first people to the scene—and therefore those nearest to the ballroom when our Thad was shot, and the closest thing we've got to witnesses—are here. You don't get blood all over yourself when you shoot a man in the back; tearing up the laundry for a stained dinner jacket won't do a lick of good. So why don't you button up your expensive little mouth and let the adults talk?"

He did just that. I won't say I didn't get a wallop of satisfaction out of it. That vicious gossip hound Algernon B stood next to Hart, looking as though he were about to get on socially with an aneurysm. Sweat wriggled off his bald head and steamed up his glasses. He put his head between his knees. But if sweating makes you guilty, they were all in on it. Gin-sweats, stroke-sweats, beef-sweats, murder-sweats—who could tell the difference? I scanned their faces. *I can do this*, I thought. *With everything I know about them, about Thaddeus, about deduction—at least the celluloid kind—I can figure it out.*

"I'm leaving," Freddy said. His face went red as a stoplight. "You're nothing but a nasty, two-bit has-been with a flat ass and the clap, and you can't keep me here."

"So am I," cried Dante de Vere. The pair of them stormed up to me, as though I'd never stared down a man who wanted my kidneys for earrings before.

I didn't budge. "Mr Edison!" I roared. "You had a dispute with the deceased over unpaid fees for sound recording on *Miranda*, did you not?"

He recoiled. I don't suppose anyone had roared at Franklin Edison since he crashed his tricycle into a swing set. But then, I did have the .22. Roaring has more *oomph* with a Martian pistol behind it. "Don't be ridiculous, Mary. I have disputes with everyone over unpaid fees for sound recording. If I started killing anyone who owes me money, the Moon would be a ghost town inside of a week."

"What about you, Dante? He fired you from *Death Comes at the Beginning*. No one's called you for so much as a footman's role since."

"Mary! I had no idea you thought of me that way—as so ruthless or so abject. I was with Maud, stargazing, just out there on the starboard rail. We heard the shot—we're perfectly innocent. I loved Thad, you know that. He looked after my dogs when I was on location."

This gave me an idea. I pounced upon it before it could get away. "I have a question. If I feel you have answered honestly, I shall let you go on your way. Who among us loved Thaddeus Irigaray? I believe that may tell us more than asking who hated him." Proper Maxine Mortimer, from first syllable to last. "I certainly did," I answered first. And it was true. He'd kept me in steady work for a decade and let me bring my cat on set. Hell, he'd proposed eight times. When Laszlo Barque left him, he stayed in my guest room for a month.

No one else spoke up. Percy stared determinedly at his feet. Maud and Dante looked quite thoroughly bored, smoking together by the piano. Finally, Maud stubbed out her cigarette and said, "All right, fine, I loved him. He looked after me post my little spot of nastiness with Oxblood. I was supposed to get the Mortimer contract, you know. The studio wanted me. But Thad wanted . . . I don't know, I suppose he wanted a blonde." She hurried to correct the bitter edge in her voice. "But no hard feelings! Why, that was ages ago."

Freddy's mouth kept running away from him. It twitched; it grimaced. It wanted to say something his brain knew it oughtn't. He was drunk as a lord, careening from side to side, as though that great huge ballroom were too small for him, that coarse, awful elephant of a man.

"How about you, Penny?" Freddy hissed. Penelope Edison looked as though she were going to split apart at the seams. She kept rubbing her arms as though she were freezing to death. She stared at her husband, such a horrible stare, full of pleading and misery. Helpless tears started rolling down her face and they didn't look like they'd ever stop. "Penny? Cat got your tongue? Who do you love, Pen? Me? Percy? How about Algernon over there? Or *that* sad sack of shit?" And he pointed to the ruin of Thaddeus Irigaray.

"Please, Freddy," she whispered. I have never seen anything quite so wretched as Penelope Edison weeping.

"Please what? I didn't do anything. But if somebody asks a question, it's only polite to answer. And being polite is so important, isn't it? If I forget one little P in an ocean of Qs, it's the end of the goddamned world, but you can just stand there and quiver and not answer the fucking question?"

"Freddy, stop." Percy put a hand on his shoulder and Edison swung wild, whacked him right in the eye. Percy doubled over, holding his face. "Fred! I'm trying to help you!"

"*You* need help, not me," Freddy snarled back. "After everything I've given you people! Without me, without my family, you cunts are just flouncing around on a stage in hell with *nobody fucking watching.* And what do I get back? What's my fabulous fee for making your entire disgusting existence possible?" He crossed to the body in two enormous strides and kicked Thaddeus's shoulder, kicked him over onto his back, and kept on kicking him. Thad's poor limp arm fell onto the floor.

Everyone started hollering, grabbing Edison, and gnashing their teeth—but all Maxine Mortimer saw was Thad's left hand, the one poor softhearted Mary had worried would go all pins and needles on him. He'd curled his fingers into a fist. He had something in there, clutched in his bloody fingers. Nobody else saw it. They were too busy wrestling a drunk tycoon, sliding around in a good man's death.

"That garbage shit-fucking cocksucker fucked my wife," wailed Freddy, dogpiled under the biggest stars in Tinseltown. "*That's* who loved him. My Penny. That's who!"

Penny shook her head back and forth, her mouth hanging open, not breathing. She flopped onto the floor. "I didn't . . ." she gasped. "I didn't . . ."

No, she didn't. Penelope Edison most certainly did not. She couldn't have. Not in a year of Easters. What the hell was going on here?

"Jesus, someone get her a paper bag," Maud Locksley said.

"Tell them!" shrieked Edison. The King of Sound and Colour was bawling his eyes out in a pool of cold blood. "That fucking whore snuck around on me while I was in Elish for the Worlds' Fair! And when I got back, you were all slim and trim again, weren't you, you *bitch*, you goddamned gold-digging Jezebel—"

It was going so well. Just like a movie. Right now, in my stateroom, in the silence of the deep, woeful night, I think it was going so well because . . . that's what happens in a movie. I cast a spell, and for a moment, just a moment, life had a script. The detective locks the door and names the suspects and, eventually, someone confesses. That's how the whole business works. It's instinct. Freddy couldn't resist it. Or Percy couldn't. Couldn't resist the desire to crawl inside the script. It's safe in there. Nice. Warm. The script will look after you.

But Percy stopped it.

"Everybody cool off!" Percival Unck, for all his faults and virtues, can yell louder than anyone I know. *Quiet on set!* "Listen to me. This was an accident. Mary, I appreciate what you're doing, but it's not necessary. I am telling you the truth. Freddy and I were having a few scotches out on the deck, talking about the new camera line. Fred clapped me on the back, and when he turned around, he saw Penny and Thad through the ballroom windows. Thaddeus kissed Penny, and Freddy saw black. You can't blame a man for that. He shouldered the door in, confronted Thad, it came to blows, we struggled—all of us, all four of us! We struggled and the gun went off. It could have been any of us who pulled the trigger: me, Penny, Fred—we all had our hands on it at some point. But it was an *accident.* And what we have to decide now is: How many lives does this terrible accident destroy?"

I had such a horrid feeling in the hollows of my stomach.

He's lying.

Like MM always said, it's bad maths. The sun might come up blue as Neptune in the morning, ice might turn to fire when it melts, I might become the long-jump champion of the world, but Thaddeus Irigaray did not kiss Penelope Edison. It didn't happen. I go for a bit of each, but Thad was true blue. I wanted to say so, but I couldn't. Not in that room. Not with all those people who Thaddeus didn't trust enough to tell when he was alive. Not with that Algernon B-for-Bastard already writing next week's column in his head. Even a corpse can be ruined. And a corpse's reputation doesn't mend. So I kept mum. God help me. I wouldn't let Thaddeus go down in the books as just another dead pervert. Because that's how we all end up, of course. No. I wouldn't let his heart be somebody's morality tale.

Or maybe I was just afraid. Of Freddy, of Percy, of all of them. I couldn't help it. I thought, *Percy, baby, you wanna run it back and do it again so you can get a better angle on the bullet? Make certain the shadows are right on Thaddeus Irigaray's eyes when the light goes out inside them? Or was there a better line you could've hurled in his face? Or at Penny, or Fred? And why would you lie for them? Why would you bother? You don't even know Penny, not really. You've been chummy with Fred since you were kids, sure . . . but the fraternal bubble never extends to wives. So what did Thad do to you, Percy? How did he really earn his bullet? Why is this happening?*

"Whose gun was it?" I asked.

"What?"

"Whose gun? Who brought a gun to a wrap party?"

"It's mine," Percy admitted. *Oh, Percy. No.* "I was showing it to Fred. Showing off, I suppose. I don't fancy ending up in a Plantagenet vault, Mary. I protect myself. Maud's got a pistol strapped to her thigh. Ask her. It's not so strange."

Then Percival Unck told us how it was going to be. His best directorial effort and only thirteen people ever saw it. Thaddeus had a heart attack. The ship doctor could be paid off; he barely graduated from medical school, anyway. We'd clean it all up, all of us together, and Thaddeus would be cremated before anyone knew the difference. The rest of us would keep the secret for our own reasons. Because we were accessories, because we wanted system-wide distribution for our tawdry little magazine, because we didn't want a divorce to leave us penniless, because we wanted a part, because we didn't care, because we loved Thaddeus Irigaray and didn't want him to be remembered as a homewrecker or worse, because we could live forever on the favours Unck and Edison could do us.

What about me? Will I keep quiet? I said I would. I promised. With blood on my cheek, I promised. I took my silver—any part I want, and the director's chair, too. Though, honestly, I think it might be time to retire.

I don't want to write about scrubbing blood off ebony with a wire brush. Or burning my buffalo fur in the engine room. But I do want to write this: While we were cleaning Thad up, I pried open his fist and swiped a wadded-up piece of paper out of the muck and the crusting blood. I didn't look at it 'til I got it safely back to my room.

It's a photograph. Of a baby girl.

I can't be certain—babies all look a bit like one another. But I think she looks an awful lot like Severin.

Kansas

**Transcript from 1946 debriefing interview with Erasmo
St. John, property of Oxblood Films, all rights reserved.
Security clearance required.**

CYTHERA BRASS: Session three, day two. Arlo Covington, C.P.A.,
Oxblood representative, instructed your crew to abandon the
Adonis set. Why didn't you follow his lead?

ERASMO: We did. We just . . . got distracted. Look, I know you
think we're a great fat lot of useless drama society layabouts,
but we are, each and every one of us, professionals. We stabi-
lized the situation very quickly. Dr Nantakarn had a mobile
ICU already set up in advance of the dives we had planned.
Retta isolated Anchises and put gloves on him so he couldn't
infect anyone else. She took Mari in hand, sliced that thing
right out of her palm, and bandaged it up before Konrad
and Franco could get breakfast cleared away. Gave her morphine for the pain. Mari was pretty doped up. She slept it off
in the medical tent while we discussed what to do about
Horace.

Venusian freshwater wells are deep. To get past the saltwater
you have to really burrow down. We had a boom mic and a
small crane. Nothing nearly long enough. Max said . . . he said

Horace was already buried. We could cap the well, carve his name on it. It would be a beautiful grave. He was trying to be kind. Maximo's kindness can be morbid. But I couldn't do it. I couldn't just let Horace rot down there, getting chewed on by who knows what blind, awful worms live in Venus's underbelly. I have too good an imagination. I could see it, some horrid night-eel laying eggs in his eye sockets . . . I couldn't leave him down there in the dark. He deserved a better final scene than that. Besides . . . he could have been alive. What if he'd only broken a leg? Both legs? What if he was slowly bleeding to death down there?

Well, the only other option was the diving cables. We had two suits left: one for the diver and one for the cameraman, and heaps of breathing tubes. We could lower someone down, just as we would from the gondola into the Qadesh. I thought it should be me. Look at me—I'm the obvious choice. I'm a big man, I'm strong, I could carry Horace back up, easy. Like a fireman. I could carry them all back.

But Iggy killed that idea. "These village wells, they narrow as they go down. You could get stuck, and, you know, *we* have to lower you and haul you and the body—and Horace—back up. We have no climbing equipment. No cleats or crampons. The tube could snap. We could drop you. You're the heaviest one of us, Raz. The lightest should go."

And all eyes turned to Arlo.

CYTHERA: Did the background noise let up at all while this discussion took place?

ERASMO: No. Maybe? I'm not sure. It wasn't *constant*. It surged and ebbed and surged again. But it never found a rhythm. If it had rhythm, we could have ignored it eventually, the way you learn to ignore the sounds of traffic late at night in Tithonus. But it never *lulled*, it just crackled and shrieked and garbled out those dreadful bursts of growling.

CYTHERA: And Covington agreed to go down after the cameraman?

ERASMO: After Horace. Surprisingly, yes. Everybody did the same mental maths: we couldn't risk the doctor, there was no way I'd let Rin go, Mari was out cold, Crissy's almost six foot of lean cheetah-girl muscle. We all had at least a stone on Arlo. If it had to be the lightest of us, he was it. You knew him—skinny as a jockey, and not so tall as all that. He was wiry, though. He must have done some sport or other—accountants don't usually have that sort of whippy physique.

CYTHERA: Rowing, actually. He was on the Oxblood crew. Up every morning at four pulling oars across the Rainy Sea.

ERASMO: Huh. I can see that.

CYTHERA: You said he agreed to this plan? You didn't coerce him?

ERASMO: Is that what the others said? That I forced him?

CYTHERA: I'm asking you. I'm having some trouble with the notion, Mr St. John, because Arlo hated confined spaces. He worked on the Oxblood accounts by the lake in Usagi Park so he didn't have to suffer in his own office. And you're telling me he cheerfully went along with a plan that required him to jump into a pit in the ground.

ERASMO: Without one second of argument. *He's your family—* that's what he said. *You don't turn your back on family.* I don't know. Maybe he lost a brother way back. Maybe his mum abandoned him. Maybe you don't know him that well. But I'll tell you for nothing that in that moment, I loved Arlo Covington like mad. He didn't even dawdle. Suited up right away— we had to strap down the suit a little to fit him. He kept the diving bell on, to protect his head, in case he fell. We rigged up a sling for Horace out of one of the hammocks and some gaffer tape, secured a lantern to Arlo's belt, and strapped Mariana's pride and joy to his chest. If she hadn't been surfing the morphine coast she would have lost her mind. Send her baby down a big black hole? No chance. See, she'd brought along a brand-new Edison-brand prototype wireless microphone. For field and stress testing.

CYTHERA: That would be the Type I Ekho Ultra-Mic?

ERASMO: You've got it. Mariana wouldn't let anyone else touch it. She had to keep notes on everything she did with it for the company back home. She kept saying it was worth more than the *Clamshell*, though that strikes me as bullshit—It looked like a little tin lunchbox. We needed it. What if something went wrong? We were happy to stroll around White Peony with parasols and a song in our hearts, but going . . . inside Venus—we couldn't let Arlo do that without some way to tell us if something went wrong. We gaffered the Ekho around his chest and tuned our field radio to seventy-six megahertz so we could pick up his broadcast. I cranked the volume up all the way and hoped to heaven we'd hear Arlo over the white noise.

CYTHERA: What time did Mr Covington begin his descent?

ERASMO: I'd say around 1100. It was stickily warm; the air didn't seem to move at all. We helped Arlo waddle into the town centre, to the mouth of the well. He stood there like a comic book hero amidst all that wreckage, all those mangled, mutilated houses, with his diving helmet tucked under his arm like Barracuda the Brave from that old Capricorn cartoon *The Arachnid vs. The Seven Seas*. He smiled at us, and I knew he was terrified, so it must have cost him something to flash that astonishing supernova grin our way. He was just trying to tell us everything was gonna be okay.

"Hey," Arlo said. "So there's this mummy snake and this baby snake and the baby snake says, 'Mumsy, are we poisonous?' and the mummy says, 'Yes, sweetums, but why do you ask?' and the baby says, 'Because I just bit myself!'"

It's not a great joke. But we laughed like he was headlining at Carnegie Hall.

CYTHERA: Did Severin record any of this?

ERASMO: [laughs] Are you joking? Of course she did. Severin and Crissy set up two cameras, one on our faces and one for the wide shot. It's a pretty amazing scene. If everything had gone differently, I think we'd be munching hors d'oeuvres at Academy Awards pre-parties right now, instead of these, frankly, dreadful biscuits and this abomination disguising itself as tea. Even after, in the darkroom, Crissy and I thought it was something else. The shards of Adonis casting hard, sharp shadows, the well in the centre of the shot, Arlo doing his Barracuda the Brave shtick, the breathing tube and diving cables tied tight around his chest, then a pan around Maximo, Santiago, Konrad, Franco, and Severin. All of us braced against the stone wall of the well like we meant to play tug-of-war with the public waterworks.

Arlo tested the Ekho mic. The radio crackled on. "Good evening, Ladies and Gentlemen! Gather in, pour yourself a cup of something nice, and sit back for another instalment of the solar system's favourite tale of adventure, romance, and intrigue on *How Many Miles Before Arlo Smashes His Skinny Arse to Bits?* Okay, down I go! Don't forget to make a wish!"

I turned away when he jumped in. I'd seen that once already.

As soon as Arlo saying *wish* whined out on the radio, the static boomed out its usual unintelligible hissing, then a voice exploded out of the white noise. This time we could all hear the words perfectly clearly: *Somewhere the sun is shining, but here it don't do nothing but rain . . .*

It was Mariana's and Cristabel's voices. Singing "I Left My Sugar Standing in the Rain," exactly the way they did on our first night at the Waldorf in White Peony Station. But it came showering down from everywhere, knotted up in ribbons of static, out of the sky, out of the trees, up from the mud and the water.

CYTHERA: How did Ossina react to that?

ERASMO: The same way we all did: it scared the tits off us. But we had Arlo hanging off of our belts—if we lost our composure, he'd fall. It was so loud! All any of us wanted to do was put our hands over our ears. We took turns, so the rest could still let the cable out slowly. Arlo called up every ten metres or so. And between his reedy voice threading out of the field radio, other voices began to pop up out of the sea of white noise like . . . like lobster cages with monsters inside.

"Ten metres down! Nothing to see, just brick. Some very exciting mould."

And Max's voice would float behind: *Heaven knows what she has known; my mind she has mated and amazed my sight . . .*

"Twenty metres! Can you imagine being the fellas who had to dig this thing out in the first place? Boy do I love taxes, accounts payable, and central heating." Then Severin's voice spooled out of the dusk: *I used to look up at night and dream of the Solar System . . .*

"Fiftyish and all's well! I'm not gonna call out the metres anymore. It's getting hard to tell. I was counting the bricks, but they've gone now, and I probably had it wrong, anyway. It's not like I have a ruler. I'll just keep talking. It can't be that much longer." Maximo's baritone snapped and sizzled out of the air: *I tell my baby it never rains on Venus, I tell my baby the sky is pink as a kiss . . .* "So . . . how do you get a dog to stop digging in the garden? You confiscate his shovel." A little girl's voice battered our eardrums from the sky: *They are all telling the story to me . . .* "What do you call a four-hundred-pound gorilla? Sir. Or anything he wants. Or the next big thing at Plantagenet Pictures, am I right? This is wonderful. I can just pretend you're all laughing. So much easier when there's only mud to give you a bit of side-eye. Ooh, there's a snail. Sort of. It's hot pink. And has little feet. You could probably make a joke out of that. What do you call a snail with feet?" *Begone, deceiver! I shall marry Doctor Gruel at the stroke of dawn!*

CYTHERA: Even for Arlo, that's a terrible punch line.

ERASMO: The punchline was "A crawlusc." Which is also not spectacular. No, the field radio started losing its connection with Arlo, and other broadcasts sort of *sagged* in over his. Seventy-six megahertz is just a frequency—and a popular one. We hadn't picked anything up since we got out to Adonis, so we didn't think frequency traffic would be a problem. But the Ekho mic couldn't quite hold its own once Arlo had gone down past . . . well, I don't know. Like I said, he stopped telling us his measurements past fifty metres.

CYTHERA: You can't possibly remember all this so well.

ERASMO: I can. We were rolling film the whole time; recording sound, too. I listened to it about a thousand times on the trip back. Before Max went on his little crusade. I remember it like it's written on that wall over there.

The tube bottomed out at one hundred and eighty meters, give or take. Arlo called up: "Don't worry! I think I can jump down from here if I disconnect the tube!"—*Behold, this is not a hospital, but my ship!*—". . . climb back up with Horace in the sling; it's only a bit of a drop to the bottom."

We all yelled at him not to disconnect, but he couldn't hear us, I'm sure he couldn't. We could barely hear ourselves. We heard him drop, grunt, and brush himself off. He said, "It's pretty dry down here. I thought this was a well? There're puddles, but nothing else. Maybe there's a sluice gate somewhere? But, Raz . . . I don't see Horace. I'll keep looking! It's *huge* down here. There're drawings on the walls. Like feathers and tic-tac-toe hash marks and, I don't know, maybe horses. Or snail shells. It looks like those caves in France. I can barely see the ceiling. Did Adonis have a cistern? If not, they were done for anyhow. It's dry as a bone down here. Not a drop to drink. Christ, it just goes on and on, like Kansas . . ."

"What's Kansas?" Severin yelled over the unbearable noise. The miserable static picked up that word from the radio and flung it out over the Qadesh, up into the dim gold clouds. It detonated softly, like fireworks going off in the next town over.

Kansas, Kansas, Kansas.

From the Personal Reels of
Percival Alfred Unck

[A black cloth lies over the lens. A demand to *shut the damn thing off* has been made and ignored, but the cloth makes Clara look benign. Shapes move indistinctly across the room. SEVERIN UNCK, sixteen years old, sits in silhouette, her hair longer than it will ever be again.]

PERCIVAL UNCK
It's for your own good, my little hippopotamus.

SEVERIN
Don't call me that. There are more lies in this house than wallpaper. Don't pile on any new ones. The roof won't stand the weight.

PERCIVAL
Ada said you can stay with her until this has all blown over. We'll go after the New Year's parade. If you'd rather a flat in the city, perhaps we can come to some arrangement . . .

                    SEVERIN

What about Mary?

                    PERCIVAL

Mary's shooting on location this year.

                    SEVERIN

[begins to cry] Why? Papa, I want to stay
here. This is my home. Don't you love me?

                    PERCIVAL

I am disruptive to your life right now. And . . .
you are disruptive to mine. I love you, but
there's a great deal of trouble at the moment.

                    SEVERIN

Oh, there's always trouble. There's always
something. Some reason I'm inconvenient. Some
excuse to stay away. What kind of trouble now?

                    PERCIVAL

People . . . people are saying I shot someone.

                    SEVERIN

[SEVERIN pulls away.] Uncle Thad? [Percival does
not answer.] Did you?

                    PERCIVAL

Rinny, it's very complicated . . .

                    SEVERIN

Oh my god.

PERCIVAL

{He reaches out for her, his shadow for her shadow.] Darling, listen.

SEVERIN

No, don't touch me. Call Ada. I won't stay in this house another second.

~~The Deep Blue Devil~~
~~The Man in the Malachite Mask~~
Doctor Callow's Dream:
The House, the Eye, and the Whale

Once upon a time, in the Land of Milk and Desire, there lived a boy who had outsmarted his birthright. Whether he knew it or not, this is a very dangerous thing to do. A birthright can't be cut off like a bit of fingernail—it hangs about, sullen, limping through the years with two wooden legs and a clay hand, waiting, slinking, sniffing for a chance to get in the game again.

Only once did Anchises, whom everyone called Doctor Callow, tell a grown person about the workings of his heart. When he was eight and believed that his biggest wishes-which-were-not-really-wishes were behind him, little Doctor Callow went to see a witch (who was not really a witch, but an ornery old woman who had once made her living as an ostentatious fortune teller in Judgment-of-Paris, one of the great cities of the southern part of the Land of Milk and Desire, very far from Adonis, a city where the laws against conflict are so strict that the slightest bickering over a supper bill is cause for expulsion). The witch's name was Hesiod—though it wasn't, really. She had been born Basak Uzun, but began trying to escape her name as soon as her mouth got big enough to say it. She tried on many new names before she saw "Hesiod" in a beautiful book about the ancient days of Home, a place she had never seen and would never see. The name sounded to her like yellow sunlight on brown, dry earth, and she took it the way some young persons take trinkets when a shopkeeper's back is turned, even though it was a boy's name. She didn't find that out until much later, and by then, she didn't care. Hesiod fell in love with a dashing diver and came away from Judgment-of-Paris to homestead in Adonis, a place so new at the time that it didn't have a name. When her beloved died at sea—brushed ever so lightly, as lightly as a lover, by the frond of a callowhale—Hesiod returned to her old ways, for telling fortunes is a hard habit to break.

Anchises strung six trout-which-were-not-really-trout on a heavy rope and brought them along to pay for his fortune. Hesiod's hut, its veranda washed by salt wind, its windows pink sea glass, sat, quite satisfied with itself, by the shore of the Qadesh. Anchises knocked three times, which is traditional. Hesiod answered him, her long grey hair plaited with cacao-husks and ocean daisies (which are not really daisies, but livid, lilac, languorous anemones that can survive for six days without water). Doctor Callow presented his gift of fish.

Hesiod plucked out one of the fish's eyes and ate it without a word. It must have tasted good, as eyes go, for she shrugged and let him into her house, sat him on a driftwood-which-was-not-really-driftwood chair, and pulled out her cards. She spread them on the table in a graceful fan, like a casino girl (which Hesiod had also been when she was young). The witch-who-was-not-really-a-witch had a crystal ball, too, but she never used it and it wore a perfect coat of dust. It was just for show, but people like a fortune-teller with a crystal ball.

"What's your name?" said Hesiod gruffly. She wasn't really gruff, but people like a grouchy witch. A friendly one couldn't possibly know anything about the world.

"Doctor Callow," answered the boy proudly.

"No it isn't," snorted the old woman.

His little shoulders fell. "It's Anchises Kephus, ma'am," he mumbled.

"That's fine, boy. I can always spot another scrap who's shucked their name. If a name doesn't fit you, best leave it on the road for someone else who'll like it better."

The witch-who-wasn't-really-a-witch and the boy-who-was-really-a-boy sat without talking or moving for quite a while. Anchises didn't know how to explain his life to her. It sounded silly when he tried to make words out of it. He had become very good at figuring things out without asking adults about anything, and he found it hard—painful, even—to change his ways now. He was eight years old, and that, he thought, was a long time to get used to living a certain way.

Hesiod coughed and pulled a cigarette (which was not really a cigarette, but a shag made of black, bilious, brackish callowkelp, more expensive than beer from Home, wrapped up in newsprint) out of her deep bosom. She lit it, and the room filled with a scent like sumac and ozone and coffee and possibilities. "You have to ask a question, you know." She chuckled. "It costs a lot more than fish for the kind of fortune where you don't say anything."

Anchises took a breath as big as his eight years. "I think that I have a curse, Miss Hesiod. Maybe it's not a curse—maybe it's no different than being born with yellow hair, or something. But I don't have yellow hair; I have this. I think I've had it since I was little—littler than I am now, I mean. This is what I think the curse is, ma'am: Anything I wish for doesn't come true."

Before Doctor Callow's words came out of his mouth, they felt as heavy and swirling and important and salty as the Qadesh. But with every word he said to Hesiod, he hated the sound of his voice in the smoky hut and the words it was making even more. These words were small and they only meant what they said, not how they *felt* before he said them. He nearly wept with the frustration of it.

"Oh, you silly little turtle. All children think that. Hell, *I* think that, sometimes." Witches, even those who aren't really witches, like to swear, and their customers like it, too. As a rule, Hesiod tried to keep to no fewer than four profanities per visit.

The boy gritted his teeth. "No, that's not what I mean. I've had a long time to go over it—and I *did* go over it, carefully, like the men from Prithvi testing callowmilk for alkalinity. I *do* have a curse! Listen to me, I brought you fish!" Anchises calmed himself down, which was not easy for him, then or later. "These are things I know about it so far: It doesn't matter if I want it very much or not much at all. It doesn't matter if it's a big thing or a little thing. I have to say the wish out loud or it doesn't count—if I just think about it, nothing happens—but I don't have to say any particular magic words. It's enough to say *I'd like rice-suckers for supper tonight,* or *I really want . . .*" But he couldn't say anything he really wanted, because he was so afraid the curse wouldn't know the difference between wishing and an example of a wish he might make, and already he wouldn't be getting rice-suckers for dinner, which he loved. He said the next part as quickly as he could, in case saying it at a normal speed would make it all come undone. "And if I am very careful and wish for the exact opposite of the thing I want, I get what I wanted in the first place, which I guess is called a loophole."

Hesiod smoked her cigarette-that-wasn't-really-a-cigarette thoughtfully. "How big can you do? If you wished for the sun to come up tomorrow, would the world end?"

"I don't know, I'd never dare!"

"You never know unless you try." The crone shrugged.

"I think . . . I think it's just things to do with me. Or, at least, people I know," he added hastily, thinking of the girl with the black ponytail. "It's *localized phenomena*," he whispered, lifting a phrase from one of his textbooks.

"Big words from a little man. If you've got this all figured out, what do you need me for? Have you got a question, or haven't you?"

"Yes! Hold on! Jeez!" It was all getting away from him, skidding out from under his feet like red sand. Anchises shoved his hand in his shirt pocket and pulled out a piece of paper, on which he had written his question in neat, round letters, in case he got confused or upset. "What Is Going to Happen to Me?" he read slowly, evenly. "Is This Going to Happen Forever? Is It a Real Loophole? What Can I Do So It Goes Away?" He looked up at the fleshy lilac flowers in Hesiod's hair and her big cataracted eyes. "Am I gonna be okay?"

Hesiod thought of fortune cards no differently than she thought of casino cards: each had a value, which changed according to its position on the table, and when it was laid down near other cards, their combined values made a winning or a losing hand. She dealt three cards from her deck as quick as breathing.

The House. The Eye. The Whale.

The House had a hut on it that looked a lot like Hesiod's hut, only made up all of locks: locks for doors, locks for windows, a lock-thatched roof. The house stood, all locked up, under a sky full of stars, and in some of the stars, faces with suspicious eyes glared down. The Eye had three old ladies on it. They all had white hair that hung down like pillars to the ground. They wore silver, and they wore blindfolds. The middle one had an eyeball in her outstretched hand, from a green eye. The Whale had a callowhale on it, but it was not like Anchises's drawing of a callowhale. It looked like a stone wrapped up in grass, only the leaves of the grass were shaped like peacock feathers, and they had eyes in them, too.

Hesiod burped. She liked to burp almost as much as she liked to swear, but her customers didn't like the burping as much.

"Fucking hell, kidlet," she sighed. Her breath smelled sour. "Just because things don't go your way doesn't mean you're cursed. You think I didn't wish to get old with my Iskender and have a bunch of babies and enough milk money for a house with central heating? You think I didn't wish to be happy? You think any of the countries that landed here didn't wish they could have it all to themselves and kick everyone else out? The world is *made* of wishing, Anki; just every bastard wishing all the time, and it's a dog's work to tell who gets their wishes and who doesn't, because everyone's wishes bash into each other a thousand times a minute, and it'll get sorted out in hell if it ever does. If you wished the sun would come up tomorrow, it'd knock into a million other sad sacks wishing it wouldn't, and no matter what happened come dawn, you couldn't say who got their way. But mostly nobody gets their way. They wish for good and they get a handful of shit, and I know you're young, but you're old enough to get right with that. If you got that curse, baby boy, we all got it. I don't want to hear you bitch before you get your beard. You got no idea how hard you can lose your wishes. You're young enough to think there's logic to time and events and desire. It's cute, but I don't go in for cute at my age."

Anchises didn't blink. "What do the cards say?" he said, stonily, his cheeks burning.

Hesiod burped again. "They say you're never gonna get what you want, and you'll just have to live with it like everyone else."

Outside, beyond the glowing crimson breakers, the seals-which-were-not-really-seals barked out their rough songs like dinner bells, and never again did Doctor Callow tell a grown-up person what he knew.

❀

As the years of July passed by, Anchises grew older—and more and more possessed by the desire to see the face of a callowhale. It was not only that no one had, but that little Doctor Callow was convinced that anything with a face had to be alive, alive the way he was, the way his parents and the foreman at the Prithvi factory and the cacao-dancers at the Nutcake Festival and the slick-suited politicians in White Peony Station were; the way the girl with the black ponytail no longer was. A face was where you kept your aliveness. It was the part of you that showed sorrow and laughing and anger and embarrassment and surprise. Other parts felt those things, but your face *announced* them. What did a surprised callowhale look like? How about sad? How about if you told one a joke, a *really* good joke, the best joke in the world, and it laughed? He had to know. At ten years old, Anchises felt that if he died without knowing, the bones of his face would be knotted up with grief. Anyone who dug him up a hundred years later would look at his skull and say: *This man died missing the better part of his soul.*

But he was only ten, and he did not yet have his own diving bell.

As Adonis began to look forward to the Nutcake Festival of the crisp, cold, lean year of July thirteenth, three things happened, one after the other. Like dreams following sleep, each one ended in wishes our Doctor Callow did not mean to make, and like morning following dreams, each wish drew borders round the territories of the rest of his life.

The village elders of Adonis put their shaggy heads and tight-stitched wallets together to plan something special for the Nut-cake Festival that year, as it was the tenth Nutcake, and also because that year had not been so kind as July third: the ampho-rae were only three-quarters full, the cows-which-were-not-really-cows were surly and recalcitrant, and every other cacao-husk had no nut in it. Everyone needed cheering up. The elders sent away to Parvati, another village in the Land of Milk and Desire, deep in the lushest and loveliest jungles of the interior, for seven barrels of cider (which was not really cider, but heady, hearty, heavenly stuff the colour of a flamingo's feathers for which Parvati was already becoming famous, as it was brewed from apples which are not really apples, but crisp, colossal, crystallized berries that grow only in the most protected and shadowy forests of the Land of Milk and Desire). They sent to the village of Dahomey on the slopes of Mount Neith where wild frangipani grows (which are not really frangipani, but fragrant, feral, fecund flowers the colour of sunset that smell like bread baking and are only the female of the species) for twelve mature Samedi moths, which are the males of the same species of the frangipani-which-is-not-really-frangipani. Every summer the frangipani-that-are-not-really-frangipani blossoms open up on the mountainside and thousands of great glossy black-green moths-that-are-not-really-moths fly out of their mothers and into the world. A single wing of the Samedi moth, properly roasted over a low, grass-fed fire, can feed twenty, with scraps left for the hounds. And, finally, the elders of Adonis sent to White Peony Station for three precious treasures, so dear they could not be purchased, only lent at robber's prices, with thrice-signed bonds assuring their return in pristine condition. One treasure was white, the second silver, the third black. One enormous, the second awfully loud, the third nothing much to look at, but more dear than the other two combined.

The first treasure, white and enormous, was a projection screen.

The second, silver and awfully loud, was a film projector.

The third, black and not much to look at, was a movie, its spools of film closed tightly into canisters like holy jars of spices buried within the pyramids back Home.

The elders kept the name of the film secret, so that everyone who was not an elder could have the pleasure of finding out what it was just as the cider was going to their heads and the world seemed very fine indeed. They had debated long and hard over which movie to request from White Peony Station—a movie the children would like, but that would not bore the adults too much, that would neither be too sad nor too cloying, too pretentious nor too stupid. Only five people in Adonis had ever seen a movie before, and all in their youths, when they had first arrived in White Peony Station, or Aizen-Myo Sector, or Judgment-of-Paris, or even back Home. Adonis was normally too small and busy for such diversions. Finally, they settled upon a film by Percival Unck, whose name the old timers remembered blazing from the marquees of those White Peony and Aizen-Myo movie halls. This film was called *The Girl Who Made Fate Laugh*, and it had an octopus in it.

Little Doctor Callow, along with his mother, who was pregnant again, and his father, and his baby sister, and the twins, thrilled with anticipation. Anchises ranged far and wide into the hills to find cacao-husks that rattled with seeds inside. He put his pole into the water off of the swimming dock, caught four lovely fish, and smoked the wine-dark trout himself. He chased cassowaries off of their nests, ignoring their squawks and caterwauling, bolting from a hen hollering *Cao ni nainai de, ni ge wangbadan gouzazhong! Sizei, ni geiwo gun huilai, wo nie si nige guisunzi!*, and carried home as many eggs as he could in an apron made from the bottom of his school shirt. All the other children did their share, wandering the jungle paths in the autumn dusk, giggling in the gloaming, chasing after wild piglets (which are not really piglets, but skinny, six-legged, spicy-tasting black miniature deer, with long searching snouts and longer teeth). Anchises tried to outdo them all, combing the beach for live scallops (which are not really scallops, and taste like slightly bitter mangoes), and clams (which are not really clams, but squirting, sallow, shell-dwelling molluscs whose meat is poisonous except in autumn).

After a long day of digging up clams-which-were-not-really-clams and prying whelks-which-were-not-really-whelks free of rocks, Anchises saw something on the magenta-mauve sand. It stopped him in his steps. It stopped his breath in his chest. He knew what it was faster than he would have known his own face in a mirror. He had drawn a picture of one a long time ago, had seen it so clearly in his head it had been like a photograph.

It was a callowhale frond.

The thing was the colour of copper and as long as three fishing boats. It lay on the beach like a dead serpent out of the corner of some old map. Fine, long hairs and thick viney stalks draped off of it, and each hair and stalk forked off into fringes like coral or ferns. Flaps of skin like flowers and leaves, silvery and mossy like verdigris, flopped helplessly in the foamy, calm water. A huge gas bladder, drained and wrinkled and empty, was sinking slowly into the wet sand. Anchises thought he could see dim lights flickering inside it, lights like eyes opening deep beneath the skin of the balloon, if it was really skin. None of the seabirds (which are not really seabirds) or scuttling crabs (which are not really crabs) would come near it.

Anchises stared at the frond for a long time. The lights burst weakly inside it, hot green and searing blue. It was still warm. It was still wet. It smelled like a thousand things at once, so many that he could not sort the stink into its parts in order to say later what it had been *like*. Its shadow stretched deep and wide.

"Hello," said Doctor Callow, and in that moment he truly could not recall any other name anyone might have called him in the history of the world. "Hi."

The frond did not reply. The lights, if there were lights, did not grow brighter or dimmer. The sea-stench of the thing did not grow less or more powerful. Was its callowhale still alive? Was it sick? Was it in pain? The boy had never heard of a beached frond. Fronds did not come off like hair in a brush. Divers who accidentally touched one came home bruised, as though they had boxed a train. Or with missing hands. Or missing eyes. Or crisscrossed with scars from wounds they had never suffered. Or not at all.

Doctor Callow put out his hand hesitantly. His bare hand—he did not have divers' gloves or a mesh suit, only his pink, fleshy fingers. He held them above the skin of the great frond. He felt nothing but the warmth rising from it like tea-steam. He took his hand away and smelled it; it smelled like him, nothing more. He tried again, going a bit closer to that copper-coloured callowflesh. Nothing—and so he drew closer still, inching forward, the rest of his body eager, impatient. When he finally allowed his fingers to fall just above the body of the frond-flesh, Doctor Callow gasped. A sort of rusty, electric, half-sour crackling blossomed between him and it. It pushed up weakly against him, invisibly. It made colours in his mind, colours without names. His whole body felt it, firing off whatever involuntary reactions it could think of: goose bumps, shivers, sweat, stomach fluttering, heart racing, pupils dilating to great black holes in his face, hair standing erect, and other parts of him erect, too. But it didn't hurt. He still had both hands, both eyes. No bruises or scars. It felt good, even, though it felt like something that *shouldn't*, like putting his fingertips in the wax of his father's candles. *Maybe because it was dying. Maybe because it didn't have its whale anymore.*

Doctor Callow closed his eyes. He was not quite brave enough to actually touch it. So he just let his arm go slack.

It fell onto the flesh of the callowhale frond with a soft wet *smack.*

Doctor Callow felt as though he were swimming in the rusty-sour electric crackle, in the nameless colours. He felt as though he had never really been warm in his whole life, even though the Land of Milk and Desire is a hot and wet and heavy place. He laughed and he cried a little. He petted it like a dog. He was so shivery and prickly and hard and short of breath his everything ached. But he would have traded every ease he'd known for that ache and called it a bargain. The boy who loved callowhales stroked the severed arm of his beloved. He whispered to it. And, after a long while, little Doctor Callow curled up in a coppery curve of the frond; pulled the fine, soft hairs over him; and fell asleep in its dying embrace. The last of the ghostlights flashed on his dreaming skin.

"I wish," he whispered as he drifted toward the cliff edge of sleep, "I wish that I'll never see your face, that I'll never look you in the eye, that I'll never know you at all."

Every night after that, while the callowhale frond rotted, he slept in its great sagging coils and told no one. The rot, as it relaxed and bloomed, smelled to him like his mother's callowmilk bisque; and Hesiod's cigarettes; and the tops of the twins' heads when they were first born; and thick, good paper that had been drawn on over and over and over so that it was all black from corner to corner.

✸

When a notice went up in the town square calling Adonites of all ages to audition for a secret Festival scheme specially prepared by the elders, Anchises scrupulously avoided wanting it too much. He told everyone it was silly and he didn't want a part even a little bit. He reported at the correct hour with a mask of uncaring plastered to his face; and thus, when the schoolteacher in charge of the whole mysterious business chose him, along with three other children, a nice lady diver with extremely straight hair, and a tall, rangy-looking milkman, he could not suppress his shock.

Doctor Callow ran around in a circle, his little heart unable to stand in one place when so much was happening.

And so Doctor Callow got to see the movie early. They all walked down the beach for several miles until they could be sure that no one back home could see the lights. Then, huddled together, they watched *The Girl Who Made Fate Laugh* so that they could play parts from it at the Festival. It was the third movie in the Mr Bergamot franchise, and suddenly the children in the cast became consumed with speculation as to what might have happened in the other films. But Doctor Callow didn't care about that. He watched in a rictus of wonder as people who were not actually there at all moved and danced silently in silver. He shushed the seals when they barked so as to hear the silence better—and to better see the face of the girl who made Fate laugh.

The girl was called Chamomile, and though she was played by two different actresses, the boy whose wishes could not come true only saw one. When Chamomile was little, the actress who played her was a small, dark, sullen child with raggedy hair and a sour expression on her face. She looked unhappy all the time, but when she danced or walked, her body seemed to have all the joy her face forgot. She wasn't in the movie very long—Chamomile grew up some and an older, brighter, sprightlier girl took over. In her big scene, little Chamomile made a dress out of poppies and ran around a field of wheat (Anchises had no idea what wheat was—it looked like hairy, overgrown rice, he supposed) with patchwork wolf ears stuck to her head, until she ran smack into a tall, severe, beautiful lady with a crown on her head and a long black dress that showed enough of the curves of her breasts that Doctor Callow blushed all the way down to his toes. A title card showed: *Better run, Your Majesty, or I'll eat you all up!* Chamomile growled like a wolf, showing her small, even teeth, and the lady laughed.

The rest was all about older Chamomile, and how Fate helped

her do fantastic things because Chamomile had made her laugh, which is a hard thing to do, Anchises agreed. Chamomile escaped a wicked prince who wanted to marry her, and went down to the Chalet Under the Sea where she made friends with a gentleman octopus named Mr Bergamot and a seahorse named Mrs Oolong, and together they had terrific adventures battling submarines and manta rays, and in the end Chamomile turned into a mermaid and didn't marry anyone but became the Queen of the Ocean anyway.

Afterward, Anchises could talk of nothing but the little girl who put on wolf's ears and the poppy dress. The others teased him about it and said he should take his pretty face and go find her back Home. Wouldn't he like to meet her and see if she had worked out how to smile yet? Maybe if he threw a coin in the well and made a wish . . .

"No!" Anchises cried on the dark beach, quite terrified. "No, I never, ever want to meet her, not ever! I hope I'll never see her in real life, not even once, not even for a minute!"

And he ran back toward Adonis with his heart screaming inside him.

�֎

On the night of the Nutcake Festival, Adonis ate itself silly, cider and moth-steaks and fried nutcake and callowmilk meringue and piglet pies and cassowary custard. By the time the projector had been set up and the screen stretched flat without a wrinkle and benches arranged in rows in front of the tower of diving bells that marked the centre of Adonis, the whole of the village was groaning, patting their bellies, and telling old Home jokes about chickens and roads and horses with long faces walking into bars, even though no one could quite agree on what a chicken was, or a horse, for that matter. *A road is like a river, right? Like a canal.* There is more water than earth in the Land of Milk and Desire, where a current is ever so much better than a wheel. Hesiod herself was as happy as a taxman, burping and yelling and singing in Turkish in a voice so deep and sweet even the English speakers cried a little.

Finally, a hush fell. Sometimes, without anyone saying so, folk know it's time for the show. A fiddle picked up—and then a viola, and a big warbly bass, followed by a zither, a balalaika, and a koto. A clarinet and an oboe joined in. Above them floated a single lonely trumpet. Below them moaned the big belly of a tuba. It was a motley orchestra, all the instruments Adonis had. They began to play a lively march, which the men in White Peony Station had assured the elders was the very one played by the big-city orchestras when *The Girl Who Made Fate Laugh* premiered in the theatres there. (It wasn't, really. It was, in fact, the opening march from another movie entirely, *The Miranda Affair*, but only one person in Adonis would ever come to know that.)

And when the title cards came up, with their lovely white writing on black backgrounds, Anchises and the others would say the lines aloud, so that the movie was not silent at all.

Better run, Your Majesty, or I'll eat you all up!

I'd rather marry a mushroom!

Oh, how I should like to see how the fish live under the sea!

Anchises said Mr Bergamot's lines. He put on a deep voice like he thought an octopus—a hideous creature he could not imagine being real—might have. Once, he said his line through a bowl of water, which made everyone laugh. He felt wriggly all over when they laughed, like bathing in the Qadesh. When Mr Bergamot danced on-screen in his eight shining spats, Anchises danced a little, too, and that made them laugh again. It was wonderful.

You're a funny-looking fish.

Buck up, baby blowfish. Just puff up bigger than your sadness and scare it right off. That's the only way to live in the awful old ocean.

I love you bigger than the ocean.

But when it came to the climactic scene, the one where Mr Bergamot and Mrs Oolong and Chamomile are swimming through a shipwreck on the run from the vicious manta ray Dr Darjeeling and all hope is nearly lost, the girl in pigtails who was supposed to say Chamomile's lines had fallen asleep at the tuba player's feet.

The schoolteacher shoved Anchises forward to say her line, even though that was a bit confusing, as he was a boy, and he had the next line, too. He tried to make his voice high and soft like a girl's, like he imagined Chamomile's would sound.

I wish the night would end and I could see the sunlight again. I wish I could stay here forever with you under the sea.

The blood drained from Doctor Callow's face. He clapped his hand over his mouth.

Far offshore, the red Qadesh trembled.

The night ended in the Land of Milk and Desire. But it did not end in Adonis. It did not end for Anchises.

From the Personal Reels of
Percival Alfred Unck

[The screen is dim. SEVERIN UNCK has awakened from dark dreams in the middle of the night. She is five years old. Her father sits on her bed, an enormous wrought-iron bower of briars piled high against the lunar autumn with embroidered quilts and an infinitude of pillows. SEVERIN drowns in it; she is a tiny ship adrift on the sea of linen. PERCIVAL UNCK wraps his long arms around his daughter.]

PERCIVAL

Don't fear, my little hippopotamus. Dreams can be frightening, but they can't hurt you.

SEVERIN

They can! Oh, they can, Papa. [She begins to weep quietly.]

PERCIVAL

Tell your papa what you dreamt that was so terrible. When something is very awful indeed, so awful you can't bear it, there's a magic trick you can do. Tell the something's story from start to finish, and by the time you get to the end, you will often find you can bear it quite well, and perhaps it was never so bad in the first place.

SEVERIN

I dreamt I grew up and I was all alone. I was the loneliest girl in the whole world.

PERCIVAL

Is that all?

SEVERIN

It's a lot! I was in a little black room and everywhere I went I took the black room with me, and no one could get in, and I couldn't get out.

PERCIVAL

That's a very short story. I don't know if the magic works when the story's so short. Do you feel better?

SEVERIN

No. I shall never feel better again.

PERCIVAL

But you will, my love. The sun will come up and shine his brightest at the scary old beasties that scamper round your poor head, and everything will be right as rainbows. That's what the sun is for.

~~The Deep Blue Devil~~
~~The Man in the Malachite Mask~~
Doctor Callow's Dream:
Teatime for Mr Bergamot

There are stories so old and strong that they travelled from Home to the Country of Seeing and Being Seen, the Land of Wild Rancheros, the Land of Purple Corn, and the Land of Milk and Desire. The stories were stowaways: they hid in the ships with settlers, only coming out to breathe and stretch when absolutely necessary. And when the ships made landfall, the stories, having conserved their energy, burst free and ran wild, changing into local clothes and dancing up on stages and wearing flowers in their hair. Stories are like that. They love havoc, especially their own.

Many of these stories involve sleep. That is because we are all afraid of sleeping. We know it deep in our blood and our marrow. A panther, a bear, a Cro-Magnon may find a child while she's sleeping. And so we tell tales of a girl who pricked her finger on a navigational array and fell asleep for a hundred years. A girl who ate an apple that wasn't really an apple and fell into a deep sleep until a handsome businessman with a Kleen-Krop patent came along and kissed her awake again. A wise scientist who gave away all his notes for free, so his assistant put him to sleep in a tree forever.

It was like that for Anchises. For Doctor Callow.

He didn't prick his finger or eat an apple—a real apple or otherwise. He didn't give away his magic books.

It was only that he had a hundred fine, long, coppery-golden hairs tangled in among his own, stuck to his skin, snagged in his boots. It was only that he smelled like sumac and ozone and coffee and possibilities; and his mother's callowmilk bisque; and Hesiod's cigarettes; and the tops of the twins' heads when they were first born; and thick, good paper that had been drawn on over and over and over so that it was all black from corner to corner. It was only that he hadn't been hungry for moth-steaks or fried nutcake or piglet pies or cassowary custard and had stuffed himself with callowmilk meringue and sweet callowmilk cheese with apricot (which is not really apricot, but a charcoal-coloured, crunchy, caramelly fruit that shrinks away from any human hand that tries to grasp it) and callowmilk pandowdy and blancmange and callowpudding and zabaglione and callownog, everything with cream and milk and cheese in it, everything with callowmilk thick and spicy and pale folded in and poured over it. He had eaten like he had never really known how to eat before. He had eaten like his bones were hollow.

In stowaway stories like these, the solution is often simple. Too simple for anyone to think of until later, when the kingdom is asleep and the spinning wheels are all burnt up and there are dwarves building a coffin of glass and a wizard has been buried in the foundations of a castle. *Oh. Oh. I should have known it. If only I had known.*

A mother knows the smell of her young. Even when she is sick, even when she is mad, even when she cannot see her own hand before her, she knows her child. Her poor, tiny child—what can have gone wrong with this one? He's so little, impossibly little— no child so thin can be healthy. What can she do, what can she possibly do to make him grow? To make him strong, to make him *right*? Nothing could be more important than a child so ill he only has four pitiful, withered fronds and a tubule that looks like it couldn't hold a mouthful of milk.

Oh little calf, little bull, come to our breast. We did not see you there. It isn't your fault, poor lamb. We have only ourselves to blame. Hold still. Don't squirm. We will make it better. We will kiss it and kiss it and kiss it and kiss it until it doesn't hurt anymore. Until nothing can hurt anymore.

Little Doctor Callow did not fall asleep for a hundred years. He fell asleep for ten. But he did not sleep a person's sleep. A person did not tuck him in and tell him: *Close your eyes, my darling— don't open them; don't even peek. Say your prayers. Count sheep- which-are-not-really-sheep. Hush now. Soft now.* He slept the sleep of a callowhale. And, in sleep, a callowhale may move, may *quiver.* The sleep of a callowhale is not like our languorous, thick, sprawling, deathlike primate slumber. It is not really sleep at all. It is a spiky, spinning sword tip pricking the surface of the world a hundred times in a hundred places (though it is really an infinite, intangible intaglio of prickings) but never cutting.

It is not really sleep. It is not really milk. It is not really a whale.

Place a strip of film in a projector. Run it forward. Stop. Run it backward. Stop. Run it forward again. Now take it out and put it back in horizontally. Diagonally. Folded in half. Folded three times. Four. Twelve. One thousand and four. Put it in front of the light. Run it forward. Stop. Run it backward.

That is how a callowhale sleeps. It is like sleeping. It is also like *jumping.* It is a sleep like a panther.

But always, always, a callowhale dreams.

This is what Doctor Callow dreamed at his spinning wheel, in his glass coffin, in the roots of his tree:

Whales travel in pods. So did Doctor Callow. The sea he travelled in was every colour. He felt no arms or legs, though he knew he had them. He felt no effort in swimming. He felt large.

Doctor Callow dove and spun through the waves, and each wave was a country like his own beloved Land of Milk and Desire, but he did not stop, could not stop, to look at them.

Beside him swam a whale, which was not really a whale but a dark, sullen child with raggedy hair and a sour expression. She wore a dress of poppies on her body that was a whale's body but also a child's body, like his own. She turned to him in the Sea of Every Colour and said:

Better run, Your Majesty, or I'll eat you all up.

He swam harder after her. Harder and harder. She was so fast.

Come find me in two years, she called back over her flippers that were not really flippers.

But I've found you now, he answered her.

And then she was sitting at the bottom of the Sea of Every Colour, her lacy dress spread out all around her, the orange flowers opening and closing like bloody kisses. The water carried her hair up, fanning it around her head like a black serpent-crown. She drew in the sand of the ocean floor with a stick. This is what she drew:

She looked up at him.

Are we going to live here forever? she asked.

I think so.

The little girl sighed. Bubbles flowed out of her mouth. *I miss someone.*

I miss lots of someones, Doctor Callow said, into the sea.

The girl nodded. *Do you know what this place is?*

It's where the callowhales live.

Yes, the girl said, though he could not tell if she was happy about it.

Chamomile?

That's not my name.

What is your name?

Severin.

Severin?

Yes?

I don't think we're in Kansas anymore.

Severin started. She gave him a strange, searching expression. Her voice sharpened, grew older. *Why did you say that?*

I don't know. It seemed like a good thing to say.

You said it like you were quoting something. What's Kansas? Is it a planet?

Doctor Callow suddenly felt confused. He forgot how to swim in the Sea of Every Colour and dropped abruptly to the sand beside Severin. *I think so? Maybe? It sounds nice.*

Maybe it's one of the other places.

What other places?

Mr Bergamot lives everywhere.

What are you talking about?

She gestured to the callowhales overhead, as massive as suns, and circling, circling forever. *Mr Bergamot loves teatime. At teatime he eats worlds. And egg salad.*

I'm lonely, whispered Doctor Callow.

Don't be. There's a million million worlds to play with.

I'm lonely, he whispered again, because he didn't know what else to say.

That's okay, Severin Unck answered. She put her small hand on his. The colours of the Sea-which-wasn't-really-a-Sea got so bright Severin and Doctor Callow had to shut their eyes, which were not really their eyes. Doctor Callow looked up through the waves-which-were-not-really-waves and saw a callowhale—thousands of callowhales—soaring through the surf. They looked back at him as one creature, their infinite faces-which-were-not-really-faces as radiant as the spasms of stars, as the first frame of a film that is perfect, that is impossible, that is complete.

That's okay, Severin said. *I'm here. There's no place like Home.*

PART FOUR

❀ ❀ ❀ ❀ ❀

THE GOLD PAGES

Goddess, as soon as I saw you with my own eyes
I knew your divinity—but you gave me no truth.
Yet by aegis-wielding Zeus I beg thee—
do not make me live on, impotent, among men.
Have mercy on me, for well I know
the man who lies with immortal goddesses
is never left unharmed.

> —Homer, "Hymn to Aphrodite"

A photograph is a secret about a secret. The more it tells
you, the less you know.

> —Diane Arbus

There lived an old woman
Under a hill
And if she's not gone
She lives there still

> —Mother Goose

The Radiant Car Thy Sparrows Drew
(Oxblood Films, dir. Severin Unck)

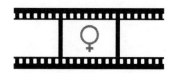

SC4 EXT. ADONIS, VILLAGE GREEN—DAY 16 TWILIGHT POST PLANETFALL 08:49 [3 DECEMBER, 1944]

[EXT. SEVERIN UNCK swims through the murky water, holding one of ERASMO ST. JOHN'S callow-lanterns out before her. ERASMO follows behind with her secondary camera, encased in a crystal canister. The film is badly stained and burned through several frames. She swims upward, dropping lead weights from her shimmering counter-pressure mesh as she rises. The grille of her diving bell gleams faintly in the shadows. Above her, slowly, the belly of a callowhale comes into view. It is impossibly massive, the size of a sky. SEVERIN strains towards it, extending her fingers to touch it, just once, as if to verify it for herself, that such a thing could be real.

The audience will always and forever see it before SEVERIN does. A slit in the side of the great whale, like a door opening. As the documentarian stretches towards it, with an instinctual blocking that is nothing short of spectacular—the suddenly tiny figure of a young woman frozen forever in this pose of surprise, of yearning, in the centre of the shot—the eye of the callow-hale, so huge as to encompass the whole screen, opens around her.]

Production Meeting
~~The Deep Blue Devil~~
~~The Man in the Malachite Mask~~
~~Doctor Callow's Dream~~
And If She's Not Gone, She Lives There Still
(Tranquillity Studios, 1961, dir. Percival Unck)

Audio Recorded for Reference by Vincenza Mako

PERCIVAL UNCK: I don't know how to end it. All this time and I still don't know. I can't change Rin's story. But I thought . . . I thought I could give *him* a better story. One where he had the means to search and find his fate, the way heroes do. One where he got saved. But answers are all that saves anyone, and I don't have any. I set the place for the ending, turned down the bed, lit the candles, and the bitch stayed out in the cold to spite me.

MAKO: But it wasn't ever going to be a *real* ending. Remember? It was going to be better than the real world. That was the whole point. That was the gift we wanted to make for her. It was going to have weight. It was going to rhyme with the beginning in some ineffable way that real endings never do. We never set out to tell a true story, only a *mostly* true one. The ending we planned *is* elegant, if you follow the logic, and "elegant" is more important than "real." That's always been our motto, really.

UNCK: The fairy tale thing was never going to work. It's beautiful, but it can only come at the story obliquely. It can only tell how it felt. It can't say anything like: "Severin Unck died by electrocution." It can't say she didn't. The language is all wrong. We have all the ambiguity we can eat already; we don't need more. And anyway, it's not a child's story. Or an adult's. It's not Anchises or Severin or anyone else, but all of them together, stuck in a room with no idea how to get out.

MAKO: There's a thought. A locked-room mystery?

UNCK: Huh. Maybe. We started him off as a detective. Maybe we can end it that way, too. Let him detect a little. But what room? We'd need a cell, a vault, perhaps a ship? We tried the grand estate already.

MAKO: Don't be so literal. Venus is the locked room.

UNCK: Things do tend to come out when there's nowhere to go.

MAKO: Let the mystery stay, but take the angry noir brooder out. Give it a bit of the old Victorian dash. A lashing of lace and leather. A room full of suspects, a brilliant genius with a flair for the dramatic. And why stick to people who really lived? Give it the shine of magic, a surreal spit-and-polish. Not too much—everyone hates the avant-garde, deep down. But enough to go out with a bang.

UNCK: But, Vince . . . I've got experience with this one. I know the song too well. It's been sung at me at top volume. I don't know if I can go through it again, even at the typewriter. That ghastly, desperate night, Mary staring at me like I'd become a hellhound before her eyes . . .

MAKO: Let's not talk about that right now. It's long over.

UNCK: I should have told Severin. Secrets seem so important until there's no one left to spill them to. I would have told her eventually. I would have found the right time. I remember she asked me once about endings. I told her you could have a story that was nothing but beginnings, but I didn't know if you could have one that was only endings. If she loved me, she'd have given me an ending I could use. If she'd loved me *at all*. [long pause] I was a terrible father.

MAKO: You weren't. Eccentric. Not terrible.

UNCK: I abandoned her. It's the one capital crime of fatherhood. Mothers can fail a thousand ways. A father's only job is: *do not abandon this child.* And what did I do? I let her run wild and never called her back in for supper when the sun got low.

MAKO: Percy . . . you don't have to finish this. You can just stop. Severin wouldn't be disappointed if you didn't finish. She'd understand. She left her movie unfinished, too.

UNCK: Oh, Vince, no. If I leave it like this . . . if I leave it, it looks just like her. A poor abandoned creature without an end. If I do that . . . she'll think I didn't love her. I can't let her think that. I let her think many wicked things about me, but not that. This is how I loved her. She knows it, recognizes it. And I promise you, if she's anywhere, she *hates* herself for leaving *Radiant Car* undone.

MAKO: Mystery on the Pink Planet, then?

UNCK: If you have a "Mystery" title, you're promising answers. If you're going to put your cards on the table, there'd better be something on them. Besides, that's just dreadful on the face of it. "Pink Planet." You're fired, Vince. I mean it this time.

MAKO: We have *some* answers. The rest . . . we guess. We lay down our best hand. Maybe it's not a royal flush, but it's enough to beat the house. And you never know. We could get it right. Stranger things have happened.

UNCK: [whispers] If I say she's dead, she will be.

MAKO: Then don't.

UNCK: I want to go back and start it all over again. From the first shot. In the thunderstorm. With the silver basket. I'll get it right this time. I can do it better. Just one more take.

<del>*The Deep Blue Devil*</del>
<del>*The Man in the Malachite Mask*</del>
<del>*Doctor Callow's Dream*</del>
And If She's Not Gone, She Lives There Still:
The Case of the Disappearing Documentarian

Begin with the widest shot possible and tighten it in: infinite lights in the infinite dark. Ten lights—shades of gold, blue, green, violet, red. One, one pink-orange lantern hanging in a wide, endless nothing without ceiling or floor. Every time it turns around, a year flies by. Closer. A city in the lantern, cordoned off by canals like velvet ropes. A single building in the city, almost a castle but not quite, thin and tall and ornamented with tangerine agate pillars, with gargoyles holding hearts in their hands and peonies in their mouths, with windows that face the sea. The doors close and lock discreetly; everyone necessary is already inside.

Begin with the most impersonal perspective, then tighten the aperture: What do the gargoyles see when they look through the windows?

Just before suppertime, in every room of the White Peony Waldorf, the telephones begin to ring. As the primrose and cornflower shadows of Venus whirl like leaves into gold, in every room of the White Peony Waldorf, hands pick up the polished brass receivers on the second ring. Lights come on like an advancing army of fireflies all over the Station, and in every room of the White Peony Waldorf, a lovely, lilting lady's voice pours out of the telephone:

"If you would be so good as to assemble in the Myrtle Lounge in a quarter of an hour, Mr St. John will present the evening's entertainment. Refreshments will be provided."

Adjust the lens: What do the windows see when they look into the rooms?

Dresses come out of closets; steam unwrinkles dinner jackets; shoes and hats are hurriedly located. Just as the supper bell rings, out of every room in the White Peony Waldorf, people emerge—hesitant, pensive, nerves and necklines sparkling. One by one they take their seats on the couches, armchairs, chaises, and barstools of the Myrtle Lounge, velvet on velvet on velvet; gowns and trousers crushing that ash-pale, fruiting moss into the thick upholstery. A gramophone plays some dainty old tune. Murmured conversations dapple the room, introductions are made—many of the guests have not met each other before tonight. Hands fiddle with cigars and cigarettes and atomizers—many of the guests have vices that prefer not to wait on the host. There is perfume, there is sweat, there is talc, there is fear—many of the guests wear all four.

Adjust the lens again. Abandon the impersonal perspective and smash it underfoot like a wedding glass. What do the players see?

Anchises St. John and Cythera Brass sweep into the lounge. The air bursts with a flurry of snapping photographs. She wears a sleek strapless number that rustles silver in the popping lights. Flashes of the palest pink feathers flutter in the hem; a slim triangle of dyed crocodile scales soars up to a daring rosette of amethyst and alarming croc teeth at the point of the gown's plunging, bare back. He wears a raisin-dark smoking jacket over dove-grey trousers and a shirtfront so white you'd think angels ran textile mills. A deep rose cravat blossoms at his throat, with a tiny tiger's eye pin to hold it in place, and his buttery-yellow leather gloves shine in the low light. Cythera beams, her posture soft as a shimmy in the dark. Anchises is a picture of health, ruddy, his dark hair glossed and thick, a beard coming in nicely, his eyes bright as the sun glinting on a magnifying glass.

Anchises and Cythera hoist up platters of cocktails from the bar and serve them with smiles.

"Good evening!" Anchises cries, his rich, full voice, a leading man's voice, bouncing off the moss-drenched walls. "Good evening, and welcome to my little party. I'm so pleased you all could make it! I know some of you have had a long journey, but you have, at long last, come to the end! Welcome to the end! Make yourself at home! Relax, put up your feet, and have a well-deserved drink!"

Zoom in again. Adjust the lens. Tighter. Tighter.

What does Anchises St. John see?

"A pink lady for you, Dad," the great detective says, and, with a flourish, presents a flute to Erasmo St. John, the man who raised him, still strong and broad as a painting of Hercules, his bright black skin free of wrinkles, of the papery thinness of his last days on Mars; as he was on the seventeenth of November, 1944: twenty-eight years old, in love, well laid, and well paid. "Real gin, all the way from London. And a gimlet with muddled mint and French lavender for you, Mum—now, now, I insist. It's my party, I get to spoil you." He places a crystal glass in the slim hand of Severin Unck, sitting cross-legged in a black silk evening gown, trimmed in raven feathers and slit up to her hip. Her aviator jacket drapes over her shoulders; she smokes a cigar. One dark, pencilled eyebrow arches up in amusement.

Erasmo leans over to kiss her. She touches the tip of his nose with her finger. Her skin flickers, crackles where it touches his; she is black and white, a film in flesh. "Thanks, sweetheart," she says. "You shouldn't have."

Cythera plops down in a dashing fellow's lap. He kisses her cheek. Thirty-seven and in his prime, with blistering black eyes and El Greco cheekbones, he looks just as he did the night before a certain silver basket landed on his doorstep. Two women share his couch. Cythera hands out the goods. "That's an aviator for Unck Senior, a Bellini for the lovely Mary P, and an old-fashioned for Madame? You've got honest-to-Betsy Madrid lemons there, Percy; real Creek Nation peaches in your bubbly, Miss P; Hawaiian sugar and California orange peel in your *extremely* stiff drink, Maxine."

Mary Pellam laughs like a toffee fountain and nuzzles the ear of Madame Mortimer. They have the same short blond hair, fine as fairy floss, but Mortimer has come to do business in her best black travelling suit, while Mary, seventeen and sweet as a clementine, wears a gold scrap of flapper froth, lavender lipstick, and no shoes.

Anchises does a quick shuffle over to a long couch mottled like a dairy cow with snowy moss. The tips of the moss have sprouted mauve spores. They smell of warm nutcake. "A piña colada with a juicy wedge of Queensland pineapple for my esteemed Mr Bergamot! A snakebite for Marvin the Mongoose—thank you so much for coming on such short notice—and a Brandy Alexander—served in a punchbowl, naturally—for Calliope the Carefree Callowhale!" A cartoon octopus in spats and a monocle wraps one hand-painted, bright green tentacle around the stem of his cocktail. A cheerful animated mongoose grabs his pint glass with both peppy, overcranked paws. Anchises sets the crystal punchbowl down on a side table so that a caricatured whale can dip her turquoise head into the booze. She sits like a lady: friendly, enormous, bright-eyed head up; long, non-threatening dolphin tail down. A steady spray of healthy milk gurgles up from her spout like flowers in a hat.

"Hey," says Marvin the Mongoose, "didn't you used to be a puppet? Or am I thinking of some other cat?"

"I transitioned to animation after my fourth film," allows Mr Bergamot. "Though what I really want to do is direct."

"No shop talk," admonishes Calliope, fluttering her long eyelashes at the boys.

"And we have not forgotten the honoured, beloved, and marvellously morbid among us," Cythera announces.

"Dead to the world, but still the life of the party—we appreciate how far you've come to be with us tonight! Don't worry, cake will be served after the festivities!" Anchises drops to one silk knee before a man and woman with dark hair very like his own, dressed in a matching summer suit and clean white linen tea dress. She sits at an angle, askew; her spine is broken. He's donned a smart bowler hat to hide his shattered skull. The couple beam with joy, blush with the embarrassment of sitting at the centre of attention.

"First," Anchises says, his voice swelling with feeling, "a bottle of 1944 Bordeaux for my mother and father. I hope you don't mind me calling those two Mum and Dad. Mixed families can get so confusing. But I know where I came from. Mostly. And the wine came from the Loire Valley." He holds a hand up to his cheek and whispers loudly, "That's in France."

Peitho and Erzulie Kephus kiss their son, stroke his face, drink in his height, his confidence, his fine clothes. "How well you look! My baby boy, all grown up," Erzulie says, and wipes her eyes.

"We're proud of you, son," says Peitho, with the special brand of gruffness that hides manful tears.

Cythera Brass selects a slim green libation from her lacquered tray. "A grasshopper for my dear, sweet Arlo," she croons.

A man in a diving costume, his jaw square, his shoulders broad, and his glasses broken, smiles like a million dollars prudently invested. Brackish water full of stones and slime pours out of the sides of his smile. He can't help it. He is so happy to see her. One of his feet is missing, the ankle chewed ragged, bloody. "Cyth! What brings a nice girl like you to a place like this?" Arlo Covington, C.P.A., kisses his old boss's cheek.

Anchises moves down the line. "Max! You old so-and-so! You had me going there on Pluto for a while, but I've got your number now. And that number is . . . a banana margarita! Am I right? Old Horace, I don't even have to ask, do I? Pisco sour, my good man. Peru or bust."

Horace St. John, his legs tied up with silk bows to keep the shattered bones at something like human angles, shakes Anchises's hand. One of his ribs protrudes from his Sunday suit like a white corsage. "You're a prince." He winks.

"Iggy, you look gorgeous! How about a stiff Sazerac?"

Santiago Zhang blushes. His mouth bleeds freely; shards of metal spike through his lips, his severed tongue. He squeezes Anchises's hand joyfully. "It's my lifelong ambition to try every cocktail known to man—this'll be number eighty-two!" His lips leave a smear of blood on the glass like lipstick.

"And last but not least: Mari, Mariana, an apricot zombie for *mi corazon*, my darling, my sugar, apple of my eye and bird in my hand—is it too soon for hand jokes? Well, you know I never had a proper upbringing, I can't be expected to know these things." The sound engineer scowls, but she can't keep it up for long. She grins girlishly and waggles her fingers. Mould covers her hand, her arm, bores into her cheeks. Fleshy fiddleheads yo-yo out of her palm. Maximo gives a mock bow and pulls a tuppence out of Anchises's ear to show there's no hard feelings. His eyes hang hollow in his face, his skin ashen, sallow, slick with Plutonian influenza, which is nothing to sneeze at.

"We'll top that off with a Death in the Afternoon for you, Anki, and a bourbon neat for me," Cythera finishes with a twirl, her feathers and scales catching the chandelier light and tossing it back up to the painted ceiling.

"You're incorrigible!" Erasmo hollers. Severin glimmers with silver-screen delight. "Let the nice man make it a Daisy, at least!"

"Never!" cries Cythera Brass.

The company roars laughter.

"Oy, Mr Grumpy Bear, you forgot somebody!" comes a voice like chocolate-covered starlight, sailing over the assembled host.

"Don't you believe it for a second, missy." Anchises snatches a final snifter from the bar and fairly hops over to the late arrival. She has always known how to make an entrance. She's buffalo fur and dragon leather from head to toe, young as the day is short, a plunging neckline and a soaring sweep of hair, her Moroccan features severe and welcoming all at once, her smile brand new, All-American. "A sweet moonlight for my sweet moonbeam, *crème de violette* for my dreamy Violet, queen of the airwaves."

Violet El-Hashem takes her due praise and her seat, scootching in between the octopus and the mongoose. She waves shyly at Calliope. Marvin curls up in her lap and begs for belly scratches.

A hush falls. Expectant, nervous silence moves like a hot potato from hand to hand. Maxine Mortimer whispers in Mary's ear. Percy makes a face at his daughter; she giggles behind her nickelodeon hand.

Anchises quaffs his absinthe and champagne in one gulp and opens his arms extravagantly, taking everyone in: everyone, everything, his life, his past, and his future.

"*Mesdames et messieurs*, ladies and gentlemen, boys and girls, octopi and mongooses, whales and wendigos, slatterns and stick-in-the-muds! We are here to investigate the early retirement of one Severin Lamartine Unck. I won't bore you with the facts of a case you know all too well. Every one of you has a piece of the puzzle, and tonight is the night we put it all together and—if we're lucky and everyone plays fair—point a finger at the baddie, have a spot of cake, dance it off, and call it a night. Are you ready? Has everyone visited the necessaries? Shall we begin?"

Mary Pellam whistles through two fingers. "Go get 'em, St. John!"

Anchises's parents clap enthusiastically. Their dead hands make no sound. "We love you, honey!" they cheer.

Marvin the Mongoose hops up from Violet's lap, spins around three times, bites his own tail, and yelps in his trademark lisp, "I am SO EXCITED. I don't know what's happening, but IT IS AMAZING. I want another snakebite! Two 'nother snakebites! HOW MANY YA GOT?"

"Why, hullo!" laughs Violet, scratching him behind one animated ear. "You're voiced by Alain Mbengue, aren't you?"

"Sure am!" Marvin puffs out his fluffy chest.

Violet shakes his paw. "My goodness, we're practically related!"

Cythera produces a brass gong from behind the Myrtle Lounge bar and wallops it with a hammer. "I've always wanted to do that," she confesses. "Enough with the patty-cake and the chit-a-chat! Eyes forward, mouths shut!"

Anchises begins. "Very well! As I see it, there are two possible solutions to this mystery. I shall lay them both out and we shall have a vote. Acceptable? Excellent. Now, the first solution is the easiest one, Occam's old standby: I propose that Severin is dead."

"Well, that's not very nice," Calliope the Carefree Callowhale harrumphs. She speaks with the voice of the actress who played her—an unsettling experience for the lady herself, Violet El-Hashem, seated one mongoose away. The whale's long-lashed eyes narrow. "And I resent the implication. I mind my own business; you lot ought to mind yours!"

"That *is* the trouble, isn't it, Miss Calliope? We *haven't* been minding our own business. In fact, we—human beings, I mean—have rather taken hold of *your* business and called it our own without so much as a by-your-leave, isn't that right?"

"Damned right," huffs the cartoon whale. "How would you

like it if I came and yanked on your personal bits while you tried to have a nap and made ice cream out of whatever oozed out?"

"How dreadful!" gasped Mr Bergamot, hiding his face with his tentacles. "I do hope none of these bandits have *my* address!"

"I'm sure we're all very sorry," snaps Mariana Alfric. Flakes of jade-coloured mould fly from her lips. "But we didn't *know*. None of us were even alive when the *Yue Lao* landed on Venus. It doesn't give you the right to go around smashing up villages and sticking your *personal bits* in my *personal bits!*" Mariana waves her tentacled hand by way of illustration. A chorus of approval echoes through the dead.

Calliope the Callowhale sniffs indignantly. "I feel we made it perfectly obvious we didn't want to be interfered with. Would you trouble a tree for apples if the branches vaporised you instantly? I should think you'd leave it well enough alone! We ought not to be castigated for defending ourselves! Ask her!" Calliope points her animated fin at Violet El-Hashem.

"I don't know what you think I had to do with any of it," the radio star opines.

"You were one of the first of the robbers to come knocking at our door."

"I beg your pardon! I was eight years old!"

"Oh, come off it. We know your voice. We've heard it over and over in our heads, sizzling back and forth like incandescent grease in an infinite pan. 'When I looked upon that new world, splendid in every way and in every way terrible, I looked upon a tiger with stars falling from his striped tongue. I looked and saw my true bridegroom!' I am *not* your bridegroom, sweetheart, but I shall be your tiger if I have to."

Violet El-Hashem laughs long and hard. "Fishie, my love, it was only radio! The first time I set foot on Venus my publicist handed me a script, a contract, a cocktail, and slapped my bottom twice."

"May I ask a question?" Arlo Covington raises his hand, still in its thick diving glove. Muck dribbles from the corner of his mouth and into his cool green drink.

"Hold your question for one moment, Arlo?" Anchises begs. "I fear some of our friends are getting rather upset. Let's remember we're all stuck in this together, shall we? We can play happy families for one evening, can't we? Mariana? Violet?"

"Fine," the girls grumble.

"Calliope? Let's see some of that carefree callowhale we all know and love?"

"Fine," spits the whale.

Anchises claps his hands together. "Now, Mum, you old scamp, get up here."

Severin Unck disentangles herself from Erasmo and skips up to the bar, where she fixes herself another gimlet.

"Come on, Mumsy. You can tell us."

"ARE WE POISONOUS?" holler Erasmo, Maximo, Mariana, Santiago, and Arlo, collapsing into helpless giggles.

But that's not Anchises's question. "Are you dead?"

Severin's celluloid eyes twinkle. She taps her nose with a silvery finger. "I don't want to spoil it." She smirks. "Never go swimming for at least an hour after lunch, kids!"

Madame Mortimer stands up, stroking her eye patch as she thinks. "The only reason anyone thought twice about the whole business was on account of the footage of your bloody great eyeball, Calliope. Normally, death requires a body; but there are many exceptions, and this easily qualified. Callowdiving is a dangerous profession at the best of times. The careless are atomized like a ball of af-yun. It's tragic, but it's happened a thousand times without all this *Sturm und Drang* and beating of breasts. Without that little filmstrip, it's an open and shut case."

Mary Pellam pipes up. "That, and the fact that Maxie-boy over there has blubbered all over the known universe that he killed her."

Anchises nods. "Yes, I do think it's time we had a whack at that, don't you, Prospero, old friend?"

Maximo Varela does not stand. He salutes with his margarita. "Ah, but I did kill her, my boy."

"Liar," purrs Severin from behind the bar. She saunters back to Erasmo, bearing a fresh pink lady. She perches on the seat of his armchair. "Oh, what a big fat liar you are."

"Are we playing the lying game?" yips Marvin the Mongoose. His whiskers *sproing* merrily. "I love that game! I'm aces at it! Pick me! Pick me! I killed Severin, too!"

"Who *are* you?" sighs Peitho Kephus in exasperation. "What do you have to do with any of this? What are you doing here?"

Marvin the Mongoose puts both paws over his mouth. He hiccups. "I don't know!" he yips. "I hitched a ride with the octopus!"

Max's plague-slicked face droops. "I'm telling the truth. I'm so sorry, Rin."

Severin rolls her eyes. "Good grief, Max, whatever for?"

"I hit you."

"I hit you, too. I'm comfortable with our score."

Maximo's sunken eyes fill with rheumy tears. "I shoved you. You fell onto the rocks."

"I had a bruised arse. Big deal."

"You fell onto George and smashed it."

"You've got me there. Your honour, Maximo Varela murdered George the kinesigraph camera in cold blood. I saw it with my own eyes. Take him away!"

"Baby, you should listen," says Erasmo softly.

"I did kill you," the Mad King of Pluto whispers. "But I did it after you died. On the *Clamshell*. Erasmo and Cristabel cut *Radiant Car* for you. As a way to say goodbye or a way to keep you alive, I don't know. It took them weeks. Konrad and Franco brought food to the darkroom and left it outside the door. We didn't see them or the boy for weeks. It was like they'd vanished, too. And all the while, I still had that static in my head. That horrible static filled with voices, our voices, sawing on my skull every minute. I can still hear it."

"You never told me that," says Erasmo.

"I don't tell you much, Raz. But it's true. And then, a month out of lunar orbit, the three of them emerged from their exile. They asked us all to come to the cantina for a screening. They even made popcorn. Trying to make some little happiness. And we watched *The Radiant Car Thy Sparrows Drew*. It was a hundred and twenty-seven minutes long. When the lights came up, everyone wept. They hugged each other, kissed foreheads and cheeks. In movies and books they always say: *A spell had been lifted*. But it had. They were in grief. But they would live."

Severin Unck leans toward her lighting master. Her breathing quickens. "Was it good? Was it *good*, Max? Did I do okay? Did I make something . . . right? Tell me it was wonderful. I have to know it came out all right."

And Percival Unck rises from his seat to take his daughter into his arms.

"That's my girl," he says. He kisses the top of her head. *It's nice to have made a person to commiserate with*, he thinks, and Severin knows his thought without hearing it.

"I always thought you were going to be taller." Percy laughs. His voice goes softer. "I always thought we'd patch it up someday."

"We did," Severin says. "Just you wait."

"It was beautiful," Max admits. "Sad, and terrible, and monstrous. But beautiful. People would have kept watching it as long as they knew how to work a projector. And that's when I killed you."

"Oh, Max," sighs Mariana.

"The static crawled in my head, and my dead, obliterated

Mariana crawled in my heart, and I couldn't get a second's peace, not a moment's quiet. The static sent hideous knives of lightning though me, and the lightning spoke with your voice. It said, over and over: *They have killed a Nereid. And she was full of roe. Full of roe. Full of roe.* Like a nursery rhyme. Once *Radiant Car* started playing, Mariana began to sing along with the killing of the Nereid in my bones. *Twinkle, twinkle, little dragon, won't you come and pull my wagon.* The two of you did not sing in harmony. Utterly atonal. I wanted to die. And when it ended, and you disappeared out of the frame like a cheap jump-cut trick, I heard you say a new thing: *A mother is a person who leaves.* I knew then how to stop the white noise from burning me out from the inside. The way princesses know things in fairy tales. The way you know things in dreams."

Maximo Varela cannot go on. He sobs, guilt and lymphatic fluid seeping out of his grey skin. Erasmo finishes his confession for him.

"While we slept, he stole everything. All the reels, the scraps, the outtakes, everything. Even the unusable stuff. He dragged it all up to the observation deck and laid it out in the sun to overexpose. You tried to stop him, Anchises. Maybe you remember. Hopefully not. I don't know how you could even have understood what would happen to film left in the light, but you tried to grab it all up in your little arms like so much black spaghetti. You held it tight to your little chest and hissed at him. And Max . . . well, he hit you until you let go. Hit a kid with his fists. Stomped on your hand. I never forgave him. Never will. *Radiant Car* fried all night. Chemical fumes everywhere. Smoke but no fire. By the time we figured out what he'd done, those four miserable pieces were all we could salvage."

"I killed you," Maximo insists. "It was all that we had of you, and I burned it. I turned the big spotlight on it and it burned and I made that child bleed and I didn't care. I killed the heart of you.

But the static burned out, too. No more roe. No more twinkling dragons. No more mothers leaving.

"We have all come here to mend. But there's no forgiveness in the Wizard's bag for me." Varela blinks and shakes his head, as though he doesn't quite know why he'd said that last bit.

Severin stubs out her cigar on her filmstrip-hand. A glowing hole pops into life in her palm, like an open mouth. "You're right," she says. "There isn't. No heart, no courage, no brains for you, Max. And no supper, either." She considers carefully, a rakish Rhadamanthus, before delivering her judgment. "Go sit in the corner. That's your punishment."

And so he does. The King of Pluto faces the wall.

"I never seriously considered Varela a suspect," Anchises informs the room.

"That's not what you said at Setebos Hall." Cythera snorts.

"I am wiser by far now. No, the evidence leads us to one conclusion: Calliope is the villain in our midst. I accuse you, callowhale! What say you?"

The callowhale tries to snarl, but she had only ever been drawn smiling, so that children would love her. She smiles and smiles, and in her singsong advertising jingle voice she trills, "She stank of death and life and a million never-sleeping eyes! Don't give me your smug primate smirks, Anchises St. John! *You* touched our dying limb and took our spores into your tiny, insufficient flesh. A new star guttered in the dream-net of the callowhales. It wanted to live, but it had no vigour. We felt you in us; we thought you were part of us, lost, dying. We came for you, and destroyed the cage you languished in. Only afterward did we understand our mistake. We are very embarrassed about it. But your parents should have taught you to keep your hands to yourself! You touched Severin's face in gratitude; Mariana struck you in fear—new stars guttering into very little of note on the edges of our dreams. We would not be fooled twice. We ignored them. Told them we were on to their tricks. But Severin came so close, right into my parlour, and her stink woke me like burnt bacon. I told her to go away, and she did. I am not sorry! She is small and I am big. She drank my milk without asking. I will not be made to apologize!"

"What about me?" asks Mariana Alfric. "I didn't come close. I didn't get a chance."

Calliope shrugs her cheerfully drawn shoulders. "You let that doctor cut us out of you. You could no longer live separately. When our child died, you died. It had already converted much of your fluid and tissue. Children are so hungry in their first hours."

"Your *child*?" gasps the sound engineer.

"What did you think it was? A disease? A wound? You guzzle our milk and think we never bear young?"

"Ooh!" exclaims Mr Bergamot. The animated octopus slides off his mossy sofa and draws himself up onto his tip-tentacles. "May I have the seafloor? I'm quite keen on marine biology, you know."

"By all means." Anchises gracefully relinquishes the Myrtle Lounge bar.

"Lemme help!" squeals Marvin the Mongoose, and scampers away from Violet's lap.

The mongoose and the octopus clear their throats. They run through a quick warm-up: *Do re mi fa so la ti do! Do ti la so fa mi re do!* Mr Bergamot produces a harmonica from goodness-knows-where, lays down an establishing A note, and snaps his suckers to a quickstep beat.

"The Lifecycle of the Callowhale!" the mongoose and the octopus sing in unison. And they begin to soft-shoe up and down the bar.

"A callowhale isn't much of a whale," sings Mr Bergamot in the key of G.

"Not a bug!" belts out Marvin.

"Not a cat!"

"Not a fungus or a snail!"

The octopus knots four tentacles together into a square while turning cartwheels with the rest. A light clicks on inside the square of suckers, though the Waldorf owns no projector. The film merrily commences, and all watch in wonder as an on-screen Calliope dances on her tail. Mr Bergamot sings his verse:

The great callowhale's got no stop and no start
Just a hundred million brains and a million hundred hearts

Hundreds of tiny callowhale shapes appear with cheerful popping sound effects, all squeezed into Calliope's big body. Marvin the Mongoose sings his turn:

They're all dressed up with everywhere to go
They might look funny but boy, how they grow!

In the film, Calliope sprouts a red bow on the side of her ever-smiling head and a string of pearls round her neck. A knock sounds—is it a date? No! It's a little boy! It is, in fact, Anchises, drawn like a lovable scamp in a Sunday comic strip. He holds up a squirming mass of fiddleheads and fronds like flowers. Calliope blushes: *For me?* And then Mr Bergamot and his mongoose assistant burst into a flurry of tap dancing, four tappity-spats and two sets of clackety-claws going a mile a minute.

If you're having trouble with the maths
Come consult our helpful graphs!

The graph's bars spring up, fountains erupting from the blowholes of two miniature Calliopes. The tallest bears the title,

"How Important a Callowhale Is to the Continued Function of the Multiverse." A very short, squat one, little bigger than an exclamation point, reads: "How Important You Are to the Continued Functioning of the Multiverse." A pitiful slide whistle sounds its note, and then they're off again. Marvin turns a somersault and warbles:

Just think of a long shiny pin!

The music scratches to a halt. Mr Bergamot protests, "A pin! Now that's just silly!"

"Not as silly as an octopus playing the harmonica," the mongoose rejoins. A rimshot echoes down the Waldorf staircase from nowhere. The octopus and mongoose join arms and serenade the lounge together:

Now think of a long shiny pin!
Stuck down through batting and muslin!
Cotton and linen, silk, lace, and wool, too!
There's so much that fantastic pin can punch through!

One of the Calliopes leaps off the graph. Her nose sharpens to a wicked silver point. She dives down from the x-axis and the image shifts: a whale shearing through quilts and blankets and veils, sending up splashes of thread behind her.

The pin holds it together, so nice and so neat
That is a pin everyone wants to meet!

The spaces between Mr Bergamot's tentacles fill with stars, with worlds none of the living or the dead have seen before, shuffling together like cards, like the squares of a quilt, lying one atop the other. All the while the bouncing cartoon callowhale dives through them.

Well, that silk is a universe and so are the laces
The cotton and linen are vast starry spaces
Where nothing goes quite as it goes where you go
And no one you'll meet will be someone you know
And the fantastic pin that we mentioned before?
Is a callowhale swimming through infinite doors

The stars coalesce into a cheerleader with GO WHALES! stamped on her megaphone. She throws nebulae into the air like pom-poms.

So cheer on the whales and treat them with care
Don't tease and don't poke, don't startle or stare
Without them, the silk would slide right off the linen
And who knows what trouble we all would be stuck in!

The cheerleader frowns and explodes into a puff of animated smoke. The slide whistle slides again. Mr Bergamot takes over once more, and the image he holds changes to Calliope with an enormous thermometer in her mouth and a cold compress on her head.

Now sometimes a whale can get hurt or get sick
Though their hearts are so strong and their skin is so thick.
But we can't go without, not for one single day
So they make a new whale to play callowcroquet!

A baby whale appears in a shower of glittery fireworks. It wears a lacy bonnet and shakes a rattle with its fin. Calliope and her baby wind up a pair of croquet mallets and whack Jupiter and Saturn through identical hoops.

Marvin the Mongoose, darling of Capricorn Studios, brings it home, while Bergamot's tentacles fill with smiling faces:

Oh, the life of a great callowhale is amazing!
We hope you'll forgive us our upside-down phrasing
And the next time your loved one gets vaporised flat
Just remember the pin, and that will be that.

A smattering of awkward applause picks up. The octopus relaxes his arms, the filmstrip clicks off, and our performers bow. But Marvin can't resist starting up again, high-kicking into a reprise:

If our song has got you spinning
Just go back to the beginning!
OH! A callowhale isn't much of a whale!
Not a bug! Not a cat! Not a fungus or a snail!

"May I ask a question?" Arlo interrupts the mongoose's encore.

"Yes, of course. I'm so sorry," Cythera says, and she means it.

"I understand the girls. But what did you do to me and Horace? We never touched the kid. We drank bottled water. We never did anything."

Calliope the Carefree Callowhale blushes, two perfect magenta circles blazing on her turquoise face.

"We ate you," she says sheepishly.

From the Personal Reels of Percival Alfred Unck

[MARY PELLAM, dressed in a black leotard and stockings, her clavicle and shoulder blades moving as delicately as swan bones beneath her skin, applies makeup in her gilded mirror. SEVERIN UNCK watches her, recording every stroke of the liner crayon with her dark pupils.]

SEVERIN

I don't want you to go.

[PERCIVAL UNCK balances his camera, Clara, on a dressing table with small blue horses painted all over it. He steps into frame and kisses Severin on the forehead before bending to hoist her up onto his hip.]

PERCIVAL

Mummy and Papa have to go to rehearsal. She's going to be Isis in *The Golden Ass*, which is a *bit* naughty for your age, I think, but you can watch it when you're . . . let's say eight. There's a donkey in; he'll make you laugh. Mummy is going to come in at the end and save the day. Won't that be wonderful? She'll wear a lovely big crown with an asp on it and carry heaps of roses in her arms. [pause] An asp is a poisonous snake. But very holy.

SEVERIN

I don't want you to *go*.

MARY

You can come along if you like, darling. You had loads of fun when we were rehearsing *The Great Train Robbery*.

SEVERIN

I ate candy and rode the train. But it was dark in there. In the . . .

PERCIVAL

In the soundstage, Rinny. [His eyes sparkle. He presses his daughter's small chin with his thumb.] Rehearsal is just practicing, my precious little hobgoblin. Mummy must practice being both Egyptian *and* a goddess, which is very hard to do at the same time! Why, it's like rubbing the top of your head and patting your belly at once. A soundstage is nothing to be afraid of, moppet. Just imagine Rehearsal has a capital R. Rehearsal is like a planet Mummy and I go to, like Earth or Mars. It's a dark cool planet with a lot of lights and people and toys and trains and candy, and when you go there you get to be somebody else and talk funny and dance a bit and say and do everything three times, because that's the law. Planets always have their own funny laws, don't they?

SEVERIN

Yes. I hate it.

PERCIVAL

Well, on Rehearsal, it's the law that you can only cry if Papa tells you to, or sing a song if Papa tells you to, and you can only fall down and hurt yourself if Papa tells you to do it *very* tragically, like Eurydice when the serpent bit her. Remember Eurydice?

SEVERIN

She let me wear her hat.

MARY

And Eurydice got right up and had a coffee when Papa said, "Cut!" didn't she? [SEVERIN nods reluctantly.] She was perfectly all right! My, my, we are just all over serpents today, aren't we? Come on, kitten! You and me are Egypt-bound!

The Graeae

Transcript from 1946 debriefing interview with Erasmo St. John, property of Oxblood Films, all rights reserved. Security clearance required.

CYTHERA BRASS: Session four, day three. This will be our last session, I think. How do you feel about that, Mr St. John?

ERASMO: Dandy.

CYTHERA: I've enjoyed talking to you.

ERASMO: Then you are out of your mind. There is nothing enjoyable in this. It's just eating ashes.

CYTHERA: Who checked on Mariana, after you lost contact with Arlo?

ERASMO: Severin and I. Rinny took care of everyone who would let her.

CYTHERA: And what was Miss Alfric's condition?

ERASMO: She was gone. Dissolved into long, stringy fern blades and spores and mud and withered leafy things. She hadn't run off. The pin in her knee from when she tried to ride Sancho Panza one last time was lying in the muck. No blood. Just . . . muck.

CYTHERA: Do you have any thoughts on the infection vector? Severin and Mariana both touched Anchises, but neither the child nor Unck had that kind of catastrophic reaction. In fact, Severin had much more contact than Alfric.

ERASMO: How should I know? Talk to Retta.

CYTHERA: Dr Nantakarn. [sounds of papers shuffling, file folders moving against each other.] *It is the opinion of this doctor that, once transmitted, the infection entered a state of dormancy in the Adonis subject. Neither Alfric nor Unck seemed to be contagious—it is possible that they would have become so given enough time. I can offer no firm reasoning as to why Unck showed no ill effects without the ability to take post-contact blood samples. Perhaps she had an immunity. Perhaps symptoms develop at different rates depending on any number of metabolic, environmental, or genetic factors. Perhaps it just liked her better.*

ERASMO: I don't know. Mari was fine until we cut it out of her. Well, not fine, but other than the fronds, she had no pain, no fever. But I think . . . sometimes I think it killed her because she hit Anchises. It defended itself. Reacted in fear. Severin just held him while he slept. It didn't have to be afraid of her. I don't know. I didn't have any time to think about the science of it.

CYTHERA: You had decided to break camp.

ERASMO: Yes. Three people were dead. We panicked. And we were still out of sync with our own soundtrack. We heard Max reciting Shakespeare to the boy hours after he stopped. Forward and backward. I was securing the gondola in the wind and I could hear Cristabel singing *I left my sugar standing in the rain and she melted away* . . . all couched in the static, sunk deep in it, the song a pin down at the bottom of the ocean. Crissy started clawing up her arms with her fingernails. Santiago . . . well, you must know. The night Severin disappeared, he took one of the machetes and hacked that Type I Ekho Ultra Mic into a hundred vicious pieces and started swallowing them one by one. Konrad stopped him before he finished his bowlful of knives, but Retta had to open up his gut as soon as we got back to White Peony. He was going into shock, bleeding into his stomach, his teeth ground half off, his tongue sliced almost in half. I never heard him speak again. Never saw him blink. He just turned off all over.

We were finished. We could take the kid back to White Peony and get a few more interviews with people who had a cousin's cousin's dog in Adonis and we'd have a movie in six months. We could heal. Everything else could be edited in, fixed in post. We had enough film shot on site to make it look like we'd been there for ages. Like we'd been thorough.

CYTHERA: Why do you think Severin went out on that dive? After everything that had happened, everyone she'd lost, why would she go out alone?

ERASMO: She didn't go out alone. I went with her. I know the cameraman is invisible, but come on. Give me a little credit for existing. Rin decided to go out to the callowhales because we were leaving.

[clears throat]

I've had a lot of time. Just . . . time. Life is long. You come to theories over time, and over time theories become convictions. And it's my conviction that Severin only went to Venus at all to make that dive. She wanted to see the callowhales. That's it. The kid, the village, sure. But the callowhales . . . they're the only unexplainable thing we found on seventy worlds. She wanted them. Maybe they wanted her. No one wanted her to go, and they all tried—she came out in her mesh suit sporting a shiner that said just how hard Maximo had tried. But I think she made up her mind that night on Neptune when the lights went out. She was going to touch one. She was going to fly through the night and the heavens to the one magical thing in creation and grab onto it for dear life.

You've seen the shot. There's nothing more to a dive than

that. You take the boat out and go down. Aylin manned the hoses up top. What I remember isn't that moment in the red dark, that moment when she was there and then she wasn't. I've seen that happen so many times on film it's like I don't even remember it myself anymore. What I remember is the night before.

We were lying on our cot with Anchises between us, for all the world like a family. We were gonna take him home and raise him—we hadn't talked about it yet, but we were going to. Just like Rin was going to go see the callowhales. She stroked his hair while he slept against her breast and she said, "There used to be a story. A Greek story, so you know it's good. About three sisters. They were actually the sisters of the Gorgons, too. You know, Medusa. They were called the Graeae. Sometimes they're painted as beautiful, sometimes as horrible and hideous. They have long white hair and they're never apart. They have one eye and one tooth between them. They share it. Pop it out of one sister's socket and into the other. I think about them a lot. I used to dream about them when I was little, when I first read about them. Oh, didn't I say? Perseus comes along and kills them on his way to killing the Gorgons. That's how it goes—as soon as there's anything interesting in Ancient Greece, some arsehole with a magic hat comes along to murder it. I used to dream about it. About the eye. In my dream I was waiting for my father to give it to me. I was blind and cold and I wanted so badly to play with it. And now . . . and now when I think about it, I think we're all Graeae. We live in a universe of lenses. We watch and watch. We all share one eye between us, the big black camera iris. We wait for our turn to see what someone else saw on a screen. And then we pass it on. All I've ever wanted was just to play with it. I still feel like I'm in that dream, jumping up and trying to grab onto the eye, and I can't reach it."

She fell asleep almost before she finished saying *I can't reach it.* I watched her. And I could see . . . little bronze threads on her cheek, tiny fronds, by her hairline, growing like gold veins across her face.

And months later when I touched Anchises's poor hand, I heard her say it again. *One eye.* And then giggle like she was three and say *oh wow, oh wow oh*—and then nothing.

And that's the end of it—nothing. I didn't hit her over the head with a tripod and dump her body, though I heard that said plenty once we got back. Always suspect the boyfriend. Maximo didn't bury her in the delta. I loved a girl and she left me. I don't know where she is. I want to know. I want to know. But I was there and I still don't.

Maybe I don't get to see the end of this show. Maybe I just live out the rest of my days between reels. Maybe Anchises will figure it out. Maybe not. Who knows, maybe death is the darkroom where you get to see it all like it was supposed to come out. Bright and crisp and clean. No shadows unless you want them. But it ended like it started, which I guess is how you know it's an Unck story. Suckers for symmetry, those two. *I left my sugar standing in the rain and she melted away.*

CYTHERA: Is that all?

ERASMO: Probably not. I'll ring if I think of anything new.

CYTHERA: Oxblood will pay for resettlement anywhere you like, Erasmo. And you'll always have a job with us if you decide to come home.

ERASMO: I'm thinking Mars. Mount Penglai. I was born near there, you know. Didn't mean to come into this life anywhere but the Moon. Still seems strange that I didn't pull it off. Mum and Dad were working on *Kangaroo Khan,* and whoops— congratulations on your bouncing baby Martian.

CYTHERA: Mount Penglai is lovely. The mangoes are amazing.

ERASMO: You'll let me take him, won't you? [Cythera says

nothing.] He's worth nothing to you. He's just a kid. He's going to be bent into all kinds of unpleasant shapes by this. He needs a father. Or at least someone who can un-pretzel him from time to time. Trust me, you don't want him. I do. Let me give him a childhood.

CYTHERA: We'll consider it. May I . . . may I ask? You wear a wedding ring, but on the wrong hand. Indulge my curiosity?

ERASMO: She didn't want to get married. Doesn't mean I wasn't her husband.

CYTHERA: [pause] Can I get you a last coffee before you go?

Christmas Card,
mailed to C. Brass c/o Oxblood Films,
Yemaya, December 1952

To be included in the manuscript of Erasmo St. John's memoir, The Sound of a Voice That Is Still, *scheduled for publication Spring 1959 (Random House)*

Front:

SNOW HO HO!
HAPPY CHRISTMAS
FROM MERRY MARS!

Inside:

Hiya, Cyth,

Well, he's gone to seek his fortune, and I'm drinking alone at Yuletide with no one else to write to.

I don't know if he ever loved me, and I don't know what the thing in his hand means. It never gave him any pain that I could tell. I don't know if it ever changed much; he started wearing gloves when we were living in New York (what a cock-up that was! Six months of yelling at each other in brownstones neither of us will be able to fish out of the back drawer again) and never took them off. Wouldn't show me the hand any more than a boy shows himself naked to his father past a certain age.

Not that I was his father. I wanted to be. I did. It would have been . . . well, there's no point in dressing it up. It would have been like Rin and me had a kid together. That's not fair, it's not a fair thing to put on a traumatized little boy, but we all put something too heavy on our babies.

It moved in his sleep. I remember that, in the days before the gloves. It moved in his sleep like it was underwater. Like it was drifting in a current, a tide that you couldn't see. I touched it once. He was sick, really sick—he was sick a lot back then. Nowhere sat right with him 'til Mars. He reached out to me in his fever, and he did that seldom enough. I held him tight and took his hands and I could feel it, moving against my palm, like it was looking for something. Maybe purchase, maybe a way out, maybe it couldn't breathe with my palm against it. But its little tendrils touched my skin and that is the only time I have heard Severin Unck's voice since the *Clamshell* made moonfall. I never told him. How do you tell a kid that?

Cristabel got her Russian citizenship six or seven years ago and came out to our little red planet. I bet you saw that coming, didn't you? She can play the bassoon. I didn't really think anyone played the bassoon anymore. It's an instrument out of books and poems and grandads manning the watch on the prow of lonely, starlit ships. It sounds plaintive and kind in the desert dark.

The plain fact is, after everything that happened in Adonis, I could never love anyone who wasn't there.

I might try to write a book. We'll see. I'm not much of a writer. Anything more than a title card seems wasteful to me. I spent the best years of my life under the law of silent flicks:

Show everything, because you can't say much. But I think I might give it a go.

It's almost dark in Mount Penglai. The way my house sits, I can watch the kangaroos out on the red plains. Who knew those funny creatures would take to Mars so well?

The Ingénue's Handbook

12 October 1947, Eleven in the Evening
Pellam's Parlour, Grasshopper City

My darling Severin,

You must know I always meant to tell you everything. You deserved to know. It was only that I couldn't be *certain*, not *absolutely* certain, and without certainty, why rock the boat?

Oh, what a dreadful thing to say! I sound like my grandmother, and she had a full set of dentures by forty-five. And it's execrable wordplay as well. You always gave me a slap on the wrist for punning in your presence. But I know you liked it, you dissembler, you.

I've settled on Miranda, of all places. It's beautiful here, really. Nothing like my old movie. Thaddeus shot Europa-for-Miranda for the tax shelter and it still looks spectacular, but it's nothing like the gentle blue hills and snowy roofs and bright red flowers no bigger than a prick of blood all over the place.

I have a horse now! She's not really a horse. Horses on Miranda are the exact colour of absinthe with white hair and rather lion-like paws. Mine's called Clementine. I thought about naming her Severin, I really did, but it's an even more unwieldy name for a horse than it was for a little girl, even if the horse does have green lion feet. I bought her from a Mirandese lady I wish you could meet. She comes round quite a bit to help me look after Clementine, and lately she's been staying longer and longer. My Miranda affair. It's funny, but she looks just like Larissa Clough in *The Man Who Toppled Triton*. Do you remember that one? Mortimer gets called to the back of beyond to investigate an assassination, or what have you. They're all starting to run together.

I miss you terribly. I've missed you on and off for half my life. A stepmother's burden, I suppose. I do hope I wasn't *too* wicked. Oh, Sevvy, my lass, there are nights out here when the sky is so full of moons you think they'll come tumbling down over the grass and roll right through your door, and all I want in the world is to show you around my little house, make you a cup of tea, and ask you, *My dearest of hearts, how have you been, really?* And you would tell me about your next movie, and Erasmo, and how old-fashioned my silly watercolours are, and who paints their parlour chartreuse, anyway? I'd make you sandwiches just like the Savoy's. You could toss Clementine a raw rump roast; she likes them especially.

And then I remember, and it's too dreadful for words.

I always meant to tell you. I'm still not certain, but I'm . . . certain enough.

Sevvy, your father didn't shoot anyone. I thought he did; everyone thought he did, though no one would say it. Batty, horrid, bear-brained Freddy Edison shot my Thaddeus, and Percy kept him from spilling it all like a bucket of paint and ruining himself because . . . well, God knows why Percy ever loved Freddy the way he did. A more undeserving shit of a man was never born. Freddy did it because he thought his wife, Penny, was sleeping with Thad. It wasn't even in the neighbourhood of true, of course. I knew that, but I couldn't say how I knew, and I couldn't understand why Percy was spitting lies whenever he spoke, so I . . . I ran away. I know I ought to have been braver. But

I've come to think you only get so much bravery in one lifetime, and if you spend it too soon, you're all out of *fuck it all to hell* by the time you really need it.

I knew Thad never touched Penny. Thad never touched anyone of the lady persuasion. When I was twenty or twenty-one, I came to his house to get a few scripts. I came a little early or a little late, I can't remember which, though I do remember how bright Thaddy's forsythia bloomed that year. It framed his door in pure gold. I walked right in because I am a rude and graceless creature and saw him kissing Laszlo Barque goodbye. They looked so lovely together, like summer in two people. We all froze like antelope who've smelled a hyena. I saw them decide to trust me, and they saw me promise to keep their secret, all without saying a word. We had a splendid afternoon playing gin rummy and complaining, my favourite hobbies.

I never told a soul. Thaddeus knew about me, too, of course. One good confidence deserves another. But I was always a spritely little Naiad; I could flow from men to women and back and forth and it never seemed the least bit strange to me, just lucky. I can hide better than some. Even if I have to come all the way out to a cold black moon to do it. If you've married men twice, nobody asks what you think about when the night breeze comes sidling in. And none of us ever forgot how Algernon B-for-Bastard ruined Wadsy Shevchenko just for the fun of it. To sell his wretched little magazine. He'd have been thrilled to shit on Thaddeus's grave so that no one ever spoke of his movies again without adding: *Oh, didn't you know? Irigaray was nothing but a nasty little fairy! And did you hear how he died? I say good riddance to his sort. They always come to a bad end.* No. Not for my forsythia friend.

Oh, I hate everything and everybody. Bother.

But what troubles me is the why. Why did Percy lie?

I think I have it figured out now. Maxine would be ashamed of me. She'd roll her one good eye and scold me. *How could anything possibly take a soul this long to think through?* So here it is, no more dawdling!

Percy lied because he had a bigger lie in his back pocket. Darling, I believe with all my beat-up little heart that Penelope Edison is your mother.

I found a photograph in Thaddeus's hand, a photograph of a baby that looked terribly like you. I did know you quite well when you were small. So the question becomes: why would he have it?

I think Penelope couldn't hold it in any longer. She'd had about a hundred thousand gimlets that night, and she had to tell somebody. Thaddeus listened to all the girls he worked with. He could listen like a funny-nosed, redheaded god of making it all okay. Laszlo Barque loved that about him—I don't think anyone listened to Laszlo much before Thaddeus. He was too pretty for people to pay attention to what he was saying. So I think Penny must have been showing him a picture, unburdening her soul, and Freddy saw them talking, pasted Thad and Penny together with a few other facts he'd collected over the years, lost his pencil-eraser of a mind, and bang. Those facts being: Freddy went to Saturn for the Worlds' Fair in Enuma Elish. He didn't come home for ten months or so. Time enough. Maybe she looked different when he came back. Maybe she felt different. Maybe she stopped wanting babies with him. I don't know. But he must have suspected her long before that night on the *Achelois*.

The thing is, Enuma Elish hosted the fair in 1914. And you were born in October that year.

That's all the evidence I have. I know it's not much. Percy and Freddy grew up together. Not in the sense of whacking each other with toy fire trucks and eating sand side by side, but in the sense of two young men on the same rocket to the Moon, both of them viciously ambitious and twenty and starving for the world. Even when Freddy turned out rotten as an old banana, Percy still loved him. Whatever part of a person can turn love off is broken in Percy. Oh, I know you don't think so. Seven wives, after all. But we all left *him,* not the other way round. Even you. And he still loves everyone he ever loved, I'm as sure of that as I am of the colour of my eyes. It's only that a real live person can never shine like a movie you haven't made yet. He must have loved Penelope like a bruise in the soul to betray his friend. And it would have killed him if Freddy ever found out. Possibly literally, considering.

Before you ask, I'm certain Penny loved you. She just got stuck, baby girl, like a needle on a record, and she couldn't get out of a story with no good end.

For a long time I thought it showed an ugliness in Percy that he never told you. Of all people! But secrets hold a sway stronger than any scruples. You were so bound and determined to put every detail of your life into a microphone and through a camera lens. You insisted on *talking* when the rest of us were happy with the quiet. Truth, reality, bald honesty—that was you in a tall glass with ice.

He would have told you someday. I'm sure he meant to. Just like I did. Maybe we all just should have used our grown-up voices a little more.

That's all I've got, Sevvy. I hope this letter finds you, somehow.

Clementine wants her evening ride. The moons are all coming up like big pale party balloons. Don't tell anyone I said so, but I love you and I will miss you till I die. Even if you weren't my child, you are my daughter, and that's worth a drink if it's worth two.

Come home, if you can.

Mary

—From a Letter Recovered from the Grave of Severin Unck

How Many Miles to Babylon?:
Episode 974

Airdate: 2 September, 1952
Announcer: **Henry R. Choudhary**
Vespertine Hyperia: **Violet El-Hashem (final episode)**
Tybault Gayan: **Alain Mbengue**
The Invisible Hussar: **Zachariah von Leipold**
Doctor Gruel: **Benedict Sol**
Guest Star: **Maud Locksley as Gloriana, the Panther Queen**

ANNOUNCER: Good Evening, Listeners, if it is indeed Evening where you are. Gather in, pour yourself a cup of something nice, and sit back for another instalment of the solar system's favourite tale of adventure, romance, and intrigue on *How Many Miles to Babylon?* Celebrating our thirty-eighth year on the waves and in your hearts, *Babylon* is a joint production of the United/Universal All-Worlds Wireless Broadcom Network (New York, Shanghai, Tithonus) and BBC Radio, recorded at Atlas Studios, London.

This evening's programme is brought to you, as always, by Castalia Water Filtration, Wherever You Go, Have a Glass of Home Sweet Home. Additional promotional consideration provided by the Audumbla Company, Bringing Our Family of Quality Callowproducts to Your Table and Your Family to the

Stars; Your Friends at Coca-Cola; the East Indian Trading Company; and Edison Teleradio Corp.

Previously on *How Many Miles to Babylon?*: Our heroine, Vespertine Hyperia, finally wed her beloved Tybault in the Halls of Hyperion, formerly Doctor Gruel's Sinister Seraglio. Her bridesmaids: two gentle callowhales. Her bouquet: the stars.

VESPERTINE: Oh, Tybault, my long dreamed-of destiny, will I ever feel more joy than I do now in your arms, with all of Venus safe and at peace and our child sleeping soundly in my belly?

TYBAULT: I know I shall not, faun of my fate.

VESPERTINE: But our adventure is not over, is it? There is so much more to do and to dare! The Mountain of Memory, the Fortress of Forty Thousand Wishes, the Dragoon Lagoon! Together we will bring each of them to the welcoming arms of the Crown!

TYBAULT: We will never cease, not even in death. This is our home for all time!

VESPERTINE: Tonight, I shall fall asleep in your arms as I have longed to do for so many years. The night wind will come through our windows and whisper sweet promises of tomorrow. I shall sleep and I shall dream of the world we made when first our eyes met and our hands touched. Farewell, Sorrow! Vespertine is your maid no longer!

~~The Deep Blue Devil~~
~~The Man in the Malachite Mask~~
~~Doctor Callow's Dream~~
And If She's Not Gone, She Lives There Still:
The Case of the Reappearing Raconteur

Wide angle. Establishing shot. Slow zoom.

The White Peony Waldorf glows like a candlelit cake. Supper waits under silver domes, ready, but not yet served. A basket of mints sits in the dumbwaiter, its contents all set to kiss every pillow with their neat green foils. The painted ceiling, like a strange chapel, depicts Venus interceding with the Trojans and the Greeks. Armies surround a patch of swamp. The goddess cradles Paris's bruised body in one perfect arm and pleads for peace with the other. She bleeds from a wound over her heart; her hair is soaked in blood. It is a famous painting, though no one presently enjoying the pleasures of the lobby looks up.

Tracking shot over the labyrinthine rose-and-cobalt pattern of the rich carpet, past the gleaming grand piano, the vases full of varuna flowers and gardenias-which-are-not-really-gardenias. A rowdy group of out-of-towners are making quite the rumpus in the Myrtle Lounge. Such manners! Passersby can hear the uproar all the way out on the twilight-washed street.

"*Ate* us?" shouts Arlo Covington, C.P.A. He thumps his fist on the helmet of his diving suit. Peitho and Erzulie Kephus cringe away from him; they remember the sudden thump of their own deaths, and they still cannot bear loud noises. "*Ate* us?"

Calliope the Carefree Callowhale keeps her cool. Her animated lines crackle turquoise to black to ultramarine with suppressed indignation and embarrassment. "I beg your pardon. But what would you do if a roast chicken flew through your kitchen window, landed on your plate, and carved itself with your knife and fork? I daresay you'd fall to, sir." She blushes her cartoon blush, two magenta circles on her cetacean cheeks. "You walked right *into* me, Mr Covington. What would you have me do?"

Percival Unck strokes his daughter's black hair. Her movietone skin flickers and skips. They have not stood together thus for so long. Severin presses her lips together. She can hardly look at the crew she lost. She knows the score, but has not yet been asked to put it on the board.

"And what about me?" Horace St. John draws himself up, with great difficulty, on a jewelled cane. His broken, bow-tied legs wobble. "I couldn't sleep. I committed the great sin of insomnia. The unforgivable transgression of taking a walk instead of having a piss inside my own tent."

Erasmo St. John puts his broad hand on his cousin's back. It is cold; Erasmo doesn't mind.

Calliope hangs her head. "You were an accident. We offer an apology—only the seventh we have ever made."

"Oh, apologize to Horace but hang the rest of us, is that it?" cries Mariana Alfric, mould flaking off of her skin and floating into the air.

"But what *happened* to me?" Horace begs. His voice drops to a whisper. "I don't remember dying."

"What do you remember?" Anchises asks.

"Leaving my tent. I walked through the village; I smelled the sea air. I thought about my equipment for the next day. I kept walking—I figured Raz would show up at some point, so I went slowly. I walked past the memorial and saw something out there beyond the houses. Beyond the old carousel. A patch of green. Not that much is green on Venus, you know. A green patch, and yellow sunlight as bright as noon, and blue water. It was a pond surrounded by long grass and bluebells and squishy mush-rooms. I dipped my hand in and tasted it—the water was fresh. I thought a swim in anything other than saltwater would feel won-derful. I popped in, just for a moment."

Mr Bergamot does a sad little soft-shoe. "Remember the pin," he says mournfully.

Calliope speaks up. "We hold countless worlds together. When one of us dies, edges begin to fray and come apart. Worlds shear off, bleed into each other, fly away into nothing, burn out. We leave a hole when we go. Through such holes, other places seep and stain. Shards of those places stick in the wreckage of us. Songs you have never heard, movies you've never seen, words as unfamiliar as new planets. Other voices may cry through, or-phan voices, unstuck from the mouths that made them. Voices that began in other versions of yourselves and became lost inside us, now seeking a way home. You saw another of our places. If you want to know, it's a tiny lake outside Tonganoxie, Kansas. It's not an important place. In your world, it does not even exist—not Tonganoxie, not Kansas, not the lake. You walked toward it. But your body didn't walk into the bluebells; it broke in ten places on the walls of a well on Venus. You did land in the sun, though, for by the time you landed, the frayed edge had stitched itself up again with you inside it. You were not on Venus any-more. You drowned in Kansas. We do not exist everywhere at once. We are always moving. Pieces of us linger when we leave like a trail of breadcrumbs. Like a staircase. Some parts of us stayed in Adonis after we tore it apart looking for our young. Arlo walked into one. You fell through the edge of another."

"If I may," interrupts Madame Maxine Mortimer, removing her sleek black blazer and folding it over the arm of an apricot-coloured fainting couch. "These little get-togethers go much more smoothly when we allow logic to lead the way. We simply cannot have the recriminations before the crime—and the criminal—has been fully examined. We must lay the events out upon our operating table, pour ourselves another schnapps, and dissect them properly."

Anchises St. John runs his gloved hand through his hair. "I quite agree, Madame. I did say there were two possible solutions, if you recall. Another round, everyone?"

"Mind if I run the bar, Anchises?" Percy Unck asks. "I made my first pennies as a barman in Truro before I managed to stow away on the *Jumping Cow* and get my arse to the Moon."

"Anything for my granddad." Anchises yields magnanimously. Cythera Brass hops up on the bar and perches there, swinging her legs like a kid. Amid much grumbling, the company gathers at the bar.

Severin laughs and holds out her glass to be filled. "You never told me we were Cornish! Or stowaways."

"Isn't that the point of leaving Earth?" Percy purrs in his own hidden Cornish accent. He spent so long hiding it away—it feels good to let the old boy run. "Leaving yourself, if you didn't like yourself—and I didn't. Making a new person when the old one's gotten worn at the knees. I met Freddy on that boat. He was running away, too. I suppose I got further than he did." Percy can't help but give the bottle of gin a jazzy little flip, catching it behind his back.

"Do it again!" cries Marvin the Mongoose.

"We are indeed Cornish, my little hippopotamus," says Percy while he pours for Mary Pellam and Madame Mortimer. "Though my mother was half French, and my father half an idiot. Your mother, of course," he clears his throat, "was Basque. Half, anyway. I believe her mother was Lebanese. There you have it: a map of your blood." He hurries on, shaking up cocktails for Violet, Mariana, Arlo, Mr Bergamot, and Erasmo with the practised hand of a juggler. He flips back easily into the voice Severin has known all her life. "Oh, I know I don't sound Cornish—funny how I thought my voice was so bloody important back then. Then I went and got a job keeping quiet. Oh, but what a glorious quiet it was! Do you know, now that Freddy's gone, they're starting up talkies again? It'll never last. You probably don't know, Rinny, but Uncle Freddy went and shot himself two years ago. They found him on the beach. Dreadful business, but I think I'm the only one who's sorry. Take that over to Max in his corner, will you, Mary? Thanks, love."

Calliope gets her punch bowl last.

Anchises presses on. "Now that we've had our intermission, if we can all remember to keep our heads? I know we all have great personal stakes here, but do let us try not to all talk at once."

Mary Pellam tosses off her third Bellini. "I do believe I've spotted a hole in your theory, kid," she says.

"Oooh, I've got one, too!" squeals Marvin the Mongoose. He scampers over to Mary and climbs her like a tree, roosting on the crown of her golden head with his ruddy animated tail round her neck. "You first, you first!"

"Let's have it, Mary," says Anchises with a smile. He claps his hands and rubs them together.

Mary pushes Marvin's fur out of her face and points a long finger at the boy from Venus. "You are not a callowhale."

"Oh, well done, darling!" cries Madame Mortimer.

"Should I be?" Anchises quirks his eyebrow knowingly.

"Well, it stands to reason, doesn't it? If that little hickey on your hand is a baby callowhale, and all this happened because they came looking for their wee one, shouldn't you look a smidge more like Mrs Cousteau over there and a skosh less like Percy's next leading man? No offense, Calliope."

"None taken, I'm sure." The Carefree Callowhale glowers.

"What's your objection, Marvin?" Anchises inquires.

"Oh, I didn't have one." The mongoose giggles. "I just wanted to be one of the gang!"

"You are quite right, Mary. I am not a callowhale." Anchises begins to walk around the Myrtle Lounge. He thinks better on the move. "Indeed, that pesky detail first alerted me to the presence of a second solution to our communal puzzle. I am either thirty or forty years old, depending on whether one counts the time I spent in limbo in Adonis, and I can assure you I have suffered no ill health, no unusual physiological developments—beyond the obvious, which I will come to in a moment—and only the expected mental disturbances of any traumatized child who has lost his parents, excepting those I inflicted upon myself with a bottle or an atomizer or a film projector. There were times when I wished for all those things. I think I would have known some peace if my fingers had become gas bladders filled with milk, if my mouth had closed over with clammy flesh and I'd grown a blowhole. My life would have begun to make sense. But the truth is quite the opposite. In fact, in recent years—" Here Anchises removes his buttery leather glove and reveals his open palm like a rabbit pulled from a hat. A great gasp goes up from the crowd. The hand is healed. A rough, hardscrabble scar runs across the skin, puckered like a bullet wound. But that is all. Mariana looks down at her own hands, crawling with feathery fronds, their fiddleheads curling and uncurling. "Even this last reminder of that morning so long ago when I found that dying callowhale limb lying, so forlorn, on the beach and . . ." He trails off, his voice thick. "Forgive me. Even that reminder has gone. So, as they say, what gives? Thus I come to my second solution: I am not a callowhale—*but someone else in this room is!*"

"Don't look at me!" cries Mr Bergamot, retracting his tentacles into his body in terror.

"I just played one on the radio!" Violet El-Hashem holds up her hands.

"Oh, all right, it's me." Severin Unck grins sidelong, putting one hand on her hip.

"Hi, baby," says Calliope, waving her blue fin.

"Hi, Mama." Severin wiggles her fingers.

"What happened to you down there?" Percival Unck pleads. "I have to know."

"Please, Rinny." Erasmo looks up at her, hurt and lost and full of an ache like a bullet lodged in a bone.

"The lights went out," whispers Severin. "The dark tasted like milk. My heart turned into a photograph of a heart."

"I don't understand you, darling," Erasmo says.

Anchises sits down at the gleaming grand piano in the corner of the Myrtle Lounge. He plays a flourish on the keys. Severin walks across the room. She shrugs off her aviator jacket, musses her hair. She slides up to the top of the black grand and lies across it. As she does so, her flickering black-and-white skin flushes into colour, her dress turns a throbbing shade of deep green, her shoes bright gold, her lips redder than Mars.

"How's your night going, Miss S?" Anchises asks, sliding into the old, comforting patter of a lounge act, his fingers coaxing the keys.

"Oh, not too bad, Mr A," Severin croons. "I was dead for a little while, but I got over it."

"Glad to hear it. You got a song for all these lonelyhearts?"

"I just might. It's called 'The Quantum Stability Axis Blues.' You wanna hear it?"

"I'm *dying* to hear it."

And so Severin Unck begins to sing, in a thick, low voice like bourbon pouring into a wooden cup.

I met my honey way down under the sea
Where the sun never goes so nobody can see
What my honey,

Oh, what my honey
does to me

Severin rolls onto her back, green sequins pulsing with light.

My honey put the moon on my finger
My honey put the stars on my plate
My papa told me good girls don't linger
When a honey comes
Oh, when a honey comes
a-rattlin' her gate

"I never said such a thing," Percy grumbles.
"I know, Daddy, it's a song," whispers Severin, putting her finger over her red lips. *Shhh.*

My honey he was dyin' without me
His heart was all locked up but I was the key
I said I should go,
but my honey said no,
Oh, no, no, no,
Let me show you what a good girl can be

Severin slides gracefully off the piano and walks through the lounge. Her green dress fades back to black, her skin to silver. She sits down on Erasmo's lap; she runs her fingers through his hair. The key changes, and Calliope begins to hum a plaintive counterpoint. Mr Bergamot joins in.

My honey and me floated out on the foam
Still I sighed: I miss my baby back home
How can I leave him so lonesome and blue?
Don't seem the kind of thing a good girl should do.

Severin snaps her fingers. She presses her knuckle under Erasmo's chin.

But with honey, ain't no such thing as leavin'
Anyone I want I can find just like that
So baby, don't you get lost in grievin'
Wherever you go, that's where I'm at.

"Because I am a nexus point connecting all possible realities and unrealities," Severin purrs seductively. "I exist in innumerable forms throughout the liquid structure of space/time, and neither self nor causality have any meaning for me." She kisses Erasmo as the song ends. Tears slide off his cheeks, onto his chin, and onto her film-shivering fingers, where they burn. "I love you right in the face."

Severin stands and bows. Marvin the Mongoose throws gardenias at her feet. She holds her hand out to her father, who takes it, and holds it to his breast. He's sobbing, a big ugly cry, but there's no shame. In point of fact, there's not a dry eye in the house.

"I'm okay, Daddy. It's okay now."

PART FIVE

✦ ✦ ✦ ✦ ✦

THE RED PAGES

The radiant car your sparrows drew
You gave the word and swift they flew,
Through liquid air they wing'd their way,
I saw their quivering pinions play;
To my plain roof they bore their queen,
Of aspect mild, and look serene.

—Sappho, "Hymn to Aphrodite"

In the end, everything is a gag.

—Charlie Chaplin

The Man of the Hours

13 June, 1971

The afternoon sun knocks politely at the doors of Mount Peng-lai. It wears a soft orange dress with red buttons and a gold sash.

Mount Penglai meant to be a metropolis, but it got a little lost along the way. You can still see evidence of its grander destiny: a pronged glass hotel rising like a trident from the central business district: the mammoth bronze *qilin* statues outside Anqi Sheng Theatre whose marquee, on this particular day, reads: *Mr Berga-mot Goes to France*. The city lies in the Chinese hemisphere, fed by the happy canals of the Mangala Valles, not so far from the enormous orange cone of Nix Olympia, a kindly volcano the size of Bulgaria that never makes any trouble. Prosperous kanga-roo ranches dot the outskirts, and that's about the size of the wealth around here—the fancier folk just didn't want to live so far from Guan Yu.

Or too close to Enyo, after everything. It's only five kilometres down the road.

Vincenza Mako knocks politely at the door of a large and handsome house. She is, by coincidence, wearing the same outfit as the sun. Orange, red buttons, gold sash. A man built this house because he wanted a place to try for happiness. Behind Vincenza, mango sellers and ice hawkers make the first market-cries of the day. She is nervous, a little. She has come bearing a gift: a box containing several reels of film.

Anchises St. John answers the door. The real Anchises St. John. Vince only met him once, when he was small and unable to speak. He turned out very tall, with shaggy dark hair, striped now with grey, soft lines around his eyes, a prominent nose. Not handsome, really—though Vincenza's standards are skewed by the bounty of available beauty on the Moon—but at least interesting looking.

"Vincenza?" he asks, smiling uncertainly. He is a man unused to company, to appointments, to strangers.

"You can call me Vince. Everybody does."

Anchises makes lunch for the two of them: 'roo steak, fried dumplings, and red beer. They watch the reels together out in the garden on a huge white bed sheet. Anchises grows sunflowers and moonflowers side by side. They race each other, up the fence, toward the sky.

The title card reads: *Radiance*.

Anchises doesn't talk while the movie plays. The images reflect in his eyes, moving in his iris, shadows and light. He chuckles a few times.

"What do you think?" Vince says when it's done. Anchises brings out goji-chocolate cake and coffee on plates with tropical fish painted on them. Crickets (which are not really crickets) hum and chirp.

"I'm not a critic," Anchises says with a shrug of his shoulders.

"Come on. It's you up there. You must have an opinion."

"Well . . . it's not really a movie, is it? Just pieces of one."

Vince sighs. She wraps her hair around her hand, tying it into a knotted bun in one quick, assured movement. "Percy couldn't figure out how to tell it. He never finished—the studio killed his funding and he just . . . stopped. Of course, you never really finish any movie, you just turn the camera off. But it was time to go, for him. The Moon wears on you after a while. I wonder if you can guess where he retired?"

"White Peony Station," Anchises says, without missing a beat. "With Penelope Edison."

"Bravo. They're living at the Waldorf. When we filmed the song and dance numbers there, he said it felt like home. And after Freddy died, she just sort of melted back into everything. Into Percy's life, into her work, into herself."

"You're not going to release this, are you? It's a bear."

"No studio; no distribution. But he wanted you to see it. Without an audience, it doesn't exist. If a movie shows in a theatre and there's no one to see it, does it make a sound?"

Anchises watches his moonflowers opening one by one, the night wind picking them up and blowing their petals open, perfect, white as screens.

"I was actually a detective for a while," he gets up to fetch himself a cigar, cuts it, lights up, settles down again. "On Callisto. Though I guess you know that. I was a little of everything. I think I always knew I'd end up back here. I was happy here, with Erasmo. Safe. I don't think I showed it much, but I was happy. I made sure I saw a hell of a lot before I came home. I was drunk most of the time and I did my best to get punched on every planet I could, but I'll be damned if I didn't see a hell of a lot. I even went to Pluto, just like you said. You did your research."

Vince smiles, shrugging slightly, as if to say: *Thanks, but you have no idea.*

"Max wasn't quite that well organized when I got there, though." Anchises St. John turns to look Vince in the eye. His gaze is still sharp. "How did you know kids used to call me Doctor Callow? And about the frond on the beach?"

"Do you remember a little girl named Lada? She was the same age as you."

Anchises rubs his forehead. Tears form at the corners of his eyes. "I'm sorry. I do try, it's just . . ."

"Don't worry. God, it was thirty years ago now, anyway. Longer, um, for you, I suppose. Lada Zhao's family moved to the Japanese sector about six months before the last Nutcake Festival. She remembers you very fondly. She has a photograph of you, standing next to the frond. She says she told you not to touch it."

"You didn't put her in your movie."

"It seemed a little on the nose, to have an actual Greek chorus there to warn you."

Anchises swirls ice cream around the top of his cake with his spoon. It melts slowly. He doesn't wear gloves anymore. His scarred hand has a tan. He doesn't speak for a long time. A few coyotes—which are not really coyotes, but have two brains, and plates on their backs like furry stegosauruses—howl out on the plains.

"Can I keep the prints?"

"Of course you can."

"I . . . I like the Anchises you made. He's better than me. He has a lantern jaw and a mission. And he gets to stand next to Severin. To play a song for her. The way he talked to everyone at the end . . . I could never talk like that. I'm no good with big groups of people. They frighten me. Everything frightens me. But some things I can frighten back. Mostly kangaroos." He looks up at the evening coming on, very blue and clotted with stars. "I wish it had never happened, Vince. I wish I'd been a diver. I wish I could have taken care of my parents in their old age. Sometimes I even wish I'd moved Earthside, so I wouldn't have to eat this shit every day." He gestures at his ice cream, made from Prithvi Brand Premium Callowmilk. "But if it had to happen, I like what you made better than what I made out of it. I'd like to keep him. I can wear him on Sundays. He got his answer, in the end. I'll take his, since I never could find mine."

"He had two. We never filmed the vote. Which one would you choose?"

Anchises St. John finishes his cake. Voices are coming up the walkway toward the house, musical, lilting voices.

"Not much of a choice, is it?" he says. "Erasmo and Cristabel will be here in a moment. They always bring gin. Would you like to stay to dinner?"

Vince takes his scarred hand in hers. She squeezes it. "Very much."

Goodbye

Look at your hands. The light on them. The light that is a small boy, head bent, turning in circles around your palm. Your fate line. Your heart line. Him.

One of the crewmen shaves in a mirror nailed to a cacao-tree. He catches a glimpse of Severin in his mirror and whirls to catch her up, kissing her and smearing shaving cream on her face. She laughs and punches his arm—he recoils in mock agony. It is a pleasant scene. You have seen it before. You will see it again. It is the best of her you hold in your hands.

There is no such thing as an ending. There are no answers. We collect the pieces where we can, obsessively assemble and reassemble them, searching for a picture that can only ever come in parts. And we cling to those parts. The parts that have been her. The parts that have been you. Your chest, your ribs, your knees. The place where her last image entered and stayed. We have tried to finish Percival's work—to find the Grail, to ask the correct question. But in some version of the tale, Percival, too, must fail, and so must we, because the story of the Grail is one of failure and always has been. He did not finish his film. We could not finish it for him. There is no elegy for Severin Unck showing in a theatre near you.

But there is a reliquary.

What you have seen in this shadowed room, this quiet corner

of a Worlds' Fair where every tiny rock has sent its best represen-
tatives to fly banners and wave, is the body of Severin Unck. All
her pieces, laid out for viewing. It does not live—we are not Victor
Frankenstein, nor do we wish to be—but it looks like a woman we
once knew. Look at her.

Now, look at my hand. I will hold it up. And look at yours. How
many of you wear gloves? One glove? Two? More and more, every
year. For the space is not smooth that darkly floats between our
earth and its morning star—Lucifer's star, in eternal revolt against
the order of heaven. It is thick, it is swollen, its disrupted proteins
skittering across the black like foam—like milk spilled across the
stars. And in this quantum milk, how many bubbles may form and
break; how many abortive universes gestated by the eternal sleeping mothers may burgeon and burst? Perhaps Venus is an anchor,
where all waveforms meet in a radiant scarlet sea, where the milk
of creation is whipped to a froth, and we have pillaged it, gorged
upon it, all unknowing. Perhaps in each bubble of milk is a world
suckled at the breast of a pearlescent cetacean. Perhaps there is one
where Venus is no watery Eden as close as a sister, but a distant
inferno of steam and stone, lifeless, blistered. Perhaps you have
drunk the milk of this world—or perhaps I have, and destroyed it
with my digestion. Perhaps a skin of probabilistic milk, dribbling
from the mouths of babes, is all that separates our world from the
others. Perhaps the villagers of Adonis drank so deeply of the pri-
mordial milk that they became as the great mothers.

I dream of the sea. Always the sea.

Perhaps we are all only pieces. But we are stitching ourselves together, into something resembling a prologue.

Go out into the Fair. Into the light. Breathe the lunar air. Eat,
drink, and be happy, for you have reached the end—which is not
really the end.

The Howler and the Lord of the World

FILM REEL FROM THE ENYO SITE ON MARS
[INT. A cinema. The seats glow a deep, heart-like red. Cherubs with the heads of fish frame the screen. SEVERIN UNCK sits in one of the seats, soaking wet. She looks confused, upset. She shivers; her teeth chatter. She turns to see if anyone else is in the theatre, but she is alone. When she turns back, MR BERGAMOT is seated next to her, a green cartoon octopus wearing spats and a monocle.]

SEVERIN

Uncle Talmadge?

MR BERGAMOT

I'm afraid not. But this was my favourite of all the bodies you remember. I like his appendages. [MR BERGAMOT flourishes his tentacles.] Can I get you some popcorn?

SEVERIN

Who are you?

BERGAMOT

Who you came for. You stuck a bloody great camera in my face, remember?

SEVERIN

Sorry.

BERGAMOT

No, you're not.

SEVERIN

I'm sorry it hurt you.

BERGAMOT

We were already hurt. Would you like to watch a movie?

SEVERIN

Always.

[A film begins on the huge screen. The camera swoops down out of the starry sky to the surface of Pluto. It is not our Pluto. There are no flowers, no cities, no glowing carousel bridge to Charon. This Pluto is tiny, without an atmosphere, a mass of blasted craters. A YOUNG GIRL walks through the barren rocks. Her hair is white, with bronze kelp growing out of her scalp alongside it. Her skin is made of scratched ice. She is crying. Blood drips from the hem of her dress.]

SEVERIN

Who is she?

BERGAMOT

That's me. My big-screen debut. Callowhales
exist throughout everything that has ever existed or will exist. We look different in each
place where existence occurs. Think of them as
sets, if it helps. Vast, infinite, enclosed realities where anything may occur, yet actions
taken in one—say, *The Atom Riders of Mars* or Universe 473a—do not affect any other—say, Universe
322c or *The Girl Who Made Fate Laugh.* A hundred
million sets together make a grand studio. The
whole of existence.

On your set, we look like callowhales. That has
proven somewhat unfortunate. Our milk was not
meant to be ice cream. In another six or seven
generations, humans are going to look very interesting. But we do not interfere. We do not resist
the progression of events on any single set.

On another set, we look like mountains. That is
safer. In another, we look like several hammers
in one particular woodworker's shed. The woodworker likes sandalwood best. He doesn't know why
he never chooses to use those particular hammers.
On the set you are seeing now, we look like her.

SEVERIN

What happened to you?

BERGAMOT

What happened to me happened on another lot
entirely. There, we look like the colour red. I
became very sick. It wasn't anyone's fault. No one
did anything to make it happen, at least not on

purpose. For us, causality is meaningless. A cow kicked over a pot of glue—perhaps that killed a callowhale. Perhaps it did not, but will 1.5 million years from now. I began to cough. My coughs have echoes upon echoes. You get sick, too—think of me as having the measles. I am young; the stronger among us would not even notice the measles. I ran away from being sick. This is where I stopped running. I was so tired.

[The YOUNG GIRL falls to the stony ground of that Plutonian wasteland. The scene changes. The YOUNG GIRL falls to the ground on Mars. This Mars is not our Mars, either. There are no kangaroos sunning themselves on Mount Penglai, no mango sellers, no moonflowers. Nothing but dust and red sky. The air is poisonous. The YOUNG GIRL crawls, dragging her fingernails on the rocks. She dies slowly. She dies crying and shrieking. By the end, her mouth is full of red dust.]

BERGAMOT

That is where I died.

SEVERIN

[squinting] Is that Mangala Valles?

BERGAMOT

Yes. But a different Mangala Valles. In the place I am showing you, no one can live anywhere but Earth.

[The camera shows a solar system without electric lights—save on one glowing world. Dark Mars, Neptune, Venus, the Moon, all many, many miles

further apart than we know them to be. No Orient
Express, no Grand Central Station, no bright cannons firing into the black. All those worlds, dead
and empty, with no air, no oceans, no rivers, no
trees. SEVERIN covers her mouth with her hands.]

SEVERIN

Oh . . . Oh, God. What an awful, lonely place. No
buffalo, no Enki floating on the ocean, no cir-
cuses on Saturn, no movies on the Moon. How can
a place like that be? How can they bear it?

BERGAMOT

Have you ever seen a movie?

SEVERIN

You're joking.

BERGAMOT

Do you know what a movie *is*, though?

SEVERIN

Is this a riddle?

BERGAMOT

A movie is a ribbon. A long, long ribbon with
thousands of pictures on it. Each one slightly
different, so that when you run through the pictures very fast, they look like they're moving.
But when the movie is playing, the thousands of
pictures are all still there on the ribbon. They
just look like one picture. There are a million
million frames, each one of them only a little

different, and callowhales move through those frames like a cigarette burn in the corner of the image. Each frame is a world; a universe. Some of them are full of panthers. Some are full of dancing. Some are so sad I think you would never stop crying if you saw them, far sadder than this one, with its teeming Earth. You and Venus and your lover and your ship and the Moon and your father are only one frame, and there are ever so many more than twenty-four per second.

This frame has only one living world. It is where I died. Sometimes we are not very tidy when we die. Pieces of my body washed up in every possible reality. A scale here, a pneumatocyst there, a frond on a beach near a village called Adonis. I spasmed all the way through my death. When I got sick, I shook and shivered, and my shaking and shivering happened not to this Pluto, but to the one you know, to a town called Proserpine. When I died, I screamed in pain, and my screaming happened not to that cold Mars but to a town called Enyo. We have no manners when we are sick. I am ashamed.

SEVERIN

If you died, how are we speaking? Am I dead?

BERGAMOT

I would prefer you not to be dead.

SEVERIN

You and me both, buddy.

BERGAMOT

This octopus, sitting with you, is just a piece of my body washing up, like the others. It will dissolve, eventually, like the rest. I wish you could stay here forever with us under the sea.

SEVERIN

But I can't. I have to go back. I have people to look after.

BERGAMOT

You were vaporised at the point of contact. You cannot go back, only forward. Back and forward are nonsense words, anyway. But you can still look after your people, if you want to.

You do not understand what a callowhale is. You have never seen like we see. In some places, we look like a camera. Like an eye shared between three women. Like a story about seeing and being seen.

[The screen shows a parade of images, of scenes, each lapping at the next like a wave. ERASMO in a small room with an espresso, agony and anger and exhaustion on his face. MARY PELLAM sleeping next to a green creature with lion paws. MARY as a child in Oxford. PENELOPE leaving a basket on the doorstep of a grand house. PERCY and VINCE, arguing over a script, swimming naked in a lake on the Moon. PERCY and FREDDY arguing; Freddy running off with PERCY's gun, shooting THADDEUS IRIGARAY, weeping. MAUD LOCKSLEY and ALGERNON B washing blood off a floor. ERASMO and ANCHISES eating biscuits on Mars, laughing. ERASMO and CRISTABEL jogging together in the morning. MARIANA sleeping in a morphine haze. MARIANA singing to the dragon SANCHO PANZA in the broiling sun. SEVERIN, very little, trying to work out who is telling the story to whom. Many more flash by, millions more. Wars that come sooner in one universe come later in another, but come all the same. There are great rockets instead of airplanes; battles stretched by transit windows and orbits until they fray to pieces, leaving fleets abandoned in the night; more and more; human bodies sailing further out, past the solar system, filling with milk and starlight until fiddleheads open out of their na-vels, blossoming with flowers; great-grandchildren playing with CLARA without understanding what she could ever have been, more; until SEVERIN is crying; until she puts her hands over her face.]

BERGAMOT

Buck up, baby blowfish. Just puff up bigger than your sadness and scare it right off. That's the only way to live in the awful old ocean.

[SEVERIN looks up. She laughs.]

BERGAMOT

Why are you laughing?

SEVERIN

I just . . . I really wish you could've met my dad. I wish I could tell him it really was an ice dragon, after all. [She wipes her eyes.]

All right, mister. Put me in the picture.

Acknowledgments

Radiance began very simply, with the desire to write about having grown up as the daughter of a filmmaker. Though my father ultimately went into advertising, his passion colored my childhood profoundly. But somehow, it grew tentacles along the way, and has been growing (and growing and growing) for seven years. In that time, even the smallest of creatures racks up a lot of debts.

My heartfelt thanks to: Dmitri, who asked for a story set on a Venusian waterworld, Neil Clarke for publishing the short story that knew it wanted to grow up big and strong from the first line, to my agent, Howard Morhaim, and my editor, Liz Gorinsky, for feeding it its spinach, Winter and Fire Tashlin for the hours spent in my living room forking nineteenth-century history off into strange and unruly paths, and Kat Howard for being a new set of eyes. I bow in the direction of all the classic science fiction writers who envisioned the worlds of our solar system as they were not but might be, but particularly Roger Zelazny.

This book owes more to Heath Miller than it is polite to admit in company. For his constant readings and rereadings, listening to me say the whole thing was terrible over and over, theatrical consults and structural advice (I hear Mom's really great with structure), for his midnight meatball sandwiches and infinite supply of index cards, he has my eternal gratitude. I love you right in the face.

And finally, thanks, Dad, for the movie of my life.